Little
Tailfeather
Publishing

CASSANDRA FEATHERSTONE

REVEALED IN THE HOLLOW

3

M.P.P.

Stalk Cassandra Featherstone in the Dark Corners of the Web

Join my Facebook group and follow me everywhere!

Want More?

Sign up for my bi-weekly manifesto for a free series sampler:

Join my Ream as a FREE follower or exclusive subscriber to get access to cover reveals, WIPs, Serial Stories, and personal chats from me!

Content Information

This is a *paranormal whychoose romance with poly elements*—our FMC, Jolene, will not have to choose between love interests.

There are many situations included that are intended for mature audiences (18+).

In this book, there may be instances/references (be they small or lengthy) that could trigger some individuals such as:

- liberal use of appropriate consent
- the fucking Fae
- group scenes
- MMF, MM, MFM, MF, MFMMM, and more
- poison
- assassination attempts
- alphahole/possessive MMCs
- cinnamon roll MMCs
- bargains made by asshole Fae
- slightly unhinged chaotic MMC
- unhealthy coping mechanisms
- spoiled, selfish gods, goddesses, and royalty
- extremely aggressive boundaries

- age gap (from 10 yrs to immeasurable)
- weird Fae drugs and tricks
- BDSM
- raw sex
- shifted sex
- traumatic childhood
- Alcohol use and abuse
- threats of bodily harm
- death
- body modifications
- fancy genitalia
- mate knots/barbs
- the goddamn Fates meddling
- bullying (in person and on social media)
- PTSD
- blood
- emotional abuse from outside poly group
- body dysmorphia
- adult language
- pop culture references
- literary references
- emotional manipulation
- power play
- adorable nicknames
- physical intimidation
- emotionally abusive/manipulative parents (MMCs)
- voyeurism
- rough sex
- wings/tails/horns/magic in sex
- masturbation play
- markings/tattoos
- Easter egg character cameos from other series in the universe
- lawyers (ugh, but Jackson is a doll)
- family dysfunction
- super awesome BFF and her poly group
- animal companions

- absolute disrespect for shitty parents
- brief mentions of non-body positive dieting culture
- brief mentions of parental death
- very liberal re-imagining of history
- ancient secret society who only cares about bigger picture
- official corruption
- name calling
- occasional misogyny
- exhibitionism
- hand necklaces
- adult bullying
- magical kinks
- impact play
- elitism
- bribery
- corpses
- fat shaming (not by MCs)
- drama
- physical threats to FMC and others
- species-ism

No sexual practices in this book should be taken as safe or appropriate for real life application.

Content information is important and I don't ever want to harm a reader with inaccurate information.

Author Ramblings

Readers,

2023 was a rough year for me, both personally and professionally. I know I've said that a bunch, but I really can't communicate the level of difficulties I overcame and the lessons I learned while I was journeying through my third year as an author.

At the beginning of the year, I was working at an amazing clip and on track to meet every goal I'd set for myself and then some. But the spring brought chaos in of the Regina George variety and by the time I got through it, my schedule was destroyed.

I didn't let it stop me, nor did I let the two months of distraction derail the entire year. I'm proud of that and I always will be. No matter what distorted reality the abuser and their flying monkeys spread, they did not win because I'm still here.

However, between that and the cons and my Evil Day Job, I struggled to get back on track. Goals got pushed and things got delayed one by one until I had to make choices to preserve my mental health and work-life balance.

In Prey We Trust and *Ruthless* came out despite my delays and I could finish *O Holy Spite*, but the longer I held onto Revealed, the more I knew it would not make it. I tried to be positive, and I worked like a Trojan, but it was not meant to be. Rushing was affecting my enjoyment and the story—neither of which I'm okay with.

I finally canceled the preorder despite my enormous reservations and took a leap.

You're going to be so very glad that I did.

The finished product is so much better than what I would have had to do if I'd kept that date and man, do I love what came out after I said 'fuck it',' and canceled.

Jolene, the animals, her men, and the #fuckingfae will make you giggle, gasp, and want to hug the shit out of some characters.

A huge 'thank you' has to go out to my emotional support wolf, Serenity, and my alpha team, the Goosebusters, because they fully supported me doing this. Their encouragement helped me write what I think is a damn fabulous book and a great installment in the Hollow series.

Now that this is done, I'm going to get my stuff together and start rotating all my different upcoming books/serials, so y'all will have an amazing year of content. Thank you for reading and thank you for supporting me, even when I occasionally fail.

Blood and guts,

Cassandra Featherstone

Reader's Note

A few things you should know...

The ***following books <u>must</u> be read before Revealed in the Hollow:*** *Home to the Hollow (containing books 0-1.5) and Rejected in the Hollow.*

TheGet your bonus scene here!ters live is set up in those books and you will be very confused if you do not read them. This is technically book **three** in the series, but I write dummy *thicc* books and they will not fit in a single omnibus. So I put out *Home to the Hollow* which encompasses *Road, Return,* and a special gap novel called *Roused in the Hollow.* Books 2-3.5 will appear in another omnibus (hopefully, this spring) and then a third one to complete it.

The series is planned to have six ***whole*** books and several ***bonuses and gap novels***. I always recommend reading those because they often contain info you'll want later on.

This is a multi-book series, so *everything will not be revealed at once.* Some plot lines will continue through series in a larger arc and not get resolved in the first or even the third book.

I write lengthy books with intricate world building, strong character development, and *lots* of tiny threads that stretch throughout a series that may not always seem important at first glance. However, I promise nothing I put to paper and leave in the book is unimportant; it may simply become *more* important later on. There is no 'throw-away' detail in my worlds, so every scene will mean something eventually.

I promise it will all get tied up and have a HEA; don't worry!

Revealed in the Hollow is a why choose/poly romance, which means our FMC will not have to choose.

I would consider it a medium burn, slow build family group. It will continue to get spicier in the following books. If you're looking for porn with little to no plot, no judgment, but this isn't the series for you. It's also not closed door or FTB, so I believe the spice will be worth the wait. I realize spice scales are subjective and everyone has different opinions on it, so forgive me if mine and yours aren't totally aligned.

There are some characters and creatures that speak in other languages. I made the *translations clickable end of chapter notes* to help.

There are some words that are slang, jargon, or foreign that may seem to be spelled wrong—*please email the author or find her on social media rather than report to Amazon* if you think something is wrong. This has been proofed and edited *several* times since release; if you believe you found errors, you may not be correct. It could be a stylistic choice or a dialect choice. Please do not assume the two ARC teams, betas, alphas, and several proofers missed everything you believe is incorrect. Contact me if you find things; I want to make sure it doesn't get taken down so everyone can read!

If you see this book *anywhere besides major retailers or my website in ebook format,* please reach out to me via social media or email. Pirating kills my ability to write full time and I am so grateful for your help.

Contact Cass for issues or to report piracy: teamcassandra@cassandrafeatherstone.com

A Note To My Loving Family Members and Their Friends...

THANK YOU FOR SUPPORTING ME BY BUYING THIS BOOK!

Do. Not. Read. My. Books.

HOWEVER...

MY MOTHER TOLD ME ALL ABOUT HER VACATION THIS SUMMER AND TO NAPA THIS FALL WHERE SHE TOLD EVERYONE THAT HER DAUGHTER IS AN AUTHOR BUT SHE'S NOT ALLOWED TO READ IT BECAUSE SHE'S PRETTY SURE IT'S PORN....

IF YOU'RE GONNA DO THAT, ASK ME FOR SOME FREAKING BOOKMARKS SO YOU CAN GIVE THOSE PEOPLE MY WEBSITE.

I MEAN, FOR REAL, I'LL TEXT YOU THE QR CODE.

DON'T WASTE FREE PRESS, GUYS.

CAVEAT: *IN CASE YOU MISSED THE FIRST PART OF MY STATEMENT* —IF YOU CHOOSE TO KEEP READING, KNOW THAT AT NO TIME WILL I EXPLAIN TERMS, POSITIONS, THEMES, TROPES, OR ANY OTHER PART OF THIS NOVEL AT FAMILY EVENTS, IN GROUP CHATS, OR ON SOCIAL MEDIA.

THAT MEANS STOP ASKING ME, LADIES—AND NOW ONE GENT.

AWKWARD.

Revealed in the Hollow Playlists

CHAPTER TITLE SONGS

Revealed in the Hollow Playlist

BONUS PLAYLIST

Fucking Fae Playlist

To the fans hoping my 'Govern me, Daddy' tee-shirt

is foreshadowing Teddy's future...

If I told you, I'd have to kill you.

A PINCH OF SOUL
WITH A WHOLE LOT OF SASS
A SPRINKLE OF NAUGHTY
AND JUST ENOUGH CLASS.
THE STRENGTH OF A WARRIOR
AND A 'GO TO HELL' GLARE
A PAST THAT'S NOT PERFECT
BECAUSE LIFE ISN'T FAIR.
A SAILOR'S MOUTH
WITH A HEART FULL OF LOVE,

THAT'S WHAT A **BADASS** IS MADE OF.

~CWPOET

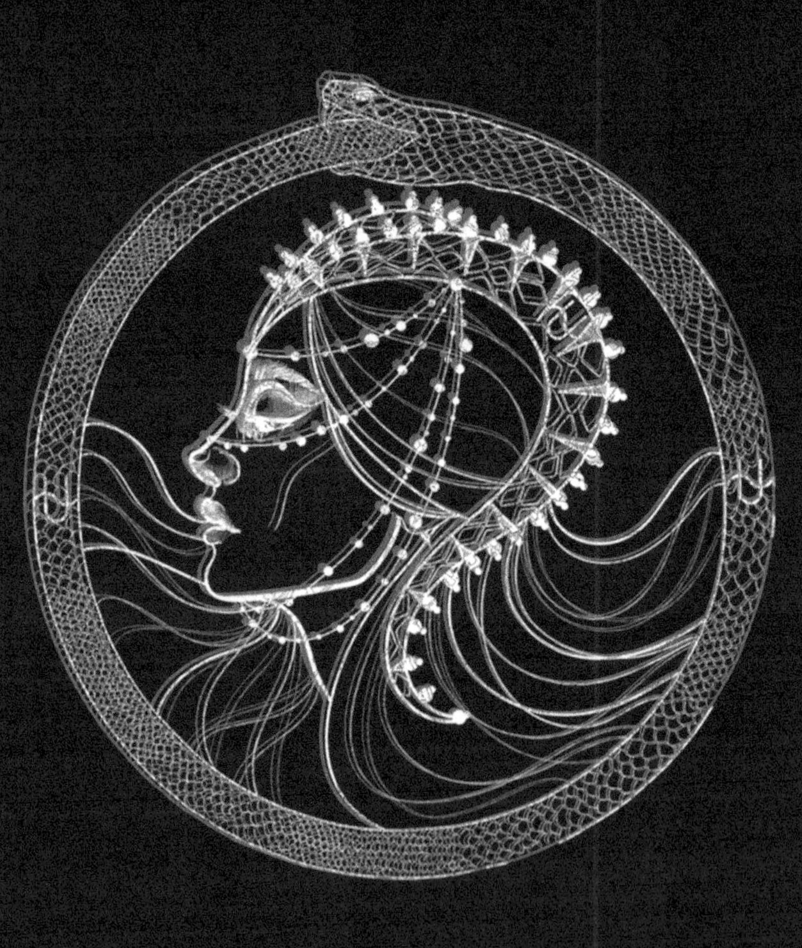

WAIT!

Previously on Rejected in the Hollow...

When our fierce FMC, Jolene woke up in the hospital, she learned the people she trusted most were keeping massive secrets from her. Julia tried to help her understand why all of her friends and lovers had to hide the truth from her, but Jolene wasn't ready to accept that as an excuse. She refuses visits from her men and best friend, except to let them know they aren't welcome in her home. Once released, she heads home with her animal companions and her pain alone.

Teddy, Wolfie, Presley, Benjy, and Saoirse head to Doyle's home to figure out how to get Jolene to forgive them. Seer mentions Jolene was hypnotized by a mysterious woman in London and since then, she's been much less willing to allow people to treat her the way they used to. That gets the guys' attention and they have Seer dig out her old albums from their time in Europe to investigate it.

Once they arrive at Doyle's, they discover he lives in a 'Mary Poppins portal', which means he's at least half-deity. He reveals his mother is a goddess who he can't name unless they find out and his father is a god from another pantheon, but he doesn't know who. They finally settle in to work on finding out who the mystery hypnotist is.

Meanwhile, Jolene is suffering the effects of pushing away those she's bonded with. She's hurt and betrayed by her friends and men, but also the wound from her past has been ripped open as well. Seeing Trevor and Antigone at the ball triggered something inside her she didn't know about, but it also tore open what she believed was healed. The pain of the past and present are melding together, making her volatile.

Resolved to survive this on her own, she goes back to work at the school right away. Ignoring the stares and even the tug to Teddy, she manages to get through the first bit until a flashback nearly floors her in her studio. It's from the night she and Teddy shifted, but she doesn't know it. Hugo finds her as she comes back to reality, puzzled by how weird she's acting. She finds out Mayor Nelia chastised the entire ballroom and forbade them from bothering her when she first came back to give her time to heal.

The search through Seer's photo albums continues that night until they finally find one with the two women posed with rockstars at a knighting ceremony. Since the pixie remembers the hypnotist being recommended by a rockstar Jolene hung out with at one point, the snapshot gives them a solid list of names to use to find out who the danger was. Their conversation shifts to how they're going to get Jolene to forgive them and they realize they have to share their secrets with one another or they can never share them with her.

At least, the ones they aren't forbidden from sharing with her.

Jolene continues to fight her way through her isolation until Jackson calls with news. She's distracted by Zelda losing her wig and ends up not getting to hear it. Once inside Atwater's, Mina Cantwell drops some very interesting info about her past and Jolene has a flashback that helps her put some pieces together about her mother. Namely, her mother was part of some organization and she definitely monitored everything about her child, hoping it would help her career. It causes Jolene to have a minor breakdown, and she heads to the farm to ride.

What she doesn't know is that her mysterious sponsor, the sheik owner of the horse she's training, is on-site today. The sheik, Dhameer, is speaking with Percy about the horse's training when he learns she is present on the farm. He has several aides with him who are unimpressed by her sassy refusal to come meet the prince. However, Dhameer finds it amusing and leaves to chase her down. We find out he is a djinn—much older than anyone in the Hollow, even Doyle. Djinn are very rare and highly sought after for their powers, but he keeps his true self hidden.

Jolene and Dhameer bond as she screams out her rage and frustration with the universe. He allows her to vent, and she can feel in control of herself again. She decides that she's not behaving like someone who went through therapy to heal her wounds and behaves like an emotionally mature person—especially with the guys. The prince merely listens, but promises they will have more in-depth contact once she is stable again.

The next time Jolene ventures out, she's getting stronger, but her trip to Derby Pies is a disaster when she runs into one of her nemeses, Sherilynn. Because mean girls never stop their bullshit, the woman picks a fight in the middle of her own restaurant. It ends with Jolene's promise to hit her back harder every time she comes at her. That incident is compounded by another altercation later in the week at the grocery store, but Saoirse steps in to save the day. Jolene's ice towards her bestie thaws and she admits she's planning to track down the crooked cop they found out about before Halloween.

Jackson Thorn is right in the thick of that, allowing Jolene to use his jet, but also letting the guys know where she's planning to escape to on the month long winter break. They come to her house, ambushing her to get back in her good graces. After much debate and some steamy makeup sex, she agrees to let them join her on the trip to Istanbul. It's a path to forgiveness, and our girl has decided it's time to bury the hatchet.

Edgar convinces her to allow Benjy to join them, and everyone, including the companions, packs up on Jackson's huge company jet headed for a new lead on her parents' death. Edgar and Benjy get some alone time with Jolene in the bedroom, cementing the new member of their family. The next morning, she has an odd experience while cleaning up for the day, but shrugs it off to have a family breakfast. They go over the plan for when the plane lands, calling

Jackson for the intel on how to get what information they need out of the embassy.

The guys discuss Doyle's theory about her unknown supe sides mating with parts of them that correspond with her own. While she sleeps, they talk about how unusual it is for someone to have a mating group of over three and what they might have to do to protect her until she emerges. Despite reservations, they come to a consensus about visiting Wolfie's mother after the stop in Istanbul. It's dangerous, but she may have heard something about a myth or prophecy that explains Jolene's odd attributes.

When they land, everyone has assigned tasks and Saoirse splits off to get her stuff done. The group heads for the house Jolene rented, finding it to be utterly amazing. They have a day to settle in, then they head for their appointment at the US Embassy. The assistant tries to block them from speaking to the ambassador, but Teddy whips out his dad's name to put pressure on. It only gets them a nasty upper assistant who gives them a strange amount of hassle until, out of nowhere, Dhameer shows up.

The jerk has to let the Prince and his entourage in, so they split the group. Jolene goes with the Prince and his people, while the others are to follow the assistant to see the sights of the embassy building. Jolene tours the gardens with Dhameer, where he invites her to join him at a thoroughbred auction the next day. They don't get to meet the ambassador, but they definitely get a read on what they need to continue their quest to find the cop.

While Jolene heads to the show with the Prince, the guys head out to break into the house the crooked cop supposedly lives in. The place is much too fancy for his income level and when they approach, Hugo has a vision. It tells him they have to find out what's in this place and they need to shift to get past the security. When they enter, the house smells like death and they find the bodies of the cop and his family. Someone got there before them.

Meanwhile, Jolene is dressed to the nines and touring the horse auction with Dhameer. Everything seems elegant and refined—until it doesn't. They run into a woman the sheik calls the 'Panther

Queen', who he met when she was hired to kill someone at another event. He sold her a special horse, and she recognizes them immediately. She's very mysterious and seems interested in Jolene, but says they will have to meet again on another day. Jolene has a weird feeling that she knows her, but can't place it. They have a long conversation once the redhead leaves, but it's obvious the Prince is worming his way into Jolene's heart.

The guys go through the entire house, hoping to get whatever the people who killed the cop missed. They find nothing, but they inform Nelia and do their best not to leave a trace. By the end, Teddy wrangles a dinner date with Jolene and Benjy for the evening so the others can meet with Seer to do a summoning for his mother. It's obvious they won't find any more in Istanbul and it's time to move on.

On the way home, they have to stop at a magic shop to gather ingredients for the ritual to contact the Cailleach. The shop is called *Destiny* and when they step inside, they find out the owner is a very odd woman. Suddenly, Wolfie recognizes her as the wildcard from the trial—the woman with the enormous wolf. She's Nelia's sister, and she's a Guardian, but of whom, she doesn't say. She sells them the necessary items, but it's clear she knows more than she's saying.

When Dhameer and Jolene get back from the show, the gang is waiting for them. The Prince says goodbye and the guys usher our girl to get ready for her date with Teddy and Benjy. Wolfie helps her get styled, and they have a lovely moment together before it's time to go.

Doyle, Wolfie, Teddy, and Prez head to a Society meeting place to do the ritual. It's guarded by a weird old supe who gives them a lot of shit until she realizes they're with the Prince and Hugo. Yet again, those two have arrived just in time to save the day. Once they get free of the old witch, they go into the altar room to do the spell and Wolfie's mother uses projection to answer them. She's rude, snooty, evil to her son, and they have to bargain to get her to agree to meet in person. She gives them a spot in Scotland to meet her in four days, but not before treating Wolfie like shit.

Teddy and Benjy have a fabulous romantic date with Jolene, where they both apologize for their teenage stupidity in the past. She accepts, and they have a steamy time on the beach. That night, Jolene has a vivid dream about her parents and the past. Her mother mentions emerging, and her father is defending her. She finds out she was adopted and her mother was definitely not who she thought. Deciding to get Eli on that trail, she puzzles through the dream until Wolfie wakes up. He comforts her and takes her downstairs to get breakfast before the others wake.

Once they share the story of their dinner, the guys let Jolene know they need to go to Scotland. Instead of fighting them, she agrees immediately, and they rush to get packed up. While they're flying, Presley tells Wolfie they may need to go to Faerie while they are there and figure out who his dad is. They worry about how they'll get Jolene through that without her figuring out things she isn't supposed to know yet. Jolene joins them in the plane's bedroom and things get hot… leading to Presley's bird claiming her, too.

From the minute they land at the airport, everyone is on edge. Wolfie's mother is not to be trifled with, and they have to make certain she doesn't spill the beans to Jolene. Wolfie explains how she works and what to watch for, hoping to protect them from her vicious games. It will be a challenge, but Jolene and the guys are definitely prepped to get it done.

Meanwhile, Saoirse is on a mission elsewhere; Andromeda Bane sent her to parlay with the Fates. Their lair is not what she expected and neither are they, but she gathers the tributes they require to have an audience with them. They tell her the troubles in Bay City and Salem will cease when specific supes rise to the challenge. She is not meant to join her friends in Scotland, but to journey to Prague to pass on a message from them.

The gang gathered in the ruins as the Cailleach demanded, waiting for her. When the sun sets, she arrives, all elegance and haughty demeanor. She pretends to know Wolfie better than she does, and he has to correct her. True to form, she says she has information, but it will come at a cost. The witch toes the line as she taunts them, almost revealing things she, too, is bound to keep secret from Jolene. Finally, she demands a hard truth from each of them as payment for her intel.

Benjy admits he never loved Sherilynn. Teddy says he liked Jolene as a kid and his parents told him to stay away—and might have set the girl bullies on her. Presley tells her off for treating Wolfie like shit, which he's never done before. Wolfie admits he only speaks to her to protect those he loves from her revenge. Doyle admits he'd like to break his oath to squash her like a bug, but he can't. The last one to give up the truth to the winter witch is Jolene, who explains that a rogue doctor sterilized her as a kid and she cannot have children.

The Cailleach accepts their payment and tells them they should go to the place Presley was considering. Jolene doesn't know she means the Faerie, but the guys do. She warns them that if they can navigate through without breaking the rules, they may find out things about themselves and the others in their group they did not know. Jolene isn't satisfied, but the witch doesn't care. She leaves them standing with her promises in the air.

After the visit with the witch, the guys are worried about Jolene. They get back to the town at the airport, but they have to wait until the next day to leave. Jolene has a very weird dream about a mysterious lady in a garden who speaks in riddles and gives her a special pair of glasses. The woman says they will help her in the upcoming trip and to not take them off once she arrives at their destination. When Jolene wakes up, the glasses are real, waiting for her in the pocket of her pants.

Prez and Wolfie wake up, letting her know they're all leaving in a few hours for Ireland to find Wolfie's father. Unfortunately for them, she overheard them talking before she let them know she was awake and she definitely heard them talking about going to Faerie…

Something they're strictly forbidden from doing.

And now….

Prologue (from Rejected in the Hollow)

The guys have been watching me like hawks since we got back from our trip to visit Wolfie's mother. I think they expect me to break down, but I let go of my emotional attachment to that part of the past a long time ago. It's something that happened and by the time I knew about it, there was nothing that could be done. That was my first time in therapy and I worked on it for a year before. I didn't get upset in the feminine aisle at the store. But after that, I had to accept reality and grieve.

You cannot undo what is permanent and there comes a time when you have to accept your fate.

That was a hard lesson to learn as a preteen and sessions with Andromeda helped. She picked up where the therapist left off and guided me through that and my mother's growing disappointment in me. Eventually, I had other things to worry about like the popular kids' wrath.

"The more I learn about the world I grew up in, the less surprising it is that my brain has blacked out most of it," I murmur to Teddy.

"You struggled a lot more than anyone knew," he replies. "I don't know how you got such good grades and did all the shit you did without once letting anyone know what was going on."

I snort. "Oh, hell, Teddy. There are people who go through much worse than I did and keep it under wraps. No one beat me or starved me—I just had a lot of emotional garbage that fucked up my head enough to make my brain misfire all the time. And overcoming that is something people do every day."

"Tilly, that secret you shared is assault. It should have been prosecuted. You were harassed and bullied so badly in senior year that you had to go to home school. That should have been pursued. Your fiancé was a tool, and your parents were probably murdered. No one is asking you to compare your hardships to people with even worse issues. Trauma doesn't need to be qualified for it to affect you deeply."

"Someone's been reading my old textbooks," I say with a smile. "That's Psych 101, Teddy bear."

He tugs me onto his lap and squeezes me close. "I have to, Tilly. You've got a degree and none of us stands a chance with all of this adult shit, especially when you manage to constantly amaze us with your strength."

"Teddy, if you don't quit doing all of this shit to make yourself look good, I'm going to think I conked myself on the head four months ago and ended up in a coma fever dream full of romance novel dudes."

"Fuck, no, magpie. Who would dream up an asshat like Haggerty on purpose?" Presley comes into our hotel room with Wolfie and carryout in tow. "Now, Lucy and I, on the other hand…"

"Oh, don't start this shit again," I say as I accept the bag with my food. "I am *not* ranking any of you—not by stamina, length, annoyance, muscles, smarts, humor… That is a hard 'no' from me. You're all different and I like that. There's… balance in your differences that I find comforting."

"Well said, Princess." Benjy grabs his food and flops on the couch. "Both diplomatic and honest."

"It would be more impressive if every time this shit came up, you fuckers didn't point at me as the sore thumb," Doyle bitches. "Because I allow all of you to live without doing something I would *not* regret, I'm the most amusing git in the room. Plus, I'm the least concerned with consequences."

Presley ponders for a moment. "He's right. If we had to send someone flying into a dangerous situation, I'd nominate him first."

Teddy's chest rumbles with laughter, and I bury my face against his shoulder. Their bickering doesn't bother me; in fact, it feels like the shit a family does. The sense of camaraderie between my guys makes it easier to accept that we all really can live together and be happy. When I stop snickering, I give Doyle a fond smile. "You can be the kamikaze psycho if it makes you happy. But I know you're more than that and so do they."

"Whatever," he grumbles and dives onto the other couch.

Uh-huh.

I open the container of delicious smelling, meaty stew and inhale before I look over at them. "So who's going to tell me where we're going and why no one told me you were considering adding a stop to our trip?"

"Once more into the breach," Doyle mutters before he looks at me. "The doc thought we should try to find the pup's dad in his hometown. We hadn't decided if it made sense to go, but since the bitch said we need to talk to people there…"

That story is full of holes, but they all seem to think I'm going to buy it.

"I don't even know where to start with this. Why are we trusting that woman? How does Wolfie know what town we need to visit? And how am I supposed to accept all of this wacky shit like that woman staging her entrance and exit with some sort of fog machine and weird effects, like she's a ghost on the moors?"

For a few long minutes, the room is completely quiet. They all look at me curiously, as if they're waiting for something to happen that doesn't.

"Hell, I told you she was crazy, magpie. She must have hired a crew or something. Callie is rich, evil, and bored, so nothing she does surprises me. You heard what she said to all of us." Prez shrugs and gives me a sad look when my gaze cuts over to Wolfie.

"Fine. She's insane and willing to go to great lengths to fuck with Wolfie. How does that translate to following her leads?" I say as I pinch the bridge of my nose. I must be hungry because my head is hurting. While I wait for them to answer, I take a bite of the stew, groaning happily as the heat slides down into my stomach.

"We picked the right thing," Wolfie says as he grins at Prez. "I can tell by her sexy food sound."

"I do not have a 'sexy food sound'; take it back!"

They all look at one another and say in unison, "Yes, you do."

"Traitors," I hiss under my breath as I take another bite. "When I get finished, I'm going to punish all of you."

Teddy shakes his head. "No, you're going to eat and then take a nap, Tilly. We've been running since we got up yesterday morning. You slept a little on the plane after you played around with the docs, but since then you haven't gotten a wink."

He's not wrong. The headache might be a lack of sleep.

"Fine. I'll eat and take a nap. But when I wake, someone better have a better reason for us to go running off to Ireland because some mean old witch said to."

That doesn't get an answer, either, so I let them chew on it while I eat.

If they think I'm joking, they'll find out soon enough that I'm not.

I'M SURROUNDED BY GLITTERING TREES AND PLACID WATERS. THE AIR IS heavy with the scent of flowers and something sweet I can't identify, but I know I should follow it. Sniffing, I pad through the forest, watching carefully for threats. I'm not sure why I think I need to watch for things I can't see, but when I look up at the starry sky, laughter echoes off the hills.

Nothing about this place is familiar, yet I feel like I know where I'm going.

Coming to the edge of the dense copse of trees, I look out into the clearing in wonder. Crystalline waterfalls spill into an oasis surrounded by vibrant plants, and there's a small table set with a tea service.

That's the smell... It's an herbal tea steeping in the pot.

I rise from all fours, though my mind can't process why I would be crawling. My body aches for a moment as I stare at the set-up, waiting for the reason I've been drawn here to become clear.

A hooded figure emerges from behind the rocks of the waterfall, gliding through the water. It seems to allow the person to move through it without soaking them and I know I have to be dreaming again. But this dream isn't like the ones where I feel animalistic or the waking dreams I believe are memories. No, this dream feels as though I'm in a world apart from the one I live in and I'm here because they have summoned me.

One hand appears from under the robes and gestures for me to come closer and I do, despite the anxiety warring within me.

"I'm so happy you accepted my invitation," the person says. The voice isn't imme-diately identifiable as male or female, but the tone makes me believe it must be a woman. Men simply don't speak that way.

I tilt my head as I take the seat she's gesturing at. "I don't believe I had a choice."

"True. You would have heeded my call whether you wanted to or not, but you made a choice to follow the scent."

Looking down at myself, I note that I'm wearing the clothes I fell asleep in, but I'm covered in dirt and brush, just like I am when I wake up from the weird animal nightmares. "Why am I here?"

"So much like me," she murmurs. "You are not carbon copies, but you all possess

the grit you need for the future. I am proud to see the world has not withered your thorns."

I give her a suspicious look. "That wasn't an answer."

"Also true! There are things I, too, cannot relay to you, Jolene, but I am not your enemy. I brought you here because you are about to undertake an important journey and it will require you to trust those around you implicitly. Like me, they are trapped by rules put in place many centuries ago to protect our kind. You are not yet at the place where you will understand, but it is imperative that you follow their lead."

"I swear to Christ, that weird drug from the club must have fucked up my brain somehow. All this bullshit with bizarre dreams and odd physical ailments cannot be normal."

"Your life was never meant to be ordinary, Jolene. However, it will take time for you to see the truth. What is important now is that you listen to what I tell you and follow my instructions exactly. Deviation could cause terrible consequences." She lifts the pot, pouring me a cup of tea before she continues. "That sounds rather distressing, but I must get you to understand."

I will not touch this crazy woman's drinks; I saw Alice in Wonderland and the Princess Bride. Who the hell knows what she put in it?

Instead, I give her a curious look. "What are your instructions? I can't agree to something if I don't know what it is. That's like signing a contract you don't read."

"Excellent! That suspicion will serve you well on your trip. Remember those words any time someone asks you a question, Jolene. The people you meet are very tricksy and they seek to trap people with their words."

"Again, you're dodging my question and I'm getting irritated. I'd much rather be dreaming about getting laid than solving riddles," I say with a sigh.

That earns me a throaty laugh. "Ah, yet again, the apple and the tree. Yes, I believe you would enjoy that more. But alas, this is urgent and you'll have to put off your spicy sexcapades until we are through."

This time, I don't even reply. I just look at her in annoyance.

"Fine, fine. I'll get to the point. Your family is taking you to a place to seek clues. There is a quirk of fate which deems that both a place they should not be taking you at this time, but it is also your destiny to go there. You are not ready for this, though the binding is loosening every day, so I must intervene to help them." She reaches into the pocket of her robes and pulls out a pair of rainbow cat eyed glasses. "These do not have a prescription, per se, but they will help your vision and your headaches. You must wear them anytime you open your eyes while you are there. If not, the consequences for your men could be dire."

Something inside of me pushes my hand out and I take them. When I put them on, the beautiful world around me turns into a grungy pub. We're not the only ones here, but everyone else seems to ignore our presence like we're ghosts.

"What the fuck?" I whisper.

"Indeed," she says solemnly. "An ancient friend who married someone he wasn't supposed to gave these to me. I have no need for them now because I have many pairs and I can spare one for you in order to keep you safe."

"Why would you do that?"

"Why does anyone do anything, Jolene? It is in my best interest to keep you safe and happy, I also want to do so. So I am here, breaking more laws than I can count, providing you with a tool to prevent you from making mistakes that will alter important events." She pauses, and it's eerie how empty the hood seems when she's not talking. "Do you agree with my terms?"

"This will help keep the people I love from getting hurt?"

"Nothing is fool-proof and your men have free will, but this will help keep you from being threatened by forces I have yet to identify while you are on this quest. That is as much as I can tell you now. There are no guarantees in life, and I would be lying if I gave you one."

"Okay. I'll do it."

"When you wake, they will be in your pocket. Keep them close and do not ask too many questions when your family explains where you are going. They will be clumsy and inept with their excuses because they do not want to lie, but also cannot tell the truth."

"Great. More lies."

"Only of necessity, Jolene. Now close your eyes and when you wake, remember only my words and your agreement."

"But I—"

I jerk awake when the alarm goes off on the bedside table. The guys are all draped in various places around the room because the bed was too small to fit everyone. They must have given me the bed, so I'd sleep rather than wiggle around until we got frisky.

"Sugarplum?" Wolfie says sleepily. "Was that the alarm?"

I nod, feeling oddly rested and groggy at the same time. When I roll over to turn the obnoxious noise off, something pokes me in the hip. I reach into the pocket of my yoga pants and pull out a pair of rainbow glasses, frowning at them for a moment, until I hear a voice in my mind.

"You must wear them anytime you open your eyes while you are there. If not, the consequences for your men could be dire."

I rub my hand over my face, trying to remember if we'd been drinking before I went to sleep. But if we had, these damn glasses wouldn't be in my pocket, would they? Someone has to be playing a prank on me—maybe it was Doyle. I turn to see if he's smirking, but he's still dead to the world in the big armchair.

Why is my life a cosmic joke? Dream glasses? I definitely have a tumor.

"It's not a tumor," Presley mumbles, and I realize I said that out loud. "The internet is ruining medicine."

My lips curve up and I wait for the others to slowly awaken as Wolfie gets up and starts packing things. There isn't much left besides the animals and a set of clothes for each of us, so I know he had everyone get ready while I was taking my weirdly prophetic nap. "Where are we going again?"

"Ireland," Doyle says. "To find the pup's da."

I frown, squinting at him suspiciously. "Wolfie's not Irish."

"Keep them close and do not ask too many questions when your family explains where you are going."

The voice in my head makes me want to cry in frustration, but I heed its words when Teddy comes over and kisses my forehead. "It's where his mother said to go, *drugar*."

"We think we'll find... clues... that will help us identify him. In... Dublin," Prez adds.

Benjy elbows him in the side and he grunts, turning to lean in and whisper something to him that makes them both laugh.

Nodding quietly, I pretend I'm going along with their charade.

After all, I don't think they meant for me to hear Presley say, "It's not like I can tell her we're going to the Faerie."

I'm pretty sure they did not mean me to hear that.

OFF TO SEE THE WIZARD

JOLENE

THE ANIMALS KNOW something is off with me. Not only is Isis curled around me tightly as I lounge on the couch in Jackson's fancy plane, but Jekyll, Hyde, Kali, and Hecate have surrounded me from head to toe. The guys are watching the pile out of the corners of their eyes, but they've also been murmuring to one another intently when they think I've drifted off. Their low tones catch my ears better than I expect, and I've picked up bits of conversation I know I'm not meant to know about.

Such as they expect Wolfie's dad—if they find him—to be worse than his mother. Fat fucking chance of that.

My eyes are closed so I can continue to eavesdrop, but my mind is whirling with their words and the weird shit that the woman said in my dream. The goddamn glasses appearing like magic in my pocket were the kick in the ass I needed to start really looking at the shit going on in my life since I got home. Since I moved back to the Hollow, unexplainable crap has been crashing into me like a tidal wave. I've been so swept away in rebuilding and nursing the wounds that reopened when I got back that I brushed it off as paranoia.

Not anymore.

I knew growing up that our town was odd and a little sheltered. Hell, I knew my mother was weirdly standoffish and unsupportive when I stumbled. No one wants to admit their parents seem unimpressed with their very existence, so I set it aside to focus on my dad. He was always there and did what he could to mitigate the bullshit kids gave me. But he wasn't the force my mother was, and she never stepped in. I was too damaged to question it, even when that Dr. Frankenstein fucker escaped scot-free when he maimed me for life.

My brow furrows as I wonder whether or not he truly lied to my parents or if my mom somehow arranged that shit. She's not a Bond villain, so I doubt it, but how *did* that asshole not end up in jail? Who saved his ass from the justice he richly deserved? And why wasn't anyone nearly as mad as they should have been?

The past is so damn hazy in my mind still… it's hard to know what's real and what I've made up to fill in the gaps.

I thought after I left the Hollow, life would be so much better. I'd get away from my bullies, make something of myself, and go on to bigger and better things. In a way, I did—teaching, going to Europe, all my escapades with Seer—but none of it made facing this stupid little town easier when the time came. Seeing Trevor and Antigone on Halloween almost pushed me to destroy the happy life I was building.

Do we ever really heal from trauma to the core of our being?

"Have you guys noticed Magpie seems to be… noticing more? Like I catch this squint to her gaze that makes me wonder if what's binding her is getting thinner and thinner?"

My breath catches and I have to force it out slowly so they don't realize I'm not dozing. This is the thing I need to hear—whatever the hell it is, they aren't telling me because of some stupid oath. I don't know if tricking them into talking freely when I'm present is cheating, but fuck if I'm not going to try. As long as nothing weird happens while I do it, I'll know I haven't been caught.

In theory.

Teddy sighs and I imagine he's pinching the bridge of his nose like he does when he's frustrated. "I don't know, doc. There was definitely something up with her this morning, but she's putting on a good front. We've all seen hints she might have memories or flashbacks or something… But she obviously isn't ready to share it with us."

"I wish she would," Wolfie whispers. "I don't like feeling like Sugarplum is hurting. One or all of us could help her."

It's hard not to smile at his tone. My little Wolfie is the heart and soul of this jumbled family. No one scoffs at his words or even makes a snarky joke—not even Doyle. They know the vet is empathetic and always working to make peace between us.

A snort follows the silence as Doyle joins the conversation. "Aye, but you all know my Tíogair is stubborn as hell, though. She's still working on forgiving us and if she's seeing odd things she can't explain, we wouldn't be able to tell her what it was, anyway. Maybe that's why she's keeping it to herself."

Damn, that Irishman is clever. I can't fool him for a second.

"Guys, so much has changed for her in the past four months. I know I'm new, but… consider it for a minute." Benjy gathers his thoughts, and I'm surprised when they let him. "Jolene was told to kick rocks by the F.B.I. after they spent months training her. She had to come back here and I don't think she ever wanted to. There are animals appearing everywhere, guys up in her grill wanting to mate with her, women trying to fuck with her, and then she finds out everyone is lying to her, but they can't explain. Add to that the shit about her parents' death and normal Hollow shit? I mean, it's a fucking miracle the Princess hasn't had a breakdown."

"She might even think she *is* having one," Presley murmurs. "If she's waking with scratches and having weird visions and dreams, plus, none of us seem concerned… she might think her brain is shutting down."

I mean, he's not wrong. I've definitely considered that I might be off my goddamn rocker. The bruises, scratches, and other injuries have been weighing on my mind. Wolfie suggested I was sleepwalking, but paired with that wavy mirror incident on the way to Istanbul, my sanity was in question. But listening to them right now… they sound like they *expect* this kind of shit. If so, their adamant denial of me having a stroke or whatever makes sense.

But why? Why is this happening to me? Why now, and why aren't they shocked?

The memories that blink in and out lately feel *real*, and so do the dreams. Admitting that means I have to allow for out of the ordinary shit to be true, and that means I have to accept that the world might not be as black and white as it seems. More than that, I might be more than I seem, and so might everyone I know.

I'm not so cynical that I don't believe there might be more out there than people realize—everything from ghosts to aliens to vampires *could* be real. Just because I've never experienced any of that woo-woo shit doesn't make it completely bunk. But… whatever is going on here feels like it's life changing. Letting in the possibilities based on my experience in the past few months is bigger than putting up a Fox Mulder poster in college.

It means believing that there's a whole other world beyond the one I've been living in and I don't know if I can do that.

"We have to make sure she doesn't think she's going crazy, guys. Even the thought of it can really harm you," Wolfie whispers.

My heart aches for a moment because I know he's thinking about his adopted mom, Aurelia. The trail we followed to the crooked cop suggested her decline started right around the time my parents had their accident and her job at the police station made us suspicious. I bet he's been wondering if she saw or heard something she shouldn't have back then and the pressure caused her to have a mental break. I need to put Eli on another hunt—this one to see what happened to the one woman who didn't willingly hurt my darling boy.

"It's okay, Lucy. We won't let our magpie suffer. Right, Boone?"

A grumpy grunt echoes in the cabin, and I realize Teddy must be brooding while they've been chatting. I think he's the most irritable about the constraints on him that are keeping him from cluing me in.

Our past makes that difficult, especially since he's grown so much since the night he stood on my porch with a cocky grin. It would kill him to lose this and he's not willing to take the chance.

"I don't enjoy keeping her in the dark, nor do I wish to die for breaking the oath. Neither allows me to keep what's mine close and happy—a fact that irritates every single one of my sides to no end. Having three aggressive beings unable to do what they want is hard to manage on a good day. I'm worried what will happen when we have to deal with the fucking Fair Folk and their need for trickery."

Fair folk? They actually meant The Faerie? *Literally?*

"I can help," Wolfie says softly. "I may not know who my father was, but I know how that half of my people work. Dark Fae are harder to predict, but if we are careful with our words, obey their rules, and avoid making any deals, we should be okay."

"Oh, is that all? I never would have thought it'd be so easy," Doyle says teasingly. "Especially when your kind exists to trick and trap the other supes and humans for sport."

Edgar's growl almost sounds inhuman this time. "Do not. Be. A. Dick. To Him. Haggerty."

"Oooooh. Touchy doggy." Doyle stills sounds amused as fuck and I can hear rumbling coming from Teddy's direction. "I wasn't being a purposeful dick, as much as being honest. His words are true, but the reality is much tougher. All the Fae will know we're there with someone who cannot be made aware of her surroundings. They'll use the oath to trap us."

"Shit," Teddy breathes in frustration. "You're right."

"How the hell do we avoid it, then?"

I smile as Benjy ignores the bickering to ask for the solution. He wasn't this peaceful in high school, but I find myself soothed by his no nonsense attitude now. He's not afraid to assert himself, but he's also not an aggressor like Doyle or Teddy.

"Honestly?" Wolfie pipes up. "We don't avoid their games as much as we have to play them better. That's really what I meant. Every word you say will be used against you, but you can also do the same with theirs. Following the rules can be as literal as you make it—because if they omit things, they aren't *in* the rules. That works both ways, of course, which is why I said don't make bargains, deals, bets, or any sort of agreement, even jokingly, without considering every meaning of every word."

Great. We're going to the land of fucking Scrabble to match wits with magical Batman villains. That's exactly my idea of a good time.

"And remember, they're bound to the oaths their rulers took even in their lands. Disobeying the Society's rules about the unemerged would ripple their kingdoms as well. We *all* have to abide by the treaties or it'd be chaos."

Doyle sighs and I imagine him stretching out with a pout. "Don't I know it. My auntie and the rest of the feckin' assholes up there hold us to their edicts *and* the bloody Society rules, so it makes getting anything done an effort one of my dear cousins would have had trouble with."

"That was a hint, wasn't it?" Presley says in an amused voice. "You love flaunting those rules, Haggerty. I think you're a bigger wildcard for this brief trip than Magpie is."

Unfortunately, I'm not sure he's wrong.

Worry

Wolfgang

My anxiety has been ramping up with every minute we get closer to Dublin. I haven't been here since I located my mother when I was younger. I only entered Faerie briefly on that visit—just long enough to realize I wouldn't find my father easily because he didn't *want* to be found. Callie, as my sugarplum is calling her, wasn't hiding as much as she simply didn't give a shit about what happened to me. The paternal side of my lineage was actively trying to cloak himself in shadows.

That kind of asshole didn't deserve my presence in his life, anyway.

However, all that means is that although this land is my birthright, I don't have contacts or strong ties to anyone who can help us. Theoretically, I'll have a species advantage that may be useful; the Fae are my people and I should be able to suss out their horseshit. But what I can't do is give us solid leads or a good place to start. It makes me feel useless and I don't like that, either.

Doyle seems pretty familiar with the culture, though, and I wonder for a second if he's considered that his own father might be tied to the Celtic pantheon. He slips into the persona of an Irishman well, and his mischievous bent certainly mimics the tricksy smugness of many of the various Fae who live there. It's not a stretch, but since we don't know who his mother is, I can't put my finger on who his father could be.

Like calls to like, after all.

The biggest problem about this outing is Jolene—both her natural outspokenness and dancing around the oath because she's unemerged. She's smart and curious, which the Fae will love, but she's also prone to telling people where they can stick it if they make her mad. That won't play well with some species, especially royalty. It will make everything harder, even with me, smooth talking Teddy, and placid guys like Benjy and Prez. Fuck only knows what Doyle will do, so he's my second worry.

"Lucy, you can't control this. You know that."

Prez's murmur in my ear makes my cheeks heat. He knows me so well. "I do, but I can't help worrying. Everyone knows how they … are."

I have to be careful what I say now because we're in the car heading towards the outskirts of Dublin where the entrance to the Veil is. Sugarplum is in the front seat with the judge, but she sees and hears more than people realize. I'm sure it's part of her law enforcement training and I know it's not to be intrusive. None of us can take chances, though, because we have her and our family to live for. Risking death when we've found our mate isn't an option.

"Relax, wee pup. I've been here more times than Boone's bent the rules." Doyle winks, giving me an unconcerned smile. "I know how the story goes once we're escorted into the… estate."

Jolene turns to look at us, frowning at me. "Do you think your father is bad?"

I sigh, shrugging. "No idea. The one time I went looking for him, he was a ghost. I got the sense that it was on purpose. Since Callie was a definite bust and he was purposely making himself scarce, I gave up. One asshole mother and one damaged one was enough for a lifetime."

"I'm sorry," she murmurs. "It's hard when the people who are supposed to take care of you turn out to be not what you thought they were or should be. The flashes of memory I've been getting have made me reevaluate my own parents. They aren't as bad as most of yours, but… I'm still having a hard time with it."

Benjy leans forward, grabbing her hand when Teddy growls in the driver's seat. "I think what Edgar would say if he wasn't focused on driving is that we didn't realize you were having flashbacks, Princess."

My brow furrows as I nod in agreement. "You didn't tell us. Why?"

"I don't know… I'm not even sure if what I'm remembering is real. Some of it comes to me while I'm sleeping. What if it's just weird dreams?"

My sugarplum bites her lip and I know why she's hesitating. Whatever she's seen—awake and asleep—has challenged her entire worldview of her childhood. She's struggling with the same feelings I had when I discovered Aurelia wasn't my mother. They only got worse when I met my bio mom and failed to locate my bio dad. It makes you spiral through the stages of grief while also wallowing in self-worth issues.

"Usually people don't dream while they're awake, sugarplum." I look into her eyes, trying to convey that I know what she's going through.

Presley squints at her. "You're having blackouts again?"

"Small ones. Mostly long enough to have these fugue dreams where I see and hear things that definitely feel like genuine memories. Like… I can place the scenes and see it through my eyes with complete confidence that it happened."

"*Tilly*," Edgar growls and I see his fingers tighten to white knuckles on the steering wheel. "That's important. You should have shared it with us."

She dips her head for a moment and when she raises it again, I feel her holding back tears. "I'm still figuring out how to deal with hearing that they adopted me as some sort of… career move, Teddy.

If it wasn't real, I didn't want anyone stomping around trying to uncover more of that truth when I wasn't ready."

Even I know he would move Hell itself to make her happy, but this isn't something he could have pushed; it's Society business.

"I might be a bulldog when cornered, Tilly, but I wouldn't force you to do anything you weren't ready for." His voice is soft, and I know he means it.

Jolene may not know that many of the children and grown adults in the Hollow were all adopted for similar reasons, but someday, she will. Abandoned hybrids like me, her, and so many others have long been sent to enclaves like the Hollow so Society members can raise them until their supe sides emerge. It's their way of making sure the world isn't full of lost ones walking around, causing chaos.

Ones they missed have fairly ugly places in human history; it never ends well for anyone.

Our girl turns back to the front for a moment, putting her hand on Teddy's arm. "I know you wouldn't. However, I also know you'd happily curb stomp anyone who stood in the way of me finding out what I need to know. I'd prefer not to risk you ending up in prison because some bureaucrat wouldn't release records Eli could hack with his eyes closed."

"Have you spoken to Thorn about this?"

The question sounds casual, but Doyle's testing the water. We need to know what shit she has him and his pet hacker looking into. Obviously, he won't break the oath, but he's not exactly skilled at hiding shit from her, either. Their time together at State U complicates the situation more than he'll admit. Jolene learned to read him, even by voice, and he refuses to acknowledge it.

"No," she sighs. "We've got Eli chasing the cop leads, Aurelia's info, shit about those club drugs, and digital breadcrumbs about my stalker. I feel bad asking about too many things at once. Jackson has other clients besides me."

Teddy snorts. "Like that fucking bloodbath up at SU in the hockey rink. The news says he's repping the rich hockey douche accused of killing his rival."

"Seriously? Why?" Presley says with a frown. "He doesn't seem like the criminal law type."

"Uh, maybe because the idiot being questioned is the heir to the Wolfenberg fortune?" The judge pauses as he listens to the GPS for a moment, then continues. "Also, because that rogue chick got made Dean and everything there is up in the air, I'd assume. It's playing hell with the odds on all of their sports teams because they could lose accreditation. I've had Billy up there watching it unfold so I can adjust things as needed."

Benjy scrubs his hand over his face, then shakes his head. "Boone, I'm not sure if it's genetic or if you can't help yourself. You've got Billy Remington running around spying? He's as thick as a tree trunk, man. Who's running the gym?"

"Billy's always my boots on the ground. *Better Booties* pretty much runs itself since I helped him replace the staff and management. His talents are *not* in business, as you know. They're much more suited to collection and intel gathering through less savory negotiations."

"Pan's hairy nutsack, I really am turning into a complete criminal since I got home." Jolene glares at Edgar, then Doyle, and lastly Benjy. The latter holds up his hands then thinks better of it. "Don't give me an innocent look. You run an illegal, unlicensed speakeasy, Benjamin Louis Foster."

She's got him there.

"Do we need to worry about any of this shit going on at the school you all attended?" Doyle sounds amused, but I wouldn't be surprised if he does his own poking around now that it's caught his attention.

"No." Teddy waves his hand as we turn onto another small dirt road. "I'm only watching because of the book. Nothing there—to my knowledge—affects what we're seeking. I'm sure Thorn will tell us if he finds anything pertinent—the last thing I saw on the gossip columns was one of his corporate planes landing in the city with an entire team."

"See? He's busy with some case," Sugarplum says. "Eli is probably helping, so I'm not adding anything about adoption to their list until I'm sure that wasn't just a weird dream."

"That's probably a good idea." Her eyes meet mine and I give her a small smile. "Finding out the truth is freeing, but it's also a field full of landmines. You'll question everything you knew about the parents you had and start aching to track down the ones who weren't there. That's a big distraction when we're already beset by bombs, puzzles, potential murders, secrets, and all this other shit. Maybe not adding it until you have to is the best decision."

The Irishman clears his throat, commanding our attention. "We're almost there. I think it's time to discuss how we're going to handle this one more time. I know it's vague, Tíogair, and that vexes you. But it's *imperative* to your safety that you're crystal clear about complying."

Her nose wrinkles, and she gives him a dirty look. "I'm not stupid, Lucky. You're all in the know about some dangerous shit I can't know and if I don't behave like a good girl, I'll get hurt. It doesn't have to be repeated over and over."

"I beg to differ, Tilly. You may not be stupid, but your head is hard as a rock." Edgar's voice is full of amusement and fondness, which makes me smile. "We're all aware you do shit just to piss me off sometimes. The cheeky idiot is trying to make sure you don't dig your heels in to spite me."

"Fair," she sighs.

You could hear a pin drop when she admits it. I'm the first to pick my jaw up, so I get the first word. "Holy shit, sugarplum."

"What? I have flaws, little Wolfie, and I know what they are. Something deep inside of me *adores*, trampling all over Teddy's fucking orders until he snaps. It makes me tingle and we have a good time afterward. Denying it would be silly and I get why you all think I'll struggle with this now."

This woman amazes me at least once a day with her self-awareness.

"Yeah, that sums it up, Tíogair. So you'll do your best *not* to make poor decisions based on pissing the doggy off?" He gives her a smirk and she shrugs.

"I'll *try*. That's the best I can do." Tilting her head, she listens to the GPS calling out directions, then pulls that weird pair of glasses out of her messenger bag. "I want Wolfie to get answers and hopefully, that helps us get more information about our search. So I'll behave until I can't. Deal?"

Doyle groans and throws his hands up. "What did we say about deals?"

This is going to be a pain in the ass for certain.

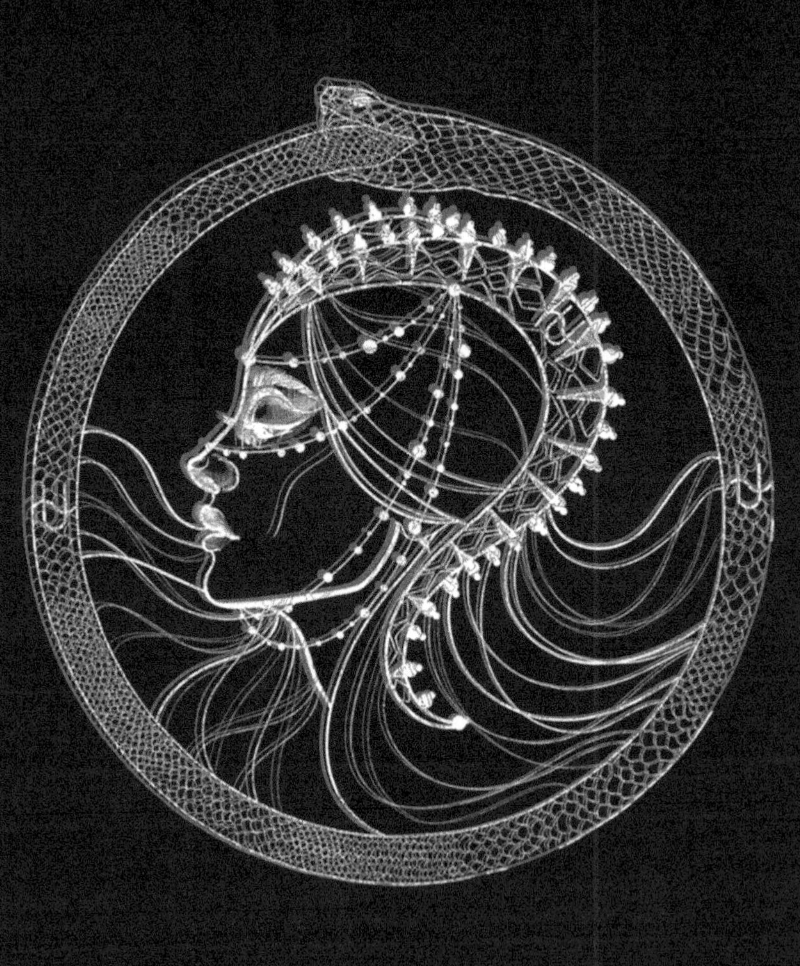

What's This?

Jolene

We pull up to a large, ornate looking house not long after my declaration. I squint through the glasses, surprised no one else is commenting on it being way out in the countryside like this. I almost ask, but a voice in my mind whispers to stay quiet. It's not my own, but I don't recognize it, either.

Jesus twerking Christ, I'm going to have a hard time with this trip; I can feel it in my bones.

"This is our destination?" I say instead, scratching my chin. "It must be bigger on the inside, like the fucking T.A.R.D.I.S. or something."

Doyle snorts, then coughs when someone elbows him hard. "Fuck, you animals. I'm only agreeing with her."

"It's a sprawling estate, Tilly." Teddy turns the car off, opening his door to hop out and head for the back of the vehicle. The trunk opens and I hear the animals grumbling discontentedly.

Isis got to stay with me as usual, but the cats and dogs were perched like sentries among the light luggage we packed. A thud on the roof of the car tells me Eury has arrived and I let out a breath. I've gotten so used to their presences that I don't know if I could deal with leaving them behind no matter where we're going.

"How long will this take, do you think? I mean, we only burned a couple days in Istanbul and another few with Wolfie's bitch egg donor, so we've got three more weeks. I'm just curious what the plan is."

Presley appears at my car door, yanking it open and holding his hand out to me. "Out you go, magpie. To answer your question, we're not sure. Since we *have* time, we'll stay until we settle this or run out of time, I suppose."

I'll have to walk around looking like a rave kid for weeks. Great.

"I'm sure we'll be greeted with some… fanfare," Wolfie murmurs. "It was the last time I came, though no one would explain to me why."

Frowning, I walk over and take his hand, squeezing it. "Maybe it wasn't because of your father, but because you're so damn pretty."

Teddy's head pops out from behind the car. "He sure as fuck is."

That makes our darling vet blush furiously and Prez laughs along with me. "Don't get shy now, Lucy. You know you're beautiful. Besides, it's more likely they greet anyone with an unknown heritage in that fashion. It allows them to get a read on the visitor and decide who in the… house… should be informed of their arrival."

They really suck at this and I'd love to tell them, but I'm not brave enough to peek and see what they're hiding yet.

"Stop it, guys," he mumbles as he walks over to round up the four-legged companions. "I know you're trying to make me less nervous, but I don't know if that's even possible."

"Pup, it doesn't matter what they say or do in here. Hell, it doesn't even matter if we find your bio dad. You have all of us, even the Irish jackass, and that's all that matters." Teddy's voice is a soft rumble, but I guarantee Wolfie is melting into him gratefully.

I don't know why, but it suddenly occurs to me that Teddy and I are the heads of this rag-tag family that's forming. We keep everyone focused and cared for without a second thought. And if you'd asked me if I thought this shit was possible when we knew each other in the past, I would have asked how high you were. Edgar Olivier Boone III is turning into the man he had the potential to become if he hadn't been surrounded by toxic assholes when we were young.

"Guys, we should probably get moving. Something is making me *anxious*," Benjy says as he joins us by the side of the car. "Like making *my hairs* stand up."

I have no idea what that means, but all of them pause in place.

"Yep, time to move," Doyle says as he slings a bag over his shoulder. "The welcome wagon is definitely waiting now."

Wolfie tugs a small rolling bag behind him as he emerges from behind the SUV. Jekyll, Hyde, Kali, and Hecate follow him towards me, all of them sporting pinned back ears. Cursing internally, I let them surround me as I head towards the enormous mansion with Teddy in tow. There's something wrong, and it's making my animals wary as fuck, but I know I have to trust the guys.

"These fuckers better have a *nice* welcome wagon waiting or I'll need someone to help me with controlling my fiery tempers," Teddy mutters to the group. "I'm getting fucking tired of all the damned surprises everywhere we go."

"Agreed," Benjy chimes in. "The feeling in my… gut… is not something I'm sure I can handle. I haven't felt this way in a long time, so I'm not used to it."

Fucking riddles. I hope to hell this place has good alcohol or I'm going to lose my temper at some point.

"Guys, I'm feeling a little left out. Can we just get to the door and find out what's behind it instead of talking in circles about it?" My voice is full of irritation, but I can't help it. The woman in my dream told me I had to trust their clumsy fibs because they're only doing it to protect me. That's simply easier in words than in practice because they really suck at it.

Doyle skips in front of me, winking playfully. "Come now, Tíogair. We're on an adventure to a place full of interesting things. You may not understand all of it, but you *will* have fun if I have anything to say about it."

"Have you been here before?" I almost smack my forehead when it pops out of my mouth. I know he has, but they don't know I overheard them on the plane.

"Mmm, yes, I have. This is a grand meeting place for people like me." He jumps up, clicking his heels together like an old timey musical character. "But don't feel bad—only the vet and I have visited the illustrious halls of our destination. Everyone else is a virgin, so to speak."

"Gross," Presley groans. "Why did you have to make it weird, Haggerty? We're all *long* past that particular rite of passage. Plus, the way people make it some big deal has always seemed strange to me. It's sound and fury, signifying nothing."

I blink. "Actually, I've always agreed with that. Down with the patriarchy and shit."

"Look what you started, doc. Now she's going to be 'I am woman; hear me roar' for the rest of the day." Teddy shoots a glare at him, his eyes dark. "That makes it *much* harder to get her pliant in the bedroom."

"*She* is right here, asshole, and we're coming up on the door. Can we *not* discuss our sex life in front of those frowning gentlemen standing next to it? They look as though they haven't gotten laid in a decade or more." I look up, making sure Eury is above us and when I see her, Isis squeezes me. They all seem to know how on edge I am about this shit.

It's damn near impossible for me to blindly trust anyone, especially so close to a betrayal.

"Everyone get ready. The first obstacle to finding out anything we want to know will be here. Remember: think about every word before you say it," Wolfie murmurs. "It matters."

This is going to be a disaster, and it will probably be my fault.

"Who approaches? Announce yourselves and be assessed for entry."

The man and woman standing on either side of the door to the immense house look tall and attractive, but not threatening. However, their scowls are almost indented in their faces. I guess this is a serious job and they have responsibilities—even if it seems like overkill to me. The woman spoke, but her companion is watching us like he'd be happy to toss us across the yard on our asses if we don't comply.

"Allow me to introduce our family," Teddy says smoothly. The guise of the perfect Southern gentleman radiates from him as he gives them his most charming smile. "This is Miss Jolene Whitley of Whistler's Hollow and her companion animals. It will be her first time here and we need to ask for your *discretion* because of her *late arrival*."

Both of the guards' eyes widen as they look at him, then at me in the ridiculous glasses, then back at Teddy. Finally, the female speaks again. "Your words are well chosen and we understand. Continue."

"I am Edgar Boone, also of Whistler's Hollow. My father, Senator Boone, has likely visited here on diplomatic trips." That gets their attention again, and I roll my eyes as he goes on. "The bespectacled gent is Dr. Presley Hamilton and his partner is Dr. Wolfgang Fletcher, both from the same town. Wolfgang has been to his homeland before."

"I see," the male grunts as he eyes Wolfie in a way I don't like. A soft growl echoes in my chest and the guard laughs. "Ah, we found the one they protect, Fiannula."

"Shut up, Lorcan."

Teddy clears his throat, sending Lorcan his own glare. "The redhead over there is Doyle Haggerty, currently of the Hollow, but of many other places prior. He, too, has been to this house—many times, I've been told. Benjamin Foster is the last of our group and he grew up with Jolene and I."

The woman straightens, reaching her hand out. "Present your hands one by one and we will determine whether we will grant you entry."

"Lorcan doesn't get to touch her."

I roll my eyes as Teddy snarls. "As if I'd want him to."

"Aye, lass. You've got enough cock to stuff a Dark Court whorehouse as it is."

Before I can shut Lorcan down, Doyle is on him, a knife at his throat as if it's a completely reasonable reaction. "Apologize to the lady or I'll get very clumsy."

"You can't…"

My Irishman looks at me. "Close your eyes, Tíogair. Just for a moment."

"But I…"

"You promised," the crazy ginger sing-songs and I groan. My eyes shut and I put my hands over the glasses. It sounds like there's a scuffle, but all Doyle says is, "Now do you see the bloody light, idjit?"

A muffled scream almost makes me peek, but suddenly, there's a warm hand at the small of my back. "Don't, Sugarplum. You promised."

Having a moral code sucks ass sometimes.

"Fine," I mutter. "Someone tell me when I can stop hiding from whatever the hell crazy pants is doing."

"You can open now, Tilly. I believe the jackass has made our point."

When I comply, I note Lorcan is still alive, but it smells like he might have just shit his pants. There's no blood on him, but even Fiannula looks spooked. *What in the fuck did he do and why does it smell like… sulfur?* Shaking my head, I let out a long breath.

"So, do we pass or what? I'm tiring of standing here like morons. We've been traveling for days and it's getting dark."

Fiannula cocks her head, looking at me with a slow, knowing grin. "Oh, yes. I definitely think I'll grant you all access to the…finest home in all the realms. How long you'll last is a toss-up, but the idea amuses me to no end."

"Great. Thanks. Glad to be of service," I mutter. "Can we go in now?"

The guard moves aside with a glare, holding a hand out as a door opens. I don't know what the hell that's about; it's not like I said something offensive. Shaking my head, I look at the other guard. Lorcan is still cowering, staying as far from my group as he can while all the men, animals, and I step inside one by one.

Something about the way she said that tells me we're in for a rough ride… but what else is new?

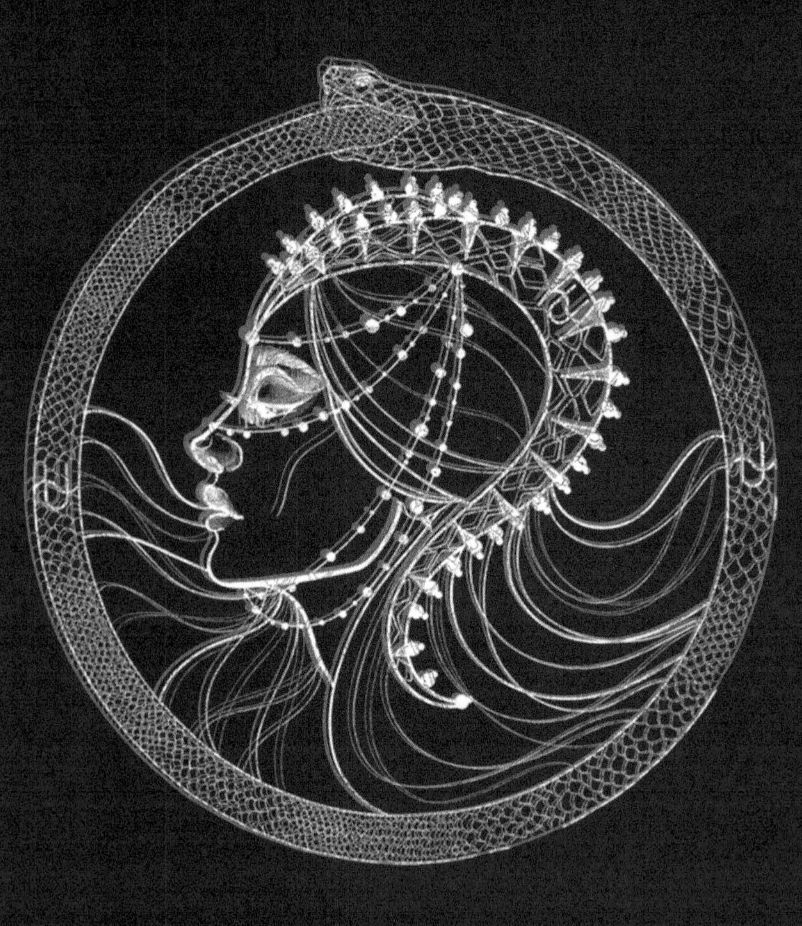

New World

Edgar

My eyes dart around the corridor that serves as a funnel to the portal to the Faerie. Everything inside of me—all three supe sides—are screaming at the danger this puts our mate in. I'm sure the pup and the doc are feeling the same; the tension is radiating off them in waves. Benjy doesn't get it yet, but that damn snarky demi-god does. He's fueled by the prospect of chaos and this unease is amping him up.

That's why he flashed his true energy at that smart mouthed guard and damn near blinded him.

Gods, even demi-gods or half-breeds like Doyle, are a reckless bunch. Their immortality makes it impossible to see things clearly in the short term. So when provoked, it's a toss-up whether they will cause a giant fucking mess for the Society to clean up. The Fae are equally long lived, so adding that to the mix is about as combustible as you can get until you factor in an unemerged supe.

"Haggerty, I'm going to need you to think with your damn brain, not your dick. You can't start a war here with your careless behavior. The balance is as volatile as ever." I shoot him a dark look, but he shrugs.

"Boone, old boy, that is none of my concern. I'm not far enough up the ladder to care about that shit, nor am I responsible for it. What I care about is our girl, and I'll do whatever it takes to make certain she's safe. Don't you feel the same?"

Before I can answer, Tilly grabs my arm and squeezes. "There's no need for you guys to fight. We didn't come here on some diplomatic mission like your father, but we don't need to piss our hosts off, either. I may not know why you're all so afraid of these people, but I assume it's money and power. I spent years in that world and they'll smell fear on you."

If only she knew how accurate that was.

"Aye, Tíogair, they will. They'll smell division as well, so it's best we only squabble in private once we're through this last door."

The faux Irishman stands at the gilded double doors, his lips curved up as he smirks at me. Tension dances in the air as he waits for me to nod, and when I do, he yanks it open with a flourish. "Welcome to Fair Lands, fellow misfits."

We walk inside, most of us looking around like Wonka just led us into the damn chocolate factory. The Fae certainly allow people to travel between their courts and Earth, but they've gotten stricter since that virus ran around the planet. It didn't affect most supes much, but the amount of expats flowing in to escape the craziness in our world overwhelmed them for a few years.

Hence, the idiots guarding the doors being such hard asses.

"This doesn't look much different from any other fancy retreat I've been to," Tilly murmurs.

Wolfie covers a laugh as the rest of us look at the lush foreign foliage and traces of magic floating through the air. "I suppose not, sugarplum."

Her head whips around and she nails him with a glare that would shrivel the balls off a fucking Minotaur. "Don't you patronize me, Wolfgang Lucien Fletcher. I might be a goddamn Magoo right now, but I can *feel* how amused you are."

"It's okay to feel left out, Princess," Benjy says as he steps in, putting an arm around her shoulder. "They're being dicks because they can't help themselves. I won't tease you; I promise."

I hold my breath for a moment, hoping she'll believe him. Since he's a recent addition to our motley crew, she's not as suspicious of his motives as she is with us now. Tilly chews her lip for a moment, squinting at him through the glasses, then sighs.

"I *hate* this, for the record. Being compliant without an explanation is going to give me hives." In contrast to her bitter words, she lets my friend pull her close. "Don't get any ideas about this being a permanent behavior—especially you, Teddy."

"I wouldn't dream of it."

She snorts, shaking her head. "*That* I do not believe, but lead the way. I'd like to get settled before we hunt down our prey."

"Shit, shit, shit."

Giving Benjy and our girl a little push, I wait until the animals follow them before turning around to see what's going on. I smile when I see Wolfie cursing under his breath as he tries to get control of his fully manifested Fae side. His wings flutter as he stomps his foot in frustration—something that makes him look even more delectable. Prez and Doyle are watching in amusement as he has a miniature tantrum, which means I need to intervene.

"Pup." I wait for him to look at me, tilting my head. "Did this happen the last time you came home?"

He rolls his eyes and pouts. "Obviously not, or I would have warned everyone. How the hell am I going to hide *wings* from her?"

I blink, realizing why he's making a stink. As long as Tilly is wearing the glasses, she won't see his iridescent skin or the pointed ears. The second she touches him, however, it will be impossible to conceal his glittery birthright. "I don't know, but we'll figure it out. Give her a bit of space until we know why you're reacting this way. I know that's not what you want, but you can cuddle Prez or I if you need tactile input."

"Boone's right, Lucy. This is only the second time you've been here and—"

"The first time he appeared with mates."

My head swivels to look at Doyle as he shrugs. "You think that's why?"

"Fuck if I know for sure, mate, but that's the difference, isn't it? Little cub changed nothing else, right?" Wolfie shakes his head and the demi-god nods. "See? The bloody land has something to say about it. We'll have to listen closely to suss out what."

"Great," Wolfie mutters as the doc pulls him to his side. "Benched by my damn homeland. Not a good start to this stupid mission."

Walking over to him, I look down and kiss him softly. "Shush, pup. It will be okay. We're going to be fine. It's just a bump in the road. Don't worry."

If we're lucky, it's not false hope because he's right—this isn't a great beginning.

WE GET ONLY TEN STEPS PAST THE SIGN WELCOMING US TO THE capital city of the Daybreak Court when a cadre of gorgeous, glittery Fae appears. They're all dressed in filmy pastel colors with layered armor and carry various sharp weapons. I blink at the variations of their wings; aside from the pup, I've never had much dealings with their people. Of the five serious looking soldiers standing in front of us, the first male has one's like a dragonfly, the smaller female has delicate moth wings, the next male is huge with bat style wings, the next male has huge ones like a bird, and the last Fae is obviously non-binary, but their wings are big butterfly-style wings. They arch a brow at me as I look, and I realize I'm probably being rude.

Shit.

"See? Something you like?" The bird man asks with a smirk. "You seem to have plenty of options already."

A growl echoes in my chest as his eyes run over Tilly first, then the pup, and finally over the Irishman, Benjy, and the doc. "None of them are available. Who are you?"

"Pardon us, weary travelers! We are the *Laochra Na Peitil*," the petite woman gives me a bright, sunshine-y smile as she claps her hands. "The Royal Family is pleased to welcome you to our home. Think of us as your official guides and escorts to the—"

"Stop." Wolfie's urgent plea makes her pause and look at him in confusion. "We have an uninitiated visitor among us."

The girl's eyes widen, and she slaps her hand over her mouth. While she panics, the dragonfly guy steps in with a sigh. "Please forgive Aoife. She's very excited to have a group such as yourselves here to visit, as is our employer. My name is Sítheach."

I nod, holding my hand out. "I'm Edgar Boone."

"Who's the lovely lass, then?" BirdMan interrupts me to look at my family again, his eyes twinkling with mischief.

Ah. He's the Doyle of their group.

"Feck, Ciarán. You'll piss them off before we get them back to the palace and the Queen will be angry again. Rein it in." Frustration radiates from the lithe butterfly Fae on as they look at me apologetically. "That asshole is Ciarán and I'm Daire. The silent dick over there is Taranis."

"Nice to meet, y'all," Jolene says as she steps in front of me. She's laying on the Southern awfully thick and I tilt my head, watching her as she bats her lashes behind those silly spectacles. "I'm Jolene Whitley, and I suppose they're calling me the uninitiated. Left to right, that's Wolfie, Presley, Doyle, and Benjy. My companions are with us, obviously. They answer to Jekyll, Hyde, Kali, Hecate, Isis, and Euryale."

Taranis looks up at the eagle, then at each of the animals. His eyes are dark for a moment before he nods at the group. "Truth."

"Bloody hell," Doyle mutters as he crosses his arms over his chest. "Of course, they send one on their welcoming committee. And this will be the *least* irritating version of this test."

Presley nods and shakes his head. "Violation of Article 3256.890123 and you know it. I don't care who you work for. We should share that tidbit when we return home."

"No, no!" Aoife says quickly. "It's not what you think. Taranis is very fond of… *animals*, not people."

I hate this fucking place already. Everything is a mind fuck.

"Ah. Very smart," Wolfie murmurs. "Someone like me is a tricky addition to their team. It doesn't break laws, but it can be very helpful in identifying threats."

Once I understand what he's implying, I glare at the group of Fae preventing us from moving. They aren't here to welcome us as much as size us up for their royals. I can grasp *why* they'd want to do that, especially in a large, powerful group like my family, but I'm not interested in human politics, much less that of Fae courts.

"Now that you've skirted the rules to figure us out, we'd like to move on. Relay our thanks for the welcome wagon, but we want to find lodging and eat before we explore your city." I put the power of the alpha hound behind my words, hoping to get their attention.

Taranis smiles faintly. "Powerful hound. Over two."

What the hell?!!

"Oh, no, just the two," Tilly says with a smile. "They're Teddy's, but they've sort of adopted me. But don't worry! All our animals will behave. I have the paperwork for them in my bag if you need it."

I turn to look at her, confused why she's suddenly playing the role of a Southern bimbette. This isn't like her at all, and I have no idea what to make of it. "That's… true."

"You won't need to do that," Daire says with a tight smile. "Our illustrious king and queen will host you during your stay. They have prepared a wing in the guest villa on the south side of their palace gardens for your group. You'll have time to get settled and freshen up, then they're hosting a small court dinner in honor of your arrival."

That's not suspicious at all.

"We appreciate your hospitality, but—"

The pup shakes his head and cuts me off. "That will be wonderful, and our family is very grateful for their kindness. We would love for you to lead us to the royal guest quarters so we can ensure we're prepared for such an auspicious occasion."

"Oh, you will be!" Aoife says excitedly. "Once we drop you off, you will have two hours before the royal tailors and merchants arrive to help outfit you for tonight and the rest of your stay. Isn't that fabulous?"

Oh, yes. It's fucking perfect.

Make A Bet

Jolene

The group of oddball soldiers leads us to a pearlescent pink SUV parked down the street while Aoife chitters away to Presley. He's the most approachable outside of Wolfie, but my darling boy is unusually quiet. I look at him, trying to understand why he's staying on the other side of Teddy and biting his lower lip. Sure, Teddy's right about how damn suspicious it is that we're barely a mile into this place and we've been accosted, but it's not his fault.

Unless he's upset about something else?

I've been using malicious compliance to amuse myself while I'm forbidden from questioning the stuff going on around us. Being ridiculously syrupy and dense is fun, especially since the guys don't seem to get why I'm doing it. But I can't enjoy myself if Wolfie is this freaked out. The need to comfort him is slowly making my chest ache and that prevents me from snarking about the fancy ass Barbie Escalade we're piling into.

"What's up with him?" I point to Wolfie and elbow Teddy in the ribs as he waits for the others to get in. "And why are you so damn tense? I'm behaving as promised."

"Tilly, that's not something we can discuss at the moment." He sighs when I growl, leaning in to look at me with a rueful expression. "You know, I'll have to keep saying shit like that while we're here. Don't make me spank you."

Rolling my eyes, I huff as he helps me into the spacious SUV. "This thing is much bigger on the inside. If you're trying to keep me from being curious, this kind of crap isn't helping. I'm not stupid and you all know it."

Wolfie leans forward, taking my hand and whispering as the car lurches forward. "Please, sugarplum. You have to just… go along with it. No one thinks you're dumb—if we could show you, you'd do better than Teddy without question."

"Hey," the judge says as he tugs the vet back between him and Prez. "I'm doing a fucking great job reigning in my shit. Diplomacy is in my blood, pup."

"Then you need to have a transfusion," Wolfie says with a grimace. "You can't… apologize… to my people. They don't like it. Take criticism and move on—that's how it works."

Well, that's never going to happen. Southern folk apologize more than they breathe —even if it isn't sincere.

"Good thing you have me," Doyle says as he winks. "I almost never need or want to express that sentiment. I should be the designated diplomat for dinner tonight."

"Uh, how about no?"

He pouts at me, making my skin heat. "Are you saying I *can't* behave like a refined gentleman when I choose, Tíogair?"

I snort. "That is *exactly* what I'm saying, Lucky. You can't hold your temper or your need to sow chaos long enough to be a negotiator. You'll get us arrested."

"That, my lovely, sounds like the beginning of a bet." Doyle stacks his hands behind his head, his eyes twinkling with excitement. "Anyone care to get in on this? We'll have to set the terms carefully. I don't want our friends up there to think I can't set proper boundaries."

To my surprise, Benjy raises his hand. "I want in. I'll put fifty on you screwing up in the first hour. I might be new, but I've seen how you operate. You'll give in and Jolene will win."

"No way. He's stubborn as a mule with bets. I hate to side with the jackass, but I'll see your fifty and add another." Teddy smirks, watching the guys with a hungry expression. "I want to know what besides cash is on the line, though. Cash I've got plenty of."

"Ooh, we're adding favors?" The redhead leans in and I can feel the testosterone amp up in the vehicle. "Now that makes it really interesting. It should have a cost and reward for our beautiful girl."

Snapping my fingers, I wave at them. "Shouldn't your beautiful girl get a say in this? If I didn't allow bets on the plane, why would I allow it in Barbie's First SUV?"

A hand lands on my knee, and I look at Presley. His expression is fond, but there's a hint of something else behind it. "You do get a say, magpie, but I think a distraction from the things you can't say or do might help. I also think that's what this dick is trying to do, not that he could ever admit it."

My eyes dart to the bet-maker and he shrugs. "It also amuses the hell out of me when people underestimate me. I feel like proving my point. Being right is *almost* as fun as being mischievous."

"Not as fun as being in charge," Teddy mutters, and I laugh. He shrugs, leaning his forearms on his knees as he looks at all of us. "So this better be good if you're asking me to back off and let this play out."

Now we're getting to brass tacks.

"What are the real stakes? You guys can call and raise like we're playing poker all you want, but it's obvious you want to pony up more than cash. Hell if I'm going to step into that as blind." Crossing my arms over my chest, I glare at them expectantly.

Teddy gives me a knowing look. "Good girl. We told you not to get cornered in a deal without making sure it was fully explained. If you win, you get to be in charge for an entire night."

"*You're* going to be submissive?" My jaw drops as I stare at him. "I don't believe you."

"Fuck no," he laughs. "However, I will let you call the shots. The rest of these clowns can submit."

Of course, that's what he meant—alpha dominant to the end.

My adorable docs shrug, looking at Benjy and Doyle for confirmation. Benjy nods, but the troublemaking ginger takes his time. "I suppose I could agree to that if we can come up with a suitable option for when you lose."

"If I lose, you get to move back into the house when we get home." Batting my lashes, I try to appear nonchalant. I planned on letting them do that anyway, but if I can make them think it's a big concession, then I win this silly bet no matter what.

"Oooh. That's an interesting offer," Presley says as he looks between the two more dominant men. "I like it."

"Me, too," Wolfie says softly. "I miss you, sugarplum."

Always the soft one making my walls crumble. Fuck.

Edgar sighs, looking between the softer three, then does some sort of 'dude eyebrow conversation' with Doyle. After a few moments go by, he looks at me again, his lips curved up. "Acceptable, but mostly because the leprechaun's place is creepy."

"Oi!" Doyle grumbles before he points at Teddy. "You've been well cared for, you spoiled dandy. I won't have you slandering my hospitality."

I roll my eyes at them both. "So you agree, Lucky? The terms of the deal are simple: if you can't maintain diplomacy for the entire group tonight, I win. If you do, you win. Teddy's books aside, the side prizes are a night of me in charge or you all get to come home. Is that accurate?"

Wolfie reaches out, squeezing my hand. "Good job, Sugarplum. You have to re-state things and make sure there aren't any loopholes."

"It's more difficult with people actively trying to mislead you," Prez adds. "But you're doing well so far."

My eyes cut to the partition separating us from the crew of royal assholes, and I frown. "Do you think they can hear us?"

"Likely." Teddy waves his hand. "Back to the deal. Haggerty, is this satisfactory? You started this little wager."

"Aye, I'll agree to it."

Grinning broadly, I stick my hand out for him to shake. "We have a bet, Mr. Haggerty."

When his hand clasps mine, his eyes seem to flash with satisfaction. "Oh, it's more than that, Tíogair. We have a pact."

Why do the rest of the guys suddenly look extremely uncomfortable?

By the time we reach our destination, I feel less on edge than I was when we got into the car. I didn't expect to get scooped up by a fancy welcoming committee, and knowing that everyone around me was hiding shit from me made that chafe worse. The motley crew of soldiers ushers us out of the vehicle, then opens the back for the animals to follow suit. When Jekyll and Hyde place themselves under my palms, the residual nervousness coursing through me subsides slightly.

"This way. We're on schedule, so as we explained before, you'll have two hours to relax, then you'll be visited by our staff." Aoife bounces on her toes in front of me and I can't help but smile.

This chick is a lot like Seer, and it makes me miss my bestie.

"Be mindful of your animals and your surroundings. This is one of the most honored guest lodges and it would be an insult to our employers if anything is broken or missing when you leave." Sítheach's voice is serious, and it's obvious they've had issues in the past.

Doyle opens his mouth like he's going to shoot back a sarcastic remark, but he pauses, then winks at me. "Of course. My family will show the housing the utmost respect while we are here. Please extend our deepest gratitude to the King and Queen."

Our escorts don't look surprised, but that might be practiced indifference. The rest of my group hide snickers as Doyle puts on the air of a reasonable person, and I see Benjy slip Teddy another bill surreptitiously. They think he's going to win, and they have conned me, but I'll show them. There's no way he can hold on to that placid exterior when we're among snooty, rich dickheads tonight.

"Follow me," Daire says as they crook a finger. "We're wasting time."

As we walk behind them, all I see is a fancy looking guest house with lots of greenery and flowers surrounding it. I know there has to be more than this—otherwise why would I have to wear these fucking glasses—and the rebel inside of me itches to look beyond the frames to see it. I won't be able to escape my curiosity forever, but I have to last longer than the first few hours. The woman in my dreams was very adamant that I could put everyone around me in danger if I didn't follow the rules.

That doesn't mean I can't do it when they're not around, right?

I chew my lip as Isis squeezes my torso comfortingly. She might agree or she might try to get me to behave; I'm not sure. It's not like I speak Parseltongue and she doesn't give me easily interpreted clues like the feathered and furry companions. "I wish you could talk," I mutter to myself.

"What was that, Tilly?" Teddy says as he puts his hand on the small of my back.

"Nothing," I sigh. "It's very frustrating that I can't ask questions and I have to walk around pretending. I'm a trained investigator, Teddy. Before I came home, I went through an entire program designed to enhance those skills. I don't enjoy being in the dark and having no recourse for it."

"Tilly, if I knew a way to get around this shit, I promise I would have after you tossed us out. None of us enjoy having our hands tied anymore than you like being in the dark. We're lucky the leprechaun hasn't thrown caution to the wind, hoping to ask for forgiveness later."

The tour guides stop in as we come to a large lounge area with an open-air kitchen and dining room on one side. Daire pauses until everyone is still, then smiles blandly. "This is the main room. Down the hall to the left are the rooms and bathrooms. You are free to decide how those are distributed. Out the doors behind me is the back lawn, which you should be able to give your companions free roaming as long as they understand to stop when they hit the barriers. It's safe within them and less so outside of them. We'll leave you for now, but please use the paging system if you have needs."

I paste a smile on my face as I look around. "This is lovely. Thank you for everything, sugar. I'm much obliged."

Teddy knocks my shoulder with his and nods at the soldiers. "Agreed. Will we see you at the festivities this evening?"

Taranis snorts. "You will see *everyone* at the dinner, hybrid."

With that, they turn on their heels to leave, and I'm left gaping.

What the fuck is a hybrid?

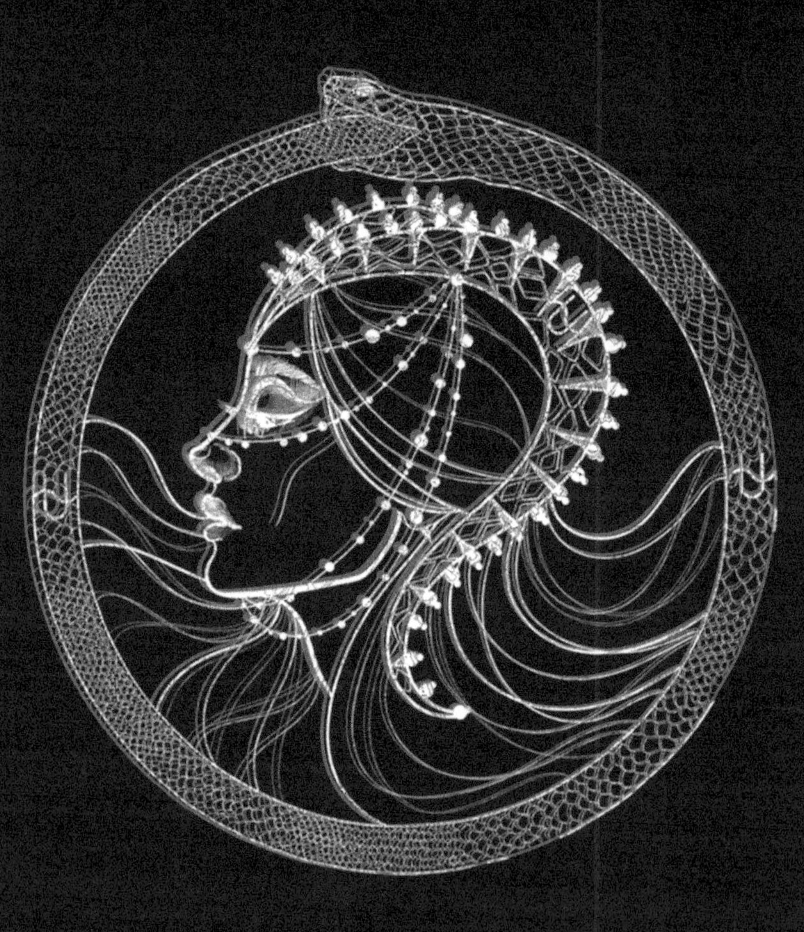

Far From Home

Doyle

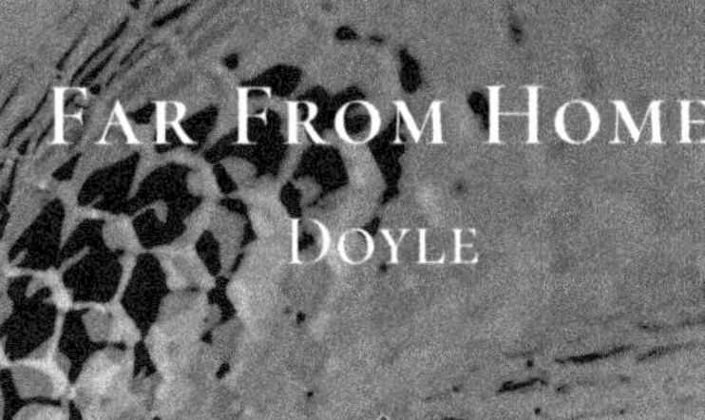

THEY THINK they're so smart, but I have a lot more bloody control than any of these young supes think. After all, I'm older than damn near anyone they've ever met; it takes a lot of skill to stay on this side of the Styx for that long. I can't be killed, but an angry relative could have us locked in some ridiculous prison if they chose. Demis like me don't have the raw power our full bloods do and I've run afoul of every type of deity in every pantheon over the millennia. Some I have no quarrel with and some I'm lucky to have survived their… attentions.

I refuse to let the sneaky-ass Fae beat me at my own game.

Luckily, the royalty of the Daybreak Court are as over-the-top as my Olympian family. This place looks rustic, but everything in it is hand-crafted or expensive as hell. There are enough rooms for us to have our own if we choose, but the docs grab one to share and the judge and his buddy take another. I'm fine with having my own; it makes it easier for me to let Odie free without our girl noticing. I'm not hiding him because I don't trust her, but I don't want her ruining his cover by glancing at him if he shows up places.

"Off you go," I mutter as I open the window in my room. The raven takes off, his wings spread as he ascends. Unlike the other companions, I've given him instructions to defy the boundaries of our supposedly generous hosts. If we're going to find the vet's father, we need eyes on the city outside of the palace grounds.

Once he disappears into the sunlight, I flop on the bed, stacking my hands behind my head. The urge to break rules and foment chaos rides me hard; I don't like being constrained by the Society's archaic bullshit. I chose my Tíogair's little bargain, so I can live with that. But not being able to show her what this world truly looks like is pissing me off.

Jolene is an artist, and she would have loved seeing all the bright, colorful flowers and plants. The outside of this building looks like a fancy, rich people hunting lodge to her, but if she wasn't wearing those damn glasses, she'd see a miniature Fae castle accented with all the fantasy flora and fauna you'd expect from movies. She's missing the best parts of this place because a bunch of people older than the fucking Crusades decided we have to stay secret until we emerge.

We know *she's a damn supe, and they do, too. What's the point?*

Kicking my boot heels against the mattress, I grunt in irritation. There has to be a damn way around this. I don't have the patience for waiting like the rest and I actually think it's dangerous that she doesn't know. Boone agrees with me, but he's in too damn deep with the whole brotherhood shit to do anything about it. Hell, I'd ask my auntie to give me permission to shove their silly rules down their throats, but she'd think I was weak for even asking.

Unfortunately, I'm not totally on my own dealing with the consequences of my rash bullshit now. I've got this menagerie of people and animals, plus the ones coming. The thought of causing them all pain or getting them put on trial is distasteful—something I've never experienced before. I actually *care* about what happens to these people in my wake.

By Apollo's oiled balls, I might be growing up!

Snorting, I shake my head. That's doubtful as hell. I don't think I'm made to be quite that serious; it comes from my absent, dickhead father. My mother is perfectly happy floating along like the perfect representation of our kind and the avatar of her powers. The most rebellious thing she's ever done is get knocked up and have me—look how well that went for both of us. I don't count on her support or help with anything because she's what the humans call a narcissist. Still amazes me they honored that mirror licking tool with a word used around the globe, but they're not the brightest crayons in old Gramps' box.

"Haggerty, where the hell are you?"

My door opens and I arch a brow as I hold my arms out. "Right here, as you can see. Why are you whispering?"

The feathery doc looks sheepish as he rubs the back of his neck. "Magpie fell asleep in her room and we're trying to let her rest before the Fae tailors get here. Wolfie says that's going to be a pain in the ass of epic proportions."

"It is. Probably second only to visiting one of the deity strongholds, if I'm guessing. Fae palaces are just as rigid and grandiose as Olympus, Asgard, or even a pyramid. I can't imagine the King and Queen of Daybreak will allow us to walk around as their guests dressed like humans."

Presley puts his hands over his face. "She's going to lose her shit. I still don't understand why we couldn't call the pixie back to help us wrangle this."

"Were *you* willing to do a spell to contact the women of the tapestry? I sure as hell wasn't in the mood to argue with them. The last time I had to visit, they took me for every dime I had on me. Never play Go with witches who can see the bloody future," I grumble. "It was a bloodbath until I used my special talents. They wouldn't have been happy to see me."

His eyes squint behind the thick frames. "Do they owe you money? Are you *serious*?"

I shrug, unconcerned with his shock. "The list of people who owe me money or favors is *significantly* longer than those who don't."

"Mother of gods," the doc mutters and I smirk.

"*She* doesn't owe me. Good guess."

"Who doesn't owe you?" Boone arches a brow as he comes up behind the healer. "You were supposed to bring him to the living room right away, Hamilton."

"As I said, very few people don't owe me. And I'm coming, keep your bloody britches on, doggy." Rolling to my feet, I make sure we cracked the window for Odie before I walk over to join them. "But don't worry… I wait to collect until it's most advantageous to me. That will be helpful at some point."

"It better be," Edgar growls as he glares at me. "Otherwise, I'll kick your ass myself. We haven't had a rematch since that street brawl."

Giving him a gleeful grin, I flip the snarly hound off. "Anytime, pooch. You, me, and a wide open space."

As long as I don't kill him, I'm sure the rest of them will forgive me.

"I'M CONCERNED WITH HOW 'SOLICITOUS' THE DAYBREAK COURT IS. As far as they know, we're nobody. We didn't request a Council clearance specifically to fly under the radar," Boone says as he scratches his chin. "I made sure we weren't tagged as diplomatic or mission-based in the system."

I frown, considering that for a moment. "Do you think Nelia or your father spoiled our cover by accident? You mentioned the Senator."

He shakes his head. "Pops isn't remotely concerned with what the hell I'm doing until it affects him negatively. I learned that as a teen. Throwing around his name doesn't really draw attention to his end."

"Then they're catering to someone else," Wolfie says softly. "Whether it's stroking an alliance or rankle a rival, the royals in this court are playing Fae politics, not supe politics."

"Your dad." The doc grimaces at his lover, stroking his hands through his hair. "It'd have to be him."

My brows furrow as I think about that statement. Supposedly, no one knows who the fuck his dad is, least of all him. How would the King of the Daybreak Court know and how would he benefit from acting like he doesn't? The Fae are known for this shit, as are my relatives, so I probably have the most experience with immortal grudges and games. It's always some sort of long con to best the other player—even when the person isn't aware they're playing.

We need to know more about how the Courts are interacting and what their treaties are.

"I believe we won't be able to suss this out without more information on current alliances *and* some popular gossip. Many times, with beings like my family or the Courts, their machinations are so far-reaching that it's hard to nail down intent. We need facts, both current and past century, paired with the rumor mill to find the truth in the middle." I steeple my fingers as I let scenarios run through my mind at light speed.

"You think they're manipulating us to get the pup on their side before he figures out who his dad is? What good does that do? And if they know, who else knows?" Edgar frowns, looking pissed as he watches the vet curl up more.

"Possibly none. Possibly quite a bit if his resentment or birthright could gain leverage in some internal bullshit. Keep your enemies closer and all," I say with a shrug. "Most of my mother's family amuse themselves by causing trouble for one another and then watching the chaos with glee. Their reason could be as simple as boredom."

Wolfie sits up, his wings fluttering as he looks at us in alarm. "Sugarplum needs us."

That stops the conversation. We all spring into action, rushing to the room where she was supposed to be sleeping. I hear nothing, but I yank the door open anyway, letting Boone take the lead. It's dark and since her animals are taking a break outdoors, she's alone. The silence is deafening and unnatural, so I let some of my power slip out so I can test for magic.

Holy fuck, look at this place.

It lights up like a feckin' Christmas tree when I turn on the juice. There's so much magic in here that it's cloaking the space, keeping the sounds coming from my Tíogair ensconced inside. She's mumbling and groaning in her sleep, but it's garbled. I walk over to the pup and shake his shoulder. "Oi, lad. Turn it on for a moment. You have to see what I'm seeing. The others won't understand."

His eyes widen and I watch as the glow envelops him, wings shimmering and his visage transforming to full Fae within a blink. Wolfie looks around and takes a step back. "Holy. Fucking. Shit."

"Anyone want to share?" Boone sighs dramatically, but the big guy and the birdman nod in agreement.

Licking my lips, I try to find the right words to explain to the shifters how big a deal this is. "The room is *saturated* with magic. It's dampening the sound of our girl having very involved dreams—not sexy ones, unfortunately, but also not bad ones. The amount of power in the room suggests this land is affecting her as much as our vet here; however, since she's not emerged, it's almost hiding itself."

"Doyle, I don't even know what that means," the doc admits. "That damned old fool who worked in the Hollow before me let these hybrids run amuck and I've never heard of shit like this. It shouldn't be possible, but then, neither should Magpie."

The judge tilts his head, his expression interested as he watches Presley. "What do you mean?"

"I mean, nothing anyone who lives in this damn town says makes any sense! There's far too many unemerged and lost ones popping out, not to mention the way you all described your emergence is absolute bullshit. You all should have been prepped and coaxed through it like I do to the kids now. That jackass let you all fend for yourself and it's not surprising shit like this happens."

He straightens his glasses and rakes his hand through his hair, seething. Wolfie walks over and leans into him, making a calm feeling flood the room. The little shit is using his empathy, but I don't blame him. A magical, sleeping Jolene is far more dangerous than shit that's already done and dusted.

"What do we do?" Benjy asks. "All this is fascinating, but blame doesn't do shit. We need a plan: wake her, leave her be, check for outside influence… pick one. Pick them all if need be; just do something."

I knew I liked him—no wishy-washy bullshit with that simian.

"Alright, Boone. What does the great and powerful *tripleskia* think?"

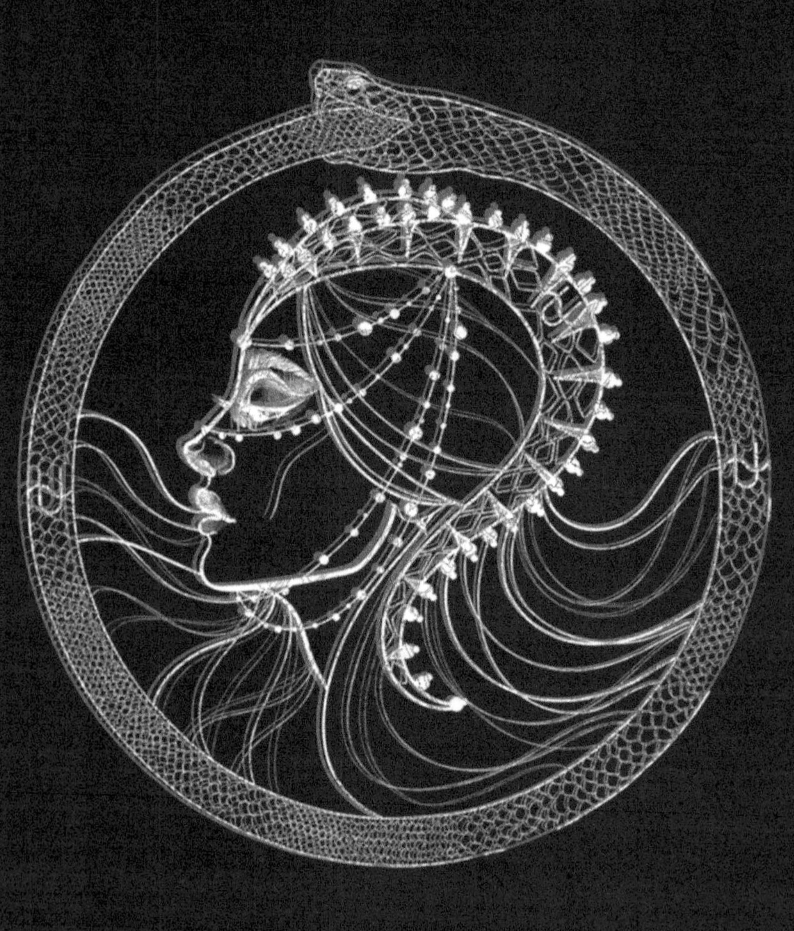

Changing

Jolene

THE BRIGHT LIGHT above hurts my eyes. I'm crying, and I don't know why. There are sounds in the room, then shadows fall over me in a tight circle. I can't see who's looking at me, except there are a lot of them. Somehow, I know they're worried; I can feel it.

I don't know why they seem so fearful until one more person leans in. Her voice croons in a language I don't understand, but the emotions behind it coast over me soothingly.

"We'll have to do it soon. Look at her; we can't hide it much longer."

That man sounds very upset, and I know he's not an enemy. The room fills with tension at his words, and I start crying again. I don't understand any of this, but I know it isn't good for me.

"I just need more time." Her voice trembles and I want to help calm her, too, but I can't.

"We've had two years to come to terms with it. It's for her safety and the greater good." This man sounds stern, but not angry.

She sniffles. "You're far too calm about this, Calix."

"He's only being pragmatic. We all knew this day would come."

All of them speak at the same time, and the tension ratchets up around me. I can't handle it, so I hide within myself as they argue. This isn't how it used to be, but now it's common. I don't know what it means or why everything has changed. Finally, the noise stops and a pair of arms scoop me up.

"It's decided. We will travel to the nearest enclave at the end of the week. We cannot risk sentiment further pushing our sacrifice out."

My eyes pop open and I let out a wail as I sit up. Once my brain catches up, I slam my eyes shut before I see something I'm not supposed to, but that makes the pain radiating through me worse. Within seconds, there are hands on me, warm bodies moving in to touch me as I try to stop yelling like I've been murdered. I don't know what's wrong with me—it's like I don't have control over myself.

"Shhh. It's okay, Tilly."

Teddy. He's on my right side; I know by the scent of dragon's blood and sandalwood with a hint of cedar. My brows furrow as that pops into my head unbidden—that's a very specific scent profile, and it came to me without a second thought. I sniff, testing out my theory, and it's like my brain is assaulted with so many smells I can barely focus.

What the hell is going on with me?

"Grab her glasses, doc. She's trembling, but she can't open her peepers until we get her covered, yeah?"

That musical lilt is Doyle and I feel him flank my other side, filling my nostrils with a spicy scent—black pepper, cloves, lavender, and Tonka bean. Confusion floods my mind as that knowledge settles because I don't know what the hell a Tonka bean is, much less what it should smell like except… him.

Am I having a stroke? No, that's burned toast. I think.

"Here you go, sugarplum," Wolfie murmurs as he lifts my chin and slips the rainbow frames on my face. "You can open those pretty green eyes now."

I give him a grateful look when I comply, hoping to reassure him. His anxiety about my state is needling against my skin; it's making his typically outdoorsy scent of allspice, patchouli, and vanilla even stronger. Swallowing hard, I clear my raw throat before I answer. "Thank you, darling boy. And… all of you… for coming to check on me. I don't know what happened."

Presley is frowning. He's not the worrier of the group, nor the gate-crashing alpha. Seeing him look less than placid makes a lump form in my gut. His fists are clenched at his sides, fingers flexing in and out as if he's trying to control his reaction subtly. I inhale, focusing on him and the fresh cedar, vetiver, and ylang ylang wash over me.

This shit is fucking weird and I'm going to have a panic attack if someone doesn't explain.

Oddly, Benjy is the one to approach, his eyes dark as he drops to the floor to kneel in front of me. "Princess, are you having trouble with something? Besides the yelling and shooting up in your bed like it electrocuted you, I mean."

He smells clean, like lemon, sage, and rosewood. Biting my lip, I murmur, "The dream wasn't… a nightmare. It was weird. Sometimes, the parts of my past that have been hazy since I was in middle school come back in bits. It used to be in my black outs, but since I came home, it's in dreams, too."

His brow arches. "I'm glad you told us that, but it doesn't answer my question. I can see your mind working. What else?"

"We don't think you're crazy, sugarplum." As if he can read my mind, Wolfie allays my greatest fears about the weird shit happening to me these past few months. "You can tell us."

I nod, raking my lower lip through my teeth again as I gather my courage. "A lot of unexplainable stuff has been happening since I came home. Most of it seems like oddball, small town shit or maybe paranoia. But… I've never had the blackouts and woken up injured or covered in brush. That's new, and suddenly, my emotions and senses randomly get super heightened."

The room is quiet and I worry I've said too much until Teddy cups my cheek to bring my gaze to his. "Tell us more about that, Tilly. What do you mean by heightened? Be specific."

"I feel shit much more keenly than before. Rage is like a burning ember inside me and pleasure is like liquid fire. Other people's feelings smack into me and, depending on what they are, it's like they're fueling mine. I react and reflect maybe? That's not normal for me. I can't lock shit down like I used to."

Wolfie tilts his head as he studies me. "Do you feel like their emotions are tangible? The stronger they are, the more substantial they become and sometimes too much in one place is overwhelming?"

"Yes. Yes, that's it!" I look over at Presley hopefully. "Is it a stroke? Or maybe a tumor? Hell, anything that won't require me to call my therapist and tell her all her work has been ruined by my hometown."

He rakes a hand through his hair, shaking his head as he chuckles. "I have never in my life witnessed someone seriously ask if they have a tumor in excitement. Magpie, you're… just one of a kind."

Pouting, I lean into Doyle. He's quiet, but it's comforting. "I don't *really* want it to be that, Prez. It's just… I spent years working through my trauma about Trevor and Antigone and dissecting all my crap from high school. My parents died while I was still sorting out the repressed past shit, and I decided I was going to leave well enough alone. Now that's amping up and I seem to be losing my marbles one by one while we're chasing murderers."

"Tilly, you're handling a lot and doing it with the grace of a true Southern woman. Don't let anyone suggest otherwise, or I'll make sure they regret it." Teddy's thumb strokes my jaw as he continues. "What did you mean by your senses? You haven't gotten to that part yet."

I wrinkle my nose when he says that, and they all chuckle. "Don't laugh, but everything stinks. Well, no, it doesn't stink. I mean, it's like my nose went into overdrive. The same thing happened a couple of weeks ago with my ears. I'm hearing shit I never heard before. It's all hyper-focused and intense. That's why I started wondering about a brain problem."

They all look at Presley, and he groans, scrubbing his hand down his face. He says nothing for a few minutes and I worry that he's trying to figure out how to say I'm fucking dying. My pulse spikes as I wait, and suddenly, Doyle finds his tongue.

"Doc, I think our girl is going to have an actual heart attack if you don't say something soon. Work it out, lad."

I don't know where chaotic, trouble-making Lucky went, but I dig this silent, supportive side, too.

"Jolene, sometimes when we're extremely stressed, our bodies go into fight or flight mode. They have tossed you around like a canoe in a hurricane the past few months. On the surface, you're doing fine, but your body may overcompensate to keep you level. Visual and auditory quirks can absolutely be symptoms of acute anxiety and stress pushing you to the limit. You only need to worry if those things become hallucinations rather than passing symptoms."

His voice is calm and his words make sense, but that same emotional awareness I mentioned earlier is telling me he's not telling the whole truth. Fear, worry, and regret are buzzing off of him like a swarm of bees prickling my skin as I focus on my sexy physician. Whatever he's hiding, it must have to do with the stupid oath I want to shove up the ass of whoever invented it.

If I find out, I just might. It would serve those motherfuckers right.

"Tilly?"

Teddy brings me out of my violent reverie and I blink up at him. "What?"

He chuckles, his lips curved in amusement. "You blanked out for a minute and your eyes had this...fire... like you were planning some-one's doom."

I shrug, trying to make light of my dark thoughts. "Maybe I was. I don't back down from fights anymore, Teddy. After Trevor, I vowed to never let people steal my agency again. I spent too long running from what the catastrophe shit and my ex did to my mental health. Now, I finish shit even if I didn't start it."

"Amen to that," Doyle crows. "I'll happily join you in destroying someone if it will bring a smile back to your face, Tíogair. I don't have a single fuck in all of my fields to give, and I'm known for being a dick."

Teddy snorts. "Amen to *that* as well."

"Oi!"

"Doyle, you can't give him openings like that if you don't expect him to take it," Wolfie chides. "Be fair and take your lumps."

They bicker amongst themselves for a few minutes, eventually including Prez and Benjy as well. It makes my chest ache in the best way, watching as I slowly wind down from the tension. I feel better knowing I shared my worries about the weird symptoms, but I know I glossed over the bits about my dreams.

I have no idea how to tell them I'm recovering tiny pieces of that past that scream my mother adopted me in a promotion campaign. Or that I just had a dream about weird fuzzy people doing something with me as a tiny child. Science says I shouldn't *have* memories that far back, hazy or not. The dream with the mystery woman and her glasses that magically appeared on my night stand makes me afraid I *am* having hallucinations.

What if I sleep-walked and stole or bought them damn things?

There were cases of people on zolpidem doing shit like driving and running around while asleep a couple years ago. Did someone slip me a sleeping pill to help me rest, and it backfired? No, I don't think Prez would do that to me. I'm stubborn as hell, but one of them could convince me to take medicine if needed—especially Wolfie.

"Magpie, what do you think?"

My eyes widen as I look at them all, waiting for my response. I zoned out, completely trying to muddle out my damn snippets of history and now I've missed what they were talking to me about.

"Um…I'm sorry. What do I think about…?" My cheeks flush, but I know better than to agree to *anything* I didn't hear around these jackals.

Teddy's grin widens. "Good on you, sugar. You didn't agree to anything you weren't paying attention to every word of. That's what you have to do tonight at dinner."

"You knew I wasn't listening and pretended?" They all look sheepish, and I point at them one by one as I glare. "Strike one, assholes. Clean up your act before we come home tonight or none of you is hitting a home run on this field."

Wolfie blinks. "Did she… just chastise us with… a sports metaphor?"

"Maybe she is having a stroke after all," Doyle jokes.

Mr. Smartass returns in time to call me out. Great.

It's Time

Presley

It's obvious some of Jolene's supe powers are breaking through the binding spell. Despite how firmly it was reinforced by the caster, her supe sides—whatever the hell they are—have mated with some of us and the magic is weakening. If pressed, I'd say each time her inner power claims someone, the enchantment will crumble a bit more until she emerges in one hell of a burst of energy. None of us are common, weaker supernaturals and she's been able to handle everything thrown at her unconsciously.

Magpie is going to be extremely powerful and mighty pissed when it all shakes out.

"It's not a tumor or a stroke, Haggerty," I chide as I walk over to our girl. "But I will monitor you and the others will let me know if they see something worrisome, right?"

A chorus of mumbles makes me roll my eyes. Some help these clowns are—they can't even put a show on to help me sell this anxiety shit. I start to speak again, but a loud tinkling sound fills the room, obscuring any other sound. It chimes four times and I realize it must be the royal Fae version of a cuckoo clock.

"Sounds like it's time to get up anyway, sugarplum," Lucy says as he rubs his ears. The noise must have been different for him, because he looks slightly pained. "The dressers will be here soon. That was a not-so-subtle warning."

Not a clock, but an alarm. Good to know.

"We should all get showered and cleaned up before they get here." Teddy rises, holding his hand out to Benjy, then to Lucy. "We don't want to be 'travel grimy' when their snooty tailors come to outfit us. I get the feeling it would definitely be dinner conversation."

Lucy nods, his eyes serious. "*Everything* will be fair game for mockery, trickery, or snobbery this evening. They will analyze every word, looking to make themselves appear smarter, more cultured, or more powerful. It's the games played at court and being visitors makes us fresh meat. Sharp wit and an unflappable demeanor will impress them, not outbursts. That is, unless you're prepared to back it up."

Boone meets my eyes and I know he understands what 'back it up' means— combat.

Hera help us if it comes to that.

A SHARP KNOCK AT THE FRONT DOOR OF THE GUEST HOUSE PUTS ALL of us on edge. We gathered there after freshening up, choosing to hang out comfortably while the animals gorged on the dinners Lucy made for them. The fridge was fully stocked, so only my secret favorite, Eurayle, took to the hunt outside. They'll be joining us at the event tonight and Magpie wanted to ensure they had food. Hungry wild animals are harder to tame and we're going to have enough trouble keeping alpha Boone and mischevious Haggerty from fucking everything up.

Fuck only knows how our family ended up with three stubborn, powerful domi-nants vying for control.

My lips curve as I think about Jolene. She's a switch like me, but she definitely leans more towards the top while I lean towards the bottom. Those two do their level best to keep her in line, but she proves they'll cave for her every single time. I actually enjoy watching the three of them duke it out and I'm not usually one for conflict. I prefer calm, easy going vibes—something Benjy and Lucy have in spades. Our girl's spark of defiance makes her irresistible to me; I would have never predicted it if you'd asked me.

"Prez? Yoo hoo?"

Blinking, I smile as Magpie waves her hand in front of me. "Yes?"

"Teddy went to answer the door. Get ready for whatever the hell is coming." She looks at each of us, her expression stern. "I haven't said it yet, but I don't trust *any* of these fuckers, by the way. Something feels off about this situation and I don't like it."

There's the bit she's getting from Lucy—it cranked her natural intuition and empathy to a million.

"Princess, I think we're all in agreement—holy shit." The simian shifter cuts off as a crew of people decked out like they're attending the fucking *Hunger Games* appear in the lounge area.

Boone's lips are pressed together tightly and I can tell he's trying like hell not laugh his ass off. A snort comes from where Haggerty is lolling about and, even with his Fae blood, Lucy is fighting a grin. The designers standing before us are almost Seussian; that's how insanely they're dressed.

"Um, not to be difficult, but I'm definitely not wearing anything like *that*," I say as I gesture in their direction. "Leave me here if it's required."

Hell if I care about cultural requirements—I'm not letting Haggerty get pictures of me trussed up like a goddamn Sneetch.

Doyle bobs his brows and I know he's figured out why I'm protesting. "Relax, doc. I promised to behave this evening."

"I doubt that extends to *after* the completion of this wager," I reply drily.

Before we can start bickering, the tallest of the magical Muppets claps their hands. "Gentlemen, gentlemen… I beg your attention. You needn't be worried about how we plan to outfit you for this royal ball. We are *expected* to appear outrageous to set trends by virtue of our positions. The selections we have available for you are much more suitable for visitors."

Adjusting my glasses, I nod as relief floods me. "Good to know."

"What do you need to get this over with?" Teddy asks. He's leaning against the wall watching them, and I see the sliver of fire surrounding his cornea. He's using the hound to sniff out what he can and if he doesn't like what he finds, he won't hesitate to shut this shit down.

"Oh, excellent question!" The tall leader with spring green hair claps again and I groan internally. Of course, they'd send a damn cheerleader to do this. "My name is Deirbhile, and these are my assistants Ríordán, Aimhirghin, Ealadha, Draighean, and Áinfean. We will each take one of you to style in your quarters. I will, of course, be working with your female companion."

That's a relief. Two of them are male and we would have had a riot if this chick assigned them to magpie.

Deirbhile cocks a brow when no one moves, then sighs in exasperation. "Off with you, men. The lady seems capable and there are plenty of companions in the room. Shoo, now."

"Go on, guys," Jolene says as she tilts her head to the hallway. Once we move, she glares directly at the assistants, zeroing on the one called Ríordán. "All of you keep your hands to yourself, understand? I won't hesitate to put a bullet in someone who misbehaves."

Boone chuckles, ruffling her hair and dropping a kiss on her head before he leaves. "That's my girl, Tilly."

"Not exactly the subtle we were going for, sugarplum." The pup is smiling though, so he's not exactly mad.

She shrugs. "I am being subtle… just not about what's mine. People should pass my lack of humor about the subject along. It might prevent awkward situations later on."

Doyle's grin practically splits his face as he follows the group. "Ha! I'm not the one planning to fuck up tonight. You're all going to lose your bloody shirts."

Who knew getting him to agree to behave would pass the shit-stirring position onto our girl? Not me, that's for sure.

I'M PLEASANTLY SURPRISED WHEN EALADHA FINISHES MEASURING ME quickly, then selects a damn fine suit in a deep forest green. It's not a perfect fit, but he rectifies that within minutes using a spring blossom smelling magic. I tilt my head at the silent tailor, realizing he will not speak beyond grunts unless I do.

"I don't recognize your magic. Not to be rude, but I'm the town caladrius and it's rare for me not to tell pretty quickly."

He snorts and rolls his eyes. "Otherworlders and their healers. You don't know everything."

Isn't that what I just said?

"True. I definitely don't know you." I don't move so his work isn't interrupted, but I'd like to cross my arms over my chest in irritation. "Educate me. I'm willing to learn."

"Not my job, birdie. But if it will quiet your curiosity, I'm a hybrid, like much of your group. Druid and brownie—we don't visit your lands much. Only the Fae and pixies enjoy the Otherworld. The other species in the Veil stay out of the reach of humans."

I blink as I think about that. He's right—I don't see brownies or fairies or goblins or druids at all. There are more species than that across the Courts, but the only Daybreak dwellers who frequent our world are the two most humanoid. I suppose that makes sense. It's harder for the others to hide their natures and the laws of the Society are strict about it.

"That makes perfect sense now that I think about it. It also explains why I've never felt your magical blend before. I didn't think there were any Druids left. My mentor said you were all gone," I reply apologetically.

"Humph." He walks around me, examining the suit carefully. "Gone because we're all here. Not dead yet, thanks."

This guy must be a gas at parties—sheesh.

Looking down at myself, I grin. It really is absolutely exquisite now that he's made his adjustments. "You could make a lot of money in my land. It's obvious how talented you are."

"There isn't enough money in the human world to replace the honor I receive for being part of the royal family's cadre. I want for nothing, birdie. Our group travels the realm similarly to rock stars, designing on commission for the most elite in every kingdom." His eyes find mine as he pauses. "You and your family know very little about my world. A word of warning: the Fae are ruthless in their treatment of Otherworlders. Be cautious."

I nod, shooting him a grateful look. "I will be."

"Let's go see what my team has done with your mates, caladrius."

Guess that's the end of the conversation.

Following the stocky hybrid out of my room, I notice it's quiet. The lounge is filled with the men in our group dressed in varying styles of suits, the same color as mine. Teddy's has a vest and muted tie, making him look very billionaire chic. Benjy's has an open shirt and pinstripes, while Doyle has tails and a bow tie. The only one of us who doesn't fit the theme is Lucy—he's outfitted in a brighter emerald with a shine to it. His wings are on full display again, but somehow, the longer jacket and flowing shirt work perfectly with it.

"Where's our girl?" I murmur. "Not that I missed how hot everyone looks, but she's—"

"Right here," an amused voice behind me says.

Spinning on my heel, I turn to look and almost have to hold my jaw in place. Deirbhile has completely outdone herself; Jolene looks like she should be a fucking advertisement for Faerie, not a visitor.

The strapless top is some sort of delicate lace in emerald green that flows down to her hips, then the bottom is made of layers and layers of filmy material like the petals of flowers. There are hints of various greens along the edges, along with random sequins dotting the fluffy bottom. Magpie has long, shining opera-style gloves with no fingers and there are matching nails on her fingers. A vee shaped choker with a fat emerald in the center has delicately beaded tendrils leading from it to lacy shoulder caps that sit above draped strands of the same beads. They pinned her raven hair up in messy curls and her makeup is light and springy, with scarlet lips.

And they put fake, filmy fucking wings that match my love's on her damn back.

"I…" No one else is talking, either, so I'm not the only dumbfounded moron in the room. "Magpie, you look stunning."

"Good enough to eat," Boone growls in agreement.

She wrinkles her nose under the silly rainbow glasses as she peers at us. "The wings aren't too silly? I don't want everyone to stare."

Doyle snorts, then coughs as he gets control of himself. "I don't think anyone will think that, Tíogair. You look delicious, more so than usual. Right, pup?"

Lucy swallows hard and I can tell he's struggling because his wings are practically vibrating with his emotions. "Truly statuesque, Sugarplum. The team has us looking like a vision and I'm certain they will be praised highly by the royals."

Deirbhile claps her hands again, a smug smile curving her lips. It's more calculating than her cheery enthusiasm earlier, and I narrow my eyes. "Excellent! I'm so happy to hear you are all satisfied. We will take our leave now, and your ride to the front entrance will be here shortly."

The rest of her team gathers their things quietly and I frown as I try to work out what I'm sensing.

"Oh, and have an *illuminating* evening. May the road rise to meet you all."

I don't like her tone one bit; something is off and we'd better figure it out fast.

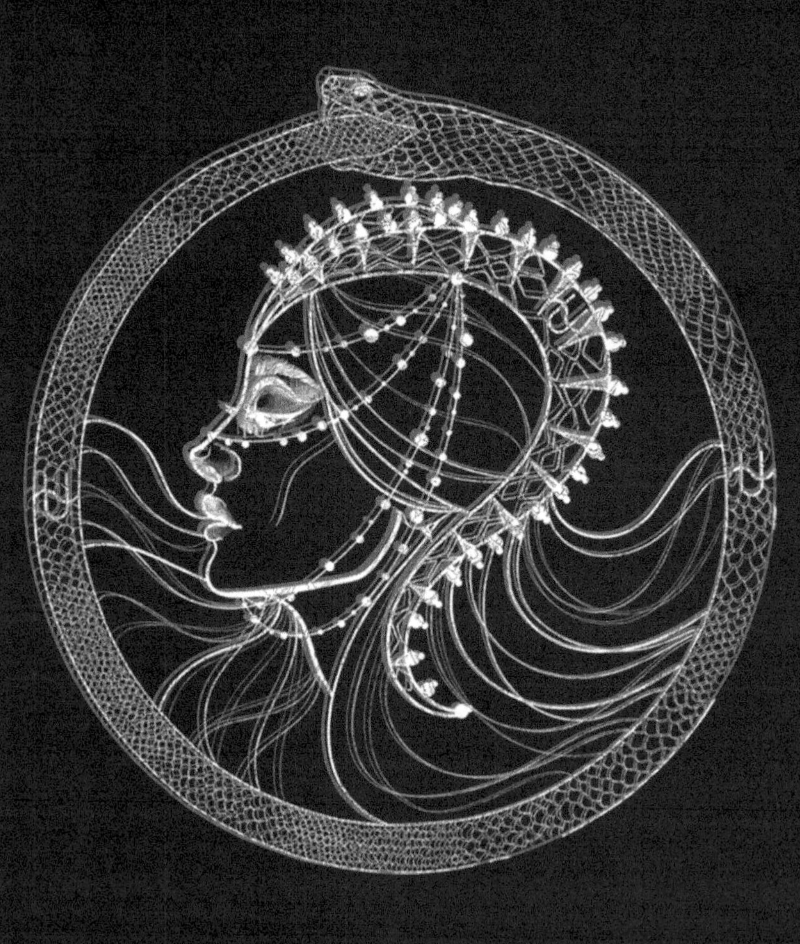

Anticipating

Jolene

As we exit the big SUV, I hold on to Wolfie's arm tightly. Ever since Deirbhile finished dressing me, I've felt this odd sensation crawling all over my skin and it's worse now that we're standing outside the big Tudor-style mansion they call 'The Castle.' Rubbing my free arm, I look around at the immaculate gardens and pristine grounds of the building, trying to figure out what's bothering me. They *filled* the air with an aromatic blend of floral and springtime scents, but nothing that hints at danger. Yet I can't stop myself from reaching out to grab Benjy's arm and threading mine through it, so I'm flanked by my men.

It's like there's something just out of reach in my mind—like a word you can't remember on the tip of your tongue.

"Are you okay, Princess?" Benjy murmurs. His brows are drawn in concern and I instantly feel bad for making him worry when it's likely only anxiety about meeting some power couple who liked to be called the King and Queen.

Giving him a small nod, I continue following Teddy and Doyle as they stride towards the entrance. Prez is behind us with the companions surrounding him and I feel his discomfort at the servals to his left. He's doing his best not to show that they make him skittish, and it makes my chest ache. Everyone in this group is making certain I'm protected, despite being able to take care of myself, and I hate to admit it feels good. Outside of Seer, I haven't allowed myself to depend on anyone for a very long time.

I just might be healing, inch by inch. My therapist would be proud.

"Halt and present yourself for inspection!"

The booming voice comes from one of the serious-looking security personnel at the door. There are six of them, all dressed in tuxedos, with earpieces just like the Secret Service. I suppose if you've got enough money to claim the monikers these clowns do, you can afford a cadre of fucking beefcakes protecting every single doorway. It reminds me of how the uber-rich in Europe or the juntas in Asia set up their protection teams. That means the money comes from mostly or entirely illegal gains—a fact that changes how I'll look at every person inside.

"What do you need?" Teddy growls as he stops the group in front of them.

A lilting voice comes from behind the wall of muscle and I tilt my head to peer around the two alpha males standing in front of me. "Don't worry, American prince. We mean your family no harm. Our search will be gentle, only taking a few moments to find out what weapons you possess and your intent is."

American prince? Barf. The Boones might be a Southern version of Camelot, but that's a simpering description if I ever heard one.

"The primary ma—er, we will examine the leaders of your family first, then we will continue with the..." The loud make from the announcement pauses, clearly unsure what the hell to say.

"Brutus means we will begin with you, fair prince and your princess. After that, your Irish rogue and lost son, then the healer and the friendly giant. To every family, there is an order and it must be respected, so we will."

Wolfie and Benjy let go of my arms reluctantly, and I step out from behind Teddy. It takes every ounce of my F.B.I. training to school my features when the guards come into view. My smile stays pasted on and I keep my eyes trained on the faces of the people before me, not wanting them to see the panic that now floods my veins. I was right to worry about the prickling feeling; it was a harbinger and I'll never ignore it again.

Standing in front of me are the same tuxedoed security men and a woman who must be the calm, lyrical voice. But now, the detail doesn't look like big, beefy ex-military types from some private security firm as I'm used to. The two biggest men who stand on either side of the female are enormous tusked orcs so muscled they might burst the seams of their suits. After them, I have to guess what I'm seeing based on playing D&D in college, but they *seem* to be a pair of gorgeous, ripped Fae men, a werewolf, and a bear shifter. The woman is petite and delicate, with dragonfly wings and multi-colored skin and hair. Fairy, maybe?

Fuck if I know. I'm wondering if someone spiked the damn food in that place.

I count slowly in mind, hoping to slow my pulse until I'm under control. Whatever is going on here, I can't let anyone know right now. This moment feels important, even without the damn hallucinations, and I can't screw it up for Wolfie. So I square my shoulders and hold my hand out, palms up. "Feel free to check me first. We are only here to enjoy your generous hospitality."

"Excellent!" The fairy woman claps her hands, then places them above mine, hovering as she closes her eyes. "Close your eyes as well, and I will determine what we must know."

Teddy literally snarls like an animal next to me, but I don't dare look at him. Instead, I close my eyes behind my glasses and focus on breathing deeply. Whatever hippy-dippy shit this chick is doing will be over soon, and I doubt it will—

Ow.. ow… ow… holy fuck… ow… ow… ow…

It takes all of my strength not to let the pain slicing through me show in my body or expression. I don't know if this is a test or if something is seriously wrong with me, but it feels like I'm peeled open layer by layer from the inside out. My teeth grit, but I force the smile to stay in place as I wait for it to stop before I pass the hell out.

Suddenly, a flash echoes in my head.

A cold room. Bright lights. Everything is hazy.

There are people hovering over me, but they're shadows. I can't see their faces, but one has weird instruments in their hand. They're all holding their hands over me and it feels like I'm being burned now from head to toe.

My mind can't handle it. I float away, leaving the cold steel below me and molten heat inside of me as they continue to mutter words in a language I don't know. In the cloud, separate from the pain, I'm safe. Nothing bad can happen to me here. This is where I can hide from what's happening. I can stay here and I won't have to feel any of this ever again.

I watch the mysterious people work covering my body in odd drawings and colorful light. None of it looks like it's hurting me, but I know the searing of each and every symbol is making the body below jerk and twitch. It doesn't leave a mark on my skin; I can't see one scratch or scar. But beneath…

Beneath that layer, an intricate mural of art lies, glowing with power.

Why? Why are they doing this to me?

They speak in hushed, fearful tones and it's confusing. How could I scare people so badly they have to do this to me?

What am I, a monster?

The second the tiny woman pulls her hands away, the vision stops and I freeze in place. She doesn't look worried; no, she beams at me happily as she nods. "You are quite truthful, Miss Jolene Whitley of America. You have no ill-intent for our royals or our kingdom. You are cleared to enter the Castle."

Stepping aside, I carefully avoid letting anyone touch me so they can't feel the trembling of my limbs. That vision was important and so is whatever the hell is going on with my brain. I lick my lips and finally raise my gaze to look at Teddy. The purple-haired tester is holding her small hands over his large ones now. His body tenses and I swallow a gasp when his visage flickers—first, a huge fiery dog that smells of sulfur, then a gorgeous man that smells like cherries and sin, and then an enormous bird that has the scent of clean air and spices.

What. The. Actual. Motherfucking. Fuck.

I whip my eyes to the others in the group and let out a slow breath when I see nothing weird—until I hit my darling boy. *Oh, sweet baby Jesus wept, look at him.* Every cell in my body activates at once, and I have to lift my hand to surreptitiously check for drool. Wolfie is always a gorgeous runway model, almost pretty, but now… His undercut, dirty blond hair is now long, sparkling silver framing pointed ears and pale, iridescent pink skin. The green of his suit perfectly compliments the pale coloring, and the gorgeous blue, purple, and pink ombré-d butterfly wings curl at the ends, fluttering bits of glittery dust as he waits his turn.

"Done! You, too, are cleared to enter, Edgar Boone the third, son of the lawmaker and upholder of human laws in America."

The irritated growl he lets out tells me Teddy is already tired of the pomp and circumstance of our hosts. He spent most of his life following his father and mother around to this kind of shit, so I'm not surprised that he can endure it, but wants to smash something. "Hurry this up. I don't like standing in the doorway like we're selling Amway."

"Patience, young prince," she chides. "Join me, Irishman. It is your turn now."

Doyle looks even *less* pleased than Teddy, if that's possible. Nothing about him looks unusual—until the woman places her palms over his. The minute she does, a blinding light flashes out and surrounds him like a goddamn painting of an angel. He doesn't grow wings, which makes me let out a secret sigh of relief. I don't know what the hell my hallucination is assigning him beyond power, but thank hell, he's not an angel. I'm the right age for a schizo-affective break and religious iconography would be a telling sign that I'm not just drugged.

Relax, Jolene, there's no history of that in your family. Even if there was, you know exactly how to manage it. Don't be ridiculous.

The logical part of my mind is working overtime at the moment, and I have to listen. Obviously, with my training, I know how to manage a multitude of mental issues. There's not a damn thing wrong with having medical conditions like that. It's just a knee-jerk reaction to thinking I'm having serious problems I wasn't ready for. But… something in my gut tells me that's not what this is and the sooner I accept that, the sooner I'll understand what's happening.

"Hurry it up," Doyle says impatiently. "You're lucky I'm even allowing this nonsense. I don't have to and you know it."

"Ah, yes. Your kind are given so many exceptions," murmurs the fairy woman. "You are now cleared, Doyle Haggerty of lands farther than even ours reach. Mind your agreed upon tenets while you enjoy our homeland."

He waves his hand at her, then gestures for my beautiful Wolfie to step up. "I will do what I've agreed to, Captain. Now, do the pup so we can get on with this fucking circus."

The second Wolfie's hands are below hers, she gasps, pulling back briefly before she gathers herself. "Oh! My goodness! You, son of winter, are exempt. You may enter."

What? The son of a senator is suspect, but not a vet?

"She must know Callie," Teddy mutters next to me. "I don't blame her for avoiding that fucking psycho's wrath."

I don't turn to look at him; I watch Wolfie frown before he walks over to join us. He seemed hopeful the woman would have some other reaction. *Maybe he thought she'd know his father?* My brows furrow and I try to reason out why I think that. It *feels* true, and his disappointment is flowing over me as he gets closer.

"It's okay," I whisper as I reach for his hand. Everything is a mess in my head and I'm not sure if I'm losing my mind, but nothing can keep me from comforting him. The smile my darling boy gives me is even more brilliant than usual, and I almost swoon.

How in the hell did this goddamn drug haze make all *these assholes even hotter?*

I'm never going to survive this night.

Bad Feeling

Wolfgang

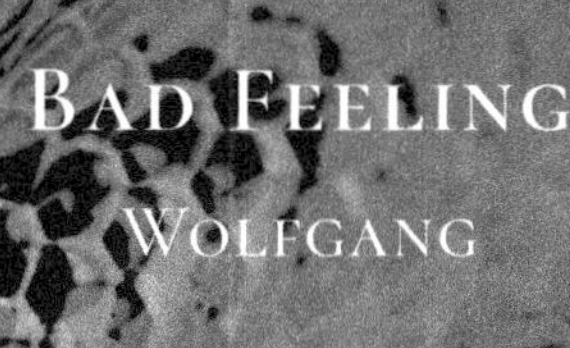

WHILE THE GUARD checks out Benjy and Prez, I watch Sugarplum out of the corner of my eye. She's fidgeting and tense, though she's trying desperately not to show it. I don't know if that's because the woman doing the testing is odd or because something else is wrong. There was a split second while their hands were together that I caught the tiniest pulse of pain from our girl, but since she didn't even grimace, I let it go. But now that she's holding my hand, my natural empathy is kicking in.

Jolene is walling herself in, keeping her emotions and thoughts to herself.

She hasn't done that since she allowed us in the house again that night before we left. I've been able to sense how she's doing and gauge when she needs support. Whatever happened between those two has her throwing up shields, and she doesn't even understand what she's doing. Of course, being bonded to more of us than before has only increased that power, so even I'm struggling to find a way past what she's doing. That's not good on so many levels, and Teddy's going to be pissed when I tell him.

My gaze flicks at the other alpha mate—a term that idiotic orc almost said out loud in front of someone unemerged. Orcs aren't particularly cunning, which is why this kind of job is perfect for them; unfortunately, this one inserted himself into a delicate situation. Luckily for him, Jolene was too focused on the psychic fairy to question what he almost spilled. That's another conversation to have with one of our hosts later, but it still made my entire body freeze until we got past it.

How do you explain that mated groups almost always have an alpha pair that leads their mini-packs that authorities defer to in this kind of situation?

You can't if they don't know what the hell mating means, much less how supernatural diplomacy works. Jolene probably thought they were being jackasses about size or something much more *human* than shifter vibes. We're not all shifters, but we've formed a family and that will often be treated just as a pack would. Without a doubt, Teddy and Jolene are at the top of our food chain. Doyle would never admit it, but he knows it's true.

For some reason, they put *me* equally with him, and that I can't fathom. I'm as submissive as they come and no one's ever accused me of being in charge of shit. The look in the fairy's eyes when she assessed me was curious, though, and I don't think it was entirely to do with my mother. I wonder if she could sense something about the other part of my heritage that she couldn't say. It wouldn't be surprising; I'm obviously not Daybreak Court, but there's Fae in me. They all have a myriad of agreements and promises made to keep their fragile peace over the centuries.

Perhaps identifying anything about my lineage would violate one of those clauses.

Looking down at my feet, I let calm flow over me so I don't show the turmoil inside. Sugarplum's glasses keep her from seeing my true nature, but the others can plainly see when I'm agitated by this form. I need to hold it together until they let us into this damned castle. Once we're away from the royal contingent, I can bounce ideas off of Prez or Teddy. One of them will have something useful to say about my experience with the court fairy.

"You are now cleared to enter the castle, brave barkeep!"

Teddy lets out an annoyed breath, then turns to us. "Let's get this show on the road. I'm already tired of being gawked at."

"Don't be such a sourpuss," Jolene murmurs as she wraps her other hand around his. "Maybe if we find our seats, we'll get to eat before anything else odd happens."

There's a tiny tremor in her voice, as if she's worried something *will* take place before we can sit down. I squeeze the hand I have, hoping to pass some reassurance to her as our brash hound leads the way past the hulking guards. I'm glad she can't see them, to be honest, because they're all huge and look like they'd enjoy tearing someone apart for fun. Their power level is lower than mine, but truthfully, we're walking around in a fairly overpowered group at the moment. I hope it warns off the more aggressive types that hang around court functions in this land.

"Psst."

I arch a brow as Doyle sidles up to me. "Hm?"

"She seem off to you, lad?"

Biting my lower lip, I decide to be honest. I'd expect the same from him, so it's only fair. "Yes. Since the woman checked her, Sugarplum has been shut up tighter than a diamond vault. Is that what you mean?"

"Mmm no. Good to know you're sensing something, too, though. I meant more like… unease. Something is making her feel very nervous and I can't suss out what it is. She's using that wall thingy you mentioned keeping us from noticing, I'd wager."

I nod at the demi-god. "She is. But it could be her reacting to not having control here. Much like you and Teddy, she hates being out of control and out of the loop. It might make her edgy."

"Not like this, pup. She's running cold as ice and just as sharp." He shakes his head and looks around, watching the elegantly dressed species from the Daybreak Court mill about. "Keep your eyes peeled for more signs. We may have to get her alone to get it out of her."

"Okay," I breathe.

Intrigue isn't my forte, but I also refuse to let something hurt our girl; I'll have to suck it up.

As we weave our ways through the glittering throng, I'm not sure which of our goals is more impossible: keeping Sugarplum in the dark or finding my father. My mother is a self-centered bitch that enjoys causing others pain, so she could have lied about damn near anything I've been told or started the rumors I've caught over the years. Aurelia knew nothing, even before her mind broke. It's clear I have Fae heritage from my shifts and powers, but nothing in the Daybreak Court calls to me. Our first stop on this vagabond tour is likely a bust—unless we can get someone to talk.

But getting people to talk when we have to keep things secret from Jolene is an obstacle itself.

Teddy finally stops at the long table in front of the dais where the King and Queen look down from their thrones. There are several males and females on smaller thrones on either side of them, which I assume are the favored children *du jour*. It's common for the Fae to have large families; they take 'heir and a spare' to new levels. Most of them will end up married off in political alliances, but not until the definite heir has ascended. The six princes and princesses we see now are likely only half of their family 'stable'.

"We're not seated with *them*, are we?" I hiss as I let go of my sugarplum's hand to approach him. My wings are fluttering with anxiety and I know he can feel the tension in me when he tucks me into his side and presses a kiss on my head.

Prez comes closer as well, then all of our family is circled around me in a group. Jolene smiles softly as she brushes her fingers over my jaw. "Don't worry, little Wolfie. We'll make sure they don't do anything to hurt you."

"It's not hurt that I'm worried about," I mumble. "It's misleading me to amuse themselves. I don't feel like this is where we'll find my father; it's far too light and hopeful in Daybreak for my mother. She'd never choose someone with this much… sunshine in their soul. So they may have rumors and riddles to give us, but they'll also enjoy sending us in the wrong direction because they can. Royals bore easily and they're immortal, remember?"

Benjy gives me a serious look. "Man, I don't know jack about this. The doc is right in saying they were really keeping us in the dark about some shit and who the fuck knows why. But I know that we have one of the trickiest motherfuckers I've ever met with us and he's agreed to a bet that ties his hands. Perhaps if we think his talents will be useful, we need a signal to relieve him of that burden?"

I swallow hard, waiting to see what Sugarplum will say. After all, this was her bet and her bounty if Doyle fucks up. I can't ask her to release him 'just in case'—can I?

"Oh, for fuck's sake." Our girl rolls her eyes and puts her hands on her hips. "Doyle can do his thing if it's going to get us information for you. Why the hell would I stop him because of a silly ass bet? Really, you boys have no faith in me at all."

Teddy grins, his eyes dark with gratitude. "Good choice, Tilly. You'll get a reward for that later."

"Stuff it, Coach," she mutters as she looks around. "There are more pressing matters than our bedroom Olympics at the moment."

Maybe, but she just sent all our trains off the track with that comment.

I clear my throat, getting the guys back as I tilt my head at the table. "We should probably sit down before we offend someone."

When the circle breaks, a smug-looking troll approaches us, bowing before he speaks. "Ah! You are ready to be announced now, yes?"

"Announced?" Presley says as he looks up at the raised thrones. "To… the royal family?"

"Yes, yes! It is a great honor to be seated here and we must announce you, then ascend to greet our most generous rulers. Once that happens, they will call the reel, and the family will join one by one. You will join as the princes and princesses do. Hopefully, you will not disgrace them with your performance."

Oh, shit.

"We'll be asked to dance… with them… in front of the entire room?" I clarify as I look around.

"Of course! Again, you are being afforded the *highest* honors for visitors from the Other Realm. I don't know why, but it is my job to prepare you. So, please, line up in the reverse order that our door sentries granted you entrance to the castle."

Jolene sighs when he moves away. "When I was little, I wanted to be a princess. Every girl does, right? After my escapades in Europe, I saw what kind of constant bullshit women like these have to endure and was suddenly glad as hell to be a lowly commoner. This needless pomp and circumstance is keeping everyone from eating, and I'm going to be hangry soon."

"Then let's get it over with before the monster gets loose," Teddy says with a chuckle. "Benjy, you're first, man. Then the doc, then Wolfie, and so on. Line up so they can call us, bow or curtsey, be polite, and we'll get through this shit. Everyone knows how to dance, right?"

"You're asking the Cotillion Catastrophe if she knows how to dance?" Sugarplum grumbles. "You've got nerve, Edgar Olivier Boone III."

"I'm not asking *you*, Tilly. I know you went through all the cotillion practice. Foster did as well. I'm asking the docs and the dick."

Doyle snorts. "I've graced many a salon with my quick feet over the years, doggy. More than you'll ever be able to claim."

"I know. I escorted someone during my time at WHFS," I admit. I would never have been considered for that part of high society like them, but I could attend with a girl who did.

"I can dance." Presley shrugs. "My mentor was a stickler for doctors presenting themselves as part of the town fabric. The damn balls and shit have different names in different parts of the world, but it's all the same. I should do fine."

"Good," the hound says as he looks up at the haughty royals. "Because I get the feeling they will judge us."

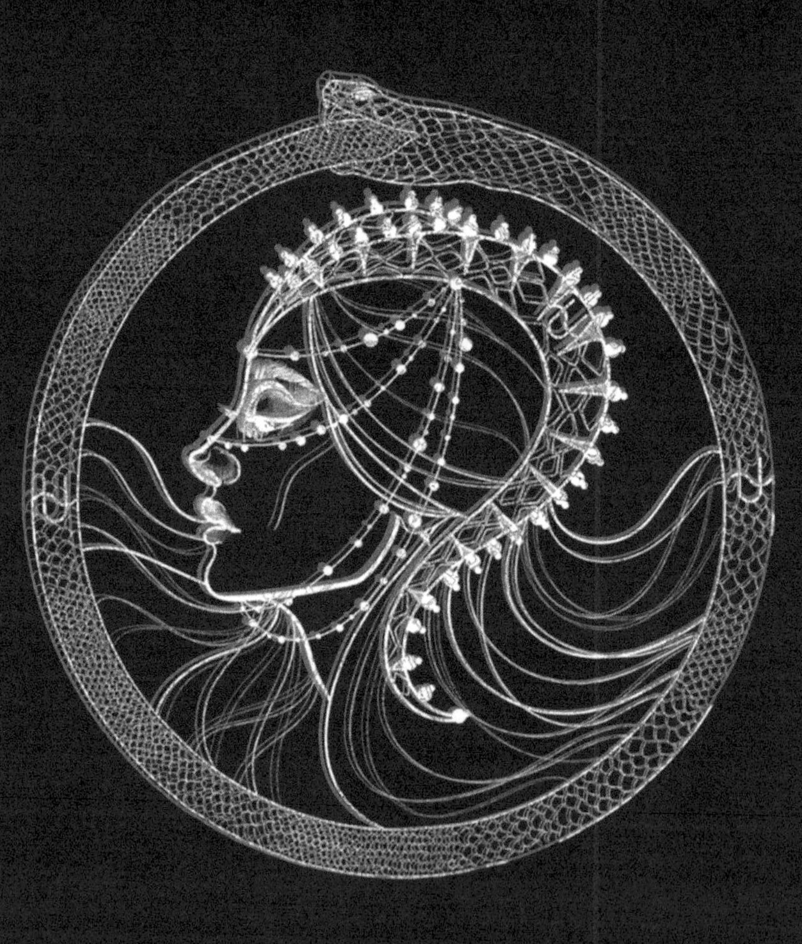

Royals

Jolene

Teddy's prediction hit me like a brick to the face and now I'm gripped with old fears about being judged at a stupid formal event in front of an entire town. It's been so many years since that damn night, yet when the anxiety from it is triggered, I still have to fight my way through an electric light show in my mind and body. The snooty Fae in this room aren't very different from the most elite townsfolk in the Hollow. Guaranteed, there are more than a few bitchy women and their male counterparts milling around. If I make one wrong move, they'll go for the kill simply to impress the royals.

They'll come for your men.

I frown, unsure where that thought came from. Before my goddamn glasses started malfunctioning, I didn't even believe this world existed. Now my mind is filling in gaps with information I can't possibly have a basis for. What the shit went on between the guest house and here that nullified the dream woman's efforts to keep me in the dark? I assume she was attempting to protect me and this has something to do with the 'big secrets' the guys can't tell me. Clara Whitley may not have been the best mother, but she didn't raise a fool.

The reality of a hidden world shouldn't be possible, yet here it is. Not only that, but my guys are part of it, which means… This place isn't a one-off. The cheerful broad at the entrance to the castle revealed all of them have… forms… I didn't know about. But she didn't seem surprised, and only Wolfie had something that appeared to connect to this world. The others had animals or glowing auras; I assume that means every myth and fairy tale I've ever been told is possibly based in fact.

Life was so much simpler when I was dealing with contrary despots and CEOs.

While I've been noodling the fucking bizarre turn my life has taken, the dance floor in the middle has cleared and guests are lining up. I hold on to Wolfie, counting in half time in my head to prepare for the quick steps. They can choose a wealth of music for this, and for all I know, there are specific Fae tunes they'll use. But reels are traditionally in a faster 4/4 time and if I just keep count, I'll be fine, regardless. Hopefully, the guys know that, too.

I don't have time to remind them, though, because we're ushered into formation and the uptempo beat begins. The beat climbs as we all move in unison, and I dart my eyes away from the crowd of multicolored Fae to make sure the guys are doing okay. Even Benjy is moving gracefully and I let out a small sigh of relief. I can't imagine what would happen if—

As if by magic, the reel music stops and everyone stands in place. I wait for the bow and curtsey, but it doesn't come. No, the music begins again and everyone moves to lines divided across the space.

Shit. They're switching to a contra.

My eyes flutter closed briefly as I wing a prayer to whatever motherfucker is listening that none of them were lying about remembering the damn cotilion training. This shit was one of their main events and I'll be damned if no one mentioned switching dance types mid-stream. This isn't a strange dance for people who have gone through what Teddy and I have, so we're able to get into position quickly. His palm faces mine as we circle, and I lift the edge of my dress with my free hand as we circle. I can feel the intensity of his gaze burning into me and for a second, I almost whisper that I know.

But I can't. If this really is the crap they aren't allowed to speak of, I don't think we've hit the flash point yet. Doyle, at the least, would have whooped for joy if whatever trigger they're waiting for got pulled. None of them have acted like they expect me to know Wolfie has fucking wings. For that reason alone, I'm keeping my damn mouth shut. I don't know what punishment they'd get, but it has to be serious for Doyle to obey.

We haven't even spoken to the royal fuckwits yet—this night may never end.

The lines move and I frown, watching Teddy slide in front of a tittering Fae woman with blue hair and an enormous dress. My gut curls in, a dark sensation sliding through me as I dance with my new partner instinctively. A soft cough brings my attention back to the male in front of me and I blink owlishly. One of the indolent princes from the stage has his palm centimeters from mine as we move through the steps. He has flowing black hair, huge raven wings, and a smirk that says he finds me lacking.

"Good evening, your highness. Pleasure to make your acquaintance," I drawl as I bat my lashes. I'd prefer he thinks I'm a clueless idiot from our world than looks too closely.

His eyes narrow, and he throws his head back, laughing as he moves in time with me. "Cute. You seek to disarm me with this guise, but I see through it. I will not break the accords by telling you how I know you are not the simpering belle you pretend to be. However, you will meet far less scrupulous royals in the other strongholds."

Isn't that grand?

"I'm sure I don't know what you mean, Prince…?" I let the question hang, ignoring the eyes of my men on me as we speak in hushed tones.

"Prince Eógan." He grins a bit as he looks around and leans in again. "Your men are very nervous about my proximity to you, especially the one who seeks his line."

"We're here on vacation, nothing more," I reply casually. "Genealogy isn't one of my hobbies, I'm afraid."

The prince huffs, bowing as our turn ends. He gives me a saucy wink as we switch to the next partner, and I roll my eyes.

Hera, save me from the tsunami of hot, asshole men who have become a daily trial in my life.

EACH ONE OF THE MALE ROYALS TOOK A TURN WITH ME IN THE contra, playfully bantering about what they knew that I didn't. I parried to each of their verbal thrusts, not breaking character for a second. Somehow, I knew letting even one of them know they'd gotten into my head would be a dangerous proposition.

By the time we make it to the last partner, I stare at Wolfie in relief. Strain is clear in his eyes as he smiles at me and I realize he's having the most trouble with tonight. His transformation probably started when he set foot in this land, and he's had to keep me at arm's length to protect me. That can't have been easy on him—my darling boy craves touch to balance out his emotions. Teddy and Prez did their best, I'm sure, but if the pull to his mates is similar for him, he's suffered.

"Well, hello, little Wolfie," I say as our palms hover together. "Fancy meeting you here."

He snorts and I see several people glare at him. I search their faces, something deep in my gut whispering dark things about what I should do to all the Fae involved in this fucking circus. The longer they have forced us to dance and endure their royal brats, the easier it was to see that this entire night is a set-up. The Daybreak Court is beautiful, but far too light and springy for Callie. We've been held hostage by tradition simply so they can gather intel or maybe just for their amusement—and I don't like it a bit.

"Um, Sugarplum?" Wolfie says quietly. His voice breaks my concentration and I turn back to him with a smile. "You're getting awfully hot. Are you overheating in your gown?"

Tilting my head, I consider that for a moment. I feel warm, but nothing alarming. "Perhaps. I think this will be our last goodwill dance. Our hosts have imposed on our desire to follow tradition for long enough."

His eyes widen, and he shakes his head. "No, we have to—"

My lips curve and I step out of the formation. I dust off my old favorite as I look directly at the bored-looking King and Queen. Seer would be proud if she could see me doing the most sarcastic, overly exaggerated curtsy I can before I walk back to my table. The Queen looked pissed, but I honestly don't give a hairy possum's ass. At home, expecting your guests to perform while you hold dinner for ransom for an hour would get you kicked so far back over the Mason-Dixon line you'd turn into a Yankee.

Once I'm standing by my chair, I see Doyle jump out of his spot, covering his laughter with his hand as he joins me. The look on his face is one of pure excitement as he leans down to murmur by my ear.

"They underestimate your sass every time, Tíogair. You don't suffer fools and you've got as much stubborn dictator in you as the doggy."

"I can't abide rudeness," I say as he pulls out my chair. "There's something rotten in Denmark here, Lucky. Nothing about tonight is what it seems, and I fucking hate subterfuge. If these dicklickers want to come at us, we won't go down like whimpering pansies."

His eyes narrow. "Amazing. Your lips are moving, but I'd *swear* I'm hearing the judge. Did you do a Vulcan mind meld?"

"Don't be ridiculous. Everyone knows aliens aren't real," Prez scoffs as he and the others take their seats.

I look around the table for a second, taking in the fantastical sights. My hand flies to my mouth as a giggle escapes, then another, until I drop my head on the table as I laugh. Shoulders shaking, tears leaking, gut clenching, laughter rolls through me as the irony of his state-ment hits me.

As if Fae, magic, winged dudes, royalty, and fucking shifters are so goddamn normal.

"Uh, Princess? Are you okay?"

I lift a hand, waving it as I try to calm the slight insanity in my mind. The blackouts and flashbacks I've had most of my life always made me think I had a screw loose. Now I'm embroiled in some plot worthy of a TV show, running around a world full of things that shouldn't exist. I continue laughing, wiping my eyes to keep my face from being ruined, and I wonder if I'm going to wake up one day in a mental hospital surrounded by dudes in white coats. They'll tell me I've been in a coma for ten years after falling off a horse and suddenly, all of this shit will make sense.

A tight squeeze under my gown gets my attention and I blink.

Nope, not a coma, because those don't involve an eight-foot snake wrapped around your torso like a straightjacket.

Sucking in a deep breath, I get myself under control. I just have to get through the rest of this fucking trip without toppling off the deep end or stabbing someone. It's been a long time since I've had to do that and I should be able to control myself. A sound from the dais floats down to us and I whip my head around. The first dark haired prince is grinning like a madman at me as I gather my wits. A pink haired sister is whispering with him as they stare down at our table, and I know it means trouble.

"Sugarplum, you should probably calm down…"

Picking up my silverware, I unfold the napkin, only to see my hands are on fire.

This can't be good.

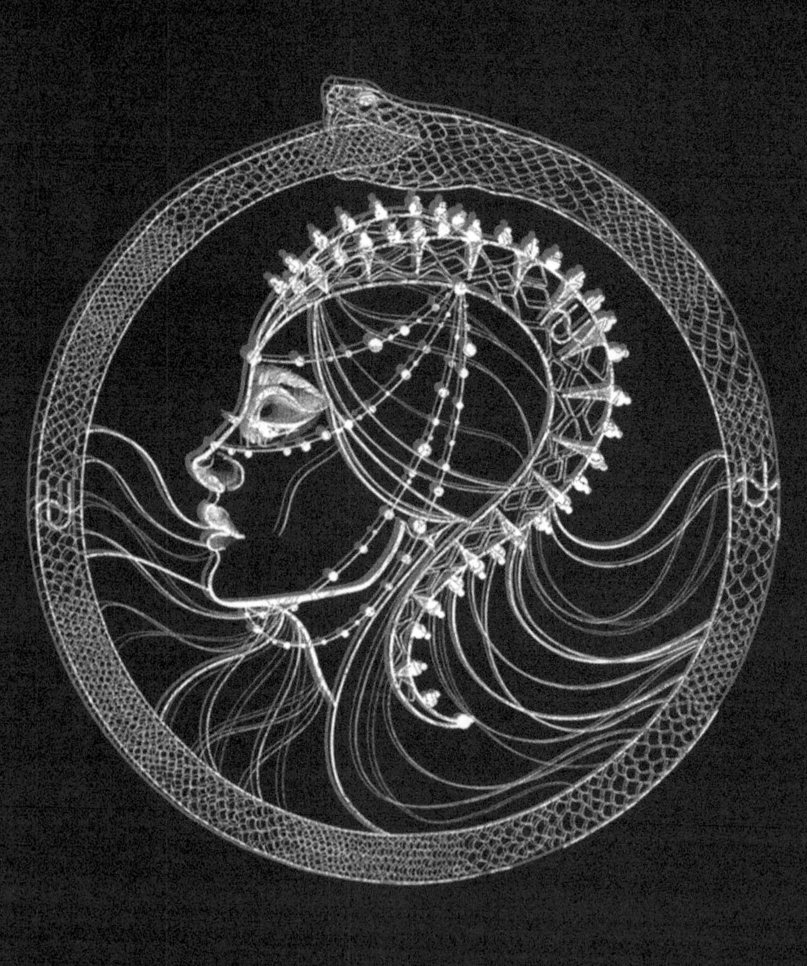

Poison

Edgar

THANK FUCK for those stupid glasses. I still haven't figured out where they came from, but I knew what they were for the second Tilly put them on. It's hard to control the protective instincts of *all* my goddamn sides as she's casually chowing down on her weird Fae salad with flaming hands. The pup tried to calm her down when he noticed, but she's obviously too worked up to be soothed with words.

Doesn't mean I'm not going to try.

"Tilly, your hands look red. Did you touch something unusual while we were dancing?" I put on an innocent expression, hoping she won't notice the strained edge to my voice.

"Other than fuckfaced rich guys? No," she says before she takes another bite. "They do feel itchy. Perhaps their gallons of weird cologne are triggering an allergy."

Doyle squints at her, his eyes dark as he watches her eat. It's hard to tell what he's thinking when he's not being a brash asshole, and I don't trust the quiet a bit. "Itchy, huh? Perhaps a rash?"

She shrugs and gives him a sweet smile. "Maybe? Who knows what those dipshits did while they were interrogating me? They sucked at it, by the way."

Holy hell, I get it now.

Tilly's hands are on fire, and her aggression has ratcheted up a thousand percent. She has to be drawing on… me. Our connection is stronger here and even though the mating isn't completely sealed from her end, somehow, she's accessing one of my powers. *Not good, not good…* It took me a long time to mostly master the hellhound, and he's the easiest of the three sides. I whip my head around, looking at Benjy, then cut my eyes to her hands. It takes him a minute, but I see when he remembers the first time my fire manifested at a football game in late elementary school.

"Princess, slow down before you choke," he says as he takes a sip from the large tankard of fizzy shit the Fae servers placed at each of our seats while we were dancing. "You're practically inhaling that stuff."

"S'good," Jolene says. "Plus, it's been a dog's age since we ate and I'm trussed up like a fluffy swan. *And* I had to dance for an hour straight. It feels like I could eat an entire hippo, honestly."

All the guys share a knowing expression—she's getting closer to emerging. Her appetite will double or triple depending on how large or powerful her form is. That might be hard for her since she's got trauma about eating, so we'll have to be very careful not to trigger that unintentionally. The fire on her palms leans towards being like me—her scent even has a trace of sulfur right now.

"Then fill up, Sugarplum. We don't want you all worn out by the time we get home."

I smirk as the pup hiccups. This Fae mead shit must hit him harder than it does us because he's giving our girl intensely flirty eyes. The doc grins at me, clearly noticing the same thing I am, and I lean back in my chair. Once we're back in our little guest house, it's going to get wild. No matter what happens here, we have that to look forward to. All we have to do is make it through dinner and whatever formal introductions these asshats want us to go through, then we'll escape.

"What are you making that face for, Teddy Bear?" Tilly asks as she pauses to take a sip down some of the mead. "You look like a cat that caught the canary and—wait, where the hell are the cats? And the others?"

"Hunting, love," Doyle says smoothly. "They're getting a read on the room for us. Don't worry; she's watching." He points up to a high railing where Euryale is glaring at the room as if it offends her. "Your feathered friend is making certain the furry ones are safe, just like your scaly companion is secretly helping you."

Little on the nose there, you idiot. What's he playing at?

"Oh! That makes perfect sense. Jekyll and Hyde are particularly sneaky when they want to be. It's cat nature, I think." Tilly nods and my eyes narrow again.

She's being quite easygoing for someone whose damn hands are flaming. I know from experience it means my hound is fucking furious when the fire moves from my veins to the outside of my body. Our lovely Jolene is playing a game of her own and I don't know who it's with—us, the royals, or everyone at the ball. There's no way she'd have magical flames dancing over her without actually burning anything, if not.

Disturbingly enough, it means she's controlling their effects somehow, too.

I was almost sixteen before I figured that shit out. The Senator had to cover up quite a few incidents when my temper blew and I accidentally committed arson before I learned how to tell the flames what to do. That fact makes my gut clench in anticipation; Tilly will be a formidable mate. We'll have a pack that possibly dwarves every group of supes within the States. Outside of Guardians, I'm not sure there's even competition.

Presley clears his throat and I look up. "Penny for your thoughts, Your Honor."

"I'd say that's overpaying, birdie," Doyle mutters.

Ignoring him, I shrug. "Considering what all of this means for the future." My gaze flicks to her hands quickly, then back before Tilly catches on. "The control being shown is not common, in my experience. It's very powerful and hard to manage."

He looks thoughtful for a moment. "I see. Perhaps it will be revealed soon, then?"

"Fuck, I hope so," Tilly mutters and we all look at her in panic. She frowns at our gaping, waving her hands around. "This formal bullshit is tiresome. I'll drink this yummy fizzy shit and eat whatever desserts they bring, but I want out of this dress. You might have to roll me home like a blueberry."

The imagery makes me snort and I lean in to nip her jaw. "Tilly, I'd happily roll you home if you're getting naked when we get there. I enjoy *all* types of juicy fruit."

That gets the attention of everyone at the table, and our girl turns bright pink as she smacks my arm lightly. "Don't be crude, Edgar Boone. We're at a ball… I think. What would your mama say?"

"Tilly, you know for fact I don't give a toad's bumpy ass what my mother would say anymore. I'll yank this tablecloth off and fuck you over the damn table if I want. Not one motherfucker in this room will stop me, I promise."

Jolene sucks in a breath, and I can scent her arousal floating in the air like perfume. Her typical magnolia and plum fragrance, with the hint of my burning embers mixed in, makes my hound thrash against the cage inside of me. I blink, feeling the heat in my eyes as the ring of fire surrounds my iris. Knowing our mate is going to emerge with our powers makes it hard to control the giant beast, but I tamp down hard. I can't do this here; even if the Court knows what all of us are, they do *not* know about the rest of me.

Only my pack—my family—knows about the rest of me, and it needs to stay that way.

"Princess," Benjy says loudly, pulling us out of the intense stare we were holding. "Have you noticed the rest of the room seems normal and we're all… tipsy, maybe?"

His words make me freeze in place. *That can't be.* Looking around quickly, I note all the other people chatting and eating with no kind of commotion at their tables. No one is ready to hop on one another and rut, nor are they getting feisty enough to have fire hands. My old friend is right; we're the only ones teetering on an emotional cliff. I suck in a breath slowly, working to process that information without all of my short-tempered supe sides losing their shit at the same time.

"We've either been drugged, poisoned, or this stuff interacts with *our kind* differently than the other guests," Presley says quietly. "Two of those options are concerning and the last is simply unfortunate. The first two would be extremely unwise on the part of our hosts. It would certainly break... laws. And it will cause a lot of... paperwork."

Snorting, I look around again. When I don't see our companions right away, I whistle low. It takes mere seconds for the cats to leap up to our table, taking seats at the small stools that appear in-between Tilly, the pup, and I. Kali and Hecate arrive next, posting up on their seats as Euryale touches down behind the doc. We need their help and I hope the Irishman's raven is somewhere nearby as well.

"Sniff the food. Scent the people. We may have eaten something dangerous. Report back."

Our girl's companions take off with mine in tow, scattering across the room to do my bidding. Jolene tilts her head at me curiously, but doesn't ask me what the hell I was doing. She's probably a bit more off than the rest of us because we encouraged her to chow down and she's been drinking the mead. Lucky for me, it's made her a lot more complacent towards me; unfortunately for the royals, she was pissed at them before this discovery.

I'm worried what she's going to do if we find out this shit was intentional.

"We need to pack up and get the fuck out of this Court tomorrow morning," Doyle says mildly. "Even if this is a mistake, it's a dead end and we shouldn't waste anymore time playing their little games."

"Agreed," Wolfie says as he looks at me. "I don't trust them. This probably isn't poison because it wouldn't affect me like it does you. But it could be some sort of drug or serum used to loosen us up before the big introduction. That's definitely against the accords and they're taking a tremendous risk."

"I have supplies in my luggage," the doc says. "I'm taking samples from everyone when we get to our rooms. I want to test them later, just in case we need proof."

Presley Hamilton is a fucking genius, and he does not *get enough credit.*

"Good idea, doc," I murmur. "We'll want evidence for Nelia and Jackson if they need to help us pursue things."

Tilly beams at me, her eyes dancing. "Jax and Eli are up at State helping that hockey player avoid getting charged with murder. It's super scandalous. I can't *wait* for him to tell me the entire story."

I scratch my neck as I consider how to answer that. We talked about this earlier, but I didn't go into detail. Being part of the Society and an alum, I'm aware of the turmoil going on at our alma mater. My father is on the board that replaced that misogynistic old fart who used to run it. The Senator was furious that they almost cost State their ability to play D1 sports and he's neck deep in all that shit. But I don't know how much of what I know has been made public.

"There's some crazy shit happening everywhere, it seems, Tilly." She nods and I breathe a sigh of relief. "Even your bestie got called off for a job instead of meeting us for this trip."

Mentioning Seer will distract her, even if it's a gamble.

"I know! I wanted her here with me, but she said she had to meet up with Julia and her fam to do something important." Her pout is adorable and I almost snicker. "I *hate* that she's missing this. She'd help me kick their rich, snooty asses for sure."

"Perhaps it's better she's *not* here then, Sugarplum? We don't want to break laws ourselves," Wolfie says cajolingly. "We just need to survive tonight and get the hell out like Doyle said."

Jolene's lip curls as she looks up at the group of fancy fuckers on the dais. "I doubt that's how it's going to work out, little Wolfie. I have a bone to pick with our gracious hosts; they won't be happy when I'm done, either."

Dionysis, save me from Fae drugged women and men tonight.

"Can we *try* not to start a war?" I ask drily.

Our girl sneers like the green Christmas thief as she shrugs. "Depends on how I feel by the time they finally call us up there, Teddy. I'm mighty fucking tired of being the bigger woman."

Just. Fucking. Fabulous.

Run The World

Jolene

"Attention, everyone!"

Turning my attention from the increasingly hot flirting at our table, I look up to see the troll from before standing in front of a microphone. An air of practiced calm has replaced the smugness. If this isn't our time to be called before those damn lazy royals, I'm taking another stand. We're leaving this ridiculous excuse for intel gathering in the next hour or I'll take Teddy up on that table fucking plan.

Zero fucks given is my new mantra with the Fae—they underestimate me and that will change.

"It is now time for our honored guests to be introduced to their hosts. If our guests will please head for the right wing in the order they entered the reel, we will begin."

I pinch the bridge of my nose, trying to rein in my irritation. This is one humongous waste of our time and these asshole Fae are doing it on purpose. What I don't know is *why* they're keeping us captive with pomp and circumstance. Dropping my napkin, I stand up, waving at the guys to follow. It's hot as hell here. You'd think royals would at least be as smart as Southern humans and provide the ladies in enormous dresses with fans.

Teddy takes my arm, his brow arching as he looks at me. "We need to cut this shit off, Tilly. You look like you're on fire."

Oh, he's hilarious tonight, isn't he?

I nod as I approach the dais, lifting the bottom of my skirts to ascend. When I'm halfway up, I look each of the assholes in the eye as I repeat my patently sarcastic curtsey. The troll looks scandalized when I don't dip my head or avert my eyes, but I want these people to know I'm serious. If everything I've figured out so far tonight is true, they're aware they can't tell me this stupid secret outright or they will be in trouble. But I believe from the bottom of my sugar and spice Southern soul that the woman who dressed me did something that fucked with my glasses or my eyes. That's when I started noticing little shit and by the time we were inside this place, it was all revealed.

The question is still: why and who does it benefit?

"Miss Jolene Athena Whitley, Whistler's Hollow, United States of America," the troll finally says.

Mustering all the saccharine coated steel I can, I smile and say, "Charmed, I'm sure."

The snicker behind me says Teddy is amused as hell. This is the first time he's seen me use the assumptions about our roots to fool people, but it's not the first time I've used it. If Seer were here, she'd be bouncing with glee; turning on the 'Miss Scarlett' always made her giggle. A glance at the Queen says she's unimpressed, but the King nods at me like I've passed inspection.

"Welcome to our home, Miss Whitley. May the road rise to meet you." His wife sniffs, looking down her nose at me for a moment before ogling my men again.

Nope. Absolutely not.

"Thank you, sir. May I be so bold as to introduce my family? We're growing weary from our travels and would like to extend our gratitude before we must take our leave."

"Leaving your own party before it's over?" The first prince I danced with gives me a predatory look, his lips curved up as lounges in his chair. "I can't imagine that's acceptable in your land."

Batting my lashes, I tilt my head at him. "A lady must excuse herself if she cannot maintain a suitable demeanor in public. I merely offered to expedite our introductions so we might express our gratitude for your gracious treatment before it becomes necessary to take our leave."

"That was a lot of fifty cent words for 'I'm tired.' It's impressive," the second prince says as he shrugs. "Perhaps we should allow her to do it. I'm interested in her… point of view."

"Fine, fine," the King interrupts. "Let the girl speak."

Unsurprisingly, the princesses and the Queen haven't been asked their opinion. This may be my least favorite stop of the trip.

"Thank you again," I reply quickly, dipping in another curtsey before gesturing to Teddy. "This is Judge Edgar Oliver Boone III, son of Senator Boone, Whistler's Hollow, United States of America."

Teddy steps up beside me, standing close enough to make it obvious he's not simply a friend. Before he can open his mouth and fuck things up, I gesture to Wolfie and Doyle. Wolfie stands at my left and Doyle joins him as I continue. "This is Dr. Wolfgang Lucien Fletcher, also of Whistler's Hollow, and Doyle Aloysius Haggerty, Ireland."

I ignore the loud snorts from the princes as I continue. They clearly have more information than me, but at this point? I'll get it from someone else. These motherfuckers have their heads so far up their own asses they can see teeth and I'm over it. Waving my hand, I see Benjy and Prez come up next and paste a smile on my face. "Finally, we have Dr. Presley Hemingway Hamilton and Benjamin Louis Foster, of Tokyo and Whistler's Hollow, respectively. Together, my family would like to formally thank you for your hospitality."

Teddy steps in front of me, dipping his head once as he looks at the assembly on the dais. "I'm sure my father and our associates would love to express their gratitude as well. Please excuse our absence now that we've had the pleasure; we have check-ins to complete with our Guardians."

What the fuck is he talking about? Does this have to do with their secret shit?

The word seems to send a ripple through our hosts, though. They've been holding us hostage with formality, but now they actually look worried. The Queen is the one who sits up, nodding at Teddy as if she's been on his side all along.

"You are all excused, Mr. Boone. Please send our deepest regards."

I frown as I realize all the women are sitting up straighter, their expressions serious, and the room has gone silent as they get involved.

Son of a bitch. They're the ones in charge, not the idiot men.

Of fucking course, they are

As we exit the car that showed up to take us back to our guest house, I look at the outside. I can see it—the real facade—for the first time and it blows me away. It's a smaller version of the castle we were just trapped in, made for the guests of the royal twats. I guess it's supposed to make us feel important, but all I feel is pissed. I don't know the rules of this game, but I recognize that until the 'right moment,' I'm not able to let my men know their secrets are out. Jekyll was studying me the entire ride back and I'm pretty sure the fucking animals have figured it out.

Luckily, they can't talk—as far as I know.

Isis squeezes me and for the first time since she arrived, it occurs to me that no matter what I'm wearing, this big ass python fits under it. I almost facepalm as I walk towards the door; I couldn't have been more blind if I tried. Seriously, what the hell was wrong with me? The snake practically sinks into my skin, two wild cats adopted me, Teddy's dogs never leave my side, and a big ass eagle from another continent took up residence in my backyard. That *alone* should have tipped me off to something being off, but I walked around like a dumbass in front of everyone.

Shit, does everyone *in the Hollow know? No wonder the Nip/Tucks are snickering behind their hands.*

Fury boils up inside of me and I stomp past the guys, heading down the hallway to my room. Even if everyone is bound by this fucking oath, I'm still the village idiot. I passed *F.B.I.* exams, for fuck's sake! My observational skills were in the top one percent, but I didn't see that my hometown was some sort of Mystic Falls wanna-be. Pacing back and forth, I rub my temples, feeling the migraine pounding in my head like a band of gnomes banging out a Sousa march.

"Why me? Why was I singled out? What the hell is going on with my memory?" I growl under my breath, looking down at my flaming hands in exasperation. "Why doesn't this shit burn me?"

"*Mow!*" Jekyll says the cats hop up on the bed, sitting perfectly straight like statues.

I frown, looking around the room to see all the animals perched in various spots as they look at me expectantly. "Guys, I don't fucking know how to answer you. Hell, I don't know if you can talk or understand me. Can you understand me?"

Kali barks, then sits back on her haunches. My gaze roves to each of them, pressing my lips together as I think about this. They've always seemed to get what I'm saying, so that might be a 'yes.' Euryale makes a soft screeching sound, her wings flapping open, then closed before she settles on the dresser.

I'm probably losing my mind. They also listen to—

"Oh. Wolfie. You understand him, too." I wait, and none of them snuff like I'm stupid, so I assume I must be right. "Okay, so that's part of his… power… or whatever. He's obviously Fae and whatever his bitchy mom is. She's not Fae, for sure. Something old and powerful, though, right?"

Hyde's tail twitches as she bobs her head. "*Mow.*"

I pull the sparkling shit out of my hair, letting it fall down my back with a relieved sigh. That helps more than I'd like to admit. "Right. So he's here to figure out his dad, who definitely isn't part of this Daybreak thing. But I bet that hybrid comment was about someone like him that's… half and half?"

This time, Hecate barks and I grin. *This is sort of working, but it's a shame I can't just talk to the guys.* While I think about my next question, I pull off the wings and undo the tight ass dress, looking down to see Isis emerging from my skin like a living tattoo. "What in the actual… goddamn it. How am I supposed to handle all of this at once?"

My snake squeezes me, and I know she's trying to help me cope with all the new knowledge being flung at me. That's *her* function— keeping me calm and even when I'm about to lose my shit. It's probably a shared duty and the fact that I need six animals here to watch me *should* frighten me, but it doesn't. If all this magical shit is real, then I suppose Fate is as well. That means everything that happens is…

Nope, not ready for that *realization yet. Putting that shit away for much later.*

"Wait a minute." I blink as the whole Catastrophe thing flashes in my mind. Why would the Richie-riches organize something that could possibly reveal them? Did they have that little control over their teens or…? *No.* "Son of a bitch. There *are* people in the Hollow who don't know about this shit. That prank was intended for that Lorelei girl, not me. Dad was *so* angry about mom for not pursuing it more…"

A brief memory makes me groan as I smack my forehead. My mother was part of this shit and my dad wasn't. She didn't go after the girls or even the boys because their families aren't just rich— they're neck deep in some supernatural hierarchy. That also explains Teddy and Benjy having odd shadows that seem to say they're like… weres? Shifters?

Fuck if I know.

But now I get why my parents were fine with me taking off and not coming back to town. Eloise decided I was a disappointment and my dad couldn't convince her otherwise. That's what that dream meant

—I was supposed to be more, and I turned out to be nothing. She was always angry at me, just like I thought growing up. She'd adopted a damn lemon and couldn't return it.

My eyes prick with tears as I finish stripping off all the layers and walk to the dresser to pull out something to wear. There's a silky set of pajamas that looks like heaven, so I put them on. Once I'm no longer bound in girly shit, I look at my servals sadly. "I guess I'm more of a failure than I thought."

"*Mrrrrp*," Jekyll says as he stares at me.

"You can disagree all you want, but obviously, whatever special shit I should have gotten isn't coming. I'm a dud," I grumble as I wave my hand at him. Then the fire on my hands interrupts my pity party and I blink. "Wait…"

This isn't the first weird thing that's happened since you came back.

Licking my lips, I listen to the voice in my mind as I consider the months since I returned to the Hollow. The dreams, the blackouts, the missing time, even the guys… Jesus Christ in a bourbon bottle, the sticks in my hair and leaves in my bed I couldn't explain. Something was happening and no one could tell me. I *am* changing; I'm just a late bloomer.

"But what am I going to do about this? I can't ask for help because I can't tell anyone I know. What if I hurt someone?"

There's no one to answer that, so I drop onto the bed next to Jekyll and Hyde, stroking my hands over their backs.

I need to figure out how to get information without putting anyone at risk, even if it means I don't tell anyone what the seamstress helped reveal.

Jolene Athena Whitley isn't human and the world just got a whole lot weirder.

Twin Peaks

Wolfgang

THERE'S something going on with Sugarplum, but I can't put my finger on it.

She's been acting resigned since we arrived here, and it's not like her. Until she squared off with those Daybreak ninnies, I was worried she might sink into a funk. Jackson warned Teddy about that from her college years and seeing her look so tired had me concerned the weight of our secrets was making her spiral. But she stood next to us and damn near gave them the finger in the most polite way possible—behavior that's right out of her typical playbook. It made my chest loosen up, despite her angry retreat to her room alone last night.

Breakfast was lighthearted, though, and we packed up our shit quickly. I remembered how to use the Flit app to call a car to transport us from Daybreak to our next stop, and we took off. I was glad to leave this section of Faerie, to be honest. The royals seemed to have ulterior motives, which isn't odd for our species, but they seemed far too interested in causing trouble for us.

I can't help feeling like they knew something they held back—something important.

"What do you know about our next destination?" Doyle asks me as he lounges on the bench seat. He scratches his chin as he thinks. "It's been more than a dog's age since I've been there."

Pressing my lips together, I consider how to answer him. The Daybreak and Autumn Courts are both Seelie, which is why we started with them. They're not likely to be where my dad hails from, but they are the less devious Fae. I spent little time in Harvest on my journey here when I graduated from college. It's a beautiful place, but it didn't feel like *my* home, so I moved on. "If I remember correctly, the folks who live in this part of the countryside aren't as fanciful as our previous hosts. They're the quieter version, if that makes sense."

"I don't care if they're chatty; I only care if they act like douche canoes," Sugarplum says grumpily. "This is your notice, boys. If these fuckers try what the people at our last stop did, I will not be held responsible for whatever diplomatic issues I cause."

Teddy smirks as he tugs her closer, moving her onto his lap entirely. "Tilly, I've spent most of my life making as many headaches as I can for the Senator. I will not stop you as long as you're willing to accept the consequences."

Has he lost his damn mind? She doesn't even know what the consequences are.

"Uh, Boone? I'm not sure you should—"

He rolls his eyes, waving Prez off with a grin. "Our girl wants to make her own decisions. The bullshit we endured at the damn mansion last night made me re-evaluate our 'lie low' tactic. Perhaps we should throw a reverse Uno in the mix?"

I pinch the bridge of my nose as I think about his suggestion. Out of all the courts, Harvest is the least likely to take affront at bold, stand-offish behavior. They're calm and logical, with fewer airs than Daybreak and less power than the Unseelie courts. If there's a place to try the aggressive stance, this might be the one that doesn't get us killed. "We could try being more direct here. Compared to the next two stops, it probably won't cause a global incident. I think."

"You *think*?" Benjy says. "That doesn't fill me with confidence, doc."

"It's been a while since I was here, and I haven't followed the… changes. If their leaders have changed, I might be wrong. The leader was quite old when I last set foot in this place, B. One of her children may have taken over—worse, one of her children may have been married off in a treaty and someone unexpected is in control. That's how these people work."

Jolene frowns. "Arranged marriage is bullshit."

Finding out about the thing with Jamie has made her bitter, and I don't blame her.

"Not here, Sugarplum. It's just a part of life. Think about how old families at home twine the branches of their trees, or even the royals in monarchies like England. Sometimes kids grow up knowing it's part of their duty and they accept that."

"Or they don't, Wolfie. Look at Prince Harry. He gave them all the finger and I approve," she says firmly. "He never looked happy at all that royal shit when Seer and I were running around. I say good for him."

Doyle tilts his head, his eyes twinkling with mischief. "What if Fate has their own idea of arranged marriages, Tíogair? Maybe some people come together because the stars said it was so long before their bodies existed."

"Don't be a Miss Cleo weirdo," she mutters as she bends to stroke her hand over Hyde's head. "Obviously, there's no such thing as Fate. It's all butterfly wings flapping in China and the other stuff Jeff Goldblum said."

"What if both chaos and Fate can exist?"

I frown at the Irishman, unsure what the hell he thinks he's doing. The last thing we need is to play with the lines of our oath and he's drifting closer to No-man's-land by the second. "Maybe they do, but I don't see how that makes a difference. Arranged marriages are cultural, particularly to families like this, and my only point was if a princess ended up with someone from another land, it would compli-cate our plans."

Sugarplum grins as she looks up at me, and the glimmer in her eyes surprises me. "I'm not sure how anything could complicate this shit more than it already is. But if it does? Bring it on. I'm ready for whatever these people want to throw at me."

Unfortunately, I'm not sure I agree.

OUR ARRIVAL IN THE CENTER OF THE HARVEST CAPITAL CITY ISN'T AS auspicious as when we crossed into Daybreak. We didn't have to pass through an immigration check and our car rolled through the quaint, picturesque city without being accosted by an envoy. I'm not sure if that's a good thing or if it doesn't bode well—do the royals here not give a shit or are they biding their time? Given my admittedly thin amount of information on them, I presume the latter is the case.

"This place looks sort of like the Northeast… like Vermont or New Hampshire," Jolene murmurs as she looks out the window. "It's very Norman Rockwell and maple candy."

Prez gives me a knowing look as he nods. "Sure is, magpie."

It's a pity she can't see all the burnished hues of glimmering copper, gold, and pewter covering the trees and gilded stone buildings.

"It seems less Hunger Games here than our first stop," Teddy says as he strokes his fingers through my hair. "The outfits at the ball, the behavior of the high and mighty… it was all a bit too pretty dystopian for me. Is everything there like that, or was it a facade for guests?"

Sighing, I ponder that. Everywhere has class systems, but humans have damn near everyone beat on the divide they've cultivated. "There are less fortunate parts of all the lands. But nothing as starkly obvious as we see in our big cities at home. At least, nothing I've seen or heard about. You know cities like the Hollow have disparity, but not at the level of other places. It's similar for our hosts here."

"While I was traveling, I was most shocked to find out how much the rest of the world is not what gets taught in our schools. Seer and I went all over—small to large nations—and it was so obvious we'd been fed bullshit. I remember being so disappointed that most people would never know any of it, you know? Is it like that?" Jolene looks at me seriously, her emerald eyes glinting with a cunning that feels out of place.

"Aye, lass. It's a bit like that in the places we'll be going. People love to tell stories about things they don't know about and once your eyes are opened, the world becomes a very different place."

I glare at Doyle, then cut my eyes to the rest of the guys. This jackass is really doing a tango along the lines and I'd prefer *not* to be called to a trial for violating one of the biggest tenets of the Society. "Knowledge always changes your perspective. If it doesn't, you're not really learning anything."

"Sometimes information changes the course of your entire life, so I agree."

Out of all of us, Benjy's the poster child for having his world turned upside down; finding out he had a fated mate made him up-end his entire life.

"How are you doing with that, man?" I squint at him, wondering how he found the courage to enrage a beast like Sherilynn and do what made him happy, regardless of the consequences.

His smile is genuine as he shrugs. "I'm happy where I am now. Boone helped me get the demon off my back long enough to escape with you guys. What I'll come back to is totally unpredictable—Mom's buried in her research up at State U with that Shadwell woman. My dad is… well, he's no better than Edgar's, as you know."

"Are they pissed at you?" Presley asks softly. "My parents haven't been an active part of my life for a long time, so I forget what it's like to have meddling bio donors around."

"At least you know who the fuck yours are," Doyle grumbles. I hold my fist out to him and he bumps it, grinning a bit. "Pup and I are chasing raging sociopaths around. Though I suppose the judge has his two a bit close for comfort."

"Mine are dead." I blanch at Sugarplum's blunt words and she shakes her head. "No, it's fine. I made my peace with that a long time ago, guys. I wasn't playing 'who has the worst sob story.' We're hunting down info on what really happened to them, but it doesn't… I'm not opening old wounds or anything."

I wonder if she knows her aura is vibrating with blues and blacks that reflect her genuine emotions.

"No one would fault you if it did. Making peace with their deaths differs from finding out they might have been killed on purpose." I reach over my head, holding my hand out to her. When our palms touch, a zap of energy flows between us, filling me with her confusion, sadness, and anger. She's not nearly as okay as she wants us to believe.

Teddy's eyes meet mine and I nod slightly. He rests his chin on Jolene's head, murmuring low. "Just because they weren't perfect doesn't mean you don't love them. The Senator and my mother are the only parents I've ever known even if they're dicks. That shit scars you in ways it's impossible to predict."

Closing my eyes, I project the roiling emotions hanging in the air to the companions. Kali and Hecate move to Prez and Benjy, while Jekyll and Hyde flank the two of us that Teddy's commandeered. The screech above the car tells me Eury would like to join, but the space here isn't conducive to the large eagle. She'll have to wait until we arrive at the hotel. It shouldn't be much longer now.

Everything quiets and by the time the car stops, the bleakness has faded from the group. I smile as I feel the vibe even out, glad I could help. Teddy ruffles my hair, making me blush, but when I catch Sugarplum's eyes, she's watching me like I'm a puzzle she's trying to figure out.

Shit. That might have been too obvious.

"What's wrong?" I venture carefully.

Her eyes crinkle, and she gives me a gentle smile. "You're just a wonderful person and you don't get enough credit for your big heart, darling boy. I feel like all of you have… roles in our family and it's why we work. Yours is the soft underbelly and warm heart."

"And yours is the center of our world, Sugarplum. Never forget that."

Before she can respond, the door to the car opens and a tall set of ginger-haired twins are giving us wide, jack-o'-lantern grins.

"Welcome to Harvest Grove, land of cozy fires and spiraling towers."

Great. We've been met by the damn Tweedles.

Slow Me Down

Jolene

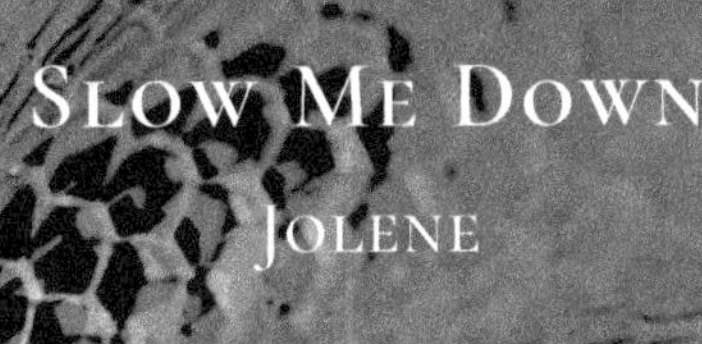

Blinking at the twins, I take a second to gather my wits. They seem harmless enough—not at all like the serious Fae in our welcome wagon in the last Court—but I don't trust anyone here as far as I could throw them. There's too much at risk to fall into a trap like I did with that friendly designer who messed with the glasses. Hyde makes a low growling sound next to me, and within seconds, the rest of the animals are flanking me.

Quite a merry band of protectors I'm amassing.

"Thank you for meeting us. I'm Jol—"

"We know," they chirp in unison. "Word of your arrival came through the grapevine."

Teddy grunts, muttering under his breath, "Fucking spooky."

He means their twin bullshit, not the gossip, and I agree. Pressing my lips together, I try not to get annoyed and have fire pop out of my hands. It's hard enough to cover up my newfound knowledge in front of the guys when we're in private, much less with an audience. Once I'm calm, I paste a smile on, cloaking myself in the Southern belle persona I've been using to deal with the wily jackholes in this land.

"How convenient! I find repeating myself tiresome, especially after traveling." Batting my lashes, I tilt my head like I'm curious. "And who might you be?"

They smirk and I can tell this twin thing must really work for them with the ladies. "We are the regents of your hosts in the city. Mick and Mack Stuart, at your service."

Okay, that was kind of impressive.

Doyle steps up, rolling his eyes at their antics. "Alright, lads. We get it. You have the twin mind meld going for you. It's not as charming or special as you think."

The twin on the left—I *think* it's Mick—gives him a wicked grin. "We know who you are, Haggerty, and it's not one of us. But I believe you *do* know about twins."

"Aye, he does. Not his mum, but in the same ballpark," Mack adds. "Sadly, none of them want to claim him, so he pretends."

I hide a grin as I tuck away new information about my chaotic lover. Despite not understanding what the hell it means, I know it'll be useful later. I reach over to grab Doyle's arm before he shoots back a response. I refuse to stand here all day and play games. "Great. Now that we've agreed twins are fucking annoying, can we please head to our rooms? The animals are hungry and frankly, so I am. I'd be happy to give them permission to find a snack right here if we're going to be detained."

Wolfie chuckles as he ruffles Jekyll's fur. "Not a bad idea, Sugarplum. They look big enough to feed them all. I'm sure Isis will clean up the leftovers."

As if summoned, the large python slithers her head out of my sleeve, flicking her tongue at the ginger bastards menacingly. I grin as her head fills my palm. "She definitely would."

Instead of looking concerned, the duo sigh and gesture at the large hotel we're in front of. "Be our guest. We would hate to make our new friends uncomfortable. Take your time and we will send an envoy to discuss your audience with our employers this evening."

My eyes narrow. "It had better not be a team to fucking dress up like dolls again."

Their eyes dance as they shrug and I groan internally. If this shit is going to happen in every new location, I might scream. I've let Seer use me as her personal doll for many years, but as far as I know, she's never tried to cause an international incident while doing so. Unfortunately, I also realize that if I don't *pretend* to play their games, I won't get to the people who might give us intel on Wolfie's dad.

I'm good at politics, but I fucking hate them so much.

Luckily for me, His Honor steps in smoothly. "Your envoys will find us much more amenable after some rest. Please pass on our gratitude for your welcome and we look forward to speaking with your employers later."

"Exactly," I add, as I smile prettily. "Teddy said it perfectly."

"Understood. Please enjoy your suite," they chirp before saluting and heading off down the street.

"So fucking weird," Benjy says as he grabs the bags out of the trunk. "Can't say I'm a fan."

"It's worse when they're male and female," Doyle says as he takes the rest of them out of the trunk. "I can attest to that."

Shaking my head, I wait until the redheads disappear around a corner before I respond. "I get the feeling they won't be the only troublemakers we run into—just the most obvious ones."

"Why's that, magpie?" Presley says as we walk to the doors of the hotel.

"Just like animals, these folks are hiding the real dangers behind the pretty, colorful things they throw in our faces. We have to look deeper than the peacocking the flunkies do if we want to get what we need and not get hurt."

"I think she's right," Teddy rumbles. "We'll adjust our strategy when these 'envoys' show up. And this time, no one is to be alone with them. I have a bad feeling about being divided."

As well he fucking should—that's why I'm in this damn mess.

"MAGPIE, ARE YOU TALKING TO THE CATS?"

My face turns bright red as Prez wakes up, shifting to reach over me to get his glasses. Realizing the movement will wake everyone up from the much needed nap, I scramble to put my frames on while he yawns and stretches. I didn't mean to wake any of them; I just have so many things to run past my companions, so I have a better chance at winning the game they keep insisting we play.

"I might be bouncing things off the animals. It's not crazy," I grumble as Wolfie stirs at my waist. "They can't talk back, so I get to untwist things in my mind without being interrupted."

"What do you need to untwist, Princess?"

I smile as Benjy looks over Teddy's shoulder, his big brown eyes soft. "Not you guys. I'm… slowly making my peace with that. More like, I'm trying to figure out how we can find out who Wolfie's dad is." I pause and shrug. "I'm also a little worried about Seer? She hasn't checked in for a bit and it makes me worry."

"We can call her," Doyle says as he pops his head up next to Prez's. "Boone's got an emergency phone for that sort of thing in his bag. Should work and then you'll have one thing off your plate."

"Think it'll work to call the Sheik and Hugo, too? They have to be wondering what the hell we're doing by now." I frown for a second, not liking that it didn't occur to me until this moment. "I hope they don't think we're leaving them out."

"I doubt that's the case, Sugarplum. You can call Seer first, while we rotate through this tiny shower. Then you get clean and while the rest of us finish, you check in with Amiri." Wolfie smiles as he drips a kiss on my belly button.

The location makes me flush pink and I grumble a little. "Alright, none of that. If you start that shit up, none of us will be ready and no phone calls will get made."

"I mean…"

My glare is sub zero as I look at Teddy. "Not an option, Your Honor. The Chair moves the committee gets their asses out of bed and moving before their supply chain is subject to budget cuts."

The room is silent for a moment, then Doyle howls with laughter. "That might be the fanciest way I've ever heard a woman say she's cutting me off. Good on you, Tíogair."

"The judge from the great state thinks the Chair has let power go to her pretty head." Teddy winks at me as he wiggles out of the pile and stretches. My eyes glaze as I watch the taut abs and bobbing cock like I'm hypnotized, then I snort.

"Good try, but we really do have shit to do. We can role play procedural shit later," I retort. "Move it, boys. Mama needs the bathroom before you all steam it up."

"You just said mama," Wolfie calls as I speed walk to the closed door.

Absolutely fucking not.

"Don't even *dream* that shit or I'll make you wake up and apologize!"

I have to keep these assholes in line every second or they'll push their way past my barriers for sure.

And that's one I'm not budging on.

I showered alone, which helped me finish more quickly, but also gave me time to inspect myself without anyone noticing.

What a goddamn revelation that *was.*

It says a lot about your mental resiliency when you can find four bites, two burned brands, and a bunch of sparkly fucking tattoos you don't remember receiving and shrug it off. Honestly, it's a credit to my therapist and I probably owe her a spa gift card. All these marks having been hidden by whatever the fuck bullshit magic is swirling around the Hollow, me, and everyone else I know.

I'm not stupid—I've watched enough shows like *True Blood* or *Buffy* to understand these are some kind of claiming mark. They obviously correspond to the guys, but not all of them, and that I'm unsure about. The sparkly shit is clearly my darling boy, and at least one bite must belong to my canine alpha counterpart. Aside from that, I haven't figured out what is what because I *think* more than one may belong to each of them.

This constant sleuthing is getting exhausting and I'm going to nut punch the person responsible.

"So they can see this shit… but can everyone else?" I make a face in the mirror as I dry my hair. "Can that cuntmuffin Sherilynn *see* these boys are mine and *still* come after me? I bet she can; she's fucking deficient that way."

I sigh as the possibilities tumble through my mind. I will not figure it all out today, nor is anyone going to help me until this big 'moment' they're waiting for happens. I have to keep gathering info and be patient—something I'm not known for doing.

Picking up the phone Teddy left me, I punch in the numbers for my bestie. I'd love to muddle this out with Seer, but she's neck deep in this shit and banned from helping me. So much for guarding me or whatever the hell she said her job was. I wonder if people with that job ever lose their charges? Seer has definitely almost lost me a couple times because of my shit, so I'd bet they have.

It would suck ass to figure out you have weird supernatural powers with no explanation or people around you to help you cope—probably fuck your brain up for good.

"Go for Saoirse."

The chipper tone of my friend makes me smile and warmth spreads throughout my chest. Even on the phone, hearing her helps me find my center. *Is that magic or just friendship?* I don't care, but I never want to lose it. "Seer! I miss you. Where the hell are you?"

A pause on the line trips my wires and I hear muffled shuffling around before she answers. "I'm on an assignment overseas. Where are you, Peanut? Still in bonny Ireland?"

"Mmm hmm. We're at the second stop on this Magical Mystery Tour of the old country," I say carefully. I know she won't give anything away, but I want her to wonder what I know. It feels like appropriate vengeance since everyone but me is allowed to know what's going on.

Her laugh is soft. "Always the jokester, Peanut. I've been running around for weeks trying to get cut loose so I can come see you. The bosses just won't let me go, and you can't really say 'no' to their clients. So I'm stuck, but you can catch me up. Tell me about the people you've met and everything that's happened since you met with your puppy's mum."

"It started with these jackasses who gave us crap at this customs gate..."

I Would Do Anything For You

Benjy

Thinking you're sheltered and *knowing* it are two very different things.

My mom married old Vlad when I was five. No one ever discussed my bio dad and I'm not sure she even knew who he was—that's why the only person I consider my father is the asshole incubus who adopted me after they got hitched. He's never thought I lived up to his expectations, especially because he's the town prosecutor and a retired agent for the Society. In contrast, I went to college, played ball, and didn't go to law school or take the agent qualifications. I married Sherilynn as agreed, which he was all for, but then I used my business degree to open the restaurant and the bar.

Vladimir Simon Foster thinks we're above 'small town pizza and beer,' so he practically ignored me after that. In fact, he stayed away right until he was in the thick of convincing me to adopt the kids with Sherilynn. The twins and their older sister aren't related by blood, nor are they any combination of supes that fit with Sherilynn or I. But my 'dad' was gung-ho and Sheri just wanted to make him happy so he'd include us in Society shit.

Before my best friend convinced me to tag along on this trip, I'd only ever left the Hollow for college and the games I played there. I sure as hell didn't come to Faerie or journey across Europe. For all her worldly affectations, my ex-wife preferred being queen bee at home rather than a tiny fish in a big pond elsewhere. Plus, someone had to keep the businesses running. Her interest in Derby Pies only piqued when it was part of the divorce settlement—not a second before.

All of this shit is brand new to me, despite emerging as a teen, so I get why the Princess is so stressed out.

"Fucking unbelievable," I mutter to myself as we walk into a large throne room surrounded by *walls* of bookshelves floor to ceiling.

If I'd thought the over-the-top fancy crap in the Daybreak Court was a bit much, this place is even worse. It's different: huge cozy fireplace crackling, large overstuffed chairs for thrones, thick rugs, and an atmosphere of crisp autumn permeating the air. But it's also insanely ornate and full of random people milling about with wine and cider as the royals look down from their perch in front of the flames.

Princess grabs my arm, squeezing it, and I smile. Her eyes glitter as she looks at all the books, and I know she's thinking about how much information they store here. Even when we were kids, Jolene was smart as a whip. The years since college, all her education and experience, have only increased her ability to look at shit in ways others don't.

That's why I've always known her secret—she knew *taking that girl's place at the cotillion would end in horror, but she did it anyway.*

"You're awfully quiet, big guy. That's not unusual, but your brow is furrowed like you're working out a play."

Blinking in surprise, I tilt my head to look at our girl. "Princess, how would you know what I look like when I'm working out a play?"

She rolls her eyes, sighing heavily. "Benjamin Louis Foster. There was literally *nothing* to do in the Hollow on Friday nights if you didn't go to the game. I didn't give a fuck about winning, but I enjoyed watching people. Figuring out how people will behave has been one of my talents for a long time."

"Ah, but you weren't just watching the QB like he assumes," I tease as we walk around the big room. "He'll be crushed."

"There is *nothing* that could dent Teddy's ego. Pull on the other leg before they get uneven," Jolene snorts, then hides her mouth with her hand as a snooty-looking Fae gives her a glare. "Why is this place set up like a library? Are the people up there our hosts? And where are those blasted, annoying twins?"

"Whoa, there, Princess. That's a lot of questions for one breath." My eyes cut to her hands, making sure she isn't getting too riled. Edgar might touch that without getting hurt and maybe his pet vet, too, but I'm not taking the chance I'll get accidentally crisped. "Close your eyes and let the calm flow through you. That's what your yoga boyfriends keep saying."

Jolene draws in a slow breath and breathes it out of her nose loudly. When I chuckle, she wrinkles her nose. "The docs are good yoga partners because they're very placid. That's true. But you're not easily riled yourself—not like Lucky or Teddy."

"Uh, we don't need more than the three of you with short fuses. I'm pretty sure that's enough plastic explosive in the group. Plus, I never would have survived a decade with Sherilynn if I was easily angered."

Oh, shit.

Instead of being mad that I mentioned my ex-wife, Jolene simply laughs and squeezes my arm again. "I don't think you could have said that any more nicely than you did. She's the worst and I admire your ability to talk about it without resorting to nastiness. It's very mature, Benjy."

I stay quiet for a moment, thinking about that as we stop at the bar. She orders us each a bourbon—thank hell they have something normal—and I sip mine before I answer. "Sheri and I were the product of old-fashioned parents playing weird politics. We were both told we should be together as teens, then stayed together at college. After that, we made the leap to marriage because our parents said it was the right move. Neither of us were strong or smart enough to question that premise once we were old enough to do so."

"I don't think—"

"Give me a moment, Princess. You'll agree once you hear the rest. I know you'd like to defend me, but I was honestly dumb as a post with blindly following what my dad said." She nods and I sip again, then continue. "Even as young as middle school, he held up the idea that him and my mom are proof that two different people can come together for a purpose and be happy. I believed him and although Sherilynn and I were never actually happy, I obeyed because I wanted him to be proud. Obviously, it never worked."

"But why? You have two great businesses, people love you, and I can't imagine you not being a good spouse or dad." Princess frowns, her expression frustrated as we head over towards the far end of the room where the docs are chatting with two scholarly looking Fae.

"I didn't go into law and Sheri couldn't conceive and give him grand-children. Not my fault, but he acted as though it was. He recruited my mom to help push adopting the kids. I gave in to that demand as well, which was a bad idea, given the state of our marriage. She's raised those kids to despise me as much as she and my father do."

Her eyes narrow, and she stops in place, whirling to look at me. "That's not right, and I won't stand for it."

"Jolene, it's okay. I mean, it's not, but it is, you know?" Pulling her into my arms, I hug her close, figuring out how to express this without saying something I'm forbidden to. "I'm not a big believer in a lot of woo-woo shit, but I think things happen for a reason. You came to town, and the world filled with color. I quit ignoring things I should have dealt with long ago. Now, I'm halfway around the world with you, my best friend, a bunch of zoo animals, and a squad of fellow oddballs. My life is changing for the better, so I don't want to focus on the hurt from the past."

She licks her lips, looking thoughtful for a second before she nods. "Yeah, I think I get that. There are things I know will upset me coming—you told me so. But… I don't know if I want to trade righteous anger for the good things I feel now."

I smirk at her, knowing what she's talking about. "I think you'll give us all hell—which we deserve—but you'll also realize we only want to protect you. It doesn't leave us with a lot of appealing choices, but life is full of times where the only options are bad ones. That doesn't mean you can't be upset; it only means you have to weigh your anger against what you truly want."

"What I want," she grumbles as we move again, "is alone time with all of you tonight. So these motherfuckers had better wrap up their welcome party early or I'm going to ruin their night like I did the last hosts. And for the love of Dionysius' pet goats, *someone* better have info on Wolfie's dad. I'm tired of wasting time on dead ends."

"I can promise you the first part if everyone behaves, but the second might be above my paygrade. You might have to see what the hell Boone and Haggerty are doing before we confirm that one."

Our girl winks at me as we join the docs and I feel my chest expand with happiness. As long as I get to stay with her, I'll be able to move on from the bullshit of the past. Together, I think our family will get over the big secret when she finally emerges, but that's only if all the players do their part.

Unfortunately, that's not entirely within my control.

"THANK YOU FOR THE INVITATION TO THIS… SALON?"

I hide my grin behind my hand, staying at the back of the group as we're introduced to the Harvest Court royals. The irritating Tweedle Twins—as Princess calls them—homed in on us as soon as we joined the docs. It took a few minutes to locate Edgar and Doyle, but once we did, they immediately escorted our group to the raised platform by the fireplace.

"Yes, we *adore* bringing together the most interesting minds to mingle and share ideas. When Mick and Mack informed us you were journeying to our home, we simply *had* to arrange a get together. Isn't that right, Hieronymus?"

The little old man in a tweed suit with elbow patches looks like a college professor, not the King of the Harvest Court. But he beams at us as his much younger wife gushes at our girl in a very familiar way. I'm not sure what the guy knows about the cougar he married, but if she doesn't quit eye-fucking the docs, Princess is going to dig them right of the sockets for her.

"Quite so, pumpkin," the short royal says as he nods at us. "I am excited to learn why we are graced with such an impressive group from across the pond. I'm sure Allora will be as well."

"Yes, she fawns over new people," the dark-haired queen mutters.

Huh. She doesn't like this chick, so given my experience, I'll assume it's the stepdaughter.

"Is Allora your daughter?" Jolene looks at the Mr. Magoo wanna-be like he's a kindly librarian and a bad feeling lodges in my gut. "Will she be joining us tonight?"

"Very subtle, Tilly," Edgar says as he glares at the Queen. She's ogling Prez and Wolfie again, but it's getting more obvious. He might be more trouble than our girl if the woman doesn't knock it off.

"Why, yes, she is!" The King claps and hops down from his immense chair. "Come, Miss Whitley. I'd love for you to meet her. She's with her new fiancé amongst our brilliant guests. Allora prefers not to sit in her rightful chair; it's the youth these days. Always rebelling against traditions, you know."

Jolene's eyes widen as he offers his arm despite his head only reaching her ribcage. I'm about to intervene when I see the old-fashioned breeding kicking in. Her eyes soften and she accepts his arm graciously, even adding a small curtsey before allowing him to lead her down the stairs. Turning to my old friend, I murmur, "We need to follow her."

"On it," Doyle says as he brushes past us. "Anyone else coming?"

I watch as the sparkling wings of our vet flutter. He mumbles an excuse to the Queen, ignoring her disappointed clucking as he pulls Presley along with him. Once they join Teddy and me, we make our escape. Doyle's bright red hair isn't as good a beacon in this land; there're gingers everywhere, as well as many people with various yellow and orange tones. It makes sense for the Harvest kingdom, but it's also annoying as hell when you're tracking someone.

"There she is," Teddy growls as he drags us throughout a knot of people blocking the way. "I can smell her. And... something else familiar."

The laughter of our girl and a tinkling giggle are our greeting as we finally get through the group of Fae. My eyes widen as I look at a gorgeous woman in a very similar dress to the one they gave Jolene, except hers is in deep gold and reds. The king is looking at them both fondly, which I take as a good sign until I see the man standing off to the side. I feel the growl of my friend as it leaves his chest, and I know we've found at least one thing we were looking for: a clue about the pup's father.

"Gentleman! I would like to introduce my daughter, Princess Allora, and her fiancé, Alistair Silkshine of the Midnight Court."

"How very *interesting* it is to meet all of you." The wicked grin of the fiancé is a dead giveaway. He's tall, muscled, and has hair like a raven's wing that tumbles over his shoulders onto his deep purple suit. The look is supposed to evoke mystery, but given his bone structure and the pattern on his sparkling wings...? It doesn't.

There's no doubt in my mind Wolfgang Fletcher is Unseelie and this motherfucker knows something.

The question is... what will we have to pay to find out?

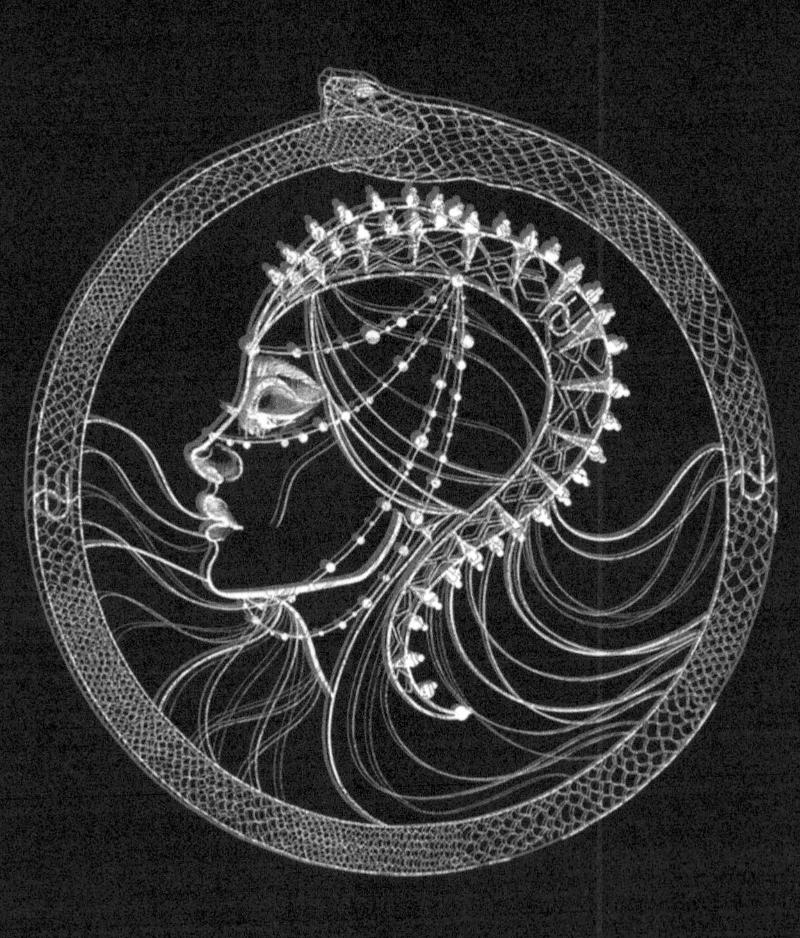

Girl on Fire

Jolene

A FLUTTER of anxiety beats its wings against my ribcage as I look at Allora, her gown a cascade of fiery autumn colors pooling at her feet. The dark Fae, Alistair Silkshine, is leaning against a marble column like he's part of the architecture—sinuous and permanent. His smirk makes me want to smack it off him and I have to pull the reins on my temper once again.

Pretending I'm not aware of everything going on gets harder with every moment, especially because some of these people are determined to fuck with me.

"It's an honor to meet you both. I'm Edgar Boone," Teddy says as he extends his hand, taking the Princess' and kissing her knuckles. I dislike him touching someone other than our family, but I realize he has to follow the protocols. "May I introduce my companions? This is Jolene, Benjy, Doyle, Wolfgang, and Presley. We're visiting your land on a research trip."

"Charmed," she replies, her voice the tinkling of crystal in a still room. She gives us all a bright smile, but I can see her intelligence sparkling in her green eyes. Allora is downplaying herself much like I am and when I realize why, it makes me grin at myself.

The Princess wants her fiancé to believe she's less capable than she is—their marriage must be very strategic to her future rule here.

"Enchantment's in the air tonight. Or, perhaps, that's the effects of a new presence in our midst? The allure of the Southern belle has always fascinated me, I must confess. The movies make your people seem so… captivating," Alistair drawls with his eyes locked on me. His words are both a caress and a slap—a velvet glove over an iron fist used to taunt my companions.

"Bless your heart, Alistair. You shouldn't believe everything you see in the media. If I did that, I might make very inaccurate assumptions about gentlemen without knowing their true nature," I return tersely, ignoring the itch under my skin that threatens the fire I'm trying to hold in. "That would be a grave tragedy, I'm sure."

Teddy smothers a snort behind his hand and I feel the tension in my guys' release slightly. "Excellent point, Tilly. As always, you know how to set the record straight in the most elegant way possible."

"She is lovely," the tiny King says with a clueless smile. "Don't you agree, Allora?"

The Princess eyes me for a moment, arching a brow as she studies me closer. "Oh, I agree, Father. Miss Jolene is quite the addition to our soirée."

Shit. She's going to be harder to fool than any of the men here.

"Perhaps Alistair would enlighten us," Doyle says as he narrows his eyes at the gorgeous Fae. "He looks keen to share his vast knowledge."

I tilt my head as I look at the cagey male, making sure I project the doe-eyed belle he accused me of being. "That would help our search. Alistair, do you have information you think we'd be interested in knowing? I'd be obliged to know anything you think is important."

"Information on what, exactly? My dear, you wound me with your directness." The Fae laughs, the sound low and wicked as his eyes dance with glee. "I'm merely an honored guest in this house, much like the lot of you. I'm not privy to any secrets or coveted knowledge in this place."

Allora purses her lips and I catch the look of annoyance she gives him. While the King is happily doddering along, she's likely keeping this court afloat and having to marry a smarmy son of a bitch like this to claim her birthright *has* to chafe. I feel she'd like to jump in and correct him, but her dim façade is preventing her from doing so.

I get it, girl. Being a woman sucks rocks when you live in a world built to cater to men and their fragile egos.

"How disappointing," Benjy says as his fingers touch my elbow lightly. The contact helps calm my sparking nerves and I breathe slowly while he diverts their attention. "Hieronymous' introduction made me think you were more integral to their family than a simple guest."

Smart, smart man.

Alistair bristles, and Teddy's grin turns absolutely feral. That tell gives him a weakness and as long as I've known Edgar Boone, he's never been one to ignore an opening. "Obviously, we've journeyed a long way and mere pleasantries aren't enough to capture our attention. Allora, thank you again for gracing us with your companionship, but we'll be—"

"Ah, but simplicity does not preclude substance," Alistair interrupts with a mischievous expression. "There are many truths I am aware of —not all of them can be shared. Your family has not asked the right questions, I fear."

I can see the gears turning in his head and the glint of malicious glee in his eyes. He'd love to violate the guys' oath for them, but they have not given him an opportunity to do so without implicating himself. If we press him to get information about Wolfie's dad, we need to be *very* careful or he might complicate our lives even further just to amuse himself.

Like all the royal Fae I've met so far, beneath the sparkling, pretty outside lies a conniving, chaos loving troublemaker with minds as sharp as thorns.

"He's enjoying the game," Wolfie murmurs as his fingers lace with mine. His jaw is clenched as he lifts soulful blue eyes to mine. "Be careful, Sugarplum. We don't know what he'll reveal—including things we'd prefer to remain in the dark."

"Games are the spice of life, *pup*," Alistair taunts.

Wolfie winces and the irritation rolling off Teddy slams into me like a wave of hot lava. If I didn't realize it before, I definitely know now— the fire has something to do with the man who broke my heart as a teen. When he's angry, my blood heats and the itch ramps up inside of me.

And he absolutely wants to beat the shit out of Alistair for calling Wolfie 'pup.'

I lean into Teddy, looking up at him for a moment until the temperature cools a little, then I turn back to the irksome Fae. "It's very bold to assume you can use a nickname with one of my beaus, Alistair. I highly doubt you'd like one of them to call Allora 'sweetheart,' now would you?"

His dark eyes narrow at my barb and he opens his mouth to retort when a loud tinkling fills the room. King Hieronymous claps his hands, looking giddy as he hops in place a bit. Allora smiles softly as she watches him and I immediately understand why she's taking part in this bullshit arranged crap. She adores her father, and whatever they need from Alistair's people is desperate enough to force her hand.

"That's the call for dinner?" Presley says, pushing his glasses up as he glances at our hosts. "I hope so, because I'm absolutely famished."

"You are correct," Allora says as she turns back to us. "You'll be seated at the head table with us once the staff is ready. Perhaps you'd like to head for the washrooms briefly while they set the room?"

Her eyes cut to the guys, and I have to bite my lip to keep from giggling. Obviously, she wants me out of this room while magical shit happens and she doesn't know how else to tell them to yeet me out of the space.

"I think that would be perfect," Presley replies. "Come, Magpie. We'll freshen up while they get ready, and then we can feed you. It's been a long time since lunch."

He's not wrong about that, but I feel dinner will not sit well with any of us.

WHEN WE RETURN FROM OUR SOJOURN TO THE MOST LAVISH bathrooms I've ever been in, there's a long table at the front of the room set for ten people. It's perpendicular to the immense chairs where the King and Queen were sitting when we arrived and the rest of the room was dotted with circular tables for the other 'salon' guests.

I'm not excited about round two of 'Guess Who's Not Going To Get Dinner,' but I don't think we have a choice.

"What a lovely table," I say as we approach the table. The King looks chuffed and Allora smiles gratefully, but I notice the Queen is still looking down her nose at us. She's certainly part of why the princess is playing a role, but I'm not sure how yet. Truth be told, it's not my circus, so I shouldn't care, but... I can't help but empathize. Allora's surrounded by sharks and she's clearly the only one concerned about it.

Alistair pulls the chair out for his fiancée, but his gallantry ends when he shrugs. "They have a quaint notion of grandeur here; I agree."

"Quaint enough to warrant your attendance," Teddy grumbles under his breath and I smother a laugh. He definitely does not like this asshole, and I don't blame him. We have more than enough problems without a smirking fuckwad trying to weasel his way to a big reveal.

"Indeed, it is." Alistair joins Allora at the table, gesturing for the rest of my guys to sit. "Sit and be merry with us, friends. I'd hate for you to miss all the fun."

"Fun's one word for it," I mutter as Wolfie claims the seat to my right and Prez flanks him. Benjy takes Teddy's right, winking at me as Doyle plops down beside him.

At least the most volatile men are surrounded by calmer heads—that is, if I can keep myself from flaming out.

"Jolene has a fiery spirit," Alistair observes, his voice low and teasing.

My head pops up and I look at my hands surreptitiously before glaring at him. He's full of shit—I'm not on fire—and I have no idea how this dickwaffle knew to push that button. A surge of warmth comes from Teddy again and I place my palm on his forearm to help him center himself. I'm not sure if he's always had this much trouble quelling his… powers… or if this place is making it hard on him. Either way, the jerk in front of us is just dying to make him lose his shit.

"Careful, darling, wouldn't want to burn down the castle."

A soft growl rumbles out of my dominant lover, but I ignore it to snap at the taunting royal. "Wouldn't dream of it. This library is far too amazing to risk, especially since we have had little luck finding useful sources of information for our research."

"You wound me, Miss Jolene," he says as he laughs. "I promise to be much more candid after the food is served. I'm sure you'll want to wait until your bellies are full before we get into the meat of our discussion."

Doyle gives him a pointed look, finally speaking up as he points a sharp knife at the smug prince. "I'm quite certain our girl isn't interested in anymore meat. She's got a veritable smorgasbord to choose from as it is."

I blink, my face turning bright red as the princess muffles a giggle, and the King looks at us all in confusion. My gaze flicks to the satisfied looking Irishman, and he shrugs as the knife spins on his palm like he's a goddamn circus performer. "I… uh…"

"Don't worry, Jolene. I'm told all men are like dogs. No matter how hard you try, some of them never learn not to piddle on the carpet."

Allora gives me a tiny grin as she picks up her water glass to take a sip and I damn near choke on the laugh that tumbles out.

Maybe this girl isn't so bad, after all. I think Seer would like her a lot.

Come At Me

Edgar

THE CEILING of the Harvest Court's dining hall stretches above us like a cathedral to decadence, garlands of golden wheat and ruby-red apples cascading down stone pillars. The tiny, absent-minded King presides at the head of the table, his eyes crinkling with delight as he listens to Doyle recount an absurdly embellished version of our experience in the Daybreak Court.

His daughter is eyeing the Irishman warily, but I think it's because she knows he's full of shit.

"By the roots and berries!" King Hieronymous exclaims, utterly oblivious to the undercurrents swirling beneath the surface of our polite conversation. "You lot have had quite the adventure!"

"Indeed we have," I reply smoothly. "But everyone has shown us generous hospitality, even if it's sometimes difficult for us to navigate in the circumstances."

Alistair leans back in his chair, a silver goblet poised at his lips. His gaze rests on Wolfie, who fidgets beside Tilly, his knee bouncing like a metronome of anxiety. I reach out and place a hand on his thigh, feeling the tremor beneath my touch. I don't like how this fucker is purposefully torturing him and it's making all my supe sides riot. It's been a long time since I felt this out of control with my powers; I spent a great deal of time in my teens with Bane learning to tamp down the hound and applying that knowledge to the other two.

However, an ill-intentioned fuckknuckle using my family for his amusement is activating the alpha protective mode.

Cracking my neck as I check on the others, I note Benjy is actively trying to keep the demigod from overloading. That helps and I'm grateful to my old friend. Tilly can take care of herself whether I want her to or not; that much is becoming more obvious by the day. But Wolfie is a far more damaged soul than her and the vibes coming off of him make me want to shift and pin this motherfucker to the wall until he cries 'uncle.'

"Your mother must be quite the character," Alistair says to my pup, his eyes glinting with mischief. "From what I understand, you didn't make her acquaintance until late in life, but her infamy casts an enormous shadow, I imagine."

Jolene's nails dig into my arm and I know she's telling me to keep my cool. Alistair told us he wasn't aware of gossip and intrigue among the courts, but knowing who Wolfie's mother is betrayed the lie in that statement. If he knows that tidbit, he also knows we're looking for his dad, and that's why the jackass is toying with us.

He's got information we need—whether it's rumors or fact doesn't matter.

"Callie has her moments," Wolfie responds in a tight voice. He doesn't look at the smirking Fae; instead, he pretends to fiddle with his napkin.

I catch the other doc putting a hand on his leg to help ground him and once again, I'm thankful for the less dominant members of our group. They provide a balance we sorely need, especially as Tilly hasn't found her true nature yet. I don't know if the two missing suitors will add to that or tip the scales, but for now, I'll take what I can get.

"You seem to be an enigma," Alistair continues, swirling the wine in his cup with a casual flick of his wrist. "I assume you don't share her heritage? One can't help but wonder about the origins of such a fascinating person."

"Origins can be very... personal, don't you think?" I interject, trying to keep my tone light despite the gravity of what he's insinuating. This dick is edging awfully close to discussing what powers our pup has, and he knows full well he can't do that in front of Tilly. If he continues, I'll have to make a scene to distract her, and I'd prefer not to. The King and the princess seem like decent people—especially the princess.

She might make an excellent ally for our girl once she emerges.

"For some, yes," he agrees, a smirk playing on his lips. "For others, tracing the threads of their lineage might lead to unexpected places. That's also exciting."

"As long as it's not harmful," Presley chimes in, his eyes narrowed in a silent challenge. The typically placid doc sits up straighter as he leans forward on his forearms. "The unknown has an element of danger to it. Discovering secrets before you're ready to grasp their magnitude has grave consequences, especially if they have hidden the truth for a reason."

Jolene sips her wine, humming under her breath as if she is bored with the conversation. When the sharp tongued Fae continues staring at her, she gives him a saccharine smile. "In America, particularly in the South, it's considered quite rude to question people's heritage in mixed company. Families often have secrets twined throughout the branches of their trees—exposing those to sunlight for one's own amusement is not something we'd consider polite."

"Perhaps not in the court of public opinion, but in courts that convene under the cloak of night or reap what others have sown, it would be looked upon differently," Alistair muses. His words are carefully chosen, tiptoeing around the secrets that hover like specters between us, but it's clear he will not back down.

My eyes cut to Allora, but she's watching her stepmother fuss at the King. Sighing, I scratch my jaw as I let Alistair's statement hang in the air. He was hoping to get a reaction from one of us and I don't want to give it to him. I can't let it sit unchallenged, though, so I look him directly in the eyes when I reply. "Courts are such mysterious entities; if you aren't familiar with their procedures, you might end up on the wrong side of the law. I'm grateful I have a thorough understanding of all the various law systems that affect our everyday life. If I didn't, I could see myself making an idiotic mistake meddling in their intrigue and—"

"Darkness?" Alistair finishes for me, arching an eyebrow.

This idiot has no sense of self-preservation.

"Darkness, light..." I shrug, feigning disinterest. "It depends on the time of day and location of the proceedings, doesn't it?"

"Or the phase of the moon," he retorts smoothly.

That gets Doyle's attention. He joins Prez and me as we lean in, his eyes flicking between Tilly and the asshole determined to fuck shit up. "I doubt the moon phase influences trials. That's a bit... out there, isn't it, Judge?"

I grin. "Some folks claim destructive behavior amps up during the full moon, but I've never seen evidence of it. People do stupid things regardless of outside forces; it's within their nature. Right, Tilly?"

"My experience with people all over the globe agrees with you, Teddy. Of course, some irresponsible fuckwits make excuses for their lack of sense, but no one takes them seriously." She looks over at Allora and tilts her head. "Particularly men with more swagger than brain cells, right?"

Allora chuckles softly as she nods. "So I've been told, Jolene. Those afflicted should rein in their baser instincts and show the decorum we have taught them as children, in my opinion."

I knew I liked this chick.

The King is still blissfully unaware of the conflict brewing at our end of the table, but when forks clink against plates, he mutters to himself. "Moon phases. Ah, that reminds me of a poem I once forgot. Something about cheese, was it?"

"I'm sure it was something memorable," Benjy assures him with a kind smile. My friend rarely passes up an opportunity to be kind and like the rest of us, he's figured out the princess is stuck managing an addled father and greedy stepmother. His dad is a real fucking treat and his mom is lovely, so the dynamic makes sense to him, even flipped by gender. "You'll tell us when it comes to you."

"Cheese," Alistair scoffs softly, a taunt not-quite-hidden in the curve of his mouth. "Very quaint."

Wolfie looks at Tilly in a silent plea for strength, and she smiles softly, trying to send reassurance to him without it being noticeable. My mind races as I consider how many ways I'd like to rip this idiot to pieces, but I have to keep my anger simmering below the surface. The Fae prince knows more than he lets on, twirling truths and lies with the finesse of a master weaver while he dances around the lines that could get us all killed. I don't know what his motivation is, but the continued pressure feels like it's about more than simply toying with us.

Does the prince have a death wish? Or is he beholden to someone even more powerful than himself?

"Quaint can be charming," I counter as I meet Alistair's challenging stare. "I'm sure many find it less taxing than your games."

"Games?" King Hieronymous looks puzzled as he speaks up. "Are we playing a game? love games!"

"We certainly are," I say to him with a forced smile. "Your future son-in-law enjoys very dangerous pursuits, and he's engaged us to join him."

The clatter of cutlery punctuates the tense air like an erratic heartbeat, as Alistair's eyes glint with mischief—a predator toying with his prey. I fight the urge to let my inner flames lick at his smug façade once again as he pauses for effect. When he finally speaks, he's swirling his wineglass with a languid motion that suggests everything and nothing. "As I was saying before we sat down, family trees can be so convoluted, don't you think?"

"Especially when the roots are tangled in secrets." The quiet words from Allora get all of our attention and it makes the annoying jackass beside her bare his teeth. She's gotten to him; I can't help but think she did it on purpose. Maybe it was to explain why she's holding back or maybe she wants to help—it's impossible to tell because Allora isn't meeting anyone's gaze.

"Ah, but the discovery of one's lineage can be quite..." He pauses again, putting deliberate emphasis on the word, "... strategic and very enlightening."

Doyle shifts beside me, looking like a storm cloud ready to burst. I sense his power crackling beneath the surface, the angry deity magic seeking release in retribution for Alistair's casual remarks. I catch his eye, willing him to rein it in.

He probably won't listen, but it's amazing he's held in his natural penchant for chaos as it is.

"Enlightenment is overrated," Doyle replies through gritted teeth, his gaze fixed on Alistair with thinly veiled contempt. "Many of us can go through life without it and not suffer any consequences."

"Perhaps remaining in the dark is acceptable for some," Alistair drawls. "However, I believe there's always merit in fully understanding one's... heritage. It opens so many doors that were previously closed."

"Heritage isn't everything. Who we are now trumps the past every time," Wolfie whispers to Tilly, his voice filled with a tremor I can feel.

I slip my hand to my lap, reaching across our girl to find his under the tablecloth. Our finger knot together in silent solidarity as I bite the inside of my cheek. The cheeky Fae from the Unseelie is making him scared to find the answer we came here to seek because of his malevolence. He's worried his father will be worse than Callie, and it's not an unfair concern. If someone as arrogant and brash as Alistair is holding back, especially given his title, the man responsible for impregnating the Cailleach has to be fearsome.

"Speaking of being more than your lineage…" I say with a smirk. I'm trying to steer the conversation away from dangerous waters, so I'm going to piss this fucker off. "There's something precious about self-made legacies. Earning respect is more impressive than gaining it through association, I think."

"An odd opinion for the son of a senator, don't you think?" Alistair shoots back, his lips curling into a knowing grin. "But I suppose you have distanced yourself from him since you left the nest. Your name carries weight on its own, granted, but we must never forget where we come from—no matter how high we rise."

"Or how far we fall," King Hieronymous chimes in, chuckling absentmindedly at his own joke. Allora looks at him in concern, but lets out a breath when she realizes he's mostly oblivious to the undercurrents lapping at the edges of the conversation.

"Exactly," Alistair agrees, his gaze flicking back to the King, then to Allora before he focuses on me. "Some falls are destined by blood, wouldn't you say?"

"Destiny is a tricky thing," I counter in irritation. "Fate is never so capricious as when people tempt its edicts."

"Ah, but rarely do they change the tapestry for a single being," Alistair says, leaning forward slightly. "The proof of that is all around us. It's present in the way we move, the power we wield, the fires we…"

His voice trails off and his eyes dart to the flickering candle between us. I'm not manipulating it, but someone is. I take a slow, steadying breath, feeling the heat within me pulsate in response.

Calm down, Tilly. Don't give him the satisfaction.

Before I can respond, Doyle is sneering at him in contempt. "Sometimes, fires are best left unlit. Some embers shouldn't be fanned for fear of the wildfire that will rage in their wake."

"Indeed," Alistair concedes with a tilt of his head, "but where's the fun in being so cautious?"

"Fun is subjective," I say, my voice steady despite the raging torrent inside me. "And some games have higher stakes than others."

"Life's a high-stakes game, Judge Boone," Alistair whispers, as if sharing a secret meant just for me. "Despite the risks, I do so love to play for big pots."

"Even pawns can checkmate kings," Tilly cuts in, her voice darker than usual. When she looks at me, I have to press my lips together because her eyes aren't emerald like normal. There's a litany of things flickering in them one by one—a flame, wings, a sparkling darkness, and a ring of red.

This is very, very bad.

Just Like Fire

Jolene

A MUSCLE in Doyle's jaw twitches, the only warning before the storm breaks. "I've had enough of these cryptic games," he growls, pushing back from the table with a scrape that echoes off the gilded walls.

"Wait, Doyle—" He's gone before I can get the words out—a redheaded blur of anger and frustration weaving through the throng of oblivious guests beyond the head table. I glance at Benjy, his eyes already tracking Doyle's departure.

We can't allow him to lose his temper, even if it's not with the royals.

He nods to me in unspoken understanding. "I'll make sure he doesn't do anything rash."

"Thank you," I murmur as I watch him retreat. Doyle's outburst pulled me out of my inner fury and I blink when I realize he might have done it on purpose to keep me from exploding on the arrogant dipstick who's watching me like a hawk. When his reaction confirms that the Fae was hoping to push one of us over the edge, my irritation simmers like coals waiting for a breeze.

I knew *we would not get to eat dinner. Son of a bitch.*

"Your friends are quite... passionate," Alistair observes, his voice as smooth as the silk shirt clinging to his lean torso. He's looking at his nails and the eye roll I give him damn near sends them into the back of my head.

"Passion fuels more than anger. My men's temperaments keep me more than satisfied in other ways," I reply with a saucy wink and Allora coughs again as she tries not to giggle. "But if you don't comprehend that, I'm not sure I can do more than express my regrets to Allora."

His eyes narrow and I see the first crack in his impenetrable armor. Alistair doesn't like when I win her favor, and he likes when she makes sure we know she agrees with me even less. I know how to win this battle; like any other male, I need to break his ego into tiny little pieces until he cries for help or admits his actual intentions.

That's child's play for a woman with my background.

Before I begin, a soft sound to my right draws my attention. Wolfie's shoulders shake ever so slightly, and he shakes his head. The sight triggers a protective surge within me and I turn to my darling boy. This is hurting him more than it's helping and since that fucker knows where we're heading next, it's bound to get worse. I wouldn't be surprised if he showed up, nor would it shock me to find out he'd tapped allies to make our journey more difficult.

"Teddy," I whisper, as I watch Wolfie. He stands, ignoring Alistair's huff of derision, and moves behind him to lay a hand on Wolfie's back. It's a simple gesture that speaks volumes about how much he cares for him, but my heart does funny flips, anyway.

"Easy, pup," my grumpy alphahole murmurs. His voice is a low rumble that resonates over both of us, and I sigh happily. His confident presence is palpable, and dominance always anchors Wolfie and makes me feel stronger.

"Is the doctor okay?" Alistair asks mockingly, his gaze flicking between Wolfie and Teddy like a predator scenting vulnerability. "Does he need smelling salts?"

"He's more okay than you'll ever be," I snap, my words laced with venom. Teddy's oddly calm composure contrasts with my fury. I watch as Wolfie lifts his head, the pain in his eyes replaced by a quiet gratitude as we defend him.

His grateful look is a reminder of what's at stake—our family, our secrets, our safety.

"Such loyalty you all show," Alistair muses, leaning back in his chair with an air of nonchalance that fools no one. "I can't imagine having to defend weaker stock all the time. Is it burdensome?"

"Only to those who don't understand the value of empathy," I counter, meeting his gaze squarely. "Either stop dancing around what you know, Alistair, or you'll see what loyalty truly looks like."

He tilts his head, considering me like I'm a puzzle to be solved. "My dear Jolene, knowledge is a currency. Why should I spend it so freely? Because you put on your big girl bloomers and ordered me to? I hardly think that's a likely outcome."

"Maybe," I lean in, lowering my voice to a dangerous whisper, "you owe a debt you're not aware of yet."

His eyes narrow, a glint of challenge flashing within them. I don't respond, holding onto my power by being the silent one. I'm honestly not sure what I'm bluffing him with, but I'll figure something out. I just need him to back off Wolfie and let us get out of this room gracefully.

Though I doubt it will hurt to have him wondering what I might do when we head to his fucking court.

"Touché," he concedes with a slow clap. "You might hold cards I'm unaware of; you certainly have the connections amongst your harem to get information. But as you know, debts can be paid in more ways than one."

"Consider this a down payment on what's owed," I say firmly. "I want answers. Whether it's tonight or within the next few days, you will give me something to work with. Understood?"

Wolfie's gaze flutters to me, seeking reassurance, and I catch Teddy's eye as he subtly flexes his fingers in a silent reminder of the strength we possess together. Once Benjy's gentle influence returns Doyle to us with his fire tempered, Teddy will make our excuses with the King and I'll handle Allora. The way he's looking at Wolfie and the sadness emanating from our empathetic vet means he's struggling as hard as I am. I seem fearless, but I know this is my last chance to force his hand.

The tension in the air is a tangible thing as the quiet stretches, wrapping around us like the creeping vines that snake their way up the palace's ancient stone walls. Alistair Silkshine toys with his wineglass, his smirk deepening as he watches me. "Perhaps there might be some merit in... exploring old texts for your answers."

"Go to the library? Is this mother fucker serious?" Presley's grumble is so unusual for him that I have to bite my lip to keep from bursting into laughter.

"We must always consider the veracity of the sources, of course," the Fae says as his eyes roam over the overwhelming amount of bookshelves lining this room.

"Books don't lie—unlike present company," I quip as I follow his gaze carefully. I don't think he'd give me clues that way, but who the hell knows with this asshole?

"The victors write much of history," he counters, his eyes twinkling with mischief. "There are those who would dispute your simple assessment."

I bite back a retort, clenching my fists under the table. This game could go on forever, and I'm done wasting time on this smug piece of shit. My hand slaps the table and the King jolts awake. The sound distracts me and I frown when I realize the Queen is gone, having left Hieronymus to snooze and their guest to pick fights with us.

I guess it doesn't matter where you go, royalty is full of snobby idiots who don't deserve the chairs they sit in.

"On that note," Presley interjects smoothly, rising from his seat with a grace that belies the power coiled within him, "we would be most appreciative if we could peruse the library archives. Tomorrow, perhaps?"

Allora smiles, giving him an appreciative look before putting her faux bimbette mask back on. "Oh, we have such wonderful scrolls and tomes. Father, wouldn't that be grand? I could give them a tour."

The sleepy King is as adorably oblivious as ever, but he peers over his spectacles with a bemused expression. "Hmm? Oh! Yes, yes. Quite right." He waves a dismissive hand, the jeweled rings catching the light. "Open the archives to our guests, Allora."

"Thank you. We deeply appreciate you allowing Allora to assist," I say, allowing a smile to soften my features. The relief that flows through me is echoed on Teddy's face, a silent thank you for Presley's intervention. I nod at the princess, hoping she knows how helpful her alliance tonight has been. "We should go, though. I'm afraid travel is still catching up with us."

"I suppose it's settled then," Alistair concedes, though his voice holds a note of reluctance. "Tomorrow, the past shall speak to those with ears to hear."

"Let's hope it screams," I mutter under my breath, catching Wolfie's eye and offering a wink to lift his spirits.

Before the jerk can start another round of bullshit, I rise and curtsey at the remaining royals. Turning on my heel, I whistle low for the companions, hoping they pick it up as we make our way out of the opulent chamber.

The heavy doors close behind us with a resounding thud and I let out a sigh of relief as I realize we're alone in the dimly lit corridor. The last thing I need is a confrontation with anyone else in the fucking place. I just want to get back to our room and order room service while someone rubs my damn feet.

Fuck this day and the horse it rode in on.

"Where'd they go?" Teddy asks, concern etching lines across his brow.

"Knowing Benjy, somewhere quiet," I reply, scanning the hallway. "He probably had Doyle breathing like a yoga master in no time."

"Found them," Wolfie says softly, his voice a blend of relief and affection as he spots the pair down at the end of the hall.

Doyle is leaning against the wall, his chest rising and falling in a measured rhythm, while Benjy rests a hand lightly on his arm. They turn towards us, and the newest person to join my family winks at me. I tilt my head, waiting for the Irishman to acknowledge our presence. When he stays quiet, I give in.

"Ready to head back?" I ask Doyle.

He nods, a grateful look softening his features as we close the distance between us. "More than ready," he replies in a steady voice. "Sorry I almost lost it, Tíogair. I didn't like how he was treating you or the pup. Made my system overload."

"Don't I get it, man," Teddy chuckles as he shakes his head. "Prez, warn *him* this time."

I arch a brow at them, but Dr. McNuggies just gives me a mischievous look. By the time we get out of the castle, it's dark out, and I realize we're going to have to navigate through the twisting streets of the Fae city. "Please tell me if one of you paid attention to how we got here. We have to get back to the hotel and back here tomorrow."

Despite the gnawing uncertainty about returning to the lion's den, there's a flicker of excitement within me. Answers are close—I feel them, as surely as the fire coursing through my veins now.

"Don't worry, Tilly. Your eagle flew above us."

Prez whistles, and the giant bird flaps in front of us, screeching as she looks at me. "This is your moment, girl. Take us home before our woman gets us all kicked out of the city."

Very funny, Birdman.

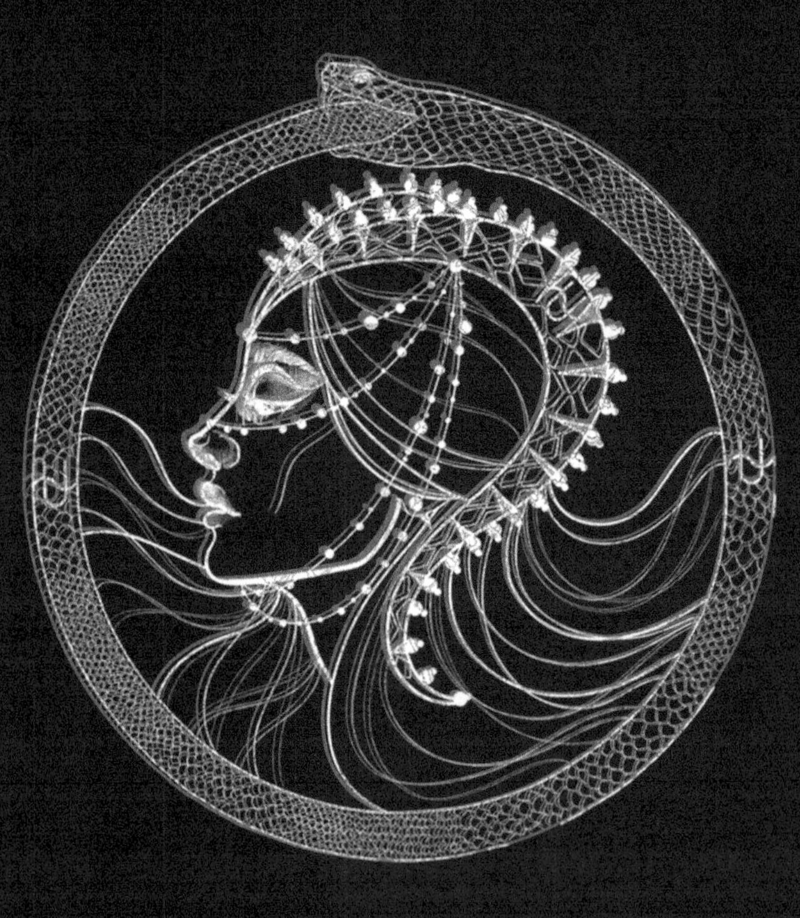

Helpless

Doyle

The great bloody bird pulled through and led us back through the disturbingly quaint capital of the Harvest Court. I'm still furious at the entire situation that forced us to endure the little shit's games all evening. I've never understood why unemerged supes who are part of the program aren't given the info they need before they leave their enclaves. Even if they don't develop powers, they're going to have shadows following them forever, watching to see if they do.

It's secret supe parole and puts them in more danger than it keeps them out of.

But we're all bound by the same fucking oath no matter what level of the Society we're part of, so we dance to their tune like good automatons. Organized shit is the worst and I hate being part of any system that takes away people's free will. My stance on that shit is why my 'family' on Olympus dislikes my presence and it's definitely why I've stayed on the fringes of the town almost the entire time they have stationed me in the Hollow.

As we head upstairs in the elevator, I notice the pup is getting less anxious by the second. Both the doggy and our girl have his hands while the doc is standing behind him, so he's well guarded. That doesn't mean I'm satisfied that no one is going to attempt to fuck with him again during this trip, especially since his marked mates are unaware or unable to use their gifts. I, however, am less hampered than they are if I do it subtly. It's not my style, but much like my tricks at that trial, I may have to surreptitiously fuck people up if they behave like the dark Fae did tonight.

"You better now, man?"

I give Benjy a wry grin, shrugging. "Never been a fan of hiding my light under a bushel, and this trip is making it hard to honor my promises."

Jolene lets go of Wolfie's hand, walking over to me. She places her palms on my chest and looks up into my eyes. "You're doing a good job reining in your temper, Lucky. I know we all appreciate the effort, but we also like that you want to protect everyone. That's what family does."

Snorting, I lean in, resting my forehead on hers. "You lot are the first people I've made an attempt for in a very long time, Tíogair. However, when this jaunt to the old world is over, I plan on wreaking havoc on every idiot who gave us shit. You can take that to the bank."

"I would expect nothing less," she says with a smile.

The elevator dings and we file out, heading to the suite with less tension arcing through the group. Boone waves the key at the door and the second we step inside, he snarls as though there's an enemy at the gates. Sighing, I push through the crowd, leaving our girl in the middle so she's covered. When I see it, I roll my eyes and pinch the bridge of my nose.

"Pull it back, you idgit," I hiss at the judge. Calling a tiny fraction of my power, I check the room out to make certain no one is hiding out of sight or in the connecting bedroom. Once I'm sure, I turn to our family. "He's a wee bit put out that someone was in our space while we were gone. It doesn't appear too malicious, but we'll have to be cautious until we inspect everything."

As we enter, the scent of roasted meats and baked bread fills the air. They parked a gargantuan cart laden with platters of food in the center of the living area with a note that reads:

"With sincerest apologies for any discomfort. Until tomorrow."

"Looks like someone is trying to butter us up with a feast," Presley says as he looks over the spread. His eyes are twinkling with amusement as he pretends to examine the food, but I catch him running his fingertips under the edges of tables and furniture as he goes.

Not much gets past our resident scholar, that's for bloody sure. I wouldn't have considered conventional spy methods.

"Or trying to poison us," Wolfie snarks. He looks like he's joking, but there's an edge to his words that makes me pause.

His words silence everyone, but I shake my head. I don't think they're trying to kill us—not even the prince would survive an inquiry from the Society involving this many inductees. It's like the princess is trying to apologize for her objectionable choice in men, especially since we didn't get to eat a bite before we had to leave. She seemed like a good sort and the King, though addled, also didn't trip my wires.

My gaze flicks to Boone, then to the half-Fae holding his hand. "I'm sure many suspicious additives would have scents. I don't smell almonds, for example."

Their eyes widen as they get my insinuation. Between the doggy's nose and the Fae's natural gifts, they *should* be able to suss out if the food has dangerous shit if they focus. We'll need to distract our girl, but that won't be hard. She hates being trussed up and the dress they sent her still has her bound up tight.

"Princess, why don't you get out of that thing so you're comfy? We'll check out the food, and if it's not up to snuff, we'll pack it up and order something new. Sound good?" Jolene looks over at the gentle giant and it makes me smile to see how easily he can guide her without being overwhelming.

I grin. "Benjy's got it right. Put on those adorable yoga things that make your ass look biteable and we'll handle this."

Her eyes narrow, but the desire to shuck the finery wins out. "Fine.

But I don't like people in our room leaving notes, even if it comes with food that smells like the goddamn heavens beamed it down."

Sharp as a tack, that's our girl.

"Understood, Tilly. Now, shoo."

WHEN SHE RETURNS IN A WELL-LOVED, OVERSIZE GUNS 'N ROSES TEE and yoga pants, I grin. Jolene's hair is down and the makeup is wiped clean, leaving her looking dewy and soft despite the sharp edges she loves to put on. Her feet are bare and when I squint at the pants I love so much, I see that she's got a knife clipped in one of the side pockets.

Wonder where she hid that in her tight autumn colored gown tonight?

"Clipped between the girls," she says as she catches me staring. Her lips quirk and I chuckle as I flop down on the couch. "Did you guys make sure this stuff isn't full of death spices?"

"Bit dramatic, but yes," the pup says as he meets her in the middle of the room. "We're as sure as we can be. Apparently, that's good enough for Teddy."

The hound whips his head around, giving Wolfie a look before he sighs. "We can't be any more sure about things brought up from the kitchen, either. So we did the best we could to verify, but we can't starve."

Jolene's stomach growls, and she flushes when we laugh. "Oh, fine. Make fun of the girl who hasn't eaten and got strapped into a stupid dress for a formal dinner. Very 1865 of you all."

"Before she makes garments out of the curtains, we should dig in," Teddy says wryly.

It doesn't take long for everyone to attack the various dishes. We're starving, and the day's frustrations have left us ravenous and cranky. I grin when I catch Boone adding helpings to her plate and have to swallow a snort when Benjy brings a few extra small plates with desserts to the coffee table with him. They're both mother hens, but from different ends of the spectrum.

I slide to the floor when the rest of them take places next to one another around the low crystalline block we're using for the food. My Tíogair is between the pup and the dog, so Prez, Benjy, and I scoot in to flank them. Our girl smiles when I pass her a glass of Fae wine, wagging a finger at her to make sure she doesn't gulp it. The ruby liquid swirls hypnotically in my glass as I watch it, content being here despite all the people pissing me off. This vintage tastes like wild berries and summer nights, leaving a hint of something exotic dancing on my tongue.

"Damn, this is good," I murmur, feeling the first tendrils of warmth unfurl within me. "I forget how good alcohol is when you're not in… the United States."

Benjy snorts, and Boone has to smother a chuckle. They both know I was about to say 'the human realm.' I need to be careful how candid I get when we drink this shit. It can loosen the tongues of the strongest supes.

"You… are being silly." Jolene points at me with her food filled fork. When I wink, she chomps the meat with a groan that makes every one of us grunt in response. "This shit is good. I think I don't care if it's poisoned."

Wolfie pinches her side before he snitches a carrot off her plate. "It's not. Everyone needs to quit saying that."

I finish my wine before I dig in again, finally feeling myself relax. "Just a bit of dark humor, doc. It's hard not to be sarcastic after the past couple of days. This was supposed to be the easier portion of the trip."

"Christ on a cheez doodle," Jolene mutters. "What the hell are the rest of the flighty fuckers going to do? They have already forced me to bind myself up twice. You know what? That's it. I'm done. No more fancy dresses. I'll go in ripped jeans and a band tee if I want. *Viva la France!*"

"Everything okay, Princess?" Benjy asks. He's very perceptive to shifts in moods, though not as good as the little vet. "You're awfully rebellious suddenly."

Our girl holds up a skewer of sizzling vegetables wrapped in a leaf I can't identify. "Better than okay. I'm re-asserting control over my fucking life. Burn the corsets and all that rot."

Mmm hmm.

"While I applaud your desire to be less constricted and suggest you take a step further to go commando…" I pause as she giggles. "I'm not sure antagonizing the hosts at the next stops will help us get what we need."

"Since when does my lack of underwear make a damn bit of difference to people who can't see my naked ass?" She waves a potato that seems to be a variant of a French fry at me, chastisingly. "It's my party and I'll free ball if I want to."

I have absolutely nothing to say to that, so I shake my head and let her go. It's nice to see her looking happy, even if it's odd timing. Laughter and conversation ebb and flow around the room as we eat. By the time we've cleaned our plates, the air feels thick with an energy that's tantalizing and dangerous.

"Is it hot in here, or is it just me?" Teddy asks, tugging at his collar.

"Maybe you ate a weird pepper, dude," I reply as I loll on the floor, sipping my wine. "Some of that stuff was spicy as hell."

"Definitely not just you," Benjy agrees, his voice dropping an octave as he looks at our girl.

"Guys," Presley starts, his usual laid-back demeanor slipping. "I think we've been—"

"Drinking too much," I cut in as realization dawns on me. The food and the wine must have been laced with something that won't kill us, but it sure as won't make us complacent.

"I suppose we should be angry that they served us jacked up booze but..." Jolene's sentence trails off as her gaze travels over each of us with a hunger that has nothing to do with food.

"Angry later. Bed now," Boone growls. He rolls to his feet, holding his hand out to her. His pupils are dilated with a cocktail of desire and whatever aphrodisiac they spiked our shit with, but I think he simply doesn't care.

"Bed," I echo as I mirror his stance. My thoughts are growing hazy around the edges, leaving only a singular focus on the surrounding bodies. "Sounds like a bloody brilliant plan to me."

"Everyone okay with this?" Benjy, ever the gentleman, checks even as he helps haul the docs off the ground.

"Oh, I'm *more* than okay," our girl says as she sashays towards the open door to the bedroom. "And if I'm not better than that soon, you're all getting your asses kicked."

Yes, ma'am.

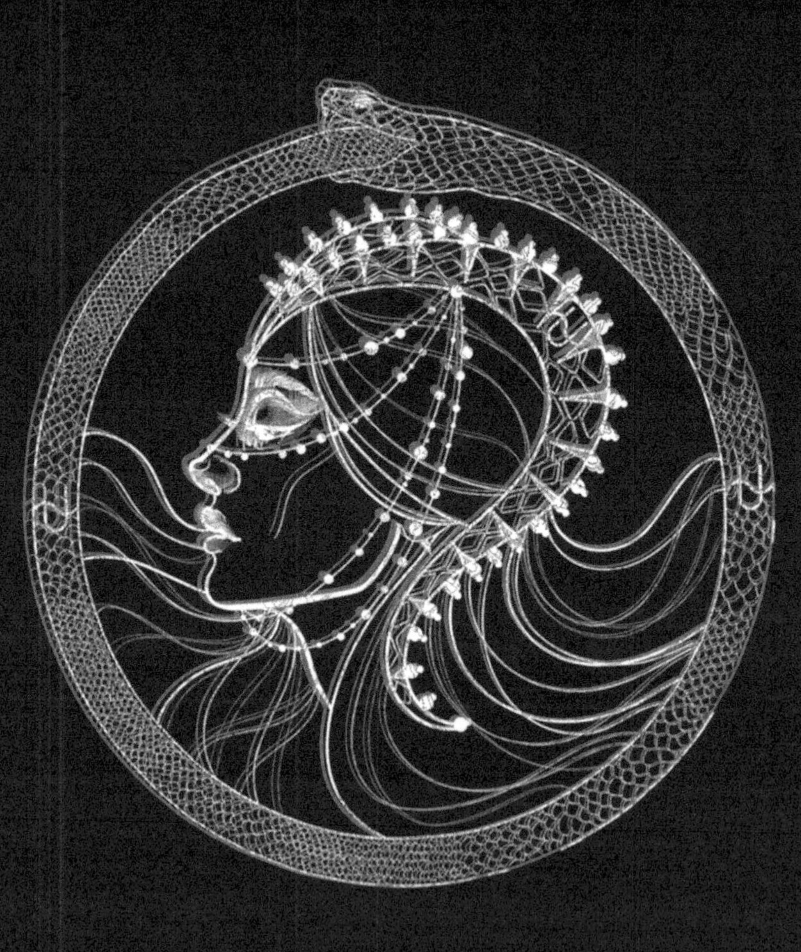

Dangerous Woman

Jolene

Clothes are flying as we enter the room and I laugh softly when Teddy grabs my waist to toss me on the bed. It's been a shitty couple of days and I'm not even upset with him manhandling me. My butt bounces on the mattress as I scoot back, my eyes glued to the muscles and skin being revealed by my guys. They're eager to burn off some of this frustration and helplessness, too, even if some Fae pheromone shit predicates it.

"Tilly, if you take those damn glasses off, you'd better have your eyes closed or you'll get three every time I catch you." Teddy gives me a stern expression and though I'd fight him on that normally, I know why he's being stern. He's worried we'll knock them loose in our haste and something bad will happen. So I nod, giving him a playful wink. Pointing out that he's admitting there's something special about my new eyewear would ruin the vibe and I'm not ready to have that conversation.

See? I can be reasonable.

"She's definitely hungry for more, Boone. You didn't even have to fight her," Doyle says as he crawls onto the bed next to me. He gives me a cheeky grin and hooks his fingers into my yoga pants. "I'm suddenly sorry I demanded these, but we'll remedy my error quick enough."

"Don't tease me," I growl as I bury my fingers in his flaming locks and tug lightly. "I'm fresh of patience for games, Lucky."

His chuckle vibrates over my skin as he kisses his way down my torso, working my pants over my hips along the way. "Tíogair, I think you'll find we're all a bit on edge tonight. It's a toss-up whether you or Big Doggy will be in charge, though."

My eyes roll up as he nips and bites his way across my stomach, trying not to groan in response. Benjy climbs on the bed from that side, his gentle smile making me melt even though he's not touching me. He's gorgeous as he kneels next to me, his bulky frame contrasted by the softness in his eyes. It doesn't hurt that he's got a beautiful dick mere centimeters from my mouth, but he's waiting for me instead of pushing.

"Why not both?" I murmur as I lick my lips. "Doyle, stop fucking around down there while Benjy fucks my face. Wolfie, take care of Daddy and Prez until I'm ready for you."

Teddy turns, his perfectly sculpted athlete body in sharp profile as he gives me a wicked grin. "Why, Tilly, I thought you said you'd never…"

"Shut. Your. Mouth." My eyes narrow at him and I flick my hand to Prez and Wolfie before I turn back to Benjy, reaching out to stroke his cock lightly. "Come here, big guy. Give your Princess a taste."

He scoots forward and I wrap my lips around his tip first, suckling gently. I use my free hand to give Doyle's hair another tug and he finally moves below my belly button. At the first wet swipe of his tongue along the seam of my leg, I moan. Sliding Benjy's length into my mouth, I open wide until I hit the root. It takes a second for me to adjust and breathe out of my nose, but once I do, my playful Irishman flicks his tongue over my clit. A surprised sound vibrates over Benjy's shaft and his hands wrap around my head to hold me in place.

"Fuck, Princess. Do that again. Holy shit."

I'd grin if I could get my mouth any wider, so instead, I do as told and repeat the high-pitched hum. He shudders and pulls back, then slams in again with his big palms guiding me. I rarely let someone have this much control over me when I give head, but it's hard to complain when my fiery lover is writing a long ass sentence on me with his tongue. I'm caught between my pussy leaking on his face while my hips writhe and my typically gentle giant picking speed as I suck him deep.

Are the others…?

A dark snarl echoes off the walls, and I ache to grin again. That sound means Wolfie has Teddy balls deep in his mouth and the whimper that follows tells me Prez is rewarding him. The noises make my skin heat and I feel my blood follow suit when Doyle's tongue slips inside of me. I suck in a deep breath through my nose and the scents that mingle in the air make my gut clench.

Beyond the normal musk of sex, there are delicious aromas emanating from my men as the lust in the room gets thicker. My eyelids flutter open to see the vague shadow on Benjy and the golden glow ringing Doyle again. The fire on my hands is flickering from orange flames to an odd pink mist as I swallow my newest lover down every time his hips pump forward. There's something just out of reach, I feel it, but the waves of pleasure pushing me towards a peak make it hard to focus.

"You're almost there, Tíogair," Doyle's voice is almost a purr and his tongue swipes roughly over my clit again as he thrusts three fingers inside of me. My walls squeeze him and I accidentally scrape my teeth over Benjy. I try to pull back when I realize it, but his fingers bury in my hair and he grunts as he continues thrusting.

"Keep going, Princess. I like it rough."

Teddy's chuckle is low and raspy from the other side of the bed. "He really does, Tilly. Mark him up; he'll like it. Benjy never lies."

Spank my ass and call me Charlotte—I can do that.

Lifting my hand from Doyle's head, I grab the big guy's hipbones and hold on tight. My nails dig into him as I renew my efforts. I suck harder, nip lightly when I can, and scratch my teeth along his shaft as his pace picks up. I feel the tension in his body build when I do and something deep inside of me unfurls. They don't know I can see the flames and mist alternating as I grip Benjy, but I know the dark satisfaction in my gut is tied to it. Every time he moans or Doyle adds another finger to slam inside of me, it spreads.

"Stop, doc," I hear my alphahole growl before he sniffs the air like an animal. "No one comes before her and she's close. Haggerty, make her come or I'm taking over."

I flick my tongue over the tip of Benjy's head, then deep throat him again, getting the vein underneath with my bottom teeth. He jerks and lets out a surprising rumble. "Fuck, Doyle, tip her over before she…"

The minute a full fist pushes inside of me, my hips buck hard and the pressure on the right spot makes me gush as the orgasm crashes over me. The cock I'm sucking on muffles my loud moan, but I don't let go as my brain leaks out my ears. Benjy thrusts one more time, then hot fluid shoots down my throat as I rock on Lucky's hand. I don't know if I've ever felt anything this intense in my entire life, but from the flood downstairs, Doyle knows it.

These sheets are definitely ruined; housekeeping is going to love us.

When the shudders cease, the big guy pulls out and closes my mouth. "Swallow it all like a good girl, and I'm sure Big Daddy will reward you."

My eyes widen, and I want to retort, but I've got a mouthful of jizz. *I'm going to kill these motherfuckers for feeding his ego.* Instead of dribbling cum out of my lips like a fool, I look Benjy right in the eyes as I swallow the rest of him down, then lick my lips clean. He groans and flops back against the pillows, his arm above his head as he looks over at Edgar.

"Brother, that was the hottest fucking thing in history. Our girl can take me like a champ."

Don't do it. No one say it and I won't have to—

"That's why we're calling him Big Daddy from now on."

Springing forward at the waist, I push a snickering Irishman off of my lower half and open my mouth to let Prez have it. Except he's the one sucking Teddy down and Wolfie is sprawled out with my dominant ex-bully's hand circling his cock possessively. I blink for a second, taking that new situation in as the rest of the scene gets clearer.

Teddy has the same flickering flames and mist in the aura surrounding him, as well as colorful feathers. Wolfie's gorgeous wings are fluttering as his hips wiggle, sending sparkles into the air. And Prez… He has the shadow of huge white wings behind him as he works his mouth over Edgar.

Even a monster orgasm isn't making this any easier. Just breathe, Jolene.

I tilt my head, pasting a satisfied smirk on my face as I arch a brow. "Big Daddy? Are you out of your goddamn minds? His head is big enough to get stuck in the doorways as it is."

"Relax, Princess. You can keep calling him asshole if it makes you feel better."

Benjy's easy quip hits just right and I cover my mouth as a giggle escapes. I want to stay irritated, but one giggle turns into two, and before long, tears are running down my face. Teddy shrugs and runs his hand over Prez's head gently, his expression full of swagger.

"Fine. Big Daddy Asshole, it is," I say when I finally get control of myself. "Although, if you keep collecting my boys, you're going to have to figure out what they're going to call me when it's my turn to be in charge."

"Tilly, get your sweet ass over here and ride my dick so the doc can fuck your ass while I suck the pup. Once you get off a few more times, we can discuss titles." Teddy pulls Prez up, winking at me as the lithe doctor scrambles across the room to our bags.

I'd bristle at the order, but it sounds like a good fucking time.

"Two in one night, Big Daddy Asshole. Don't let this shit go to your head," I whisper as I hover over his cock. When he laughs, I sink down on him, spearing myself on his dick with a soft moan of pleasure. "Holy fuck, that feels good."

"Woman, you're so wet I can't even…" Teddy trails off as his hand tightens on Wolfie. "Pup, you'd better get ready. This is going to be a rough ride."

"Aye," Doyle says as he moves up the bed. "Because she's got one more hole to fill and I aim to get our girl airtight."

My eyes move to Benjy, noting he's hard again and stroking his hand over himself with a lazy grin. "Don't worry, Mama J. I like to watch sometimes and I have a feeling this is going to be hot as fuck."

If I wasn't trapped between a dick in my pussy and one pushing at my lips, I'd strangle them all.

That's when Prez comes back, and I hear the bottle opening. I shift on Teddy, squeezing his dick until he growls at me, and lean forward to take Doyle into my mouth. His ragged breaths pick up as I take him deeper, and the golden halo around him gets brighter. I wait for Prez to line up and slide home, filling me full enough to draw rough sounds from everyone, then I move.

Presley's hands on my hips and smooth thrusts help me rock on Teddy and the forward motion brings Doyle to the back of my throat. The rhythm consumes me as the tasty scent permeates the air, and my cunt grips Teddy with every downstroke. My eyes are closed just in case the stupid glasses fall off, but I *know* all the weird shit has to be getting more intense. The stuff I saw when I was with Benjy and Doyle was a precursor; I feel the intensity in my body building to another out-of-control peak.

Something is coming… something beyond an orgasm that will make me black out…

With Doyle in my mouth, I can't warn them, but as our bodies move and skin slaps, the sensation gets bigger and bigger until a loud cry escapes. The climax explodes within me like an atom bomb, and my eyes stay squeezed shut as the feeling of being ripped apart slams into my consciousness.

The last thing I hear before I pass out is an unearthly howl, the beat of wings, and a pounding sound.

Then it all goes black.

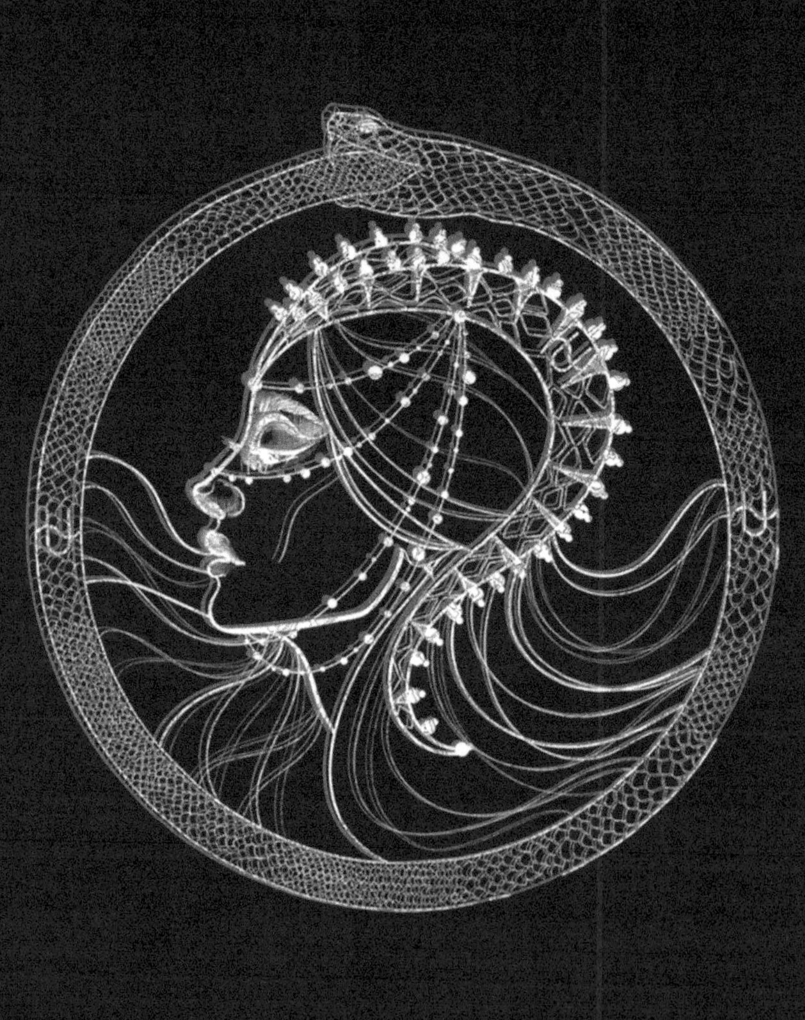

Half A World Away

Dhameer

My eyes pop open, and I sit straight up in my bed.

Something is happening.

The oracle awakens immediately, looking at me with concern from the couch. "Amiri, what is it?"

I close my eyes, connecting to the universe that only ancient powers can. Once I sort through the threads, I see it clearly. My smile is genuine as I look at Hugo. "It's begun, my friend."

"Shit," he says as he scrubs a hand down his face. "I didn't think it would start until she was home. The visions were murky, though."

His position prevents him from sharing much regarding his gift, but I know he is trying to give me what he can. We've been traveling around, using my wealth and status to open doors the others could not while they searched for the Fae's kin. Our mission has been moderately successful and when they return to Whistler's Hollow, I plan to share the information we've gathered with our fated.

But we both believed this process wouldn't begin until she'd marked all of us—the Fates must be playing their little games again.

"The others will help her. They have the good doctor to guide them and our fated through the beginning phases. It will be okay," I tell him. "We cannot lose focus; our tasks are vital. This turn of events makes me feel more than ever that we must solve the mystery of Jolene's adoptive parents' death. Once we do that, we will follow the clues to her true heritage."

"Why is this so important?" Hugo asks softly. "My kind rarely get mates and my entire body is screaming that we should be there while she's emerging."

Ah, the short-sightedness of youth.

"Patience, my future-seeing friend. I feel the pull as well, but we are not as tied to her yet, so we can use that to our advantage." I run a hand through my hair as I consider how to explain what the stars are telling me. "I do not have visions like you, but my first tie to Jolene was through granting a wish. That connection twists us together even further than mating—it twists our threads together in the great tapestry. I feel a distinct urgency around uncovering her past, so it must be irrevocably tied to her future."

He stays silent for a moment, then nods. "I understand now. Your magic is tied to the fulfillment of those desires. It must have mistakenly given you access to the Fates' plan—or part of it."

"Perhaps. We both know they enjoy being cryptic, but they enjoy re-weaving things to teach people a lesson even more. I do not want to upset the balance by acting outside of the current bounds."

"Then we continue on as we have been?"

I nod, stroking my beard. "We do, and we trust that the rest of her mates will keep her safe among the sharks they are swimming with. Our purpose has not changed, nor has that of her friend."

"Saoirse checked in with her when they were at Daybreak. She was worried that Jolene seemed distracted. Perhaps this started there?"

"A sound assumption, Hugo. We will call her tomorrow and have her fill us in on what the weird sisters have demanded. For now, we should get some rest."

He huffs, thumping his pillow as he lies down. "As if I'm going to be able to sleep now. Just make sure when the damn visions come I don't swallow my tongue, please?"

I chuckle, giving him a thumbs up. "Agreed, friend. I'll safeguard your person and keep Isra from bursting in like we're being stormed by invading Huns."

"Thank hell. That woman is terrifying."

"Are you certain the man they have asked you to guard is human, Saoirse?" My brows furrow as she squawks about her current assignment like an angry goose. "The Sisters have you and your cadre babysitting… a human criminal?"

"I didn't stutter, Prince Ali." Her tone is irritable, and I truly can't blame her. "They rerouted me after Budapest, told to meet Julia and the guys at their safe house in London. They'd been keeping some dude they scooped up there since they left after Halloween. He's been sedated, so he won't need his memory wiped, but whatever sign we're supposed to wait for hasn't come yet. I'm pissed as hell."

"Do you know who this unlucky gentleman is?" I frown as I try to understand why in the heavens a team of Guardians would be asked to guard a human. "Have they given you any hint as to be why he must be protected?"

"Not a word. He's too doped up to ask, and none of our magical probing has indicated a link to our world. He's a computer guy, and he got injured in a bombing—they picked him up afterward. That's all I know."

The frustration in her voice is understandable; They trapped Saoirse far from her best friend and charge at a crucial time.

"Don't worry about Jolene. I promise we will keep in contact with you and I am certain the others can help our girl through her transition. If the Fates deem this crucial enough to tie up four Guardians, it will become clear eventually. Do your job so you don't tempt them." I look at Hugo and he nods. The visions he had last night were unchanged from the last time, so we believe everything is still on course.

Saoirse sighs heavily, and a loud crash behind her rings out. "Fine. I have to go see what's going on, anyway. Tharin deals with being cooped up *really* poorly, and he's been a nightmare to deal with, especially since Zasha is amusing himself by torturing him."

My lips curve and I chuckle softly. It seems no matter what year it is or where one is located, there will always be a troublemaker and grump within a group. Saoirse has her work cut out for her someday, I fear. "Go deal with your cadre and we will look for the next location we need to visit. We must find the team that killed the policeman and his family, just as you must guard this charge."

"Be careful, yeah? My girl likes you and that other one a lot—she might not know how much yet, but if you get hurt, she'll be upset. I don't like how involved these ancients are and how little the Society has to say about it."

On that point, we are in absolute agreement.

"We will. Keep in touch."

"Always."

Turning to Hugo, I sigh. "It is very odd that the ladies have that many supes watching a human. Even more odd is that their handlers have not made noise about tying them up with something any agent could do."

"It's very strange. Four Guardians to a full human is like using a nuke to drive a nail. What value could this guy possibly have to warrant such heavy artillery?" The oracle frowns, shaking his head. "Maybe we could run his information past Jackson's tech geek?"

Arching a brow, I give him an amused look. "Do you not think I have resources of my own? We do not need him contacting Jolene and worrying her. Although, until Saoirse and her team figure out who their charge is, we have nothing to research."

Sighing, he nods. "Then we should pack up and move on. The last clue I got was in Brazil. We'll have to head there if we want to track down the people responsible for the massacre in Turkey."

"Then Brazil it is. Allow me to speak with Isra and Fazal, then we will take the easy way across so many miles. I don't relish the thought of a flight that long, even in a private jet."

"The easy way?"

I grin and wink at him. "You'll find out soon enough."

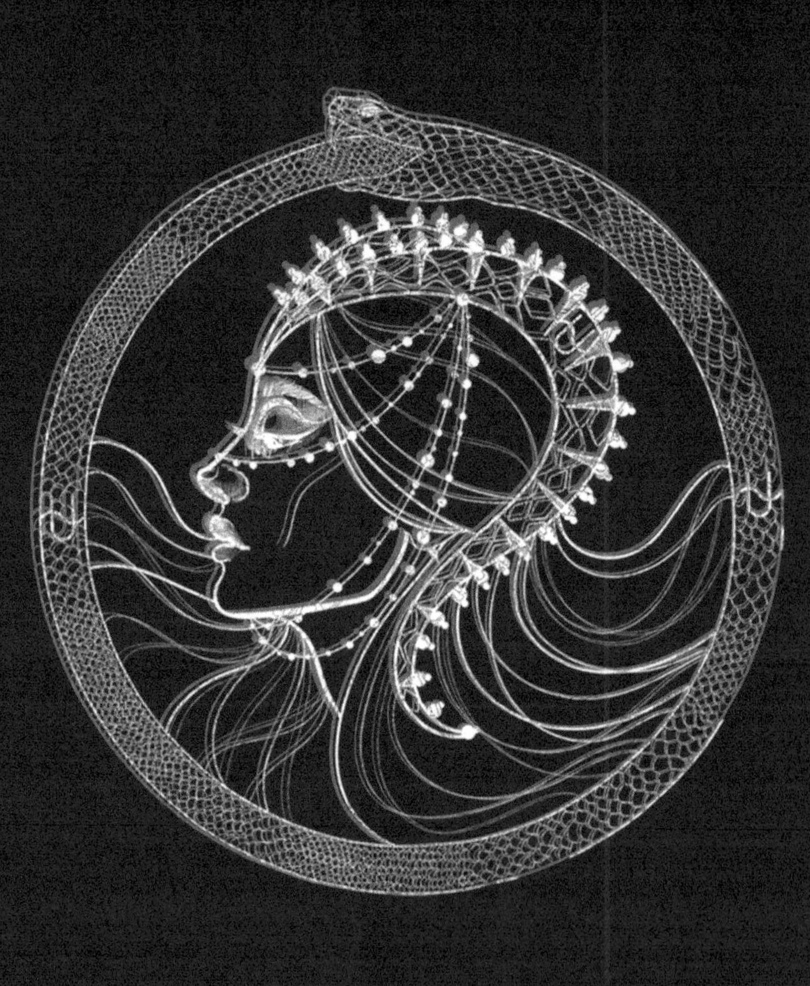

Morning Light

Jolene

My eyes flutter open only to be greeted by the aftermath of indulgence. The morning light filters through the curtains, casting a warm glow over the tangle of limbs sprawled across the bed. The scent of musk and sweat lingers in the air, a remnant of last night's revelry.

"Morning," I murmur, my voice still hoarse with sleep. I'm not sure who's awake—if anyone—but I'm feeling so damned good that I can't help saying something.

"Hey there, Princess," Benjy replies, his voice a low rumble that resonates through my bones. He leans in to press kiss to my temple and whoever he squashed to do so grumbles good-naturedly.

This is my idea of Paradise and knowing we have to get up and move sucks rocks.

I stretch, the sheets slipping to my waist. The damn glasses perched on my nose are a necessity for keeping the illusion that I don't know about their world. Surprisingly, they didn't budge during the night's escapades. When I look at the warm bodies on the bed, it's obvious something's different this morning. My vision isn't just clear; it's... revealing more than ever before.

"Guess hot sex turned up the contrast while I wasn't looking," I mutter to myself as I marvel at the change in scenery.

The guys' still look hot as hell, but I can see vivid auras surrounding them that show me the full extent of their supernatural natures.

Sniffing delicately, I shudder when their scents tickle my nose, provoking a visceral response from my body. *Holy fuck that's potent; is that what they smell all the time?* I shake my head a little, trying in vain to clear the tantalizing aromas from my brain. They make me want to stay here all day, luxuriating in my boys until… something happens. I don't know what, but the dark spot in my gut has blossomed into a voice that whispers to me.

"Not good, Jolene," I mumble as I shift. I need to get up and pee, but more than that, I need a fucking minute. I feel like I've stepped into a paranormal romance show; it's wigging me out. Wiggling a bit, I untangle my limbs slowly so I don't disturb everyone.

Teddy lifts his head, concern etching his features as he frowns at me. "What's wrong, Tilly?"

"Just need the bathroom, Teddy," I lie smoothly. He arches a brow and I know he must not be buying it, but my guileless expression makes him pause.

I hate having to keep my knowledge a secret. When the hell will I be able to let them know?

Benjy stretches and I watch as the silhouette of a gorilla flickers around him. His strength has always been apparent, but now it's almost tangible in its intensity. It's more than human—primal, powerful. Yet his eyes and his touch are so gentle that I can't see him doing some movie magic shift into King Kong.

Does Sherilynn know about this? I bet she does and that's completely humiliating.

My gentle giant stretches again, rising from the bed to walk over to the bar. The lines of his back, the muscles, and the power in his form are so magnified now that I can see him as he truly is. I can't believe it took me this long to see how fucking gorgeous this man is; it's almost a crime that it took this long.

"Wow." The breathy comment escapes my lips before I can help it and I feel my face heat.

"Like what you see, Princess?" he teases as he turns to look at me. He's unaware of the depth of my newfound perception, so he doesn't realize I've got a view of the full monte, plus the extra bits.

I shrug and give him a soft smile. "Always, big guy. You're damn near sculpture-worthy."

Teddy chuckles, stretching his arms out above his head. I tilt my head as a combination of flames, pink mist, and feathers swirling through his aura. So far, he's the only person I've seen with three competing signatures and I wonder how rare that is. His presence is usually so solid, but the multiple pieces make him enigmatic and mysterious. I'm not sure what it means, but I'd like to know. It feels important that our alpha hound has more going on than most and I wonder how many people know about it.

Teddy's known for being strategic, particularly when it's to his advantage.

I reach out to trace the line of Teddy's jaw, my fingers passing through the mist but feeling the warmth of the flames beneath. They don't hurt me, much like the ones on me don't harm me or the others when I touch them. That, too, must mean something important. "You look like a cat who ate a canary, Judge Boone. So much for your legendary poker face."

He snorts, rubbing his cheek in my palm. "I promise, no poker face for you, Tilly. As much as we can, we will be honest with you, even when it's painful."

The room is silent save for the soft breathing of Wolfie and Presley, still lost in slumber. I smile at the two of them curled together at Teddy's waist. They were draped over both of us, but I moved to alleviate the pressure on my poor bladder. I'm struck by an over-whelming urge to stay in bed again and the dark voice whispers more.

"Speaking of pain… How are you this morning, Tíogair? We were a bit rough, so it would be natural if you're a bit achy." Doyle's eyes meet mine, and I'm caught in the radiance of his golden light—an aura that speaks of powerful magic and secrets. It's breathtaking, and for a moment, I'm lost in it, wondering at the source of his power.

"Um, not too bad, really." That's absolutely true and I'm kind of surprised by it. My limbs move and my girly bits don't feel like I need to hobble, so I'm taking it as a win. I expected to be damn crippled this morning after that intense romp.

"Good dreams?" Doyle asks, his voice laced with something akin to curiosity. He's watching me closely and I get the feeling he expects to see something specific.

Scooting to the edge of the bed, I put my feet on the ground and stand, then stretch up to the ceiling. My back cracks loudly, but my muscles don't even pull. In fact, I feel pretty damn good. "Who needs them when you have wild orgies?"

The Irishman laughs, his eyes dancing as he props his face in his hand. "Good answer, love."

Wolfie stirs first, his blond hair a stark contrast to the golden sheen of his skin. He's opposite in every way in comparison to the dark fae of fairy tales we met last night. While he has an ethereal beauty, especially when he's fully Fae, Wolfie doesn't look like you'd think someone with his heritage would, nor does he look cold and pale like Callie. I'm not sure where on earth my submissive vet got his Cali boy looks in his human form, but I love both versions of him.

He's model-gorgeous and the fact that he's mine is as astounding as the other sexy men here. What the hell do they all see in me?

"Sugarplum, you're staring again," Wolfie chides playfully, though his eyes sparkle with mischief.

"Can you blame me?" I challenge, my heart swelling with a mix of affection and awe. "You're all sprawling or strutting around like a fantasy calendar. It's scrambling my brains—all before I've even had my morning coffee."

Prez opens his eyes, sighing as Wolfie hands him his glasses. He's been the least readable in terms of the secret power shit, but now his aura sports the feathers of the caladrius. I'm not sure I'd ever heard of the mythical bird believed to heal the sick and dying before, but that flash last night seemed to upload the knowledge directly to my brain. It's a revelation that leaves me breathless in its simplicity.

How could I have missed the signs when he's so talented at taking care of everyone in town?

"Presley," I start, but words fail me because I can't admit I know what he can do. "You're absolutely lickable in the morning."

"Thanks," he says with a shy smile. "I'd share my thoughts, but you seem to be having enough trouble tearing your eyes from us as it is. And you did say you needed to.."

"Oh!" I turn red as I remember and the pressure is obvious again. "Yes. Damn. Be right back."

With that, I run to the bathroom, cursing my idiocy in my head.

Why can't you just be normal, Jolene?

ONCE I'VE TAKEN CARE OF HYGIENE, I STAND IN FRONT OF THE mirror looking at myself. I'm surprised to see a myriad of marks that don't look temporary dotting my form from neck to hips. Each one is a little different and when I touch them, a rush of desire floods my system. I pretend not to hear the groans in the other room because that's enough evidence to confirm my suspicions.

I'm not sure if I want to be mad about this or not—it may not have been a conscious choice.

My nose wrinkles as I roll around all the fictional information I have on supernatural shit. I have no idea what's myth, what's truth, and what's a load of bullshit. It's not fair, but life rarely is, so I have to suck it up. We don't have the luxury of wallowing in philosophical tripe—not when we have a deadline and specific goals for this trip.

"Discussion about possible mating marks *later* then," I mutter as I put my hair up in a high ponytail. "Dealing with egomaniacal Fae now."

Of course, the list of questions about this situation is far *longer than that, but I'm keeping them filed away until it's time.*

Looking at myself in the mirror again, I fight off the never-ending urge to cover myself before I go back into the room. Body dysmorphia isn't something you get over and move on from. It's a constant battle with yourself and it's for the rest of your life, even after you've done the work. I *know* there's nothing wrong with my body in my head and the guys didn't have a single complaint last night. But I hate the thought of walking out there nude in the daylight where they can see every imperfection clearly.

"Are you coming back, Magpie?"

Prez's voice brings me out of my head and I close my eyes for a moment, murmuring my mantra until the anxiety in my veins dies down. When I'm calm, I answer. "Just a minute…"

One more look in the glass has me straightening my spine. These men may have fallen out of the pages of a damn Playgirl, but I'm Jolene Whitley. I partied my way around the globe like a rockstar and not once did *anyone* make a remark about what I looked like. That trauma belongs to high school Jolene and though two of my guys remember her, they've both admitted they liked her.

My past pain does not define my future happiness.

I smile, squaring my shoulders, and head out the door into the room. The hottest men I've ever known all look at me with hunger in their gazes and my gut flutters with pleasure. "Here I am."

"We can see that," Teddy growls softly.

My gaze travels over them, taking in the nuances of their true forms. They're more than men; they're legends brought to life. Suddenly, the sexy factor seems less important than knowing I'm a part of a world so vast it threatens to swallow me whole. I wish I could let them know what I can see; I want to share that with them, but deep down, I know I can't. I have to wait for whatever the sign is or everything will get much more complicated. Instead, I distract myself by bringing up another topic.

"Last night was… " I trail off, not able to find an adjective that feels accurate.

"Definitely one for the books," Benjy says as he pulls on a pair of jeans.

Having some of the skin on display covered helps and I laugh softly. "Indeed. Sorry I did that passing out thing. I swear, this shit only happens with you guys. Seer never had to find me blacked out after sex in Europe or anything."

The growl coming from Teddy makes me smile and I walk over to perch on his leg as he sits on the edge of the bed. He buries his face in my neck for a moment and I sense the struggle he's having with not being a super possessive dick. "We're the only ones it will *ever* happen with, so don't apologize."

Presley rolls his eyes as he heads for his bag to grab clothes. "You know that's not entirely true, Big Daddy, so get yourself sorted."

Ugh, I'd forgotten about that for a few, blissful moments.

"We aren't *really* going to keep feeding that monster ego of his, are we?" I laugh as Teddy nips my neck in response, rubbing my cheek on his hair. "I thought you guys were joking."

"Nope," Benjy says in a sassy voice, popping the last letter for emphasis. "We decided we're all in with you two being the big dogs, Princess."

I scrub my hand over my face, knowing this is going to bite me in the ass at some point. "Great. I can't wait for that to come out today."

"It's going to be a tough day," Teddy reminds us as he lifts his head. "We only have a certain amount of time to browse and that assface is definitely going to be there, hovering like a wasp."

"No shit. Alistair Silkshine is the epitome of the spider his name suggests," I quip. I ponder for a moment, wondering if that's some sort of clue or I'm just reading too much into things as I try to make sense of this world.

"He's something else, that's for sure," Wolfie says, his expression unusually feral. "I don't like him and I definitely don't trust him. He knows something about me and what's worse, I think he knows something about Doyle, too."

We all stare at the typically passive vet in shock. He's normally not so vehement, nor is he quite as anxious as he was at the dinner. Could this be why he was having such trouble with Alistair's taunting?

"I didn't catch that," I confess, my heart racing with the thrill of the unknown. "Did any of you?"

The rest of the guys shake their heads and the shining golden man in question glares. "Well isn't that fucking peachy? Now I'm going to have to actually deal with the smarmy shite until I figure out what his game is. Nothing to do with my family is simple and their secrets have quite the price."

"Does it mean we're in more danger?" I ask quietly.

Doyle snorts and rakes his hand through his hair. "If we don't find out who he's been bargaining with, it leaves us very exposed in ways I can't tell you. But I will say it's not something we want to risk."

Just when I thought we might make progress, we're in the middle of yet another mystery.

Who did I piss off in another life?

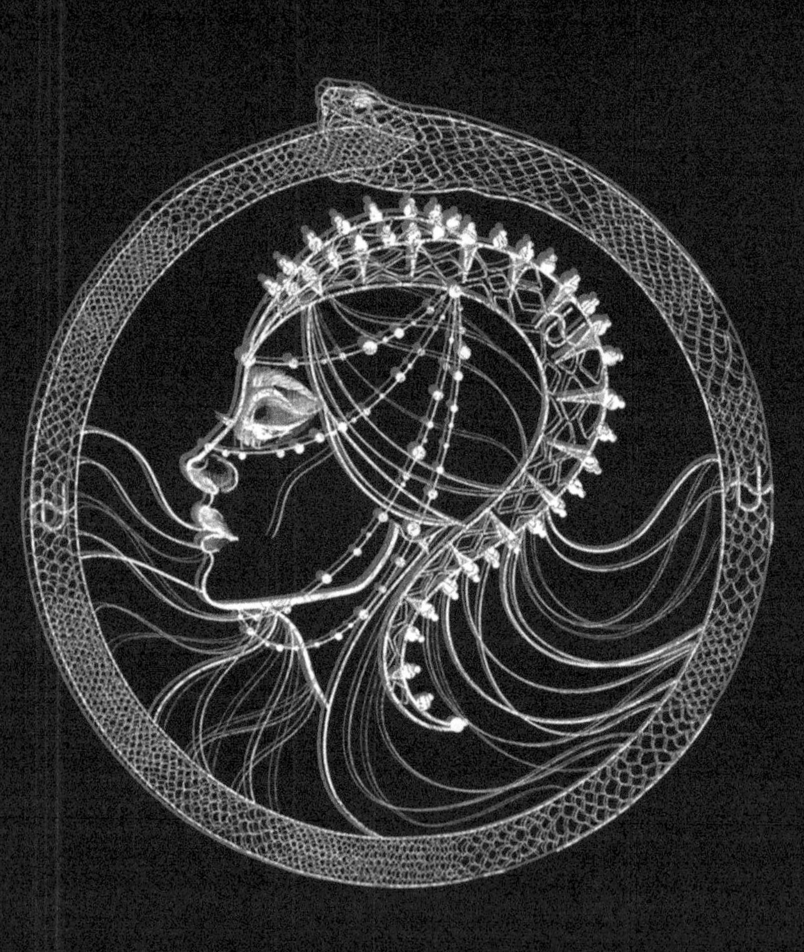

Family

Wolfgang

THE SCENERY FLIES by as we head for the palace, but I'm trapped in my thoughts. I wasn't joking when I dropped that bomb this morning; I'm just not sure *why* I believe it to be true. So much about my empathy is cloaked in vibes and feelings that sometimes I feel like I'm a seer predicting a nebulous future. I'm not, but there's a certain amount of big picture shit that I can sense without knowing what the tiny pieces that formed my view are until everything comes together.

It's the Cassandra effect, Prez says, because most of the time, people don't believe me.

But my family does and they accept that I can't give them solid reasons why I think that jackass knows a hell of a lot more than he's letting on. I spent most of that dinner curled in, but it wasn't about his taunts in regards to my father or Callie. I'm not stupid—I realize my bitchy mother wouldn't stoop to fuck around with someone she considered beneath her. That means the bio dad is a big kahuna of some kind and he's stayed hidden for a good reason.

Who knows what that reason is or even if it's as valid as he thinks, but having to hunt him down makes me believe I'm right. Callie's reticence about details also confirms their union would not have been acceptable. She's not one to give a flying fuck about that shit, so the secrecy must be at my father's demand. To get her to comply, he's either *very*powerful, *very* connected, or has something *very* bad on her. The Cailleach isn't known for doing anything out of the kindness of her heart.

If she has one, it's frozen like the tundra.

"You okay, darling boy?"

Jolene's voice brings me out of my thoughts and I give her a soft smile. She's perched on Teddy's lap in the back of this damn limo, looking completely at ease despite all the challenges we're facing. Once she made her decision about not playing people's games anymore, she pulled on the ripped jeans that hug her like a second skin and shoved her feet in worn combat boots like she was declaring war on the Harvest Fae.

Our girl doesn't do anything half way and I fucking love it.

"Yes. I'm just pondering my theory from earlier. I hate that I can't give you guys better clues as to why I think Alistair knows about Doyle, too." Running my hand through my hair, I give her a sheepish look. "I'm also not used to anyone but Prez believing my weird not-premonitions."

"If you say you have a feeling, we believe you, pup," Teddy says with a shrug. Like Sugarplum, he's dressed more casually than yesterday and we all followed suit. He's a natural leader like his dickhead father and the constant support is more of a balm than he realizes. Even Prez has let go of reins because he knows our alpha dog and our girl have it covered. "I don't give a shit if you can't hand me courtroom proof. There's something to be said for instincts and your gut."

Benjy nods, giving me a thumbs up. "Exactly. You guys aren't really sports folks, but we always trust our captain even if he's running on vibes. This family is our team, so if one of us has a theory, we support it."

"The scary part is none of you realize how often Lucy is right," Prez says with a grin. "It's downright eerie how good he is at reading shit when he can focus. That's why I didn't bother him yesterday; he always looks like a sad panda when he's doing that shit."

Pressing my lips together I give my lover a *look*. "I do not."

"You do, but it's adorable. Shush. I'm trying to be supportive."

I give him another look then turn back to Jolene. "Are you ready to kick some snooty rich guy ass, Sugarplum?"

Her lips curve up and the sparkle in her eyes answers before she speaks. "Today is all about 'come at me, bro.' I'm not seeking out trouble, of course, but I'm done letting that twat fuck with us. If we don't find anything before lunch, we're going back to the hotel to pack up and move on. As cute as this place is, we don't have time to dawdle."

Teddy arches his brow, running his eyes over her with a smirk. "Not looking for trouble, huh? Dressed in… that."

All eyes go back to the holey jeans with her torn Clash tee-shirt and knee-high Docs. She shrugs, one shoulder of the tee slipping to reveal her creamy skin. "I'm wearing normal clothes for a normal errand. Anyone who doesn't like it can catch me outside, how 'bout that?"

I almost choke on the snort that escapes my lips and within seconds, everyone is howling with laughter. She's chosen her armor for its battle cry and her attitude this morning is right in line with the genre. "Prepare for parking lot fist fights…. got it."

"Damn straight."

Doyle squints at her, his hand dropping to pet Hyde absently. "Are you sure you want to provoke them this thoroughly? They have the ability to be very indiscreet about our stay to our future hosts."

Jolene shrugs, looking at us as if waiting for someone to correct her. When we don't, she grins at the mischievous Irishman. "We're sure. If you feel the need to be… *you*… we won't stop you, Lucky."

That gets his attention. Doyle sits up straighter, tilting his head as he studies her resolve, then nods. "Right then. We're here to show them when you fuck around, you find out. Message received."

"Damn," Prez says before he whistles low. "You're *asking* for a show-down letting him off his leash, Magpie. You know that, right?"

"Was she unclear?" Teddy asks mildly, his big hand squeezing her knee. "Tilly said we're done playing nice, so we are. That means within certain boundaries, we're all free to do what we need to in order to get our information or defend our family. Saddle up, gents. This dog and pony show just got interesting."

THE DOUBLE DOORS TO THE PALACE FEEL MORE FORBIDDING TODAY than yesterday, but I think that's because I know Sugarplum's let everyone loose. It felt right when she did it, but standing here, I have yet another flash of intuition—something is going to go awry here. I don't know if it's a good or bad thing yet, but I *know* this visit is going to go off the rails in a major way.

"Let's not keep them waiting," she says as she grabs my hand and squeezes. "I don't want that idiot to think we're scared to see him again."

I lick my lips and nod, but I can't help adding, "Be on your guard, though. I have an odd feeling that this won't go as planned."

Teddy nods, striding up to the doors and pressing the button on the intercom. His posture is full of that 'big dick energy' he and Doyle have going for them as he waits for someone to answer. It makes me smile and when I look at my Sugarplum again, she's doing the same.

Big dogs are gonna strut no matter what, I suppose.

"State your business," the voice snaps.

A wave of irritation rolls over the group and that bad feeling digs into my gut again. Not a good start, especially when we've all been pumped up by our coaches.

"Jolene Whitley and family. We're invited guests of Allora. I highly doubt she forgot to inform you of our imminent arrival this morning."

My eyes widen when the charming, diplomatic Edgar takes his leave completely and puts the barking bully in charge. "Holy shit."

"Guess we're not waiting for them to fire the first shot, Lucy. Prepare yourself for a lot of spiky anger when we get inside," Presley says as he comes up behind me.

I'll say—unless we get the Princess herself, we're going to be greeted by pissy ass staff after that declaration.

The doors open and our leader winks at us, holding one as he gestures for us to precede him. As we step into the corridor, my pulse throbs in time with my footsteps. There isn't any opposition so far, but I can't imagine the steward will be pleased when they get to us. Sugarplum squeezes my hand again and tugs me forward, her gait confident as her ponytail bounces.

I suck in a deep breath, schooling my features like I've watched her and Teddy do, then straighten my spine. Benjy and Doyle are following with their heads held high, eyes moving over the hallway as they take in our surroundings cautiously. It might be the same way we entered last night, but we're not here as compliant guests today. Our family was invited to peruse the archives by the princess so we're not here to kiss anyone's ass.

"Was that tone necessary, Your Honor?" A short Fae appears in front of us, his arms crossed over his chest as he glares up at Teddy. He's obviously required to observe protocol and use the honorific, but he doesn't want to. The expression on his face and the ramrod posture he's projecting make that abundantly clear.

Jolene steps forward before he can answer, looking down at the brownie. "It was. The greeting was rude, which I doubt is normal for someone who works for such gracious people as the Hieronymous and Allora. It makes me wonder if you knew who was there and *chose* to be snide. Is that what happened or did you make an error on a bad day?"

The mustachioed man looks even more furious at her question. He huffs, then turns on his heel. His voice is less aggressive when he calls over his shoulder. "Follow me to the archives. Do not dawdle or deviate from our path. You have not been cleared for any other area of the building."

I get the feeling this fucker works for the Queen; she seems like the type who would employ a nasty little weasel to greet people.

We follow the steward down a hall, around a few turns, and down two separate staircases until we reach another large set of double doors. He sneers at us as he pulls a big key ring out, using it to unlock the doors. The room he reveals is *not* the book filled hall from last night—no, it's an enormous, dimly lit underground room with row after row of ancient looking tomes and scrolls.

"Allora will join you shortly to review the archivists' guidelines for using our treasured library. You may wait inside until she arrives, but *do not* touch anything. There are..." he pauses for a moment and looks as if he's searching for a word. "...*security measures* in place to ensure none of our most valuable records are used or taken. It is a rather aggressive system and I do not recommend trying your luck until she disarms it."

Excellent. He's telling us this is guarded by nasty magic that will hurt or kill us if we get impatient.

"Thank you for informing us," Jolene says as her eyes roam the room curiously. "It must have been difficult not to leave us to our own devices without relaying that knowledge. You made a good choice."

The stout Fae gives her a sour look, then marches off, leaving us standing in the room alone.

"You really are ready to do battle today, aren't you, Princess?" Benjy says with a soft chuckle. "I thought you were going to curb stomp that little dickwad when he mouthed off to Big Daddy."

Her head whips around and she gives him a venomous glare. "Shh-hhh. If that nickname gets around, you'll be the one in my hot seat, Benjamin Foster. We'll see just how much *you* like a red ass."

He shrugs and gives her a bright grin. "For you, I'll try anything once, Mama J."

What the hell life am I living right now?

Jolene Whitley has torn every one of us down and we're all building back up together and I am *here for it.*

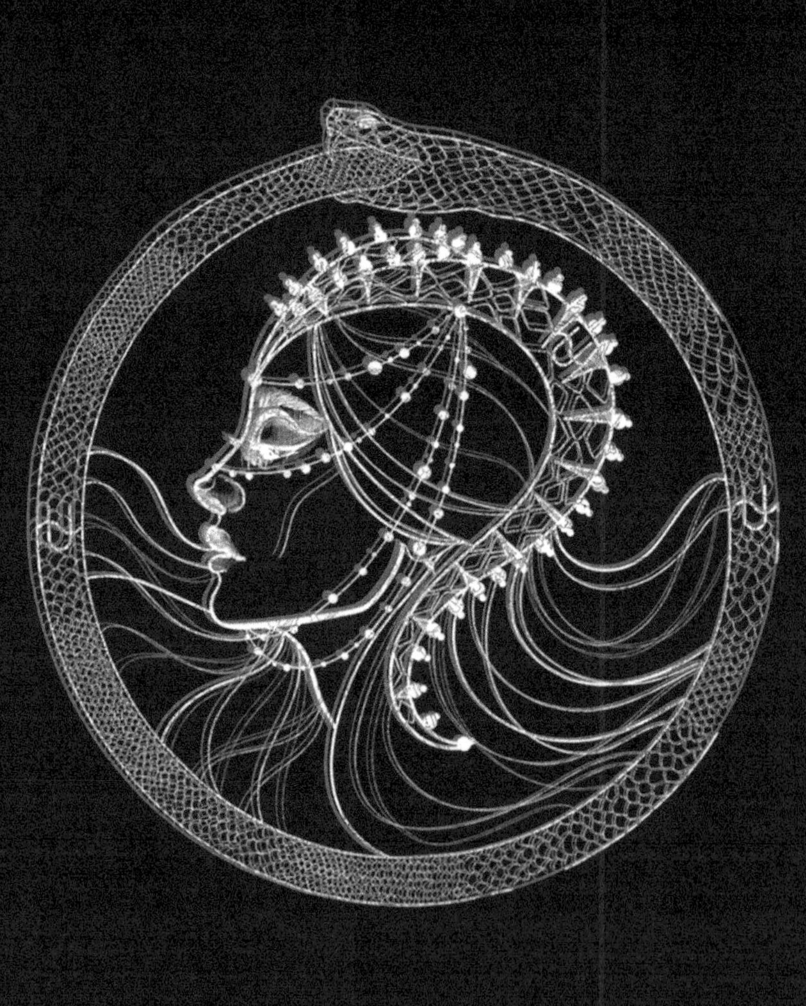

Secrets

Jolene

The air is thick with the scent of old paper and dust, a perfume that stirs an odd sense of reverence within me. My gaze drifts over stacks on stacks of ancient tomes, their bindings etched with time's tender caress. It's like stepping into a world where history pulses through the very walls, whispering secrets of ages past. I've always loved libraries and one of the extremely geeky, touristy things I made Seer do in every city we visited was to go places like this. It always feels like knowledge is just pouring into the air, waiting for you to grab on to it.

The guys haven't seen this side of me yet, though I know Teddy and Benjy remember how much time I spent in the library as a teen.

"I'm so happy you were able to return," Allora's voice is melodic yet hushed, as if the library itself demands a certain solemnity. She moves with an ethereal grace as she enters.

I step aside as she walks over to a pedestal by the wall, glad we have at least one ally in this damn place. She places her hand on a piece of glass above it, and a series of intricate symbols glow with a pale blue light. Her fingers are quick as she pushes various fast moving things on the screen as if playing a very high tech version of Simon. A tinkling sound echoes through the room and I hear something that sounds like a pop before she turns to us again.

"There we are. The security systems are quite particular. It's keyed to certain people and requires a light touch," she explains vaguely.

She doesn't meet my eyes, so I simply nod. Feigning ignorance is my only option until I'm allowed to know shit, but my mind reels with curiosity. That seemed like it might be magic mixed with tech—something that fascinates the hell out of me. I don't know that I have innate abilities that would allow me to work with such a fancy system, but I'd love to feel that secure in my house.

Damn the assholes who put this stupid ban on telling people like me what the hell is going on.

"Over there, you'll find the handling gloves and special cloths for the more delicate pieces," Allora continues, gesturing towards a neatly organized cart.

Bottles of what I assume are preservation liquids line the top shelf and various instruments gleam even in the dim light of the library. They obviously take their stuff seriously, so I shoot Doyle a narrow eyed look. He smirks, holding up his hands in surrender and I turn back to the princess, satisfied none of my crew will fuck around with their important shit.

"Thank you," I say, plucking a pair of white gloves from the pile. They're softer than I expected, almost like they're woven from clouds. I pull them on, and they fit perfectly, as though they were made just for me. No way *that* isn't magic and now I'm even saltier about this situation.

Imagine what that kind of power could do for sheets…

As we walk, Allora points out the different sections, her words carefully curated to keep from violating my silly ban. "This area holds volumes of political history—power struggles, alliances formed and broken over centuries—including with other families and peoples." Her fingers trace the spines of bound leather, the embossed titles indecipherable to my untrained eye.

"Social and practical histories are through here," she gestures towards another row, lined with scrolls sealed with ribbons and wax.

"You'll find accounts of cultural practices, economic developments, and other significant societal evolutions."

I can't help wondering who they're significant to, but I keep the question to myself. I don't want to fuck anything up and get her in trouble, either. She's doing us a huge favor allowing us into this vault of knowledge. We can't make her life any more difficult than it already appears to be.

"Of course, we have our mythological annals as well." Her smile is tight as she nods towards a section that seems to hum with an energy all its own. "Tales of heroism, tragedy, creatures of legend... they provide essential context for understanding the broader picture."

"Sounds fascinating," I reply, my throat dry. I'm itching to dive into those stories, to see the hidden threads of magic and Fae that I know must be interwoven in the text. I can't let that show, though, because nothing she's describing would warrant that enthusiastic response. If I look like I'm going to lose my shit, she'll suspect that I know—Allora's not dumb.

"Lastly, newer information from the last century is stored here," she says, indicating a set of shelves less burdened by the weight of time. "It includes various interactions and events involving multiple groups, even some pertaining to sister courts."

Sister courts? Was that slip on purpose?

My heart skips a beat. I'm so close to the knowledge I crave, yet it feels just out of reach, veiled in Allora's careful phrasing. There's a dance happening here, one where every step and turn is measured, deliberate.

"Allora," I start, trying to sound casual, "have you ever come across something in these histories that surprised you?"

"Constantly," she replies, her eyes finally locking onto mine. There's a depth there, an ancient knowing that sends a shiver down my spine. "History has a way of unfolding in unexpected patterns. Sometimes what we believe to be true is merely a fraction of the story."

Her words echo in my mind, a puzzle begging to be solved. But for now, I simply nod, my hands itching to peel back the layers of the past hidden within these walls. I follow her lead, each step taking me deeper into the labyrinth of knowledge, the threshold between what is known and what is meant to remain secret.

The scent of ancient leather and dust fills my nostrils in the next part of the library. The air is cool and still as if it too is holding its breath in anticipation. Allora's slender hand traces the spines of books so old I fear they might crumble under her touch. Something about the way the tomes here are displayed gives me a hint and my eyes widen when I figure it out.

"Genealogy?" I ask, my voice a whisper amongst the towering shelves. "We're hoping to find something on lineage."

Teddy grunts and I note him putting a hand on Wolfie's shoulder. They've been quiet as our guide led us around, but I imagine they're concerned what would happen if I were to be allowed to dig into this section.

"Ah, yes," she replies, her gaze lingering on a heavy tome bound in dark green leather. "There is a section for that, but Wolfie will need to go through it with Teddy." She pauses, her cough delicate like the flutter of moth wings. "You understand, such materials require... specific clearance."

"Of course," I say, nodding even though frustration knots my stomach.

Everyone around me plays their part perfectly, faces schooled into understanding. I know better. It's not about clearance; it's about keeping secrets from my 'human' eyes. The same secrets my now useless dream glasses are supposed to shield me from. I bite back a bitter smile – if only they knew how clearly I see through their charade.

"Benjy, Doyle," Wolfie calls out, "you take ancient history. Teddy and I will handle genealogy."

They nod, making their way toward the dustier end of the library where time seems to have stilled, leaving whispers of the past clinging to the air.

"Magpie, you're with me," Presley says, gesturing toward the newer archives. His eyes glint with a scholar's fervor, unaware of the unease tightening my muscles.

"Let's get started then," I reply, trailing behind him.

As we approach the sleek terminals set against the stone walls, the juxtaposition of old-world charm and new-age tech strikes me. I sit down at a computer, my fingers hesitating over the keys.

This is where I'll either find answers or more riddles.

"Look for anything related to notable figures in the last century, especially if they seem to be avoiding the media," Presley instructs before he gets absorbed in his own search."I think that's where we're going to find this guy—in the shadows, not in the spotlight."

"Agreed," I murmur, my heart pounding as I delve into digital records.

The screen illuminates my face as I comb through an intricate web of sites and services. There's a whole other world of communication sprawling before me. *How could I have been so naïve?* Supes have their own networks, thriving and pulsating right under human noses. No wonder everyone from my past was scrubbed clean from the mundane internet.

They're keeping the profile low where they can't be seen as extraordinary without drawing attention.

"Anything interesting?" Presley asks when I sigh in annoyance. He doesn't look up from his screen and I see him navigating all these unfamiliar windows with ease out of the corner of my eye.

"Somewhat," I answer, careful to keep my tone neutral as I stumble upon a website for message boards. Once I navigate to our home town, I blink in surprise. My men are talked about as if they are celebrities in the Hollow messages. Fame and adoration drip from every post, painting some of them in a light I never considered. The fawning over Teddy isn't shocking, nor is the ire for Benjy because of his split with Sherilynn. But the thirsting over Prez, Wolfie, and Doyle is… intense.

"You seem to be getting the hang of this pretty easily," I comment. Using a half-truth to mask my real discovery is the best I can do. A lot of the gossip on the Hollow board is salacious or downright nasty, so I'm wading through dreck to hunt for nuggets of gold.

"It's pretty simple. I've had to deal with programs like this before at school," he says with a shrug. Prez is too focused to notice my distraction and I know it's because he's assuming the glasses are doing their job.

Too bad that designer chick fucked with them and now I'm getting all the tea I've wanted since they admitted they're hiding shit—or least, some of it.

My curiosity propels me deeper, past the innocuous pages, to forbidden territories. Hybrids, Andromeda Bane, the schools—they're all pieces of a puzzle that's slowly clicking together as I surf their internet. Memories from my childhood align like stars in a constellation, revealing a picture too grand and terrifying to fully comprehend. I lean back in my chair, the weight of knowledge pressing down on me.

"Are you alright?" Presley finally looks at me, a look of concern creasing his brow.

"Fine, just... I'm overwhelmed by how much there is to go through," I admit, offering him a strained smile. "Our hosts and their reciprocal families have lots of connections and get a shit ton of attention online. More than I ever would have realized."

"Do what you can for now," he says, turning back to his work. "We have visits to the last two families left before we jet home. I have a feeling we'll pick up things while we're there, too. This is more like extra credit, you know?"

I grin, looking at him as he pushes his glasses up. Prez is so adorable and so damn easy going. He and Wolfie made the first couple days I was home much more tolerable, especially since I was still fighting Teddy. *Speaking of which…* "Prez?"

"Hmmm?" he murmurs from his computer.

"Not that I'm complaining *at all*, but what the hell happened with you and…" I make a face at my screen as I choke it out, "…Big Daddy Asshole last night?"

He bursts out laughing, swiveling his chair towards me. I do the same, my cheeks flushed as he grins. "Surprised you, didn't I?"

"I mean, yeah?" I tilt my head as my eyes dance. "You're hot as fuck together—in a different way than he is with Wolfie."

"Probably different than Doyle will, too," he says as he takes my hands. "And don't tell me you can't see *that* cause you're not blind, Magpie."

I laugh softly as our fingers twine together. "I'm not dumb enough to think that putting those two tigers in a cage won't result in fighting, fucking, or both. Doyle's about as fluid as they come. He does whatever the hell he wants no matter what anyone thinks."

"Yep," Prez murmurs as he lifts our hands to kiss my knuckles. "I, however, choose people based on emotions. And making Lucy happy is *always* a good way to worm your way into my good graces and perhaps, eventually, into my heart."

Now I get it—the way Teddy takes care of Wolfie made him more attractive until Prez couldn't help himself.

Wrinkling my nose, I lean forward to whisper to him. "I get how you arrived at what happened last night now. What do you think went on with Teddy?"

He snorts and shakes his head. "Oh, Magpie. That man is a sucker for people who love you as much as I am for people who love Lucy. And he's likely always been curious but had no way to explore it before you demanded he accept us. Now he has an entire room full of people to boss around and protect. Edgar Boone is living his absolute *best life* right now."

"You're pretty smart, you know. It's really sexy," I whisper before kissing his lips lightly. "But we have to get back to it or someone's going to come in and threaten to spank us."

"I'd literally *pay* to hear that conversation."

Prez winks at me and scoots back to his computer, leaving me grinning like an idiot as I spelunk my way through the supe internet looking for clues.

I'm living my best life, too.

Destiny

Edgar

The air in the genealogy section is thick with dust and the musty scent of ancient leather, a tangible reminder that history is more than words—it's a living, breathing entity. Harvest Court's secret archives aren't as vast as the Society's, but they're focused on a species determined to keep much of their internal history and strife to themselves. Tilly can't appreciate how rare an opportunity this is until we can be completely honest, but she's going to love it.

The amount of people allowed into this kind of place within Faerie can't be more than a handful a year—less than the Vatican archives, I'd bet.

"Do they feel different to you?" The pup's eyes scan the spines of countless tomes with a mix of reverence, his fingers trailing over the embossed titles. Despite the time crunch, I've noticed he seems wistful at times when we look around these lands. Perhaps a vacation with the family where things aren't so urgent? I file that away in my mental notes for later.

Considering his question, I shake my head. "No more so than the rest of the room. Does it feel different to you?"

"Very. They're humming with energy until I touch them. Once I make contact, they sing."

My brow is furrowed as I take in his words, then I squint at the volumes. "Do they all sound the same, pup?"

"Nope. Some are louder, some are soft, and some are almost silent. Do you think that means something?" He pauses, looking at me with unsure eyes as his hand hovers near a shelf.

That damn doctor wasn't wrong about the submissive Fae—once his hooks are in, you're a goner and I already went down with the ship.

"Probably," I scratch my chin as I pull out a thick book on the history of the Unseelie Courts. "I'd look at the loudest ones first; they might be trying to give you a hint."

Carrying my chosen book to a nearby chair, I leaf through the ornate volume looking for sections that stand out. We don't have time to read everything, so I pull out my phone to snap pictures of anything that catches my eye. We can print this out later and add it to Tilly's board at home if we need to. I doubt the Fae are involved in the mysterious cover-up involving her parents' death, but I think the clues to who and what she is could be anywhere. There's too much unexplained about her and the way she's emerging for it to be anything simple.

Wolfie finally settles on two books, bringing them over with him as he settles on the ottoman to my seat. He curls up on the wide, cushioned footrest, leaning against me as he opens his books. My lips curve up and I drop a hand to run my finger through his hair as we read.

If someone told me I'd be gallivanting through Faerie with my mates and family a couple months ago, I would have laughed in their face.

"Look at this," Wolfie murmurs, pointing to a faded painting of a being shrouded in shadows. The text below the image says it's an advisor to the court known for his cunning, discretion, and power. "Do you think this might be him?"

"Maybe." I squint at the image, then the page, noting there's no name associated with the figure. The book he's flipping through is definitely old as hell and even I feel the buzz coming off of it. It's not calling to me like it did the pup, but there's magic in that book. "We need more than speculation, though. Can you find more references to this advisor?"

"I'll try." He goes back to scanning the text and I watch for a minute. The kid reads so fast it's like the pages are going by in blur. He's so unassuming that I forget he skipped grades and flew through vet school like a blur because he's a damn genius. Looking at him in his element, though, it's impressive as fuck. Wolfie researches like that skinny kid on the crime show Tilly likes and for a moment, I grin when I think about it.

She's forming her own team with a hard-nosed leader, a boy wonder, a kind muscled alpha, a troublemaker, a wizened old soul, a visionary, and a laid back doctor. No wonder she enjoys that shit so much. Hell, now that I think about it, there's some of her in the dark haired chick.

"Teddy?"

Whoops. Got distracted thinking about whether she'd let Benjy call her 'baby girl.'

"Did you find something, pup?" I ask as I return to reality.

"Maybe. More of a question…" Wolfie's voice is laced with frustration as he taps the book page. "If the Society made strict rules about interbreeding, why did they allow people to break them? Why create havens to take care of the results of breaking that edict? I mean, why not hunt down the people who were thumbing their noses at the decree?"

"Rules are for those who fear consequences, not for those who write them," I reply as I turn another page of my book. "Most species aren't forbidden to inter-breed anymore, as you know. There's some historical shit, probably in Benjy and Doyle's section, that will clarify who those rules apply to now. The program was designed to keep lost ones whose parentage might be dangerous from being dropped in the middle of humans to live their lives like normal people. I mean, there are lots of human tales that likely describe that very situation still happening. Look at shit like Hercules or X-Men or Superman."

"So they created the program specifically to monitor the kids who might emerge with multiple sides or powers that would be dangerous. That means the only supes or beings dropping kids at the assigned spots have to be… extremely powerful," Wolfie says, piecing together the history. "Deities, demi-gods, ancients, overpowered shifters, magicals… Anyone who was adopted through the program has the potential to become a huge issue if they aren't watched. That's why they have the Guardians, especially for adoptees who don't emerge when they should."

"Exactly. The Society inducts or employs the unpredictable ones, like us. They monitor the ones who haven't broken their barrier spell because they didn't emerge." Teddy agrees, glancing toward the door as if expecting someone to overhear. "Nelia said there was one a few years ahead of us that seemed like a major concern, but according to her Guardian, she disappeared off the face of the planet. The chick reappeared with suspicious skills that can't be explained, which is why they're so worried about Jolene."

"The Hollow was never just a town," Wolfie whispers as it dawns on him. "It was a crucible for something bigger."

"Likely. They had to wait until the opportunity was right to get control of the town so they could increase cloaking and barrier spells for the humans and non-emerged. The Senator was part of swinging that deal; I remember him being so damn proud of it. Even as a kid, I knew it was a big deal. Whistler's Hollow was the last enclave they got full control over and it was the most important one, he said."

I pinch the bridge of my nose, feeling puzzle pieces slot together from my life, our current situation, and my work with the Society. The people who are pulling these strings aren't evil; they're trying to protect everyone. By the lengths they're willing to go, it stands to reason that there are beings out there that everyone needs protecting from.

They must be working with the Fates to prevent something; that's the only thing big enough to span this many centuries and the entire globe.

"That's why they have Bane in the Hollow," I breathe. "The woman is ancient as fuck and she's been in charge of making certain the emerged here are trained and developed. But lately, they've been sending her on away missions again, which says to me that they feel it's safe to have her absent from town. Why?"

"They've got some chick with powers and no info running loose, as you said. Plus, there's been a lot of Society chatter about supe activity in other parts of the country." Wolfie looks at me for a moment, his brows drawn together as he thinks. "If they were worried about a specific being or events, they'd send their strongest people to deal with it. Andromeda is one… and Saoirse's team must be another. They're being directly instructed by those wacky sisters."

"Christ," I mutter as I scrub my hand down my face. "This shit is hitting the bottom of the ocean. It feels like they've all been moving chess pieces for centuries—or longer."

"Maybe they have," he whispers softly. "So many supes *never* find their mates, Teddy. All of us have landed smack dab in the same town—right at the time our unemerged girl comes blowing in like a hurricane. Doesn't that feel… coincidental? Like *too* coincidental?"

Well, now it does. Fuck. Me. Running.

"To be clear, we're surmising that we are all part of a millennia-long experiment—a test to see how much we could change the game without breaking it. But now whatever the fuck they were worried about is happening, so they're scrambling to 'Avengers Assemble' and make a team?" I shake my head. "Too surreal, pup. This is tin foil hat level shit."

"Maybe," Wolfie says quietly. "You have to admit it's weird. You being the only *triplásia* we've heard of, Doyle and I having mystery dads, Prez being a healer, Jolene reacting to all our supe sides, all being fated… all of that is a lot. And that's without throwing in the companions, a fucking *djinn*, and a *male* seer. It's too much to be random. Mathematically speaking, random isn't…"

"Either way," I sigh, closing the heavy book with a decisive thump, "we're far more entwined than we imagined. All of us might have been drawn here—bound by a secret destiny or some shit."

"Bound by fate," Wolfie muses. "Not something you can plan for, huh?"

I snort. "I spent most of my life rebelling just enough that the Senator couldn't force me into some world-shouldering responsibility. I definitely wasn't looking to get recruited for a Scooby team. Can't we just… run off to the Maldives and buy a fuck hut? I could get Tilly on board; I know it."

He blinks then bursts into laughter. "A fuck hut?"

My eyes narrow and I give the pup my best version of a pout. "Yes, that's what I said. We all chip in and buy a hut on the water. We'll laze in the sun all day and fuck and eat delicious shit. No dangerous world saving fuckery involved."

"You don't like the idea of anyone being in danger," the Fae says with a soft smile. "I get it. Making sure you're not responsible for anything is a reaction to the disappointment your father expressed and—"

"Pup?"

"Hmm?" he asks as he pushes his hair out of his eyes.

"Shut it," I say with a fond grin. "We've got more research to do on your sperm donor before we leave. I want to get as much done here as possible so we don't have to keep working when we get back to the hotel."

Tilting his head, he gives me a serious look. "We didn't talk about what happened last night and even if we can't include Sugarplum, we need to."

I frown. "Because of the doc?"

"No, because I had to magic away a pound of faerie dust, feathers, fluids, and that weird solid dust your mist turned into once our girl passed out." Wolfie makes a face and points at me. "*You* didn't tell anyone your… mist… is solid."

Uh-oh. Admission time.

"That's because it's *never been* solid before," I mutter. "Jolene is changing us in ways we aren't aware of until it happens. I mean, you haven't released that much glittery shit before, either. The doc doesn't leave feathers everywhere. I highly doubt Benjy left sheds like that at home or Sherilynn would have thrown him out long ago. This is *all* new."

"We're getting stronger as she bonds to all the parts," he murmurs. "And she's definitely bonding to them more deeply each time. Did you see her eyes?"

"Yep." I lean back in my chair and look up at the ceiling, blowing out a breath. "We are so fucking screwed, pup."

His head rests on my lap as he responds, "On the bright side, no one's trying to open a Hellmouth, so we have that going for us."

Oh, well, I suppose everything's peachy, then.

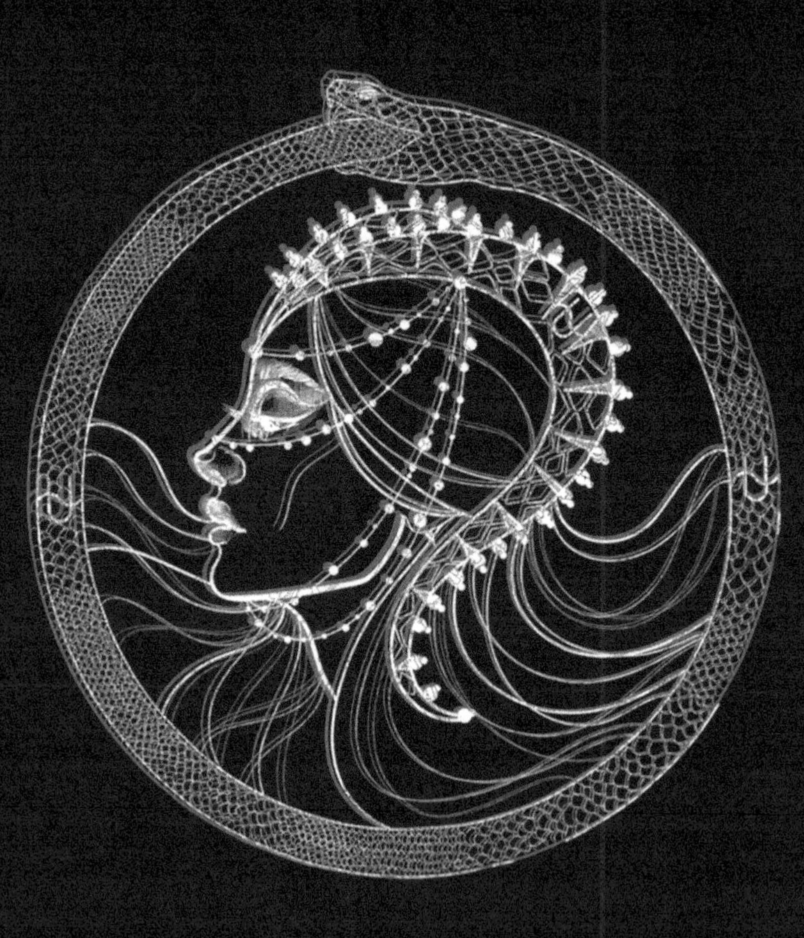

Wish That You Were Here

Hugo

The world folds like origami, edges sharp and sudden, before it bursts into new shapes. I stagger as reality solidifies around us, the air thick with the scent of salt and humid earth. Temporal magic has always had its quirks, but nothing quite compares to the prince's brand of travel.

"Welcome to Brazil, my friend," Dhameer says, a hint of amusement in his voice. He's used to this, as is his staff, but moving through time and space by accessing the object where he exists outside of time is rough.

Not that I have any idea what that object might be—djinn guard those secrets like the Society does the identities of their highest ranking members.

I nod, trying to keep my balance and dignity intact. The once-familiar sensation of ground beneath my feet now seems alien. My words come out shaky, mirroring the tremble in my legs as I finally reply, "That was... intense."

"Quicker than a flight, though, wouldn't you say?" He sweeps an arm grandly, indicating our lavish surroundings, the sun casting glimmers over Rio's skyline visible from our penthouse suite.

"It's perfect if you don't account for the migraine." I press my fingers against my temples, hoping to quell the pounding behind my eyes. My visions, usually a trickle of foresight, are now a deluge of images, crashing over me with no regard for my sanity.

"Ah, yes, your gift can be... inconvenient at times," Dhameer acknowledges, his concern peeking through his usual stoicism as he watches me closely. "You should rest. We have time."

"Rest, he says," I mutter under my breath in half amusement, half exasperation. Those who don't have the 'gift' of sight rarely comprehend what a physical toll it takes on your body. The mental weight is enough to destroy lesser beings, but the bodily symptoms wreck even immortals like me. "As if lying down will stop the kaleidoscope in my head."

"Sometimes, Hugo, you must allow the body to catch up with where the mind has been thrust." His tone brooks no argument—the prince's natural imperiousness ever present in his demeanor. "Do as I say or we won't be able to achieve our goals when you break down."

"Fine." I relent—not because I want to, but because arguing with an ancient royal when I feel like I've been tossed in a cosmic blender is futile. I sink into the plush king-sized bed that looks like it belongs in a museum rather than a hotel room. Closing my eyes, I pray for relief, but the darkness only serves as a canvas for the flashes of places I've never seen and people I've never met.

"Let me know if there's anything you need," Dhameer says, worry creasing his brow. "We could call for a healer—"

"No healers. Just time." I force a tight-lipped smile, opening my eyes to meet his gaze squarely. "It'll pass. Always does."

He nods, though I can tell he's not entirely convinced. The prince moves toward the door, pausing to glance back. "Remember, we have all the comforts of Olympus here. Use them."

With that, he steps out, leaving me to wrestle with my own turbulent senses. Finally alone, I focus on breathing.

Inhale. Exhale. Repeat.

My thoughts drift despite my efforts to anchor them. I try to piece together any coherence from the maelstrom of my visions, but it's like grasping at smoke. All I manage is to catch glimpses—a street carnival exploding in color, a woman's cry, the flit of a shadow just out of reach.

Hours pass, or minutes—it's hard to tell. Slowly, the flashes subside, and the migraine dulls to a persistent throb. I sit up, testing my equilibrium, relieved to find the world holding steady. I rise, steadier now, and walk to the window. Rio sprawls before me, lively and vibrant. I watch the city pulse with life, and promise myself that I'll partake in it—as soon as I'm truly able. For now, though, I am content to observe from this quiet refuge, gathering strength for what lies ahead.

THE SUN DIPS BELOW THE HORIZON, SPILLING MOLTEN GOLD ACROSS the opulent room. I stand by the window, a silent sentinel, fingers tracing the chiseled marble of the windowsill. Outside, Rio de Janeiro hums with unceasing energy, but within these walls, there's a different kind of intensity brewing.

"Any improvement?" Dhameer's voice ripples through the stillness as he enters, bearing a sheaf of papers that whisper promises and secrets.

"The visions are clearer," I answer, turning to face him. "No more riddles from the ether—for now." Relief is a tangible thing in my chest, yet it's laced with caution; my gift never allows for complacency.

"Good. We need clarity if we're to unravel this mess." Dhameer spreads the documents on the mahogany desk, his brow furrowed in concentration. "Our thread leads here, to Brazil. The assassin—or assassins—who executed that officer in Istanbul and decimated an entire family... they've left traces. Infinitesimally small traces, of course, but Isra was able to track them down for me."

I join him at the desk, my gaze flitting over the pages, each one a breadcrumb on a trail we must follow. "Human criminals?" I muse aloud, the notion foreign yet plausible amidst the chaos we've encountered.

"It would seem so. Saoirse's intel suggests they're operating under the noses of human law enforcement with ease. Though in the Society's defense, I can understand why no one understood this particular assignment had bearing on the supernatural world. We don't interfere in human affairs without just cause, so this group hasn't been on the agents' radars, either." He taps a photo of a group of people in black with obscured faces gathered in shadows, and I feel the weight of their deeds like a yoke around my neck.

"Then we'll shine light into those shadows to see what they're hiding." Determination steadies my voice even though getting involved with humans gives me pause. Oracles don't interact with them much anymore, except for me, and my assignment has always been to observe and report. I've kept myself apart from the citizens in the Hollow purposefully to honor that agreement, but this skirts the line of what my people are allowed to do.

I could get in a lot of trouble for taking part in this—maybe even be recalled to the temple—but it's worth it for her.

"Exactly." Dhameer's agreement is fierce, a warrior's pledge.

He rifles through the stack, showing me a few more clues his faithful guard gathered. Isra found records of their individual entries into the country, a few clues about where they might have gathered after they arrived, and the last part is what led us to Brazil—four separate identities that left Turkey. They snaked around the globe before ending up in Brazil, but their trail is here in black and white.

I look around, taking in the lavish surroundings—the villa is grandiose, sprawling. It's hard not to feel dwarfed by the scale of luxury, by the sheer opulence that seems to mock my Spartan tendencies. The Temple of our lady is luxurious, but the acolytes who live there do not stay in that environment. Our quarters are nearby and virtually barren to prevent clutter from clouding our visions. My apartment in the Hollow is similar—it's what I know and feel comfortable in.

"Is something wrong?" Dhameer catches my gaze, a corner of his mouth quirking up in understanding.

"Olympus wasn't built in a day," I quip, trying to shake off the discomfort. Riches have never been something I sought; I've always found more value in the unseen, in the visions that guide me.

"Consider our journey practice," he says with a chuckle. "This is nothing compared to the halls of gods and heroes you've tread. I'm aware of the Greeks' love of exorbitant surroundings."

"True," I concede, a smile tugging at my lips. "Though I doubt Zeus concerns himself with air conditioning glitches or Wi-Fi passwords. He's more of a delegator."

"Ah, but does he have a view like this?" Dhameer gestures towards the panoramic vista of Rio's night skyline, winking with endless lights.

Olympus moves, so he could if he chose. But that's information I definitely cannot share.

"Point taken." I allow myself a moment to marvel at it all—one does not simply overlook the beauty of the mortal realm when you have the chance. All the work various deities put into this world as it developed is breathtaking, even after so many years on this plane.

"Come, let's focus. There's much to do, and time, as ever, is a fickle ally." He turns back to the papers, his demeanor shifting to that of the general he truly is, mapping out the terrain of our investigation.

As I lean over the desk, poring over maps and notes, I can't help but feel a surge of gratitude. For all its strangeness, this journey, this mission—it binds us together, a fellowship cast against darkness. And in the heart of this gilded cage, we forge our resolve, ready to confront whatever may come.

THE HUMID AIR OF RIO CLINGS TO MY SKIN LIKE A SECOND, STICKY shadow. Fazal and Isra have already melted into the throngs outside, their silhouettes fading among street vendors and pulsing samba rhythms.

"Think they'll get what we need?" I ask Dhameer, watching the crowd swallow his two closest advisors.

"Isra's instincts are sharper than a viper's fangs," he replies without looking back at me, his eyes scanning the sea of humanity with an analytical gaze. "And Fazal has a way with words that could sell sand to a desert."

I nod, the weight of the mission nesting uneasily in my stomach. We need connections, threads to pull us closer to the web of assassins we're hunting. The thought of what those threads might lead to sends a chill through me despite the sweltering heat.

Once we put together all the intel Isra gathered, Dhameer called Jolene's Guardian and she insisted we wait until she arrived. She's been losing her mind cooped up with her family and the human; I think the prince took pity on her, so he used the same method of travel to bring her to Rio while Fazal procured earwigs for us. The careful inquiries Isra made in the marketplace this afternoon gave us the time and place for a private party at a villa in the hills we believe will help us make contact with an informant.

Now he and I are on the guest list of the affair, which allows his staff and the Guardian entry to snoop around the mansion.

"Got it," Saoirse's voice cuts through my reverie, her determined tone ringing clear even over the din. "Lead confirmed. I'm on it."

"Alone?" Isra's voice is cool, but the disdain for an operative so opposite of her isn't lost on me. The lesser djinn does not like all the new people in the Prince's life and I suppose after centuries of working for him, I don't blame her.

But Seer knows what she's doing or the Society wouldn't have her guarding an unemerged lost one.

"Listen, grumpy. I can handle myself. Besides," Saoirse retorts in irritation. "Hugo and Dhameer will see me safely to the rift once I accomplish our mission and you'll be rid of me. Don't get your armor in a bunch."

"Let's make haste, then," Dhameer says, breaking the tension. "We have a party to attend."

The castle looms before us, its walls steeped in history and secrets. It reminds me of *Schloss Neuschwanstein*, but any whimsy is snuffed out by the realization of its dark past. I feel a shiver travel up my spine as we pass under the archway, the sense of walking through a portal into a time best forgotten.

"Escaped Nazi legacy in full effect here," Saoirse mutters, her eyes flitting across the grandeur, the opulence built upon the bones of atrocities. She speaks for the ghosts who can no longer cry out. "This shit makes my skin crawl."

"Tomorrow," Dhameer whispers to her, his voice a low growl of promised vengeance. "Isra will return, and the past shall fear the future."

"Good." Her lips curve into a smile, but there's no joy in it—only the sharp edge of a blade thirsting for righteousness. The Valkyrie in her has never been quite so obvious as right now—Dhameer's promise of justice for the innocent makes it shine like a beacon.

I watch the two fierce warriors, cloaked in the finery of a gala but armored with conviction stronger than steel. As I stand beside them, I realize that while I falter amidst the luxury that feels foreign to my touch, I am anchored by something far greater— faith in the visions that guide us.

"Let's not linger any longer than necessary," I suggest, the mansion's tainted legacy weighing heavily on me.

I do not want to get trapped in visions here; the rancid atmosphere is crawling over me as it is.

"Agreed," Dhameer says, his eyes briefly meeting mine before returning to the task at hand. "We dance with wolves tonight, but we do not join their pack."

With my friends by my side, I step further into the lion's den, ready to face whatever beasts may lurk within.

Hopefully, the risk is worth the reward.

Quiet

Jolene

The air in the digital archives hums with a kind of static energy, as if the magic vibrates through the cables, connecting us to the outside world. Silver-blue screens cast an eerie glow on Presley's determined face as he methodically captures the last bits of data. I'm saving photographs of scroll after ancient scroll like a thief of knowledge in a treasure trove that stretches back centuries.

Too bad I have to continue this ridiculous charade of not understanding what I'm screenshotting.

"Do you think we've got enough to piece together what we need to know?" Presley's voice cuts through the silence.

Suppressing the urge to roll my eyes at him—because how the fuck would I know since I'm not supposed to be able to see the real texts—I push back from the table with a sigh. "More than enough. Their past is written in more than just words. It's in their actions—the deals they made and broke."

Presley nods, tapping his phone before he frowns at his screen again. "Allora mentioned the 'sister' courts, right? Hopefully, you found references to them. I think our current and previous hosts pretend they're the sunshine twins, but I bet their shadows cast just as darkly as the others when it comes to politics."

"We're about to walk into part of that shadow later today. I don't know if this will help us, but I made sure to get anything that seemed noteworthy." My mind races as I reflect on our next destination—the Midnight Court. Home to Alistair, with his eyes like twilight storms and a demeanor just as unpredictable, it's not known for being the most vicious, but it's a close second.

We're willingly entering the belly of the beasts despite being hampered by that damn oath; I don't like it.

"Jolene," Presley leans closer, lowering his voice, "these families play the game differently. Like our snooty friend from dinner, they craft confusion until you're trapped in a labyrinth of your own making. We all need to be more cautious with what we say and do—even in private."

"Gee, I was hoping we'd go somewhere that makes me worry I'm being spied on while we fuck. It was on my 'to-do' list for next year," I quip. I sound like I'm joking, but based on the tricks and traps I've been reading about, it's not outside of the realm of possibility. It's not like they'd release revenge porn, but they will use shit they have no right to in order to get ahead in negotiations. Every court dances around truth as if it were a flame—beautiful to behold but perilous to touch—but the next Fae we visit seem to have mastered intrigue.

That is, if you believe everything you read online—which I don't.

"I'd say fuck this, but we need them." His reminder is like a pin to a balloon, deflating any illusion of avoiding their bullshit. "We're more likely to find details about Wolfie's father or perhaps even the man himself in these destinations. It's important to him, so we have to make it work."

"The risk is why most people avoid them entirely unless they have specific needs. It's pretty clearly outlined in everything I found— don't fuck with the dark houses." I shrug, leaning back in my chair as I try to dance around what I know again. "But they have a big industry and whatever it is they provide is in demand, hence all the tales of *caveat emptor* about making deals with them."

"Big gains," the doctor muses, "big risks. People know what they're getting into when they come calling. That doesn't make it right, but it does help us figure out what to watch for, I suppose."

"Exactly." I exhale, the weight of what lies ahead settling on my shoulders. We're about to dive headfirst into a world where even the flora may have fangs and every bargain is a beast waiting to pounce. I thought the crap the rich people in the Hollow put me through was bad, but I have a feeling this is going to much worse.

No room for mistakes with this one, Whitley.

"Ready to pack up?" Presley asks, glancing at the clock. Time has slipped away from us, hiding in the crevices between each revelation and secret we've unearthed and we definitely need to get moving if we want to arrive in the next place before dark.

"Ready as I'll ever be."

My affirmation is a battle cry tinged with trepidation. As we gather our devices and exit our section of the library, the light shifts, casting long shadows that mimic the ones we're stepping towards. I squint, tilting my head as I watch them change in the flickering light. They grow, mimicking horrified faces, then change back to our normal profiles.

Hell, even this damn place knows we're heading into the great unknown... fantastic.

THE ANCIENT HISTORY SECTION OF THE LIBRARY IS A SANCTUARY OF hushed whispers and the musty scent of time-worn pages. This looks like some of the old libraries I toured throughout Europe more than the section we just left. I close my eyes, inhaling the scent of lignin with a smile. No matter how many people try to make candles and shit that carry its scent, there's nothing like the real thing.

Hovering between rows of towering bookshelves, I run my fingers over the texts carefully. Some are well used—their spines are cracked and faded. Others look as if they've rarely been touched and I wonder if the royal library takes donations or if they simply gather copies of everything they can like literary hoarders. I'm all for it either way, but a girl could get lost for weeks in this damn place.

How do they get anything done when they could be down here?

"Over here, Magpie," Presley calls out softly. His voice is barely more than a whisper in the quiet atmosphere, but it echoes through the large section. The dimly lit historical archive has architecture that amplifies sound and I haven't the foggiest idea why anyone would do that.

As I ponder that odd feature, I navigate toward his voice. He's gone deeper into the stacks to find our companions and though my steps are muted on the thick carpet, he turns as soon as I get close. Benjy is at a big mahogany table, poring over a pile of scrolls so ancient, I fear they might crumble under his touch. He doesn't look up, keeping his hands steady on the equipment he's using to ensure he doesn't damage them. Doyle, however, is the picture of idleness, sprawled out on a high-backed chair with one leg lazily thrown over the armrest.

"Did you wear yourself out lounging about while we were all working?" I ask drily as I peg Doyle with a disapproving glare.

"Appearances are deceiving, Tíogair." The Irishman flashes me a roguish grin and lifts his phone, the screen aglow with images of text in languages that twist and coil like serpents. "I snapped these while you two were digging into digital dirt. These scripts are relics, but we can unlock their secrets with the right tools."

"Show-off," I mutter. His brows bob and I walk over to peck his cheek in apology. "Sorry for jumping up your ass without any proof. I know you're trying to contain the chaos as much as possible."

"Ah, but you weren't wrong to suspect me. I have been doing this the easy way while Foster took the worst of it," he admits, eyes twinkling with mischief. "But I didn't sit around with my thumb up my ass, so I'll accept your gracious apology."

The Universe is testing me, I think as I pinch the bridge of my nose. *And I'm going to fail eventually because my patience snapped.*

"Found anything juicy, Benjy?" Presley distracts me from strangling Doyle as he leans over the giant's shoulder, looking at his current focus curiously.

"Legends and lore," Benjy rumbles. "Tales of ceremonial… wedding things, cryptic references to original treaties... It's like piecing together a puzzle without the picture on the box."

"Sounds about right," the doc says as he blows out a breath. "Most families like this are so intertwined that they're almost incestuous. It changes the dynamic from strictly political to a very dangerous familial one. That means what you find will include influences beyond the normal business of the land intrigue—it's tainted with interpersonal shit as well."

"Family secrets are difficult to uncover when people want them buried badly enough," I murmur, my thoughts drifting to the truth about my mother. "People will do anything to keep some things from becoming public knowledge. That's pretty true in the normal royals around the world, too. Europe is full of random people connected to old royal lines through adultery or marriage. They only trusted people of their own station."

"Those people made powerful allies or formidable enemies—many leaders will choose the former. That's why there was so much inbreeding going on." Prez grins, pushing his glasses up as he looks at me.

"Often that led to finding out the object of their alliance was both, if they were not careful," I say thoughtfully. "Alistair's family are like sirens luring sailors to their doom for Allora's family. Their beauty masks the danger beneath, but the risk involved must be worth the price."

"Charming analogy, love, but that can't be our concern right now," Doyle says grimly. "You may like the girl and I do, too, but our biggest concern has to be getting what we need. Once we do, we can go home and leave the expert level bullshit here."

"There's still bullshit to deal with in the Hollow," I correct him as my gaze flicks over the snaps of foreign script on his phone. "We're not going back to a rose garden, Lucky."

Benjy puts down his work, looking up at us with a sigh. He rolls the scrolls carefully, his large hands gentle as he puts them into the casing. "You're both right. However, we can't stand around and argue because we have a date with a bunch of manipulative asshats tonight."

"He's right," I whisper. "We have to get on the road in time to arrive before dark; that was a very stringent recommendation in the things I read today."

"Then let's not keep them waiting," Prez says with a wink. "We'll grab Boone and Lucy, then get back to the hotel to pack up the animals. We're not going to give these fuckers anymore advantage than they have before we get there."

His resolve steadies my nerves and I nod. "Let's blow this joint."

WOLFIE'S VOICE CUTS THROUGH THE DENSE SILENCE OF THE genealogy section as we walk in. "Honestly, this is a mess, Teddy. Alistair's marriage to Allora is all political maneuvering. Dumb crap about heirs and lineage that the royals care about far too much."

"Isn't it always that way with your kind?" Teddy mutters as he flips through a book that looks like it's going to fall apart. "I mean, sometimes there's other stuff like—"

"Money," Wolfie continues as he looks up at him seriously. "They don't want to join forces with Midnight, but the Queen seems to be pushing the King. I wonder why." He pauses, eyes narrowing, as if seeing the chessboard of intricate politics in his head. "Hieronymous isn't exactly in good health, particularly mentally. If something happens to Allora, there will be a fight. I can smell the greed coming from her stepmother."

"Charming family dynamics," I say when they notice we're here. "It's almost like we're not the only ones with fucked up relatives. Oh, wait… that's everyone."

I think I'm funny, but apparently none of them do.

"Tilly, you spent a shit ton of time with lots of rich assholes and celebs. Do you think their problems are the same as normal folks?" Teddy grins and shrugs. "Everyone's family has issues, but when you throw in money, fame, and politics… dysfunction takes on a life of its own. As much as I'd like to write off this stuff as 'not our problem,' I worry it's going to affect our time in our future locations."

"You're right," she exhales sharply.

"Alistair is the oldest of seven siblings—all sisters. His mother died young, and his oldest sister is the heir apparent. He never had a chance when it came to taking control of their family. That definitely means he's up to something," Wolfie says softly as he looks up at me.

"Alliance through marriage," I muse aloud. "That's why his father offered him up—to cement peace between the courts—but I doubt it's why he agreed. He's got other motivations and he'll screw with us simply to see if it helps him get ahead."

"Exactly," Teddy says grimly. "Neither Alistair or Allora are thrilled, but it's a union meant to strengthen their bloodlines, not their hearts."

I can't imagine being stuck with fucking Trevor now that I know who he is; having to deal with Alistair has to be no better for Allora.

The door creaks and I wave my hand, hoping to quiet them without saying anything. When no one shows, I frown and make a slashing motion across my throat. If someone's listening in, they can't hear us speculating about this topic.

"Tell me we have something to eat in this trove of knowledge," Wolfie grumbles as he rises to his feet. His eyes dance as he winks at me and I have to cover my mouth so I don't laugh.

Definitely never assigning him any undercover duties.

"Later," I promise. "We've got to make tracks if we want to hit the next stop by nightfall."

"Night travel isn't wise where we're going. You guys ran into that advice, too, right?" Teddy asks as he runs a hand through his disheveled hair.

"Speaking of which," Allora appears out of nowhere to interrupt us with a smile. "I've arranged transport for you. My driver will ensure your safe passage."

"That's more than kind of you," I say, studying her face for any sign of deception. I don't find it, but there's a feeling of something unsaid that prickles the back of my neck.

Could she have overheard Alistair plotting to mess with us?

She smiles again, looking me in the eyes. "I'd feel terrible if some-thing happened to people who were under our care when traveling through such difficult terrain. It's my pleasure to ensure your safe arrival."

The way she's looking at me speaks volumes even if she's not saying it out loud. We need to be cautious on our way and she's hoping her staff will deter any shenanigans. I hold out my phone, giving her a knowing grin. "We should keep in touch. Share your contact with me and I'll do the same before we go."

"Excellent idea, Jolene," she replies as she whips out a device to do so.

Of course the weird iridescent, winged thing she thrusts forward is not a damn thing like my iPhone, but I have to pretend I don't see it hovering mid-air.

"We'll head out now and gather our things. Will your cars know when to meet us?" Prez asks as he extends a hand to help Teddy up.

"Of course. They'll follow you to your hotel and wait for you to come down with your animals," Allora says. "Though I am sad I did not get to meet them properly. Perhaps in the future?"

Teddy snorts. "Perhaps if you're alone."

Allora does her best to hide a laugh and I wink at her. "Enough jokes, guys. Super un-fun assholes await."

That's about as much as I can say about our future hosts without wanting to smash something.

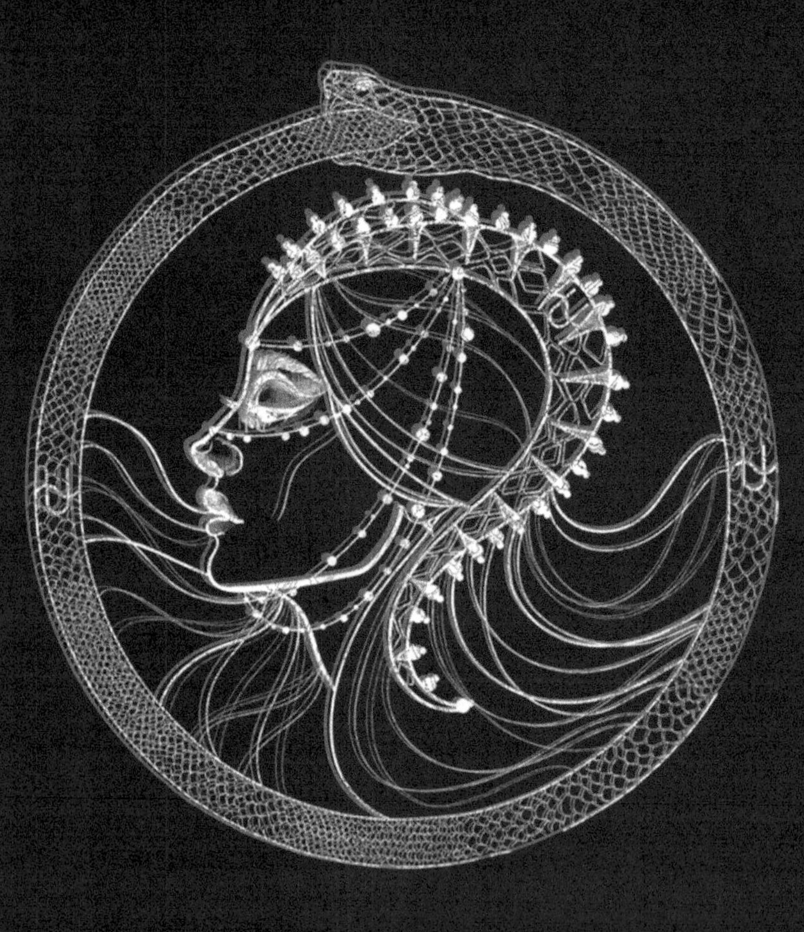

Rise

Benjy

The hotel room is a stifled mess of suitcases and animal gear when I step in.

Teddy's hovering over the King Danes, whispering last-minute instructions that sound more like pep talks. "Stay close to Presley, you two. We're in for a bumpy ride," he murmurs, stroking their glossy coats with a gentle hand. The servals are less compliant, their golden eyes flashing with mischief as they swat at the judge when he tries to dangle leashes in front of them.

I doubt that's going to work; Jolene never makes them wear that shit.

"Ready, Benjy?" Presley calls out as he steps back from Euryale. The giant bird is even bigger inside a building, but he acts like it's tiny parrot. It's weird until you realize his shifted form is a bird that dwarfs the eagle in size by leaps and bounds.

"Almost," I reply, zipping up my duffel bag with a final tug. "Just need to grab my—"

"Your what? Your sense of impending doom?" Teddy interjects, his voice laced with dark humor as he eyes Allora's cars outside the window. To anyone else, they are sleek black SUVs, but through our knowing gaze, they shimmer with enchantment, transforming into majestic royal carriages waiting to whisk us away.

"Can't forget that. We're going to need it," I shoot back grumpily. My gut churns with the kind of apprehension that precedes a storm, and Jolene's obliviousness only amplifies it. She sits on the edge of the bed, scrolling through her phone, the very picture of calm, but that's only because she doesn't actually understand how dangerous our next two visits will be.

This bullshit about not telling her has made everything ten times more difficult and I want to strangle someone every time I think about it.

Once everything is settled, we head downstairs to the cars. Doyle and Presley lost the rochambeau, so they get to take up the rear with our menagerie and luggage. Allora's guards nod to us, their faces unreadable masks as they takes the reins up front. I wonder what Princess sees when she looks at this crazy Cinderella-esque get-up? Probably some Secret Service SUV bullshit, I suppose. Shaking my head, I climb into the damn thing, settling next to her on the opposite side of Teddy.

"Teddy," Jolene says firmly. "I appreciate your skepticism, but I really believe Allora is our friend. She didn't have to offer this, nor did she have to hint that something might be coming on the horizon. She took a huge risk, I bet."

"Forgive me if I can't simply accept it at face value, Tilly," Teddy grumbles. He understands Allora's plight: forced to marry Alistair, used as a pawn in a game we're all too familiar with because the Hollow politics aren't much different. That doesn't mean my old friend is going to entrust someone we just met with our girl. "I've learned to question everything and it's kept my ass out of the fryer many times."

He's not saying that if she were less trusting, she would never have become the Catastrophe years ago, but it's true.

"I get it; I really do," Jolene says softly, "so are these night family folks —are they really as cutthroat as the forums say? Do you think they actually do the whole mafia-style make them disappear shit? If so, I know how to deal with it, but I need to know if you believe it so I can prepare myself."

"Cutthroat?" Wolfie laughs without humor, pushing up from where he'd been lying with his head in Teddy's lap. "They'd consider that a compliment. They're masters of manipulation, always angling for the upper hand. And yeah, I absolutely think they kill anyone who crosses them or gets in their way."

"Think of them as ultimate chess players," I say, trying to keep my voice light. "Every move calculated, every bargain a trap disguised as opportunity. The history books make them feel more like psychopaths, not sociopaths. They play the game because they enjoy it and they don't care if everyone involved knows the rules."

Of course, now's probably not the time to mention the only folks who have managed to best them are the Court of Reaping and the Society.

"Sounds like Alistair's got competition, then," she muses, unaware of how close to home her words hit. "He won't be the only one trying to fuck with us while we search. Maybe that will work in our favor."

"Maybe," I mutter, looking out the window to see Odie flit between shadows above us, a silent sentinel ready to alert us to danger. Euryale soars higher, her keen eyes fixed on the road ahead. I wasn't keen on Doyle sending them ahead as sentinels, but maybe he was right.

"Are we safe as their guests? I mean, I assume the whole diplomatic stuff should keep them from really trying to harm us, right?" Jolene asks, a slight furrow in her brow as she looks at Teddy.

"Safe as one can be when dealing with the night families," Teddy says as he watches her run her fingers over Isis. "Rumors say their hearts are as dark as the night sky they adore—which explains a lot about Alistair. It also makes me nervous about Allora because aligning with them is... problematic. Her stepmother has hidden schemes up those designer sleeves."

Princess frowns, stroking the python wrapped around her thought-fully. I can tell she doesn't like Teddy's train of thought and that means she's already considering taking Allora under her wing. That protective streak is the other reason she got humiliated in high school, but even the trauma hasn't made her less willing to stand in front of the cannons if someone's in danger.

That's part of why we all love her, even if we can't say it yet because she gets wigged out.

"Problematic," she echoes, rolling the word around like it's a puzzle piece she's trying to fit into place. "We'll just have to be smarter than them, won't we? It shouldn't be too hard with our darling boy genius, the clever troublemaker, and our slick son of a senator, right?"

"Smarter, or luckier," I mutter under my breath. "Though good to know you, the doc, and me are just here to look pretty."

Jolene rolls her eyes at me as she bumps my shoulder with hers. "You *are* pretty, Benjy, and so is Prez, but we're gifted in other ways."

"Such as?" Teddy smirks as he preens about being named a smooth operator with the damn Irishman. "Tell me what you see us all as, Tilly. We have plenty of time."

"For the love of…" I give him an annoyed look. Edgar's always loved praise, though he enjoys giving it even more. "She doesn't have to do that, buddy."

"I don't mind," Princess chirps with a sly look on her face. "Benjy and Presley have a lot of very useful jobs, but one of the biggest is being the calm center of our little family. When the big dogs are going off the rails—even me— or the tension is off the charts, they help us come back to Earth. And that's so necessary that I don't know how we'd survive without it. Plus, they're pretty, kind, strong, and gentle."

My smile is broad as I look my friend smugly. "We're the center of her storm, dude. Suck it."

"Don't tempt me to start shit in this car," Teddy rumbles. "Our girl will get mad when we make a mess of her friend's vehicle."

"I will once I stop screaming; you're right," she says happily. "So don't get him started until we get to our destination. I don't want to arrive grumpy about the mess, even if I would be satisfied in other ways."

"Fine…"

I settle in, stretching my legs in front of me as I get comfortable. Jolene smacks my leg, her eyes dark. "Don't start flexing, either."

Laughing softly, I bump her back and we all sit back to watch the road that stretches before us, winding towards a destiny shrouded in uncertainty and shadow. As we drive, I can't shake the feeling that we're heading straight into the belly of the beast.

And we simply don't have the food to bait the damn thing.

A SCREECH SPLITS THE AIR, A PIERCING ALARM THAT HAS US ALL snapping to attention. Euryale's cry is urgent, and as I struggle to wake up, I lean forward to look out the window. The eagle is circling above a snarl of twisted metal strewn across the road ahead.

I have a bad feeling about this.

"Dammit!" Doyle's voice crackles through the intercom from the other car. His tone is laden with disgust and resignation as he growls, "It's definitely 'wounded gazelle' setup."

I'm about to ask what that means when our vehicle shudders violently beneath us. It feels like invisible forces are slamming into us with the intent to crush. Teddy's eyes light with fire as he snarls and I know we don't have a choice—we have to get out and fight. Within seconds, we're spilling out of the vehicles in a wild cascade of bodies, fangs, fur, and fury.

"Tilly, stay back." Teddy's command is sharp, his eyes shooting daggers of warning her way. But she's already moving, dashing past him with an unapologetic look and dual middle fingers extended.

"Try and stop me," she shouts over her shoulder, and there's fire in her eyes that rivals anything Teddy could conjure.

I shouldn't encourage her, but hell yeah, that's our girl.

My heart is hammering as I watch her dive headlong into the fray. One hand is brandishing the knife she always carries and the other is gripping the polymer gun she managed to sneak in under the Fae's noses. I'm not sure which will be more useful to her, but since she has no idea she's going to be fighting magic, it's a toss-up.

"Shit," I breathe out in irritation. We've been so damn careful to keep things under wraps, but now, there's no room for caution. I feel the change rippling under my skin, a call to something ancient and powerful.

We're all going to shift and whether she'll figure things out afterward, I don't know.

Teddy explodes into his hellhound form, massive and monstrous, flames licking around his maw like tendrils of the underworld reaching out to claim souls. Smoke coils from his nostrils, sulfur tainting the air as he jerks his head at me then takes off into a group of black clad assholes in masks.

"Cover our girl, B," he roars in a sound that vibrates through my bones.

Despite being the soft compliment to our group, Wolfie doesn't hesitate to let loose. His transformation is fluid—dark fae majesty made flesh. His wings unfurl, vast and shadowy, while his ears sharpen to lethal points. The air around him shimmers with magic, a pink iridescence that paints the world in shades of danger. He looks both beautiful and deadly, making me realize he's never really shown any of us the extent of his full form before.

This one makes it impossible to believe he's from the lands that spawned Alistair.

"Let's dance," Wolfie growls softly, and there's a gleam in his eye I haven't seen before. "I don't like people trying to hurt my girl."

Before I can pick my jaw up, I see our other friends coming out of the second car. Doyle's aura pulses with a golden light so bright it almost blinds me. The power he wields is raw, unbridled—a force of nature that refuses to be leashed any longer. He moves with a purpose, his every step a statement of divine wrath.

"Benjy, now!" Doyle commands, and I don't need telling twice.

Muscles bulge and my body stretches until I'm an eight-foot tower of primal strength. My fists are hammers and my roar a challenge to the very sky. "Let's bash some heads," I bellow, giving in to the gorilla within.

The inner beast is thrilled with this shit because I almost never let him out and definitely not like this.

Presley leaps skyward, transforming mid-air into the majestic caladrius, his cries echoing Euryale's. Together, they dive towards the melee, two sharp beaked birds bent on tearing into their enemies. No wonder he has such a rapport with that eagle; they look like a perfectly matched squadron of predators in the air.

"Watch it!" I yell as one of the black-clad assailants produces a bow, aiming at Presley. A swipe of my massive hand sends the attacker sprawling and I run for the next one before they can find their own weapon. We're a storm of supernatural might, but even storms can be unpredictable.

That's when it happens—the twist none of us saw coming.

I stop dead in my tracks, almost dropping the dickhead I'm shaking when my Princess shifts. Unlike new shifters, her body snaps into the form of an enormous hellhound like Teddy, her body wrapped in blue flames and exhaling mist the color of his incubus. Quetzalcoatl feathers adorn her tail, but dark fae wings sprout from her back. The glitter flying as they flap is black as obsidian, sparkling in the air with unknown power.

"By my maiden auntie's dusty panties," Doyle whispers. "I've never seen anything like it."

For an ancient demi-god, that's saying a lot.

Her transformation isn't just shocking—it's a revelation, a display of raw potential that none of us anticipated. When one of the attackers lands a lucky strike, drawing a line of crimson across her side, we all freeze, our battle-lust replaced by sudden fear.

But then, a soft, gentle golden glow radiates from her wound, spreading outwards in waves of silent fury. The attackers, previously so confident in their numbers and skill, turn to ash before our eyes, crumbling away like shadows at dawn.

"Did you see that?" Wolfie's voice is tinged with disbelief, his normally unflappable demeanor shaken.

"Impossible..." The word is a whisper from my lips, my thoughts racing.

What does this mean? How did she...?

"Focus!" Teddy snaps us out of our stupor, his fiery gaze sweeping the scene. "We have to keep moving."

"Right," I say, shaking off the shock. "Let's get out of here before more show up."

We glance at Tilly with trepidation as it hits us that while she's going to be an amazingly powerful supe, that won't come without even more challenges. Until she's fully emerged and aware, the news of this event getting out would have put her in serious danger. It still might if anyone managed to zip out before her atom bomb of god-like power cleared the field.

She's out again, a sure sign that this still isn't the final leg of being emerged, so Teddy picks the now human form in tattered clothes gently. As we pile back into our battered carriages, my mind whirls. We're all going to have to keep this secret, especially if she wakes up not knowing what happened.

I don't know how much longer that gambit is going to work, especially in a court where they delight in revealing weaknesses.

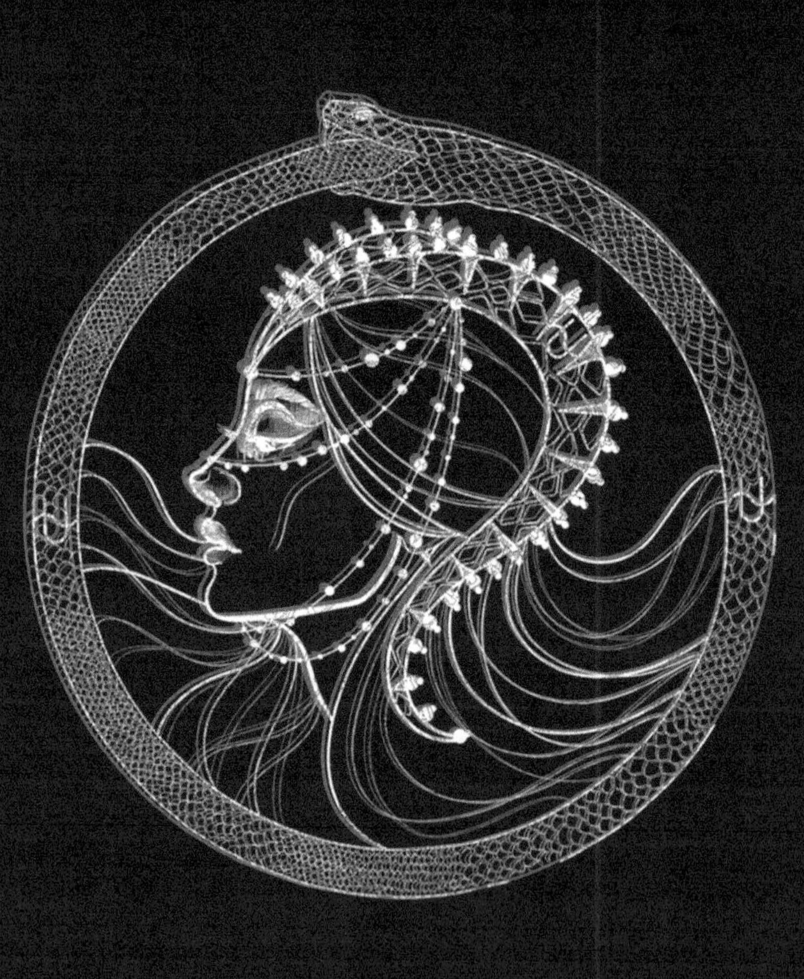

Nightmare

Jolene

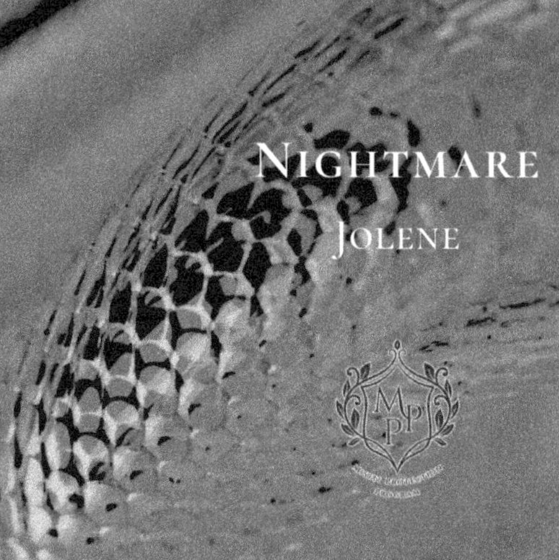

My eyelids flutter open just as the car shifts from the smoothness of the road to a gravelly ascent. The sky is bruised purple and orange as we pull up to the castle that looms ahead. The giant, gleaming structure is less a building and more an eruption from the very bones of the earth. The style is unsurprisingly gothic, draped in a verdant shroud of vines and flowers that whisper concealment. Fae creatures, their eyes like shards of moonlight, skitter across the blackened masonry. It's an odd paradox: dark yet sparkling, as if this realm has purposefully decided to don night-time regalia and forsake the warm cheer of summer.

I suppose it has—that was one of the oft repeated rumors I came upon while reading from the digital forums.

"Overcompensate much?" I grumble as I stretch my limbs. My sarcastic quip cuts through the thick aroma of night jasmine and lilies that saturates the air within the car. Patchouli and myrrh linger underneath—darker scents that feel like warnings. I press my palm against the window, half expecting the glass to frost from the magic outside. When it doesn't, I breathe a sigh of relief.

There's only so much I can take at once.

"They really went all out with the 'midnight' vibe," Teddy agrees. He's making light, but his laughter sounds hollow, like he's trying too hard to make this seem less daunting.

"Eccentric rich people are so over-the-top," Benjy adds as he gauges my reaction. He's very perceptive because he's often quietly observing, so I have to be careful how much he sees when I'm not paying attention.

"I bet this place is a hoot at Halloween," Wolfie chimes as he smiles at me. His expression doesn't reach his eyes and the solemn undertone in this car makes me worry about what shit happened while I was supposedly asleep.

I study them all through my lashes, noting the scrapes on Teddy's knuckles and the way Benjy's lip is split at the corner. Wolfie's jacket is torn, like he's been grappling with more than just his inner demons about his family. My stomach knots because now I know for certain something serious happened while we were driving here—something they're keeping from me.

That can only mean one thing and I don't like it at all.

"Guys," I start, my voice betraying the edge of anxiety. "What aren't you telling me?"

"Tilly, it's nothing. Let's get inside and—" Teddy begins, but I cut him off.

"Nothing? You look like you've gone ten rounds with a boxing champ." I point accusingly at his hand, then to the others, piecing together a story they refuse to voice. "What did I miss?"

"Bad blow out on the road. We were in a rough area and some jackasses tried to mug us while the driver changed the tire. Can we talk about this later?" Benjy pleads, but there's a firmness in his tone that says it's not up for discussion.

"I'm not an idiot, Benjamin Louis Foster." My words are sharp, laced with rising fury. They exchange looks, and I know—it's got something to do with this place and our so-called hosts.

"Sugarplum..." Wolfie says, trailing off as he catches sight of the disquiet in my eyes. He knows I hate being left in the dark, yet here I am, blindfolded by my own mind's gaps. "Just... let it go. We're all safe and no one is truly hurt. You have to trust us until we can be more specific."

Of course it would be him that asked—I can't say no to his big blue eyes.

"Fine," I relent, folding my arms as a defensive shield around myself. "But when I *can* be let in on the secret, you assholes are going to tell me everything you know even if it takes a fucking *week*, got it?"

"I promise we'll share everything when we can. In fact, I swear on my bottle of Pappy, Tilly." Teddy gives me a serious look and I believe him—mostly because that's a five thousand dollar bottle of bourbon he looks at like it's made of gold.

As we approach the gates to the creepy disco castle, the sparkles from the castle's embedded gems catch the dying light, flinging prismatic colors across our path like a mocking celebration. I snort. "Can't wait to see what they've got lined up for the welcome party. Maybe a diamond studded platinum carpet instead of red?"

My grumbling gets a genuine laugh from Benjy, and even Teddy cracks a smile. They know I get more sarcastic when I'm irritated, so the jokes tell them I'm not worried as much as ready to stab someone. Sadly, I doubt I'm going to get the chance, but a girl can dream.

Especially when we'll be seeing that fucking tool, Alistair.

"Knowing these folks, it'll be woven from the fur of an endangered species or a goddamn unicorn," Wolfie adds, shaking his head. "People who need this much bling to feel good about themselves make me uncomfortable."

"Even if they were real, unicorns would be off limits," I retort, trying to find solid ground in humor. "Even fucking rich people have standards."

He arches a brow at me. "You know they don't. There's assholes racing to send themselves to the moon for street cred out there, Sugarplum. Bored people with more money than sense will always push the boundaries of acceptable behavior; they lose touch with reality after the seventh zero."

I chuckle at his assessment as we come to a stop. The engine dies and the silence feels heavy as we all prepare for whatever nonsense is in store. Finally, I crawl over Teddy and Doyle to step out of the car with my back straight and chin high. I'm ready to face whatever waits inside this twisted place, even if it pushes me to the edge of my boundaries. I look determined, but inside, I'm stoking a small fire of rage.

Even if I accepted their fake ass excuse about the injuries, I know the mother-fuckers in this castle are responsible for whatever happened.

I swear on my dying breath if this castle's masters are behind the attack that hurt my guys, they're on my list. While I may not be able to act on it today, I will keep it locked up tight inside of me until the time is right. When it is, I will unleash everything at my disposal to show them exactly why people don't want to piss off a Southern woman.

Bless their hearts, they just made an enemy, and they better find someone to pray for them, because I'm coming.

IT TAKES A FEW MINUTES FOR THE GUYS TO GET OUR LUGGAGE AND the animals out of the cars. As they thank the reluctant chauffeurs Allora provided, I take in our surroundings. The four men who rode in the front of the vehicles have grim expressions on their faces as they look around and I take note of it. We're not the only ones who find this place off-putting.

"Thanks," Teddy grunts to one of the men, his voice strained through the courtesy. "We couldn't have made it without your... expertise."

"Ours is but to serve," the man replies with a bow so shallow it's almost an insult. I narrow my eyes at him, but I let it slide.

After all, Allora's private guards have no reason to be loyal to us and I have far too many enemies on my chessboard to add disrespectful idiots.

The air is a tangle of animal excitement and apprehension, mirroring my own emotions. Jekyll mrrps as Hyde follows him to my side and I smile. I miss them when we have to split up and this trip has been a *lot* of separation from my furry companions. Eurayle traces circles in the sky, her silhouette cutting through the thinning light. Kali and Hecate bark, eager to escape confinement, and I snort as they run for a place to relieve themselves. I kind of hope they piss on something important; it feels like a fitting tribute.

"Keep watch," I murmur to my servals, hoping they understand. My eagle's sharp cry is comforting, even as I spot the raven tracking her every move. *Déjà vu* prickles my skin; I've seen that bird before. It has to be someone else's shadow masquerading as a friend. I press my lips together, not liking the possibility that we're being followed.

Would one of the people who demanded that stupid 'oath' send a bird to keep watch on us? Fuck if I know.

"Sugarplum?" Wolfie's voice breaks through the hum of my thoughts. "Are you okay? You… slept pretty hard."

"Never better," I lie with a tight smile. Poor Wolfie struggles with the lies even more now that I know they have to do it. It's not in his nature to be so secretive, I think, and he hates it. But he can't stop himself from worrying about me, so he had to ask.

"Come on," Teddy says with a sigh. "Let's face the music."

We turn to face the castle as a group. Its opulence is a stark contrast to our disheveled appearance, but I don't give a fuck. Whatever happened on the way here was arranged ahead of time and our survival is probably more surprising than the state of our attire.

Within seconds, a group of men exit the huge double doors. They're dressed to kill and look like a fucking fantasy calendar lineup. Alistair stands out because he's smirking like he owns the place—which, unfortunately, he does. I assume the others are his sisters' suitors. They range from the casually confident to the brazenly brawny, but not one has a single hair out of place or crease unpressed.

Fantastic. We're being greeted by the Fae mafia.

"Welcome," Alistair drawls, stepping forward, his designer clothes whispering of wealth and indifference. "I'm so glad you made it to our home safely."

"I wouldn't miss it for the world," I say, pouring sarcasm into each syllable. My eyes narrow behind the glasses as I look at each of the seven men who are courting Alistair's sister carefully. There wasn't a lot of information on them, which I found shocking, but I suppose keeping their assets under wraps is what criminals do.

"Delighted," says one of the smaller Fae. His eyes gleam with an intelligence that suggests he's more dangerous than his stature implies. The others nod in agreement, a chorus of predatory smiles shining at us in the waning light.

"Tomorrow night will be... enlightening." There's something about the way the largest Fae—part orc if I had to guess by his short tusks —grins that sends a shiver skittering down my spine. He looks like a mountain with a vendetta.

"Can't wait," I manage, my words edged with faux enthusiasm. So far we've heard from the smallest and the largest, plus the biggest dickhead in town. I'm not sure what the others in the rainbow of rich douchebags bring to the table, but this is a lot of treacherous people to manage at once.

"Please, follow us," the medium build masked man offers. He doesn't say another word as we look at him—not even an explanation as to why he's wearing the half mask over the top of his face.

Fucking weird ass Fae, I swear to Hades in a hamper.

These men are all different shades of threat dressed in silk and arrogance. Alistair may be the devil I know, but the rest of them are question marks. They could be from anywhere in the four kingdoms, with any powers, and any connections. Until someone actually introduces us and gives me something to work with, I have to consider them all threats to me and my family. I'm sure Teddy feels the same way because he's shifting towards me as we all stare one another down.

"Lead the way," Benjy finally says. He shoots me a look that tells me he's as wary as I am, but we can't stand here all day.

Our band of misfits moves forward when our hosts do, but my mind is racing faster than my feet. *What kind of special event requires such an ominous invitation?*

Tomorrow night might hold answers, but I'm not sure I'll like what we find.

As we walk down long stretches of hallway, my knuckles itch with the need to give Alistair a piece of my mind the old-fashioned way—right across his smug nose. He made the purpose of the event tomorrow clear while we traversed the miles of castle to the wing we're going to be staying in. They're throwing another fucking ball and I'm fresh out of patience with this shit. As a woman who grew up in the damn debutante world and then traveled the world as a fixer, I've been to a shit load of fancy events. They're not my favorite thing, but I can bend when it's necessary.

But we've been in this place for a little over a week and I've had it up to here with these high-society shindigs where they treat me like some kind of dress-up doll. I'm here for one thing, and that's to dig up dirt on Wolfie's elusive dad, not to waltz around in glittery gowns.

I am not their Barbie girl in their Barbie world.

Before I can open my mouth to let these asswads know how I feel about *another* formal event full of bullshit, Alistair stops the group. The men face us, all giving us a different form of creepy smile.

"I'm Lucien, husband to Elara," says a Fae who looks as if he could charm the scales off a snake. His eyes glitter with mischief and I can *feel* the trouble wafting from him. I don't think he's fully Fae, but I haven't the foggiest what else he could be.

Another one bows, his voice as smooth as the velvet cloak draped over his shoulders. "Julien, betrothed to Celestina," he says as nods at each of my men.

Note to self: That one doesn't think women should be in charge. Restrain yourself, Jolene.

One by one they introduce themselves, each name tied to a sister like a badge of honor—or a shackle, depending on how you squint at it. Then Alistair steps forward, and I can almost hear the air sour.

"Alistair, intended of Allora," he declares, an edge of defiance in his tone.

The snickers from the rest are almost imperceptible, but I catch them —little ripples of contempt across a very exclusive pond. When they turn their backs, Alistair's facade cracks for a fleeting second. His eyes darken, his jaw tightens, and that smirk? It slips away like it was never there.

How very odd. Why do they find the alliance lacking and why does he look like he actually cares what they think of Allora?

"Let's get you settled, then."

A maid pops out of nowhere and I almost scream. I was so focused on this clown car of men that I wasn't paying attention to anything around me. *Bad Jolene*, I think as I jerk my head at the guys. The animals gather in close, and Hyde gives the bevy of buttheads the stink eye as we look at the staff member waiting for us.

"Thank you," I mutter, my brain churning with fresh suspicions. There's more to this Allora-Alistair alliance than meets the eye, and I'm itching to unravel it. Once this stupid oath shit is behind me, maybe I'll come back and help Allora—if she really is a friend to be had.

"Right this way, esteemed guests," the small woman chirps as she leads us down a corridor that looks like it was ripped straight out of an epic fantasy novel.

"Esteemed, my ass," I mutter to myself. "These dudes think we're rubes."

Teddy shrugs and winks at me. "Perhaps that's not a bad thing, Tilly."

He might be right.

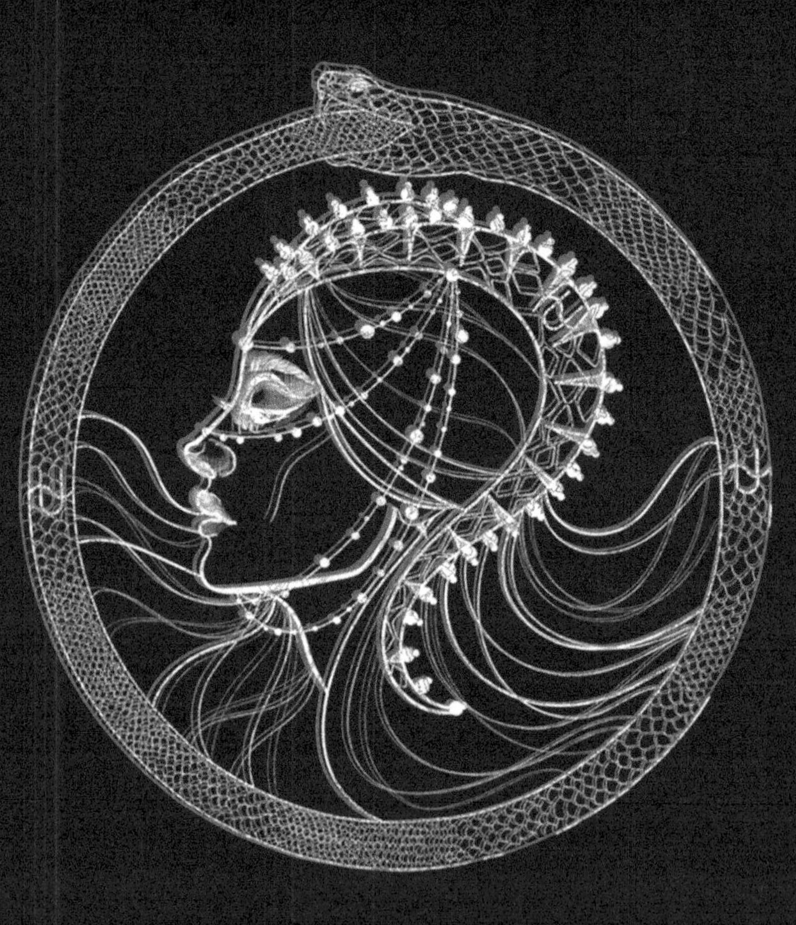

Walk Through Fire

Presley

The door to our suite swings open, revealing a scene plucked from a dream—or a particularly inventive hallucination. Starlight dances across the ceiling, casting a soft glow on the colossal bed that sits like a throne in the middle of the room. An enchanted forest mural wraps around the walls, so lifelike that I swear I see the leaves fluttering. In the corner, a spring bubbles merrily, its music a soothing counterpoint to the chaos of my thoughts.

Jesus salsa dancing Christ, how are we going to keep the damn oath if these shitheads keep throwing our girl into situations like this?

"Wow," Benjy breathes out, his awe echoing my silent admiration. "This is the most swank set-up yet."

"Of course," the pixie maid nods, oblivious to the frustration on most of our faces. "Should you need anything, please do not hesitate to ring the bells. The cord is over there by the…jacuzzi."

I snort as she fumbles for a normal word to describe the bubbling spring without letting our unemerged mate know what's really going on.

"Thank you," Teddy swoops in to save me before I crack up. "We appreciate all of your hospitality."

The maid curtseys and scurries out, leaving me to look at the rest of our group. Jolene is walking around oblivious thanks to the weird glasses. Benjy is still gaping at the spread as Wolfie eyes every inch of the place. The only one who seems relaxed is Doyle. He's heading for the couch at the sitting room end of the giant suite with a skip in his step.

I have no idea how that idiot maintains such a happy-go-lucky exterior right up until he bursts into a rage.

"We should check for bugs," Teddy whispers, already scanning the room with trained eyes. Given his less than legal side hustle, I'll bet this isn't his first rodeo with that particular challenge.

"Every nook and cranny," Magpie confirms as she nods at him.

The weight of exhaustion pulls at my limbs, but we can't afford to let our guard down, not even in this fairy-tale sanctuary. "I'll take the en suite."

"Sitting area," Doyle says as he drops to his knees.

So that's what he was doing; I'll be damned.

"Tomorrow's another day, as the belle said, but tonight isn't over yet," Wolfie sighs as he lowers himself to the floor by the bed.

"Another day, another firing squad," I grin. "At least this one seems to have cracks." I wink at them, heading for the room I claimed.

"Let's get to work, then," Benjy says, rolling up his sleeves as he passes me on the way to what I assume is a large closet.

"Then we sleep," Jolene says firmly, "because gods know, we'll need our strength in the morning if we want to get through this without murdering anyone. We can dismantle spy equipment and double-check shadows now, but after that, we're on geezer time. I want to be alert as hell when we have to face that squad of fuckwits."

"As you wish, Princess," Benjy replies.

I knew he picked that nickname for a reason—how clever.

THE GROWL THAT WAKES ME IS LOW AND GUTTURAL, A WARNING THAT ripples through the predawn silence like an ominous breeze. My eyes snap open, heart pounding in the stillness, and I'm immediately aware of the tangled mass of limbs around me—my arm thrown over Wolfie's waist, Doyle's calf draped over mine, and Magpie's fingertips touching mine as she snuggles into Boone. We're a jigsaw of bodies, interlocked in an accidental intimacy that only a night spent in the same bed can create.

"Prez," Wolfie whispers, nudging me with his elbow, "something's at the door."

"Ugh," Teddy grunts, his voice groggy as he disentangles from our human knot, gets up, and pads barefoot across the room. The animals are all standing with their hackles raised, ears pinned, and lips curled back to reveal an arsenal of teeth. It's a canine and feline chorus of distrust aimed squarely at the unexpected interruption.

"Easy, guys," I murmur at the group, though I'm not feeling particularly calm myself. Pushing myself up on one elbow, I watch as Boone opens the door to reveal a stack of neatly wrapped packages. They sit innocuously enough, but in this place, even gifts feel like thinly veiled threats.

"Looks like Alistair decided to play dress-up with us," Teddy announces as he hauls the boxes inside with a wary eye.

"Great," Jolene mutters. "Because nothing says 'Welcome to our home' like complimentary yet also obligatory wardrobe choices."

It didn't occur to me that sending clothes was a way to control us, but I'll be damned if she isn't right.

"Stylish spies, that's what they are," Doyle says as he climbs out of the pile. He pokes a box with his toe suspiciously, frowning at us. "Guaranteed these wankers know we found all their surprises and mucked them up."

Disengaging from Wolfie reluctantly, I rip open the packages aggressively to find clothes that are my size while also comfortable with a touch of elegance that doesn't sacrifice mobility. The rest of the wrapped boxes have similar contents for each of us, including a pair of pre-worn, punk rock looking jeans for Magpie with a faded Sex Pistols tee shirt and Union Jack flag combat boots.

"It's fucking creepy how well they have us nailed," Benjy says as he pads over, "but then again, Allistair's probably got the staff wired to snoop better than the NSA."

"Maybe he asked them what sizes we wore at the Harvest Court," Wolfie offers reasonably. He sounds casual, but his eyes are tight with concern, mirroring Benjy's unease.

"Either way, it's unnerving," Teddy agrees as he grabs his parcel of clothes. "I don't like them knowing this much, especially because it gives them an advantage we don't have. Hell, they didn't even give us everyone's name yet."

We dress quickly, each lost in our thoughts until a staff member knocks on our door. Their impeccable timing has us exchanging glances laden with trepidation.

Did we miss a fucking camera? We'll have to check again.

"Breakfast is served," the lady says when we open the door. The maid gestures for us to follow her and I look to the rest of them.

"Let's go," Magpie says with a sigh. She crooks her finger at the servals and dogs, grinning as they jump to flank her.

Teddy's expression hardens when we head out. "I'm interested to find out what kind of circus awaits us today."

"Keep it cool," I murmur, knowing some of their 'pre-coffee' tact is about as refined as a sledgehammer. "Remember, we're in their house and we have to play by their rules for now."

"Doesn't mean I have to like it," Magpie grumbles. "I get the feeling I'm going to want to beat the shit out of them no matter how much caffeine I suck down."

"None of us like it, Princess," Benjy reminds her as he herds the dogs through the doorway.

Though, unlike the rest of us, her, Teddy, and Doyle are the most likely to get us arrested.

We make our way down to the dining room through an open court-yard where Euryale disappears into the morning light immediately. I don't blame her; I wish I could take to the sky and get a better view of this shit. There's so much going on in front of our faces that I think we're missing a bigger picture, but I haven't been able to put my finger on it.

"Are we ready for whatever this breakfast charade brings?" I ask, as we approach another set of double doors.

"As ready as we'll ever be," Benjy says, a forced smile on his face as he corrals the dogs with practiced ease. "We have no idea what they're hiding or even what they want with us. It feels like we're going in blindfolded; I don't like it."

"Guess we'll find out if the food's as good as the fashion," Doyle adds, a dry edge to his voice.

"Or if it's poisoned," Wolfie says, half-joking but his eyes are scanning for exits and potential threats.

Why did he have to say that? For that matter, how did it become completely normal for that to be a serious question?

"I just want to get through this meal without any casualties," Magpie says as she shoves her hands in her pockets. "I wouldn't mind kicking someone's ass, don't get me wrong, but I'd prefer to do it when I have a clue what I'm up against."

"If we can make it through the meal without one of you volatile folks lunging across the table at someone, I'll be surprised as hell," Benjy teases.

"Hey, I'm always a lady," Jolene retorts, "even when I'm plotting murder. Maybe more so then, actually, because I like to bat my lashes and simper to distract them.

"Can we keep the plotting to a minimum?" Wolfie sighs as he adjusts his new jacket. "We have to learn as much as we can about them before we try to play their game better than them."

"Fine," Doyle acquiesces, "but only because you asked so nicely."

Apollo help us.

With a final look shared between us, a silent agreement to stick together no matter what, we step into the fray, ready to face the courtly masquerade that waits beyond the dining room doors.

THE MOMENT WE STEP INTO THE DINING HALL, THE AIR THICKENS with tension and unspoken questions. The prince and his 'brothers-in-law' are already waiting for us. An array of Fae masculinity that spans the spectrum from Lukas's diminutive elegance to Julien's towering presence looks up at us with interest when the door opens. They're clustered at the far end of a long table, their conversation halting as if snipped by shears when we enter the room.

"Where in the world are the sisters?" I whisper to Wolfie. It's weird that we haven't heard or seen a thing about them, but they're the entire reason these clowns are here.

We're seated by staff at the close end of the table, facing the eight men like chess pieces poised for a game neither side knows how to play. No one says anything, we all just stare as servers bring out food and drinks like they're feeding an army.

Alistair finally takes charge, introducing us one by one, his voice carrying an odd note of formality. "Jolene Whitley and Judge Edgar Boone," he begins. "Drs. Wolfgang Fletcher and Presley Hamilton," he continues before pointing to the last two members of our family. "And Benjamin Foster and Doyle Haggerty."

"You've met Lukas and Julien, but the others are Finn, Declan, Riordan, Keegan, and Angus." Alistair's voice trails through the introductions, naming each Fae man in turn. Their eyes are curious, watchful mirrors reflecting back our own wariness.

"Where are your sisters this fine morning?" Doyle can't help but ask and I have to hide my smile. His voice is laced with sarcasm he doesn't bother to hide, plus he's starting to lay on the faux Irish charm.

"Off having new gowns made for tonight," Lukas answers with a smile that doesn't quite reach his eyes.

When I turn my head to look at my magpie, she looks like she's fighting the urge to slam her forehead on the polished wood of the table. Teddy puts an arm around her shoulders, keeping her place as he whispers in her ear.

"New gowns," she mutters before Doyle steers the conversation towards safer waters.

When asked by one of the predatory looking Fae, he explains our land tour is inspired by finding out more about Lucy's heritage. I catch snippets of interest flickering across their faces—that is except for Alistair, who seems to be pretending he's clueless for some reason.

It's probably time to get their attention off Lucy before Alistair pounces again.

"Tell us how you met your respective princesses," I say as I lean forward. "I'm dying to know."

Julien answers first, recounting a tale that has more gloss than truth, and one by one, they chime in with stories of encounters orchestrated by destiny or clever matchmaking—tales from all corners of the dark lands that were featured in some ridiculous reality TV show.

"From nobility to business families," Lukas adds, his voice tinged with pride. "The search was... extensive."

"Sounds romantic," I comment dryly, and from the corner of my eye, I see Alistair's lip curl as he gazes off into the distance, no doubt recalling the spectacle.

"Indeed, it was quite the event," another chimes in, oblivious to Alistair's disdain.

"Event," Jolene echoes, her tone heavy with irony. She glances at me, then Wolfie, her concern clear.

I know she worries about his sensitivity, but there's something about Alistair's irritation that feels significant. "What, no comment, Silkshine?"

He glares at me and I hear Doyle snort. The Irishman clears his throat, giving the princes a charming grin. "Obviously, he was overcome by your grand overtures for his sisters."

"Aw, but it's your turn, Alistair," Teddy says, unable to keep the edge out of his voice as he taunts the Fae. "How did you and Allora cross paths?"

The smirk he gives us is infuriatingly familiar. He's put his mask back on as he leans back in a picture of arrogance. "We met in the most romantic way possible: our parents decided we were a good match."

Guffaws erupt from his brothers-in-law, their laughter echoing off the vaulted ceilings. I can't imagine why that's any less admirable than a fucking televised audition tour, but for some reason, these dimwits think they're better than the real prince of this land.

"Didn't have to strut your stuff on the marriage market like us, right, Allie?" Finn teases, elbowing Alistair.

"Unlike some, I didn't need to audition for love," Alistair retorts sharply, his eyes flashing with something that might be anger or pride —I can't tell.

But he's echoing my sentiments rather than making a shitty comment about Allora, which I find odd.

The room falls silent, those around us suddenly finding their plates fascinating.

"Love is so... unpredictable," I mutter, trying to defuse the tension.

Unfortunately, it's too late; Alistair stands abruptly, his chair scraping loudly against the floor. "Excuse me," he announces, his voice cold enough to chill wine. He strides out, leaving behind a wake of awkwardness.

"Guess that's our cue," Benjy says, standing up as Kali and Hecate whine. "We should take the animals out."

Before they can protest, Teddy nods and rises to his feet, holding his hand out to our girl. The rest of us join her as the watch us herd our zoo out of the dining hall quickly. In the hallway, we nearly collide with Alistair.

His eyes are stormy, his jaw set as he glares. "Watch yourself. This court is more than it seems."

"Is that a threat?" Teddy growls, pushing him against the wall with surprising force. "Did you send those black-clad goons after us?"

"I have no idea what you're talking about."

"Right," I chime in, not fully convinced but seeing the truth in his bewildered expression.

"Believe what you will," Alistair bites out, regaining his composure. "But know this—there are layers here you don't grasp. If you want insight, watch the show. It's... enlightening."

Frowning at him, I try to work out what the hell he wants us to know. My gaze flicks to Doyle, who shrugs, and then to Wolfie, who shakes his head. Finally, Magpie blinks and I see it dawn on her.

"The tailors will come by tea time," Alistair adds before shoving Teddy away and stalking down the corridor.

"Looks like we've got some binge-watching to do," Jolene says, a wry twist to her lips.

My mind churns over what we've learned, what we haven't, and what lies beneath Alistair's carefully constructed indifference.

Jolene is right; there's a puzzle here, and we need to put all the damned pieces together in order to survive this shit.

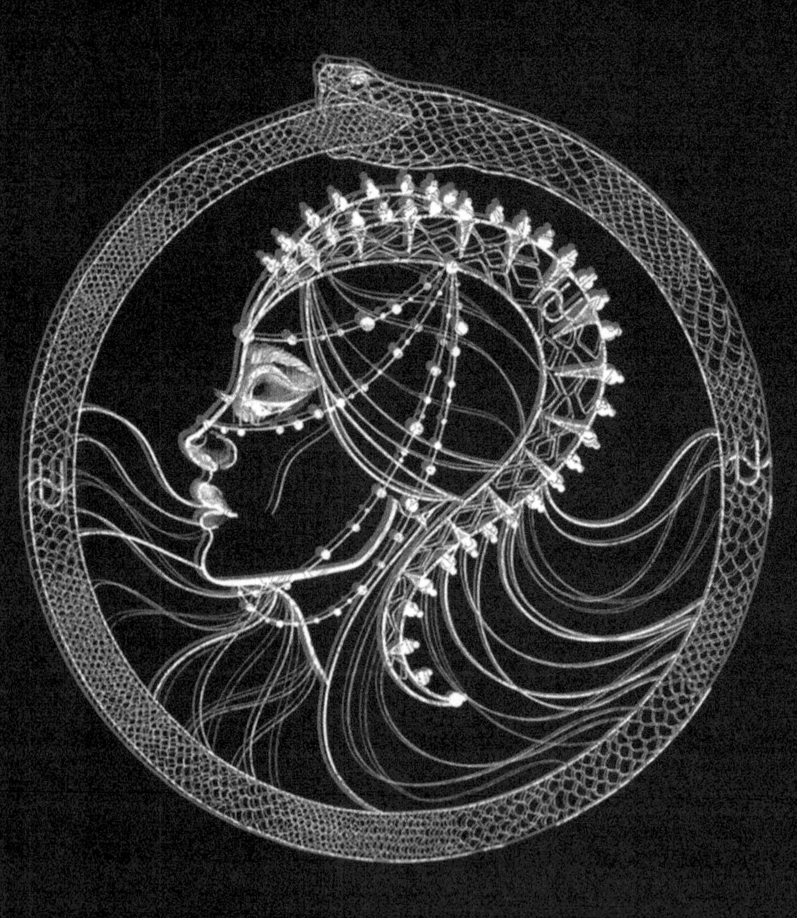

Everybody Wants To Rule The World

Jolene

"I never watch shit like this at home, you know. I'm making an exception because there's something hinky about the way Alistair told us we needed to see it." I look up at Teddy, who arches a brow at me.

"Sure, you don't, Tilly," he says as he drapes my legs over his lap. Benjy picks up my feet on the other side of him, his strong hands massaging them and they both chuckle when I groan.

Wolfie scoots closer on my right, making me grin as Prez runs his fingers through my hair with the arm resting on the back of the couch. Doyle returns with the tray of drinks he made at the in-room bar—a luxury I'm extremely grateful for, despite the time of day— then settles on the floor in front of me. His head leans back against my hip and Teddy's leg as he rolls his eyes up to look at us.

"I sent the beasties on an exploration trip. Seems best if both the winged and furry ones get the lay of the land inside and out just in case we have to sneak out or hide."

I've been on my own for years, outside of Seer, so I don't think I'll ever get used to these guys simply doing shit before I even think to ask. It's eerie.

"I'll admit I'm curious about how they handled this," Wolfie says softly. "It's odd for these kinds of families to allow the kind of access a show like this would require. I mean, half the things we read about in our research were based on rumors and speculation because they're all so secretive."

"Politicians are, too, pup, but I know the Senator allowed ridiculous access to our family during the last campaign. Everyone is looking to go viral—getting famous without doing anything. Regular people don't get how painstakingly orchestrated much of that 'viral' fame is. The ones benefiting from it put large investments of time and money into being declared an overnight sensation. It's all rigged and I'm sure this is no different. It is reality TV, after all."

He frowns at Teddy, then looks at me. "All of it?"

"Most things, darling boy. It's fairly common knowledge in the circles I traveled in that awards, bestseller lists, some elections, and more than a few romantic liaisons are simply business deals. You, too, can have a number one album or book or movie if you've got the cash flow to back the launch and continue promoting afterward. Sorry to burst your bubble," I say as I lean in to kiss his cheek.

"That sucks," he says as he wrinkles his nose. "It's not surprising, but it's also pretty disillusioning. I hate that we can't trust a damn thing anywhere."

"Only us, pup," Doyle says as his hand comes up to pat Wolfie's knee. "Everything else you should question. I sure as fuck do and it's kept me from getting boxed in over the years."

I'll bet it has.

"Shhh," Teddy scolds us. "The damn show is starting and we have to pay attention or we're wasting our time. Behave, children."

Benjy huffs a laugh and mutters something that sounds a lot like 'Yes, Big Daddy,' which sends us all into peals of laughter. My grumpy alpha pauses the TV, narrowing his eyes at all of us imperiously until we're quiet, then unpauses it when we're quiet again.

The glow of the screen casts a pallid light across our faces as we sink into the depths of 'The Princess Games.' Nestled in with the guys, I watch the first season begin curiously—will I be able to see the real deal or will my glasses magic hold up with something on video? I don't know, but I hope like hell the shit that the first designer did will help me unravel this mystery. I'm relieved when the first few episodes introduce Elara, the eldest princess of this court, and the fifty supernaturals who are vying for her hand in marriage.

She's a more patient woman than me because five is straining my ability to cope. Fifty would make me homicidal.

Luckily, the episodes of 'Princess Games' aren't too long and we speed through her various dates and challenges with ease. But when we get to the second to last show of the season, I find myself enthralled with the story—even rooting for a competitor that I know won't win. Suddenly, Elara's laughter is cut short by a screech that sends a shiver down my spine—an ugly avian creature with talons sharp as nightmares and cries that curdle blood swoops on screen. The weird Fae animals focus on the carriage she and Lukas are riding in immediately. In a flurry of dark feathers, engineered chaos unfolds as the bird things continue to batter the vehicle.

The breath in my lungs freezes and I stare at the show in horror. *Why does this feel familiar? Why am I humming with the need to punch something?* I look around at my men and note they've tensed, but they aren't nearly as wired as me.

"Real or rigged?" Prez asks, skepticism lacing his tone.

"Does it matter?" I counter, not taking my eyes off the ensuing melee. "I doubt Elara was aware either way. She looks absolutely terrified and I'm an excellent micro-expression reader."

Lukas leaps into the fray, dispatching the creatures with practiced ease, but it's the cloaked figures emerging from the treeline that draw our collective gaze—black-clad attackers that make my pulse spike even higher.

"Those can't be extras," Doyle says, his voice low and dangerous.

"Definitely not local theater troupe material," Teddy agrees, his frown deepening.

I gasp when one of the people pull Elara out of the carriage and a fight ensues as Lukas battles to get her back. It's obvious the fucker who yanked her out was going to take her, but the smallest of the princes fights like a man possessed until he's able to get her free. Then a blast comes out of nowhere, knocking Elara to the ground and I know in my gut this is serious. She's barely breathing and Lukas launches himself into the fray until he scatters their attackers to the wind.

Our group exchanges loaded glances, a silent consensus forming that there's more to Lukas than meets the eye. When he drops to Elara's side and starts working some sort of emerald tinged magic on her, it becomes obvious that he's a healer of some kind, though I don't know enough about this to identify what kind. Elara shoots up, coughing up blood, but breathing and the episode ends. The one that follows is the last and she obviously chooses Lukas despite favoring another suitor for most of the season.

I don't know if that's because he was always supposed to win or if it's because no one but him was there to save her.

But as soon as one mystery begins to unravel, another spins onto the screen. Celestina, the vibrant second oldest princess, is introduced at the beginning of season two. Unlike Elara, it's not clear who she's leaning towards picking because she seems quite unhappy to be taking part in the show. In fact, most of the episodes depict her being annoyed and sarcastic as they primp and polish her, as well as her shooting down the men with a bored expression. It makes me grin and for a second, I think I could like Celestina if this is the real her. But yet again, tragedy strikes near the end of her season, when she's successfully snatched during the merriment of a Harvest Court festival. Julien—a mountain of orc-ish might and Fae cunning—storms after her, a relentless force plowing through fields and foes alike.

"Staged fights," Benjy scoffs, crossing his arms over his chest. He's easily as massive as the current prince on-screen, but his lip is curled at the way the hunt for Celestina is playing out.

"Look closer," I urge, pointing at the screen where Celestina's terror is palpable even behind the mask of reality TV drama. "That's not acting."

"Security's tighter this season," Teddy observes. "They're playing for keeps now."

The pattern continues, each season a variation on the theme of peril and providence. Finn's rescue of Aubrette from the clutches of a unpredictable storm on a lake in Daybreak; Declan's tussle with a pack of fae wolves keen on tearing Nissa apart in Reaping; Riordan and Marin's disorienting dance through a portal mishap on their way to our world for a trip to Disney.

"Every suitor's challenge is just outside their reach," I muse aloud. "It's almost like they're being tested beyond their limits."

"Or set up to fail," Doyle adds, stroking his chin thoughtfully.

But why? What could anyone hope to accomplish with so many others, including Alistair, left to pick up the pieces if one of the sisters is gone?

THE LAST EPISODE LEAVES US WITH ANGUS AND FLORA, THEIR JOYOUS banquet in Midnight turned sinister as they unwittingly consume enchanted edibles. The healers who rush to help them barely manage to keep them alive before the cameras go dark and I swallow hard.

"Poisoned at their own table," I whisper, the realization cold in my stomach.

"Seems like someone's playing a very long game," Prez notes, his eyes narrowing.

"Whatever's happening, it stinks of desperation," Doyle concludes.

"Or ambition," Teddy counters. "Whoever's behind this wants power without the spotlight."

"Power..." Wolfie whispers. The word hangs heavy in the air, leaden with implication and dread.

"Let's remember why we're here," I say, trying to anchor myself to the present. "Answers about my parents, Wolfie's dad, and maybe... maybe something bigger."

The last flicker of the 'The Princess Games' season finale dies on the screen, and we sit in a loaded silence. I can feel the weight of their eyes on me, but it's the unspoken words hanging heavy in the air that press down on my chest.

"Right," I start, breaking the hush. "So, that was... educational." My words feel clumsy, like trying to tiptoe through a minefield with clown shoes. The truth is unwieldy, especially because I can't let them know I'm seeing everything they do. But I am, and it's damn clear someone is trying to fuck with the Midnight Court and possibly the others as well.

Is it a coup? I don't know what de-stabilizing all four would accomplish besides chaos.

"More than that, Tilly," Teddy says, leaning forward earnestly. "That damn show told us something we should have already admitted to ourselves. We're painting targets on our backs by poking around." His hands move as if gesturing to the entire world around us being an enemy.

"The stakes are higher because someone thinks we're getting too close. They may be right or our search may have nothing to do with their machinations," Doyle adds in a low rumble. "But until we know more, we're stumbling around in the dark."

Wolfie, who's been quiet for too long, finally speaks up, his tone so soft it makes my heart ache. "Maybe our presence here isn't just about finding what we lost. Maybe it's about seeing the bigger picture —the one we've been missing."

"Seeing or being led to a specific conclusion?" I say absently. "It's not like events haven't cropped up that didn't seem random."

"Exactly." Benjy suddenly stands, decisive, as if casting off doubt like an ill-fitting cloak. His eyes cut to Teddy's and I wonder what he's trying to tell him without words. "Someone—or *several someones*—thinks they can play us."

I nod, feeling a sliver of determination wedge its way into my thoughts. "Alistair knew what he was doing when he pointed us to this show. It's like he's trying to clue us in without actually telling us. Do you think he's got some kind of… oath… like you guys he can't betray?"

Teddy frowns and looks at Doyle, who nods. "It's quite possible he's been forced to submit to a geas."

"That means," I say, ignoring the word he used as my gaze drifts over each of them, "we need to look at this from every angle. Question everything and trust no one."

"Especially those closest to the throne," Teddy adds, the suspicion clear in his steely gaze.

"Or those who stand to gain from the purposeful chaos," Doyle interjects, always the strategist. "We need to figure out who that might be. What we found in Harvest isn't enough to form a complete picture."

"Chaos…" I murmur, rolling the idea around in my head. Like pieces of a puzzle, events and warnings begin to click into place. "A butterfly's wings in China…"

Prez laughs, shaking his head. "Yes, Magpie, life finds a way. I don't know if that theory applies here, though."

Rolling my eyes, I look to the ceiling for patience before I respond. "I didn't mean someone's breeding hyper-intelligent dinosaurs—though if they are, I'm *so* in for the first tour. I'm much smarter than those idiots."

"Tilly, focus," Teddy says as he laughs and scrubs a hand down his face. "I can't believe you still have a thing for fucking extinct reptiles. It's been decades, woman."

I cross my arms over my chest, wishing I could shoot back that if I have to believe in goddamn Fae, orcs, were-animals, magic, and any number of shit that would get me thrown in an asylum, I should be able to hope someone resurrects T-Rexes for me to ride. "Fine. My point was that there's too much coincidence in this chaos for it to actually *be* chaos."

"She's right about that," Doyle says as he rolls to his feet. "I can *feel* that it's not right."

"Whatever's coming our way, we have to trust each other and no one else. That's how we keep people from manipulating us into dancing to the tune. Besides," I add with a wry smile, "we've dealt with worse bullies than those grumpy princes."

"Sherilynn, for one," Benjy cuts in with a grin. "Their machinations can't touch her and that band of harpies she hangs around with."

"Exactly. We can't forget our purpose for being here, even if we're caught up in Alistair's games," I caution them, even as warmth floods through me at their confidence. "His marriage to Allora might be more than it appears, but he could have told us before now. The bullshit is layered thick in this stupid place."

"Then we cut through it," Teddy declares as he joins Doyle, then holds his hand out to me.

"Let's not get ahead of ourselves," Prez cautions, though his eyes hold a spark of rebellion. "If we don't step carefully, we could end up in a web similar to the one we believe Alistair's caught in."

"Forward is the only move we have, Prez. It's not like leaving will erase our names from anyone's minds." Wolfie sighs and I have to pretend I can't see his wings fluttering nervously.

"Then we keep going until we get answers," I say firmly. "I'm not about to tuck tail and run. That's not something I do anymore. Let the assholes slinking around in the shadows bring it."

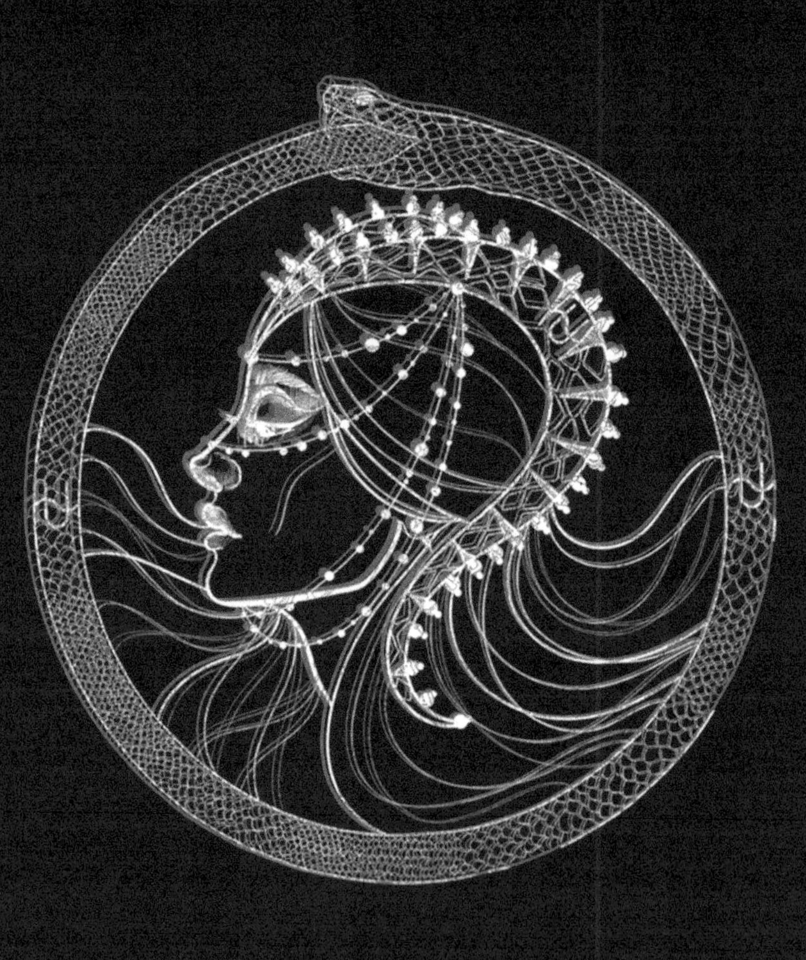

Glory

Edgar

My gaze wanders around the room as I take in my family. I was worried that the talk of this formal event would end up with us dressed like something out of *Interview with A Vampire*, but the designers who accompanied the tailors were actually less outlandish than the previous ones in the other courts. Midnight seems even more concerned with protocol than Harvest or Daybreak, but somehow more relaxed at the same time. However, what we got wasn't a bunch of plumed and ruffled weirdos, so I guess I should be grateful.

"When is she coming out?" Doyle asks as he fiddles with the dark plum vest. "I'm not putting this stupid hat on until she does. I feel like the git from that sailor cartoon—masks, tails, and fucking top hats."

Notice I didn't say we weren't dressed in something ridiculous—just not in crazy Gothic costumes.

"Soon, I'm sure," Wolfie replies as he straightens the doc's bow tie. "They always take longer with her than us. There's a lot of crap involved in dolling up women."

Prez snorts, batting his hands away to tug at the jacket. "She doesn't *need* all that shit, babe. Magpie's gorgeous just as she is."

Time to redirect or we'll wander off topic discussing our girl's attributes when we need to focus.

"Tonight," I cut in with a sharp tone, "we're going to need eyes and ears on everyone—the princes included." My eyes flick to the door as if expecting a staff member to waltz through it at any moment. "One of them could be part of this... whatever it is."

Benjy leans against the wall, looking large and in charge in the black and maroon tuxedo they sent for him. "Even if they're not, the likelihood of someone attempting shit at a big event like this is high. We thought the other courts were messing with us by giving us amped up booze or putting aphrodisiacs in our food. It might not have been them fucking with us at all."

I nod, feeling the weight of his words settle in my stomach like stones. He's right; we can't afford to overlook anyone, especially not those bathed in the spotlight of royalty. "Question everything," I murmur, "and trust no one's story without scrutiny."

Wolfie stands by the window, his silhouette outlined by the departing light. The perfect cut of his emerald and onyx suit makes him look both delicate and wicked at the same time when he's fully shifted. It's sexy as hell and I catch Prez looking, too.

The pup is a magic of his own and we're all entranced by him.

"Are you thinking it's a coup?" he asks. At my nod, he frowns, then shakes his head. "Fae courts are brutal in their transparency. This.." He gestures vaguely to the space between us, encompassing the unseen threat with a sweep of his hand, "... is shrouded in secrecy. Whoever's playing this game wants the power shift unnoticed until it's too late."

"Secrets within secrets," Doyle says, pacing back and forth like a caged animal. "That's how they're moving—like shadows in the moonlight. That's how deities work, but I don't think this is any of their doing. They'd have to contend with their brethren here if they played games in Faerie."

A chill runs down my spine as his words make the wheels in my mind turn. "Whoever it is might want people to think the gods are involved somehow. They obviously wanted us to blame the courts previously," I say slowly, reluctantly voicing the fear that has been gnawing at the edges of my mind. "What if someone who knows how all the players operate is involved? Someone who can see the whole board would know how to manipulate all the pieces, even the Fates. Hell, what if Wolfie's father is involved? What if he's aiding our unseen enemy?"

Doyle stops pacing and Benjy's grin fades. A heavy silence falls over us, thick and suffocating. It's as if the suggestion has deflated all of us. I had to say it, though, because the only thing about our trip here that could have drawn attention to us is looking for the guy. Even traveling with an unemerged like Tilly shouldn't have made this so hard. We're being sucked into things we don't understand but it doesn't feel personal. This shit is more clinical—distract and disarm us rather than kill anyone.

What better way to discourage us from continuing to look for the missing bio dad than waste our time?

"Then we'll deal with it however we have to," Wolfie says, his voice barely above a whisper. His words are brave, but the doubt in his eyes speaks louder. For a heartbeat, no one moves or speaks. We stand frozen, each lost in our own thoughts of betrayal and the painful decisions that might lie ahead.

"Guys, we don't need to borrow trouble," Benjy finally says, but there's a tightness around his eyes that belies his casual tone. "Worry is a misuse of imagination and we've got more immediate issues to consider."

"Right," Doyle adds, though his hands clench and unclench at his sides. "We stick to the plan. Watch, listen, and learn—that's all we can do for now."

Our raging Irishman isn't usually an advocate for self-control, but I think he's trying to keep Tilly from doing whatever the hell she did when we were attacked in public.

I glance at the fading light outside. The first stars are starting to prick through the velvet sky in a beautiful but deceptive calm. The view confirms why the land of summer is choosing to embrace the night; it's stunning . The staff is preparing the huge outdoor area where the ball is being held. Everything trimmed in midnight blues, silver, and black with sparkling accents and lights outlining the lavish gardens.

"I'd ask if you're ready, boys, but it seems like I'm last to the finish line again."

"Holy hell," Benjy mutters as we turn to look at Tilly.

The gown is beautiful, but it doesn't hold a candle to the woman wearing it.

I'm still gaping as she steps out like a celestial phenomenon, her gown a cosmic burst of midnight blue, black, and silver sparkles that contend with the dimming light. A crown of stars is sitting on her dark raven waves and the silvery mask draws attention to her darkly rimmed emerald eyes. The mating tattoos on her skin shine, rivaling the luminescence of her dress, casting an almost divine hue around her.

"Damn," Benjy murmurs from beside me, his words barely a whisper. We both stumbled through our teen years, tripping over reckless decisions, yet here we stand, united in our love for the incredible woman Jolene turned into.

"Is it too much?" Tilly asks, her voice laced with self-consciousness. "I *hate* letting these people treat me like "Dress Me Up Barbie,' but I have to admit this damn dress is almost worth it."

"Never," I assure her as I continue staring. I can't stop looking at her and I chuckle when I figure out that Wolfie and Prez are similarly struck. Their expressions make them look like love-struck fools who'd follow her to the ends of any realm—which probably isn't too off-the-mark. Doyle's eyes narrow slightly, assessing her like a man who's been alive long enough to classify the most beautiful things in history.

"You look…" he starts, a tremor of hunger in his voice, "… astounding. A vision worthy of the women in my family for certain."

Considering his known relatives are goddesses, Tilly has no idea how flattering that sentence is.

I feel a hum in the air, as if the essence of her power is sending shivers down my spine. It's a siren's call, even to the demi-god blood coursing through Doyle's veins, and I don't blame him for struggling not to answer it.

Jolene rolls her eyes, a gesture so like her that it cuts through the enchantment of the moment. I know she's trying to hide the blush staining her cheeks with assertiveness, but even that is so damned attractive I can't help but grin. She strides forward, the fabric of her dress swishing audibly as she twirls before us. "Pockets!" she exclaims, her face lighting up with childlike glee. "For my phone and of course, my knife."

"Of course," I say solemnly.

Laughter bubbles up among us, a release of tension in the revelation of such mundane concerns. I'm not that sheltered; I know women adore garments with functional pockets, but most of them aren't looking to slip a weapon in them—except our woman.

It's why she's goddamn amazing.

"Wait, you're all unarmed?" Her brow furrows in disapproval. "We know this thing will be filled with snakes. You can't go in unprotected." A head slithers out from between her breasts, letting out a hiss that almost sound affronted. Tilly looks and sighs. "Not good snakes like you, Isis."

"Relax," I say as I walk closer, reaching out to smooth the line between her brows with my thumb. "We've got it covered. Sometimes you've gotta trust the rest of us to watch your back."

The snake hisses at me and I glare at it as Tilly's lips pout up at me. When I arch a brow, the stubborn set of her jaw softens and Isis backs off. "It's just—" she starts to explain when Doyle interrupts her.

"Just because you need to be battle-ready in your ballgown doesn't mean we have to be weighed down with armor, Tíogair."

"You hush," she warns, her tone playful yet edgy.

She walks over to him, giving his lapels a yank to straighten him out, then quick as a viper, her heel comes down hard on his foot. His grimace speaks volumes, but he doesn't chastise her. Instead, he chuckles—a sound that holds a tinge of respect for her spirit.

"Okay, okay, truce," he concedes, lifting his hands in surrender.

"Calm down, you two," Prez, ever the voice of reason, finally speaks up. "We have specific goals tonight. That doesn't mean we can't have fun, but it does mean we need to be aware of what's going on around us."

I nod at him, grateful for the injection of logic. "Stay sharp, everyone. The night is young, and this place is full of secrets waiting to be uncovered."

"Real secrets draped in jewels and masked by fake smiles," Tilly muses, her eyes flickering towards the entrance where our evening awaits. "We'll have to be careful where we dig."

THE GRANDEUR OF THE OUTDOOR BALL UNFURLS BEFORE US, THE scene drenched in opulence that even rock stars would envy. As we enter via the sparkling path that leads to the party from the patio, Jekyll and Hyde slip away, all feline grace as they slink among the sparkling throng of people. Kali and Hecate stand sentinel at the periphery, their dark eyes vigilant as they watch every one who leaves the palace. Eurayle, the embodiment of predatory elegance, soars overhead as she keeps tabs on the movement around the vast borders of the party under the stars.

Our girl's entrance is nothing short of majestic, walking into the crowd with Isis coiling around her arm with an air of possessive warning, in a gown that seems to mimic the night sky. Doyle chuckles as we follow behind her, his slight limp a testament to what happens when you cross our woman, even in jest.

"Always the dramatic one," he says with an approving nod. "She knows how to get everyone's attention on what she wants them to see without being obvious. It's a useful skill."

"The best way to make a statement is loudly," I reply as I scan the crowd before I head to the bar. The setup encourages mingling—staging a perfect opportunity for us to weave through the whispers of the court in search of clues about Wolfie's enigmatic father. "Remember, we're looking for someone who can match Callie's years—and her cunning."

"Got it," Benjy says, saluting as he follows Tilly towards a cluster of elder Fae.

Wolfie and Prez veer off in another direction, their senses tuned to the undercurrent of gossip that might lead us to our quarry. They're looking for younger, but less tight-lipped prey. Doyle winks, walking backwards away from me before disappearing into thin air.

That motherfucker and his slipping in and out dimensional pockets—what if Jolene saw? Reckless.

Once I get to the bar, I place an order. It arrives quickly and my hand wraps around a chilled glass of Gooseberry Whiskey. This shit is expensive as fuck and I'm surprised they're serving it. I'm about to comment on it to the bartender when he gets distracted by a man who sidles up beside me. The newcomer is quiet, but his presence commands my attention—a picture of weary aristocracy, clothed in a pinstripe suit that whispers of wealth and power. The purple sparkle of Phantasm swirls in his glass and I wince. That is not a drink meant for the faint-hearted or light-walleted.

"Careful with that," I comment, nodding towards his drink. "Phantasm is known to reveal more than some wish to see."

"Ah, but sometimes revelation is exactly what one seeks," he responds in amusement.

I study him closer now, noting how the silvery threads of his suit glint with a magic signature that sends a shiver down my spine. It clicks suddenly—those are no ordinary pinstripes. They're spells, stitched in silver thread from collar to hem. Something like that had to cost enough to set back a small state budget.

Could this be the elusive Midnight King? No one has even mentioned the patriarch or matriarch of this court.

"Interesting choice of attire," I remark, keeping my tone neutral. "Protection spells?"

"Observant," he replies with a tired smile. "One must always be prepared, don't you think?"

"Indeed." The dance of riddles between us is a subtle duel of wits, but there's a hollowness to his gaze that suggests his true target might not be me. We sip in silence for another moment until I finally excuse myself, leaving the king—or whoever he really is—to his devices.

I need to find Tilly and Benjy; the royals might be mingling amongst us in disguise.

I locate them deep in conversation with two couples whose elegance is striking. One pair shimmers like moonlight, the other dark as pitch, and their masks obviously conceal more than their identities. As I approach, my hound's instincts kick in; these strangers bear the same scent as the king I just left. The men are princes, which means the women are two of Alistair's sisters.

"Teddy!" Our girl greets me, radiant as ever as she sparkles in the moonlight. I lean in and kiss her cheek, drawing curious stares from our company.

"Your... family structure is unique," one of the women observes. There's a mix of fascination and puzzlement in her voice, so I know she's not being nasty, but I dislike nosy questions.

Tilly's easy laughter rings clear as crystal. "We're polyamorous. There are three more guys wandering the party. We're all very happy together, I assure you."

"Quite the modern arrangement," comments the darker of the men. His tone is unreadable, but I wonder if any of the competitors for that stupid show had considered a family like ours.

Probably not. Despite monogamy not being the norm in supe communities, the old guard of a lot of species still encourages it so we blend in.

"Our love doesn't follow outdated rules," Benjy adds and I grin at my friend. He's really coming out of that shell he was stuck in for so long.

I kiss Tilly's knuckles, sealing our explanation with a gesture of endearment. The couples look a bit ruffled, so we take our leave not long after.

The air is thick with unasked questions until we get far enough away that I feel safe murmuring to my companions. "Did you learn anything useful?"

"Maybe," Benjy says, his brow furrowed. "Though I feel like it was more about how unhappy they seem."

"Trouble in paradise? How could that be when you enter a relationship based on a TV show contest?" I feign surprise and they both snicker.

"The glitz has definitely faded," Tilly snarks as we encounter Wolfie and Prez. "Those women seem about as sexually satisfied as a group of nuns."

"Guys, listen," Wolfie starts, urgency lacing his words. "We might have found something."

I close my mouth, letting my response to Jolene's quip fall away. "Tell us, pup."

"We heard about a fae who tried to unite the kingdoms a long time ago. He moved through all four, advising the royals and trying to stop a lot of the petty bullshit wars. When it became obvious it wasn't working, he vanished for a decade. When he returned, he was a different person—cold, manipulative, and power hungry."

"Sounds like a delightful chap," I muse. "I suppose that could be your dad, Wolfie."

"Having to fuck Callie would do that to anyone," Tilly muses and I give her a look.

Wolfie dips his chin and shrugs. "I mean, she's not wrong, Teddy."

"We should keep digging," I say with a sigh. "There's more to this court than meets the eye, and we're going to uncover it all."

Legendary

Jolene

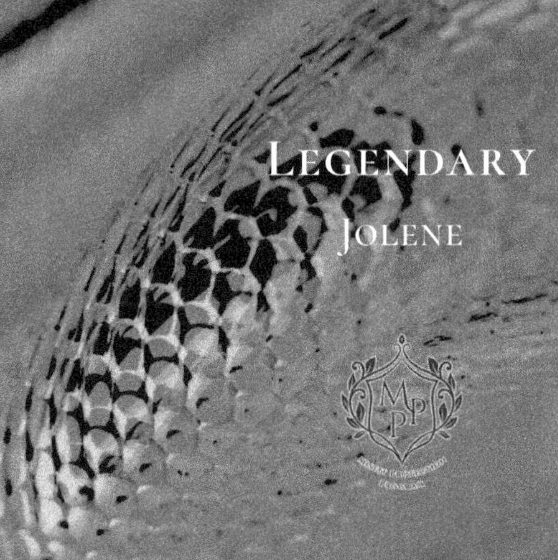

Everything here glitters like a constellation of nobility and deception swirling in dance. I watch from the outskirts, my eyes scanning for clues among the fancy people drinking and mingling. My heart thuds a rhythm that matches the undercurrent of dread in my gut. I don't like hearing that we're probably hunting a bad guy, especially because it will disappoint my darling boy.

He's had enough bullshit in the parental arena and I'm ready to tan someone's hide if it doesn't stop.

Wolfie's profile stands out from the group he's in, his expression etched with growing concern. Once he sees me, he excuses himself, making a beeline for me. His voice is steady as he speaks, but there's a tremor there—fear, anger, or maybe both. "Any luck, Sugarplum?"

"Snippets of stories, but nothing solid. It's like trying to catch smoke," I reply as a frustrated sigh escapes me. "Some say 'he' moves through shadows; others claim he's waiting for war. There's no substance, only specters."

"Same here," Prez chimes in, his brow furrowed as he joins us. He tries to lighten the mood with a wry smile, but it falls flat. His hands land on Wolfie's shoulders, squeezing them gently. "It's like this dude is their Boogeyman."

"Or a ghost story," Teddy adds as he comes over to pat Wolfie on the back. I smile as the vet turns to lean into both of the men, loving how they take care of him. "We'll get to the bottom of this if it kills me. I hate feeling like we're in an episode of Scooby Doo, though."

Wolfie nods, but I can tell his mind is racing with possibilities. He's far too sensitive and kind to not feel bad if both of his biological parents are complete psychopaths who get off on torturing people.

"Hey," I ask, lowering my voice to a softer tone. "Are you okay?"

He shrugs, a gesture meant to be nonchalant but laden with sadness. "I just hoped for... something different." His gaze flickers downward, then towards the regal and detached Fae court, and then back. "I guess madness runs thicker than blood."

"Lucy," Prez says as he pulls him closer to press his lips on his forehead. "We have you—all of us. You're not alone and you're not crazy, even if all your bio-donors are."

Teddy nods as he joins them, his protective instincts palpable as he rumbles softly. "The doc is right. You're ours, pup, and nothing is going to change that—especially not asshole parents."

"Thanks," Wolfie murmurs before pulling away to straighten his tux and gather himself. "I don't want to be needy, but this shit is harder than I expected."

"Tilly," Teddy says, turning to me, "stick with the women. They talk more around you."

"And even more when she walks away," Doyle snorts. "They're as bad as the belles back home with the mean girl shit. Our girl should watch for a knife in the back from damn near anyone in this garden."

Fucking fabulous. I just make friends and influence people everywhere I go now.

"I'll go back out there," I say with a sigh. "But keep an eye on our boy or I'll be pissed." When they nod, I nod and turn away to weave through the throngs of guests. Now that I know what to look for, I see when the princesses flit by. Their smiles are tight and their eyes betray the sadness lurking beneath. I also catch glimpses of the princes with stoic masks firmly in place. Both seem equally out of tune with the grandeur of the ball, but I can't figure out why.

"Something isn't right with them," I mutter under my breath as I pass a group of teen girls who titter at my proximity. "Obviously Doyle was right about the fucking rumor mill, too."

An older woman hears me growling and pauses, her lips quirking as she looks me up and down. "Darling, this whole thing's a sham. Ever since the show started, it's as if the entire court has been bewitched."

Ooh. Now this *is interesting.*

"Perhaps they're enthralled by their own misery?" I suggest, baiting her to see if she'll bite.

"Or cursed," she returns. Her voice drops to a fearful hush, and I tilt my head as I pretend to think about that.

"By whom?" I gasp, feigning ignorance as I put my hand on my chest. "Wouldn't that be very dangerous to attempt?"

"Who can say?" she replies, her eyes darting around nervously. "They whisper of a shadow, a phantom advisor who vanished and returned to pull strings from behind a veil of darkness. It could be him."

Paydirt.

I have to hide my grin as another woman scurries up, giving my new friend a reproachful look. "Those are tales for children," she scoffs. "It's more likely the royal family are embroiled in a power battle between the new princes and the true heir. Alistair is known for his vicious temperament; it's why they're sending him to Harvest."

"Do you think it's only a fairy tale or are you scared it could be true?" I challenge. My mind races as Alistair's words echo in my mind *'That's when shit started going wrong.'* He meant the show and the pairing off of the princesses.

He must think a guiding hand was messing with all of it.

"Perhaps you're right," I concede with a smile that doesn't reach my eyes. "But if not, your rulers have a serious problem on their hands."

"They're royals, darling. They always figure it out," the second woman says with a shrug. "We're not responsible for their troubles. Come, Priscilla. I see a fresh tray of hors d'oeuvres circulating."

I frown as they walk off, disliking their snooty dismissal of troubles in their land.

All it takes for evil to win is for good people to do nothing, after all.

"I'M GOING TO RIOT IF WE DON'T ACTUALLY GET TO EAT THIS TIME," I declare as I slide into a chair at our secluded table.

From our table, the royal family's grim faces are on full display—a veritable theater of quiet despair. The man Teddy suspected to be the King sits with the weight of the world bowing his shoulders and his wife is beside him, her face masked but her expression unmistakably hollow.

What the hell is going on in this damn place?

"It feels like we're dancing on a knife blade, doesn't it?" Doyle murmurs as he takes a seat across from me. "Our hosts have been nothing but gracious, but they're treated like pariahs among their supposed sycophants."

"Maybe it's not what they've done," I suggest, picking at the bread in front of me, "but what they're expected to do that scares them."

Before any of my guys can respond, an unnatural shadow blankets the stars above. My heart rate kicks up as a swarm of winged beasts darken the sky, their shrill cries drowning out the music and laughter. Panic ignites the ball, a fire fueled by fear of the shrieking monsters diving from above.

"Tilly, get down," Teddy growls as he leaps to his feet. He shoves me toward Prez, but I'm already ripping away from his grasp.

"I'm not helpless," I spit out with my teeth clenched. I give him the fingers and stomp away before he can get his hands on me. Pushing through the chaos, I feel my dress billow around me in an impractical sea of fabric. Cursing, I consider ripping it away, but I don't have a damn thing on under here that wouldn't be humiliating to show off in public.

I'll be damned if I'm letting these motherfuckers watch me fight in goddamn Spanx—that's a line I won't cross.

"Damn it. This is going to be really hard to explain later," Prez mutters somewhere behind me, but his words fade as I spot Alistair under attack—from Prince Finn, whose form is monstrous and covered in white fur matted with blood he didn't shed.

"Yo, Fuzzball," I yell, drawing the beast's attention long enough to dart forward and jam my knife deep into his shoulder. Finn's pained roar confirms he's still in there somewhere, but trapped in his body as it betrays him. I have to do something or he's going to get killed and I *think* Princess Aubrette might be upset. I don't hesitate, swinging a fist with all my might, connecting with a crunch.

I don't have many options, but here it goes.

Gathering my fury at every stupid thing going on in my life right now, I swing my fist in a vicious right hook, grinning when it connects with a sickening crunch. Finn collapses, and I'm left panting over Alistair, who's more vulnerable than I've ever seen him.

"My sisters," he croaks, blood spilling from his lips. I'm pretty sure he'll be okay, so I nod.

"Stay alive," I shoot back before turning on my heel to find the next afflicted couple. Grumbling, I head for the next fight on the stage. "I can't wait to blast you for this fucking mess, you absolute goddamn biscuit."

"Tíogair, get back," Doyle shouts as I approach him and Celestine. She's dangerously close to receiving a fatal blow from her prince in his hulking orc form. My cheeky Irishman is clearly holding back, causing a desperate dance of evasion as he fights the green monster man. "I'm going to finish him off."

"You can't kill him," I breathe as my mind races for a solution. Closing my eyes, I feel a strange surge crawling up my spine as I stare at the two men fighting. When wings unfurl behind me, I try not to freak out. Doyle doesn't look surprised when they sprinkle the air with black sparkles that settle like a whisper over the chaos.

Son of a bitch. Am I fucking fairy like Wolfie?

The feral prince and terrified princess slump to the ground, suddenly enveloped in slumber. Doyle's wide-eyed shock mirrors my own pounding heart, but before I can process it, he's pulling me away, hand locked with mine.

"Nobody can know what you just did," he hisses as we dodge through the fray.

"Over there," I point, spotting Benjy in gorilla form giving Keegan the elf a thrashing that might end in death. I don't know what to do except reach out to touch the primal fury in him. It takes a moment, but I see clarity return to his gaze. He stills, panting heavily, his fists unclenching as he looks at us in confusion.

Benjy doesn't have a lot of human in him when he changes—good to know.

"It's not just the princes," Doyle says as realization dawns "Something—or someone—is driving the men wild, stripping them of control. That's why I almost… and Benjy… Fuck, who could wield that much power? I'm not exactly easy to…"

He looks frustrated as he mutters to himself, obviously trying to keep his full thoughts from me as he works through this newest complication.

"I think the better question is: why turn it against the Midnight Court?" His eyes meet mine and he shakes his head. My brows furrow as we look over the people fighting all over the lawn. "Whoever it is, we need to put a stop to this… fast. Otherwise, someone is going to die, Lucky."

I have a feeling our secret enemy has a fall guy lined up to take the blame—it could easily be someone in my family.

I'll be damned if I'm going to let that shit happen on my watch.

Cello Suite No. 1 in G Major
Dhameer

The clink of crystal and the murmur of the elite weave into a symphony of decadence. Here, in this ballroom awash with golden light and laughter, we are hunters cloaked in the finery of our prey. Hugo stands beside me, his posture relaxed but eyes keen beneath the low glow of a chandelier. Saoirse's elegance is effortless, her gaze sweeping the room with a predator's precision. I can't help but admire how she carries herself—like a blade sheathed in silk.

It's very different from how she typically presents herself; her Guardian training is more apparent tonight than I have seen in the past.

"Patience," I whisper to myself, scanning faces and fine jewels, searching for one particular glint of auburn. She appears at last, the *Reina Pantera*, slinking through the crowd. The woman from the horse show in Turkey materializes like an enigma wrapped in emerald velvet, her famed red locks a fiery contrast to the subdued hues around her.

"Found her," Hugo murmurs, his voice barely audible over the chamber quartet's crescendo.

"Let's not rush," I counsel. "She's dangerous and easily spooked. My experience with her was not typical; most do not survive being the center of her attention."

We glide through the throngs of guests until we stand before her. There's a weariness to her eyes that wasn't there in Turkey—a shadow beneath the blaze. It's jarring to see such fatigue on a creature known for her ruthlessness. I cannot help but notice the change and wonder if I'm picking it up because she allows it or because she cannot conceal it.

What could possibly have this serious effect on such a powerful supernatural?

"Good evening, *Reina*" I greet, masking my emotions with a diplomat's smile.

"Ah, you've arrived. And you're traveling in a charming trio this time," she responds, her voice a melody laced with hidden notes. "You've been busy since our last encounter—building an alliance, Your Highness?"

"Simply enjoying the company of good friends. Are you here with your companions this evening?" I ask as I look around discreetly. "Or is this meeting an extension of an assignment?"

Her lips curve in the ghost of a smile and she shakes her head. "No guests this evening, Prince. I am far too busy to pause for revelry at the moment. But your associates' probing for answers drew my attention and I decided to handle this situation personally."

I arch a brow at her, my expression curious. "How would our subtle digging show up on your radar of all people, *Reina*?"

"Just as you have your sources, I have mine." She sips the martini in her hand, twirling the stem in her fingers with the dexterity of a master thief. "You've shown up on reports you don't want to be on. Eyes far less understanding than mine have noticed your efforts. So I made time that I did not have to meet with you."

"Saoirse," I say as I turn to her. "Is your family as discreet as Isra?"

"Always," Saoirse replies smoothly, the corner of her mouth ticking upward.

Reina smirks and shrugs. "They likely were, but the people I'm referring to have more resources than you can imagine. Which, given your wealth, isn't a small feat, I know. You do not want to continue fumbling around and catching their eyes, Prince."

She's trying to help us, but I have no idea why—that worries me.

"How do you know this and why would you risk coming to tell us?" Hugo cuts in. His face is a mask of distrust as he studies the lethal woman.

"Especially since I *technically* still owe you one," I mutter. That gets a laugh out of the woman and she shrugs, but it's not enough for me. "Why can't we locate this team of assassins who slid in and out of that house without leaving a trace? We've been looking everywhere, even in human circles."

"I suggest you search for those who dwell where your sun's fingers cannot pry," *Reina* advises cryptically. "It takes more than mere mortals to bypass the wards that protected that officer's home."

I feel a chill despite the warm air. *What are we stepping into following this lead?* My face reveals nothing of my concern; I've learned to school it into impassivity over countless negotiations. She tilts her head, her bright blue eyes flashing emerald for a moment and I have to hide my reaction again.

Reina Pantera is not human, either—a fact I doubt many know since the Society has never mentioned her.

"An intriguing suggestion," I say as my mind already sifts through possibilities while discarding the impractical. There could be a team of supernatural mercenaries operating outside of the Society's purview, but it seems unlikely they wouldn't at least be aware of them. I wonder if the cover up we're tracking isn't one orchestrated by our people, but one purchased by an outside party from skilled criminals.

But how does she know?

"Consider it a free piece of advice. You can take it or leave it, Prince. Now that I've warned you, my responsibility is done," she says cryptically, then drifts away like smoke, leaving us to ponder her words.

"More than mortals," Hugo echoes thoughtfully, glancing at me with a frown creasing his brow.

"A surprising piece of information indeed," I reply, watching the space she vacated. "It makes you wonder what sort of darkness hides within her own silhouette, especially since she comes and goes with such skill."

Saoirse touches my arm lightly—our shared signal to regroup later. None of us want to be seen entering or leaving as a group for fear of drawing too many eyes on where we'll end up afterward. I'm particularly well known, so keeping my staff with me while the other two slink off allows them to disappear into the crowd easily.

We disperse among the revelers, and I'm lost in contemplation. This night has yielded more questions than answers, which is not my preference. Our hunt for the killers continues, but now we must pursue phantoms that slip between worlds, it seems. I wasn't prepared to hear that, nor to find out that we've been pinning our efforts on a conspiracy that may be coming from another source. I will have to contact our family and let them know there are more enemies than we were aware of.

Especially since somewhere, behind tired eyes, the Reina Pantera watches, a puppeteer holding strings we have yet to see for reasons we cannot fathom.

As I MAKE MY WAY THROUGH THE PARTY, PRETENDING TO MINGLE with the guests, the music pulses like a heartbeat in my ears. The thrum of urgency quickens my heartbeat as I continue to mull over the possibilities. While I have to stay a bit longer to keep my cover, I'm barely able to focus on the banal conversations of the elite around me. I lean closer to Isra, the din necessitating proximity as much as secrecy does.

"I'll delve into the *Pantera*'s advice," I tell her, the words nearly lost amidst the cacophony of laughter and bass. "You and Fazal can gather leads on these shadowy supernatural criminals."

Isra nods, her golden eyes reflecting the strobe lights, giving them an otherworldly glow. "I'll consult with lower beings and leave more respectable ones to Fazal. Your friend should speak with her handler. The Guardians know much about beings that prefer obscurity; some of their teams monitor them."

"Supes were sent to erase that human family because other supes were protecting them with wards. It feels as though there is a problem in the Society's ranks," I muse aloud.

Humans aren't the only ones who are corruptible, but it's disappointing when any of our kind go rogue.

We move slightly, allowing a couple laughing drunkenly to stagger past us, their carefree antics a stark contrast to our grave conference. My faithful general shrugs as she scans the crowd to make sure the people who bumped us weren't a precursor to something darker.

"A lot of money is involved then, Amiri," she says in a low voice. "A team of killers who can do that and make everything disappear, a mole high enough to have the right information… I do not believe this is the work of an individual and it surely is not last minute. This reeks of a very long term gambit."

"Too many coincidences lately," I respond thoughtfully. My mind paints the recent chaos in vibrant, violent strokes. "The witch disturbances during Halloween in Salem. A mafia upheaval shaking the West Coast. Northern Europe's Snow and Ice Kingdoms rattling sabers over trade routes. The death of that elder dragon. Young heirs being accused of murder."

It didn't occur to me until now that the small eruptions I've seen in the supernatural news might tie together.

"None of those issues intersect," Isra frowns. Worry is etched into her fierce features momentarily before they smooth into practiced calm. "That sounds as if we have discovered a much larger plan beginning to unfold."

"Agreed." My jaw tightens. "An unseen hand agitating the supernatural world's chessboard. But to what end, old friend?"

"Let Fazal and I do our jobs once you are safely ensconced in the hotel." Isra jerks her chin at him as he joins us. "We should take our leave, Your Highness."

"Of course." I reach out, focusing my energy. The air around us shivers, reality bending to my will as I open a pathway for us. "We will regroup with Hugo and decide what happens next."

THE MOMENT WE ARE BACK IN THE HOTEL, MY CLOSEST ALLIES check every inch of the suite until they are satisfied that we are safe. Hugo watches in amusement, but I know they are simply doing the things that have helped me stay both alive and free for many years.

It's difficult even for him to understand the life of a djinn.

Once they complete their sweep, my staff do exactly as promised—they head out into the night to see what they can glean from the local supernaturals. Hugo arches a brow as I retrieve my laptop, beckoning him to join me in the sitting area.

"Time to report back to Nelia," I say as I dig through my valise to find the files we've been compiling.

He nods, his face set in lines of concern as touches my arm when I'm about to hit the call button. "Are we certain she can be trusted?"

"Yes. Nelia isn't quite as ancient as I am, Hugo, but she's been part of the Society for longer than you. Her loyalty is unquestionable, which is why they put her in charge of a town like the Hollow."

"Okay. I'm just..." he trails off for a moment, then continues, "... feeling a bit paranoid after this evening."

I nod, understanding his hesitance. "As should we all."

When I hit 'call,' it only takes a few seconds before Mayor Nelia's face flickers onto the screen.. "Dhameer, Hugo. Any progress?"

"Only cryptic hints so far," I admit, watching her expression carefully. She's trustworthy; I didn't lie about that. But I'm not one to show all my cards to anyone until I know what I'm looking at.

"Have you heard anything from Jolene's family? They're still in Faerie, last I heard and they've only got about two weeks left to accomplish their goals before Jolene has to be back here."

"Harvest Court was their latest stop when I spoke to them. No luck finding Wolfgang's father yet though." I keep my tone neutral, but the news clearly troubles her.

"Things here are... unsteady," she confides, glancing off-screen as if expecting eavesdroppers. "The Hollow's balance is teetering with so many strong citizens out of town. The more... ambitious… townspeople are causing quite the stir with their gossip."

"Will this affect Jolene when she returns?" Hugo asks, his concern mirroring mine as he leans in.

"Undoubtedly." Nelia sighs. "She'll have to navigate a sea of old grudges and fresh whispers. I'd put a stop to it if I could, but mean spirited gossip is not a crime—especially not when it's shielded by influence and heritage."

"We'll prepare her as best we can," I say firmly, feeling the resolve steel within me. "I appreciate you making us aware of the increased pettiness and venom, Nelia. I know it's not your job to monitor this sort of nonsense."

She sighs and rubs her hand over her face. "Unfortunately, this is part and parcel when you live in a small town. I just don't want to see the girl harmed again. I wasn't there to help prevent it the first time."

"Understood," I rumble as my frown deepens. "I will send you any pertinent findings before we head to our next destination tomorrow. Have a good night, Nelia."

The mayor returns the sentiment and our call ends with the click of a button.

Hugo looks at me, his gaze unsure. "What now?"

I think about *Reina*'s words, my determination a match for any darkness we may face. "We follow the shadows, and we brace for the storm to come."

He nods as I close the computer, ending our duties for the evening. We will sleep while my associates do their work and in the morning, we can regroup. I have faith that Isra and Fazal will bring us something we can use to determine our next path.

They haven't failed me in over a thousand years and I highly doubt they will start now.

MORNING LIGHT SLICES THROUGH THE HALF-DRAWN CURTAINS, casting a geometric glow upon our belongings strewn across the room. I'm bent over my valise, methodically packing the materials I do not wish to have leave my person when we travel.

When Isra and Fazal gave their report this morning, I decided we would head to Argentina next then back to the States. My general heard rumblings about a facility off the coast of the nearby country, while my assistant caught wind of a possible lead in the Midwest at some bar. It was hard to decide which one would yield more results, but since Argentina was close, I chose to stop there first.

We're about to leave the suite en masse when the sound of voices coming closer tugs at my attention. I poke my head out the door, frowning as I wait.

"Keep it down, assholes." A woman's voice hisses the rejoinder as she turns the corner to come into view. Her electric blue hair is long and it sways around her hips with each step she takes.

I shake my head, turning back to pretend to zip my bag shut as they near our open door. They don't need to know I'm watching or listening to them as they walk by.

The girl is flanked by a woman and three men—one of whom's face tickles the back of my mind as if I should know who it is. The tallest man is rough around the edges—clearly the type who knows the back alleys of the world all too well. Another companion leans heavily on crutches, the clack of his progress rhythmic and steady as they head toward us. He trails behind the first two with the other woman. Their incessant stream of chatter spills from their lips as if words were currency. That's who the leader was chastising, for sure.

It's almost too *distracting, in fact.*

"Hey, isn't that—" Hugo begins, but his words falter, his eyes glaze over, and I recognize the distant look that precedes his visions.

"Damn." I reach out to steady him, my gaze still locked on the group now disappearing down the hall. "Is it over?"

"Many heads... animals..." Hugo's voice is a hoarse whisper, his brow creased in concentration. "A darkness—so vast it devours the light. And there... the hooded figure from the trial."

"Do you have any idea what it means? Is that even something you can share or is it going to violate your ethos?" My question hangs in the air, heavy with the burden of our unknown adversary.

Hugo shakes his head, frustration etching lines into his face. "Not yet. But it's vital, Amiri. I feel it in my bones."

"Visions are never just smoke," I sigh. The unrest, the supernatural undercurrents, the hooded figure—it's a puzzle with pieces scattered across a shadowy board. I love puzzles, but this one has parts flung around the globe and possibly throughout the years.

We need to catch up.

"Let's get moving." I sling my bag over my shoulder, determination fueling my stride. "We have a lot of ground to cover, and I don't intend to let these threads unravel without us holding the ends."

"Right behind you," Hugo replies, though his eyes remain clouded with the remnants of his vision.

As we leave the room, I glance back once more at the corridor where the blue-haired girl vanished. There's a story there, another piece waiting to be placed.

I'll be damned if I let it slip through my fingers.

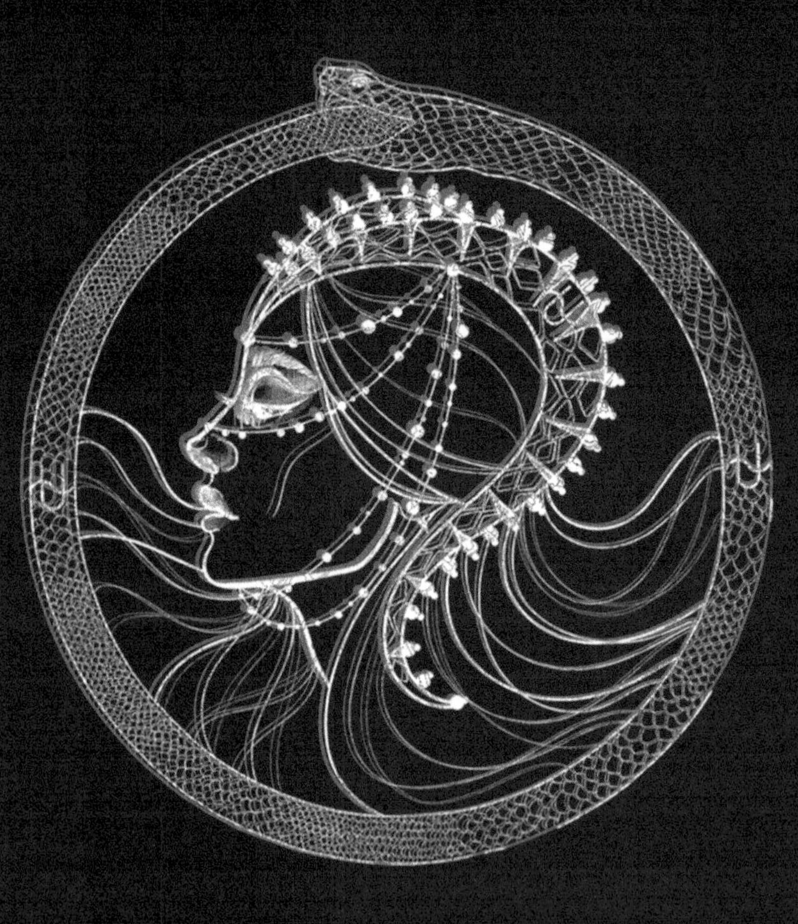

Dead Man Walking

Jolene

"Damn it, Riordan!" I shout, the words torn from my throat as another bolt of magic sizzles past my ear, singing the ends of my hair. The air crackles with energy as the half-Fae prince charges up again. I dart to the left while clutching Princess Marin's arm to keep her behind me. "Stop it, you idiot. You're going to hurt her."

This cannot be my life… ducking magic bolts with Fae royalty was not on my goddamn bingo card this year.

The fae prince grins, his eyes wild with some rogue spell or enchantment. He looks completely off his rocker and I have no idea what the hell to do about it. My heart pounds in my chest, each beat echoing my rising anger. My hands are ablaze again, flames licking up my wrists, turning my internal fury into scorching heat.

"Tilly, watch out!" Teddy's deep growl reverberates through the mayhem. He's enormous—a monstrous black hellhound man with thick fur flickering with fire. Once I nod, he pounces on Prince Angus, holding the squirming scaled fae beneath him. Water sprouts from Angus's fingertips in a futile attempt to quench Teddy's inferno and I realize he must be part mer… something.

Fuck, I'm so behind when it comes to this shit.

"I think he's trying to dampen your spirits, Teddy," I mutter under my breath. I'm trying to find levity in the horror, especially since I get the distinct feeling I'm not going to remember a damn bit of this when it's over. The more I think about it, my inconvenient blackouts feel like they're a protective measure. It's like they're meant to help me stay sane until that one moment when everything makes sense the guys keep referring to.

"Focus, Tilly! He's behind you," Teddy barks, voice rough with the notes of the canine he's shifted into.

I steal a moment to glance upward where Prez, now shifted into the huge white bird again, clashes with winged beasts that darken the sky. Euryale is striking at anything that comes too close to him; my girl is fierce as hell as she works alongside my adorable doctor. Their aerial ballet is a desperate fight to defend those of us on the ground while we try to temper the hyped up men.

"Your men have Angus and the sky covered, but Riordan's coming!" Marin's voice trembles as she rushes closer to me, her gown dirty and torn from the fray.

"Shit. These damn women can't keep themselves out of trouble for a second," I grumble as another blast from Riordan narrowly misses us.

Note to self: Alistair needs to get his sisters some fucking self-defense classes.

Grabbing her hand, I tug Marin out of firing range while I gather myself. I see my sweet, dependable Wolfie, weaving through the throngs of possessed partygoers. His wings shimmer, dusting the air with fae dust that I think is meant to soothe the savagery surrounding us. I watch as a couple, moments ago locked in a vicious duel, now cling to each other. It's effective, but for every pair he calms, ten more are still fighting as if they want to end one another.

"Come on, Wolfie," I whisper under my breath, "we don't have all night."

"Princess, duck!" Benjy's command snaps me back to reality just in time and I take Marin with me as I hit the ground.

I'm tired of this dick trying to fry me and I don't care if he's Marin's fiancé—the motherfucker is done.

"Enough," I grit out as the burn creeps up my forearms. *I have to end this, but how? How do you stop a tidal wave with a teacup?* "One cup at a time, just like eating an elephant, Jolene."

Marin frowns at me as she dusts herself off. "You want to eat an elephant?"

I shake my head, looking around for a second to get my bearings, then give her a crooked smile. "Not literally. But we have to do something about this mess; it's getting bigger and more out of control by the minute. So, how do you eat an elephant?"

The princess looks confused for a moment, then gives me a grim look. "Ah. One bite at a time, yes?"

"Yep," I say as I wipe the blade of my knife on the ruined gown. "You stay over here while I try to remove your prince from my plate. I'll do my best not to maim or kill him, I promise."

"Be careful," she pleads, reaching out to grip my wrist for a moment. "Please. I don't think anyone knows what they're doing right now."

I know that, but if you can't stop a rabid animal, you may have to put it down to protect everyone else.

"Careful went out the window three princes ago. I have to stop him, Marin, but I'll try," I reply.

With a feral cry, I rush toward the magic-wielding Fae. It's him or me —and I didn't put on this ridiculously elaborate dress to be outshone by a man, even if he is a sparkling fairy prince.

I have to dodge and weave around the stupid magic blasts—which sucks in a dress—but I finally see my opening when he spins to look at a loud sound from above. Euryale is flying above him, taking swipes with her enormous claws, and I could kiss my damn eagle if I wasn't busy.

Now's my chance.

Leaping onto Riordan's back with a force that knocks the wind out of him, I hold on tightly as we crash to the ground. The impact jars my bones, but I twist until I can clamp my thighs around his neck like a vice. He flails beneath me, sputtering desperate words in a language I don't know while I squeeze. He starts to go limp and I feel a vicious satisfaction when I finally get the upper hand. Slamming the butt of my knife against his temple, and I pant while Riordan sags into unconsciousness.

"Yoga isn't just for chanting wusses. I've got thighs of steel, baby," I mutter as I push the hair sticking to my forehead away from my eyes. The heavy fabric of my dress is in my way, so I gather it to free my legs. Once I do, I frown in sadness before using the knife to cut a ton of it off so I can slide out from under the fallen prince.

That was a damn fashion crime and I'm adding whoever made me destroy that thing to my 'getting their shit stomped' list.

I look around, seeing the world around me is still in chaos. The entire garden is a cacophony of screams, spells, and wingbeats. My heart hammers against my chest as I try to figure out what bite I need to take next to help end this thing.

~Jolene,~ the voice in my head begins—her tone oddly serene amid the turmoil. *~Use the mist.~*

"Are you kidding me? *Now* is when I lose my marbles? *Here* is when the voices in my head start? Very funny, universe," I mutter, more to myself. "What the chicken fried *shit* is the mist? How do I use it? Why are weird voices in your head so damn vague?"

Note to self number two: Call your therapist when you get home.

~Look inside of yourself. Find where you are connected to your canine. Push aside the fire to find more..." the voice instructs with infuriating calm.

Rubbing my eyes as I make peace with the fact that I may be having a psychotic break, I flick my gaze to Teddy, fully in the form of a colossal hellhound made of shadow and flame. He's battling the watery wrath of Prince Angus still. The voice says the mist is connected to Teddy, which means like some of the Fae, he's got more than one supernatural part. He's a man, a beast, and... something else that I need to figure out quickly.

"Okay, okay. Fine, weird dream lady. I'll give it a try." I take a deep breath, focusing on looking inside of me without closing my eyes to carnage around me. "Push away the fire..." I envision the flames licking up my arms, the heat that mirrors my anger, and mentally shove it aside.

A shiver runs through me as I reach deeper into the bond I share with Teddy, toward a soft pink glow. When I realize it's the odd pink mist I saw at the Harvest Court, I feel like a dumbass. The mist swirls around, pulsing with a warmth that I didn't notice before because it happened at the same time as the flames. When I reach out to touch it, the vapor soaks into my skin immediately.

Well, okay, then. I am one with the mist.

"Here goes nothing," I whisper as I look at the fighting Fae surrounding me. I take a deep breath and hold my hands out, reaching for the mist with trepidation. "Hopefully, you don't kill everyone. That would suck and I'll be very cross."

The mist unfurls, shooting out of my fingertips and spiraling out into the night. At first, it's just a wisp—a tendril curling through the air. Then it grows bolder, spreading its influence across the garden party in pretty pink curves of smoke that curve around the warring factions.

"What. The. Actual. Fuck?" I murmur to myself. I'm awestruck as the mist caresses each frenzied guest, altering their behavior almost immediately. Every being it touches stops the fighting, and replaces their grunts with ones of a different nature.

Everyone is no longer kung-fu fighting—they're kung-fu fucking.

"Hoooooooleeeee shit," I breathe in shock. My eyes widen, taking in the results of my experiment. Across the garden, couples are entwined as their aggression transforms to lust. The effects are hitting everyone except for my guys. They're all standing, frozen as their expressions range from shocked to bemused.

"Sugarplum, what did you do?" Wolfie asks, his voice tinged with concern.

"I don't know," I admit as the strange heat from the mist swirls inside of me. I feel like I'm the conductor of a symphony I barely recognize the music for. "But it worked, I guess."

The moans and grunts around us are better than screams of agony—marginally.

"Tilly, do you know why suddenly everyone is fucking?" Teddy says sternly. He's shifted back, which means he's standing with his arms crossed and his Dom face on—stark naked.

Wolfie chokes and I have to smother a very inappropriate giggle before I answer. "Apparently, I'm Cupid? Hell if I know, Big Daddy Asshole. This shit seems to just happen to me."

"Sugarplum," Wolfie scolds before he snorts, covering his mouth as he looks away. I know he wants to say more, but he's struggling to keep the laughter in.

"Quite the party trick, amirite?" I bob my brows at Teddy, who looks ready to turn me over his knee. Prez lands and walks over—*naked*—to scan the crowd going at it around us. His gaze cuts to me and I shrug. "I don't *know*, Doctor McNuggies. Trouble follows me like a bad penny."

"Speaking of bad pennies," Doyle says as he saunters up. He's not naked, but the gorgeous man following him is. Benjy just winks at me and I feel like I'm going to over heat on the spot.

Too. Much. Sex. And. Candy.

"Magpie, are you okay?" Prez asks, but his words are distant, echoing as if from another world.

I blink, feeling the world tilt a bit and that's when I know it's coming. I'm going to fucking blackout *again*, and I'll be lucky if remember *any* of this shit when I come to.

"Tilly? Tilly? Are you okay? Guys!"

And then my body surrenders to the void, leaving my allies to untangle the aftermath of this nightmare while I float in nothingness.

Someone in this damn universe has a sick sense of humor.

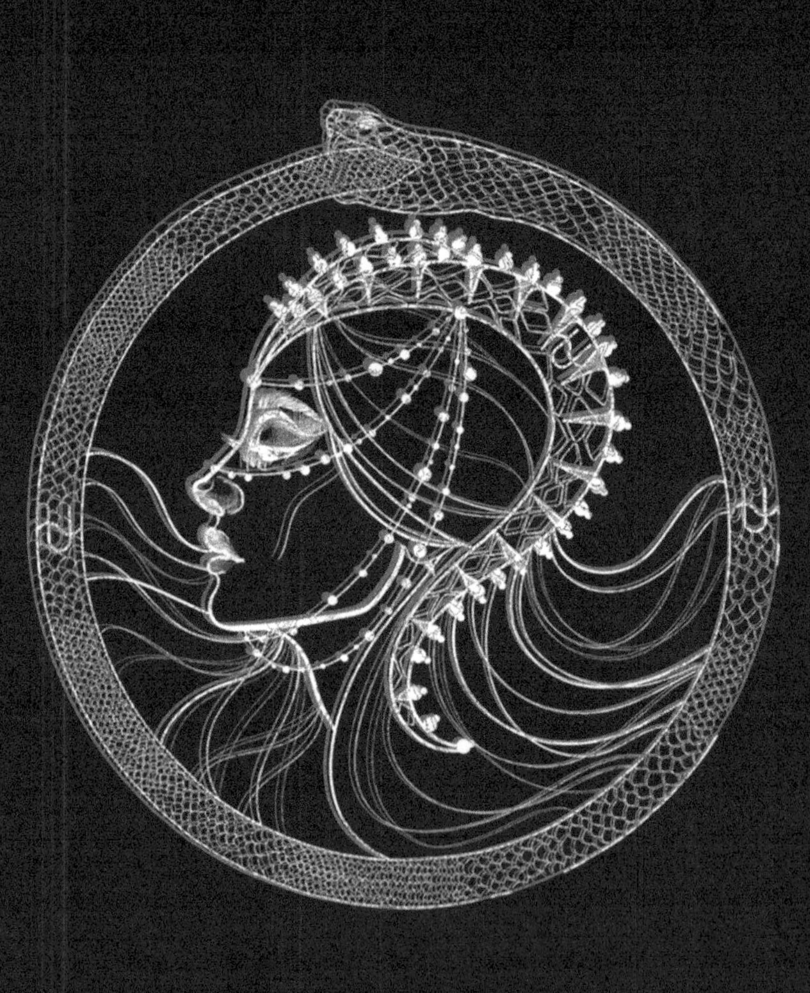

So Suspicious

Doyle

The air is thick with the stench of sex and sweat as people continue humping all over the damn lawn. I normally wouldn't object to the way it clings to my nostrils and coats my throat, but it's not my family producing it—it's a fucking arse load of random Fae. Trudging through the piles of bodies, my boots stick in places where blood from some of the fighting has congealed with…. other fluids. My irritation simmers just below the surface, threatening to boil over at any moment as I make a disgusted face.

I've been alive a long fucking time and this might be one of the grossest outcomes of battle I've ever seen.

"Breathe through your mouth and it will get better, mate," I mutter to myself as I sidestep a healer. The woman stumbles past me hurriedly, her mask fogging up with each labored breath. Jolene's borrowed incubi mist remains like a stubborn specter unwilling to release its grip on the castle grounds. It's a miracle most of the royals avoided a worse fate. Getting by with scrapes and bruises that seem to be immunizing them against the lust fog is a pretty light punishment considering what could have happened.

Teddy extricated my Tíogair from the chaos as quickly as possible. Her dress was in tatters, skin smeared with grime and flecks of someone else's blood as he carried her to our room. We decided to clean her up while the castle staff cleared the grounds little by little. Prez handled her with care that belied his shaking hands, stripping away the ruined silk and washing her wounds with water that turned pink before swirling down the drain. She was unconscious, blissfully unaware of the result of her tapping into Boone's power.

While she was out, Benjy and I came outside to look around. I wanted to see the bodies of the damn winged motherfuckers Hamilton took out in the air, plus we were all curious how long this weird orgy would last. The answer is nebulous, obviously, because it's still going despite an hour going by.

"Man, these things are ugggg-ly," Benjy says as he kicks the corpse of a buzzard thing. "And they stink to high hell."

I snort. "How can you tell? All I can smell is jizz and blood, mate."

The big guy laughs, shaking his head. "You're not a shifter. I can smell… everything out here. If you think jizz and blood is the worst it could be, you're sorely mistaken."

Before I can fire back a retort, my phone buzzes in my pocket. I don't bother to answer; I know who it is. "We gotta split. Our girl must be moving."

"Shit, let's go. Watch your step over there," Benjy says, pointing to the pile of Fae writhing on the ground behind me.

"I never thought I'd see the day when I was turned off by a garden-sized fuck fest. This is surreal," I grumble as we walk toward the back of the castle.

Benjy just grins. "Our girl's just that special, man. I didn't feel a thing out there."

Neither did I—not even a spark of excitement about the chaos.

How very unusual for me.

We're all standing over her when my Tíogair finally flutters her eyes open and gives us a confused look. I tilt my head as she pushes up on her elbows, groaning low.

"My head feels like a brass band and a group of tin men are having a slap fight," she says as she blows a hair out of her eyes. "What the hell happened?"

"Tilly, do you remember anything at all?" Teddy asks gently. He's closest to her, and he takes her hand as we all wait with baited breath.

"Not a damn thing," she replies with a disgusted look. "This is getting *really* old. I've had these blackouts for most of my life, but never this often. It's getting worse."

Honestly, it's probably better that she doesn't remember, but I can't say that out loud. Every one of us knows we can't talk about this shit until she's done emerging. Based on my theories, she's not done and won't be until the others join us. I'm not sure what the fuck we'd do if she had memories of the battle.

I don't want to gaslight the shit out of the woman I love just to please those stuffed shirt Council dicks.

"Where is Alistair? And the princesses?" Jolene frowns, rubbing her temples again. "I feel like I need to check on them, but I don't know why."

Wolfie's eyes go wide and he moves closer, putting a hand on her shoulder carefully. I know what he's doing—he's reading her emotions. A small shake of his head at Boone tells me that he believes she doesn't know. "I think some of them are in the infirmary, Sugarplum. They needed medical attention."

"Medical attention?" she squawks as she spins to put her feet on the ground. "Are they okay? If one of you doesn't tell me what the hell is going on right now, I'm going to be really pissed."

Teddy sighs and rolls his eyes toward the ceiling before he turns back to her. "Tilly, something poisoned the whole damn party. When everyone started getting… sick… a group attacked and tried to harm all the leaders. There was a lot of fighting and some people got hurt while others are still not well."

Her brow furrows and she looks at us suspiciously. "Okay. So you assholes swept me away when I passed out, cleaned us all up, and waited until I woke up?"

"That's about it," Prez says. "You were out for about an hour, so I assume they've got most of the family triaged by now."

The truth isn't too far off from her summary, so I don't feel like a rotten fuckwad.

"Do you want us to take you with us to the infirmary?" I ask. The words pop out of my mouth before I realize what I'm saying and I find every eye in the room on me. "She's going to insist on it, anyway. You know I'm right."

Heaving a frustrated sigh, Boone nods and holds his hand out to her. "Come on, Tilly. As much as I hate to admit the Irishman's right, you'd be throwing a hissy fit the minute we tried to leave. Let's cut out the middleman by just taking you along."

"I'm never going to let you forget you said that," I say as I wink at him.

Jolene lets go of his big paw and comes over to kiss me on the jaw. "Good job, Lucky. You're my favorite today."

THE CASTLE INFIRMARY IS A SYMPHONY OF GROANS AND WHISPERED comforts with harried healers flitting between beds like hyperactive toddlers. Alistair catches my eye from his cot, a grim smile pulling at his stitched-up side—a fate much less painful than what my Tíogair could have handed him. As we approach, he clears his side of the room with hushed commands, leaving only our tight-knit group at his bedside.

"Start talking," I demand once no prying ears remain. "What the hell happened out there?"

Boone is standing behind Jolene and he looks at the injured Fae with a menacing expression as if to remind him of our girl's handicap. "Carefully."

Alistair winces, and I can't tell whether it's from pain or the difficulty in explaining the situation without revealing things he shouldn't. He nods toward Jolene, who folds her arms defiantly, as he asks, "If you want to know, why bring her? It only makes this harder."

"Because *she* has a mind of her own and refuses to be left out," my Tíogair says firmly. "Danger doesn't discriminate here and I'm not staying in our room alone like a sitting duck when there are kidnappers running around."

I have to hand it to the asshole—he didn't even twitch at our big ass lie.

"Convincing her would have taken longer than we were willing to wait, " Prez chimes in, a smirk playing on his lips. "And her… companions… are occupied with their own pursuits, so she's not wrong about being alone."

The animals are all outside sniffing around the battlefield for clues at Wolfie's behest. Since the flying tank helped Prez ward off the ugly air beasts, I can't really complain about having the circus around. They're watching our backs and helping us keep Jolene calm, so they're okay with me. Plus, Odie's watching them as well, so we've got even more eyes on what's happening at the sex fest.

"Since you were injured in the line of duty, we thought you might be more amenable to our questions, Alistair," I add as I wink at Jolene. "Are the painkillers not very good? I'd think your people would be lauding your name and giving you the very best shit."

"Doesn't sound like they think he's a hero," she says with a mix of sarcasm and genuine amusement. "Maybe it's his sparkling personality."

Every time she plays along with my need to poke and prod, I realize again how fucking perfect this woman is for me.

Alistair gives her a rueful expression, accepting the narrative we've painted and her snark with a surprising grace. "You're not wrong. I don't have the most… gentle reputation. But since you asked, my pain medicine is more than adequate."

"Damn. I was hoping if I poked that stab wound, you'd feel it," Jolene mutters. "Whoever got a piece of you did a great job."

The prince chokes, coughing as he tries not to laugh. "Yes, the woman who stabbed me in just the right place to incapacitate me but not damage any organs was quite skilled. And maybe a little merciful, though you wouldn't know it now."

"Watch it," I warn him as he looks at her in amusement. "We don't know who attacked the party, so we can't assume they had mercy on their mind." My irritation simmers below the surface like a beast waiting to pounce. This entire scene is a farce, and I find myself not in the mood for the amount of playacting we need to do to keep it up.

Stupid rules have always been my downfall—the need to flaunt them drives me insane.

"Calm down, Haggerty," Teddy interjects, slicing through the tension with the precision of a surgeon. "What's your take on the attack, Alistair? How could someone have gained access to the grounds to… poison… the affected people?"

Alistair's eyes flicker over to Jolene for a fleeting second before landing back on us. His fingers twitch against the linen sheets as he tries to figure out how to respond. "This mess is bigger than any of us realized, including me."

"Mutiny always is," I mutter under my breath before I can stop the word from coming out. Everyone looks at me and I shrug. "We're not pirates, but it's the same shit, right? This is some betraying motherfucker giving your enemies what they need to accomplish a coup. The target was the entire next generation of your family, mate."

"You're right, of course," he says finally. "But I believe we're mere pawns on a chessboard so vast we can't see the edges."

"Or who's moving the pieces," Wolfie agrees as he looks around.

"That's how I feel about our journey here as well. We're dancing on a knife's edge and there are people constantly trying to push us off."

"Let's not slip, then," Jolene replies, her voice a beacon of resolve. "I say we should be the ones who move first so we surprise the hell out of whoever's orchestrating this nightmare."

Says the woman who has absolutely no idea what's going on, but is willing to jump into the fray without hesitation.

Her determination is infectious, and I feel a reluctant smile tug at the corner of my lips. We've been through a lot of shit since this trip began, but somehow, she always manages to pick herself up and keep moving. It's admirable, if not a bit naïve, and I'd follow her straight into Hades if she asked right now.

"Right," I say, clenching my fists. "We can do this together. Tíogair has the right idea."

The rest of our crew give me proud grins and I shrug. *Even an ancient demi-god can learn new tricks.*

"Into the fray together," Benjy says. "Has a nice ring to it, Haggerty."

For a moment, I let myself believe that it's enough—that our united front will shield us from the storm that's brewing just beyond the horizon. But as I steal another glance at Alistair, the furrows in his brow tell me that the tempest is closer than we think.

"That's great, but I don't think you understand the breadth of this issue," the prince says with a sigh.

"Before you say anything else, I have to know," Benjy starts, breaking into my thoughts, "At the Harvest ball, were you just putting on a act? If so, you're a damn good actor. I wanted to knock your block off."

Good question because I did, too.

Alistair sighs, the sound heavy with fatigue. "Yes. To protect Allora and our people, I have to pretend to be what everyone expects me to be." He pauses, his gaze flickering to our girl for a moment. "There's a rot setting in among the families, and it's spreading fast. Allora and I made certain to convey that our arrangement was unwanted and motivated by parental pressure."

"Parental pressure," I echo, snorting. The absurdity isn't lost on me. "Here I thought those smiles were a bit too tight. You both looked like you had poles shoved under your fingernails and that seemed like a bit much to me."

Wolfie leans against a wall, arms crossed and expression thoughtful. "I don't think your mole is any of the princes from the show. To be certain, I'd need to dig deeper, and they'd sniff me out before I could uncover anything."

"Then we keep our noses clean for now. Good job, pup," Teddy interjects then peers at Alistair with concern. "Anyone else aware of something off-kilter?"

"Daybreak's women rule from the shadows," Alistair reveals, a note of respect in his voice. "It makes their men visible targets and I think it's why they've had the least trouble with this shit."

"Ah," Jolene mutters, her lips twitching, "that explains the peacock display." Laughter ripples through us, a brief respite from the gravity of our situation due to our woman's undefeatable sass.

Prez steps closer, scrutinizing Alistair's injuries like he's assessing the state of a prized fighter. "They've got you stitched up well, it seems."

"Luckily, your lady is quite the blade master," Alistair retorts, a glint of mischief in his eyes before he winces. Tíogair's brow furrows, but before she can question it, he clears his throat. "The poison must be muddling my head still."

Teddy smirks proudly, exchanging looks with Prez and Wolfie. "What's our next play, then?"

"You need to head for the Court of Reaping. They're insular and secretive. If there's a scheme brewing, they'll have the least leaks," Alistair says, conviction steeling his tone despite his weakened state.

"Spies, plants... bloody garden of treachery," I mutter under my breath. Suddenly, it occurs to me that I love that kind of atmosphere. "That should be the most fun we've had since we got here."

"Those closest to me, like Allora, are working to contain this... internal blight. But if these conspirators seize control—" Alistair doesn't finish the sentence, yet the implication hangs heavy in the air.

"Then we'd best help you root this out before it strangles us all," Teddy says. "Otherwise, the effects might spill into other places."

"Exactly," the injured prince says. "That's what I've been worried about."

Well, isn't that bloody great.

Good Riddance

Jolene

I watch Teddy and Doyle , the silent communication between them almost palpable as they play the eyebrow talking game. When I get tired of being an odd man out, I put my hands on my hips and glare at them both. "Doyle, what the hell does finding Wolfie's biological father have to do with any of this? Why do the two of you seem to think that it's putting us in the middle of all this crap?"

Alistair shifts on his hospital bed, grimacing as he re-settles. "I don't know who he is exactly," he starts with his gaze locked onto Wolfie, "but the resemblance is striking. I've seen those features before—in our history books. I can't imagine there wasn't at least one person at Daybreak who recognized them."

There's a weight to his words, like each one is a piece of a puzzle we're not seeing clearly. I look at Doyle, but he's solely focused on Alistair, his expression intense. Teddy crosses his arms over his chest, sighing as he waits for the injured prince to elaborate.

"During dinner, I pressed you because…" Alistair trails off, squinting like he's thinking hard about something before he glances at me. "I knew it would make you more likely to believe my ploy and I could give you what I knew when you came here. Doyle, I felt the same about you. Your attitude, your signature—it's familiar. It reminds me of someone who once visited our homelands quite some time ago. You know I can't name him, though. Your kind don't take kindly to being outed."

His kind, huh?

I roll my eyes, throwing my hands up in exasperation. "Great, yet another taboo topic. As if we needed more secrets to prevent us from actually figuring anything out."

Alistair nods solemnly at us, his expression grave. "Be ready to leave for Reaping under the cover of darkness. We must move swiftly, before dawn exposes more than just the light of day. I fear your presence will cause those looking for answers to point the finger at the convenient outsiders."

"Trust is a luxury we can ill afford," Teddy says as he takes a scrap of paper Alistair pulls from under his blanket. The gesture feels like an anchor, a lifeline in a sea that's determined to swallow us whole. Between him and Allora, we have at least two people who aren't trying to kill us. "Don't make me regret extending you the courtesy."

Doyle, ever the one to find humor in the abyss, snorts as he rolls his eyes to the ceiling,"Looks like destiny decided to dump its entire burden on our doorstep. We're adding your shit to the load we're already hauling now."

Alistair lets out a brittle bark of laughter and we join in, the sound echoing around us—a chorus of discomfort. Deep down, I know the stakes have to be impossibly high for him to risk sending us away like this. As much as we try to fend off the creeping dread with humor, it still clings to us like a second skin of unease.

After all, we seem to be fighting something much bigger than my parents' death or finding an absent father—when did that happen?

"Go and keep in touch with the information I gave you. You don't have much time."

People keep saying that.

THE STERILE TANG OF ANTISEPTIC NIPS AT MY NOSTRILS AS WE LEAVE Alistair to his staff. His warning hangs like the sword of Damocles in my head, swinging back and forth until the rope snaps. I'm pretty good at juggling a lot of balls—see my bedroom for proof of that— but this feels like more than I can handle. In the past few weeks, I've gained another man in my family, two more seem to be headed for joining us, and then the whole supernatural thing hit me.

It's a lot. I don't know if I'm ready for destiny level responsibility right now.

"Time to pack up again," I murmur, more to myself than the guys as we enter our room. "I can't wait until we're home. Moving around like we're part of a traveling circus is fun when you're in your early twenties—not so much in your early thirties."

"When we're home, Sugarplum?" Wolfie says quietly. He gives me a soft smile and I feel my chest tighten.

Goddamn cheaters—always sending in the adorable one.

"Yes, when we're home, darling boy." My brows furrow and I tilt my head at Benjy. "I don't know what that means for you, big guy."

He shrugs, winking at me. "I hope it means no more apartments over the store for me. That place is cramped as hell."

Teddy whistles low, his lips curved up. "Sparks are gonna fly in Dixie."

"Oh, stuff it, Your Honor," I grumble. "We have to get moving. Everyone stop farting around and help me get us ready."

Prez straightens up, the ever-ready spark in his eyes as he nods. "I'll locate our animals," he says, heading for the door.

Doyle's gaze latches onto him, but he just nods. It's another silent conversation, and though I catch it, I decide to release it into the ether. We're about to slink our way from one dark haven to another cloaked in shadows. There's no room for petty mysteries right now; I simply don't have the spoons.

After he leaves, Teddy goes back to pacing in front of the window and the others help me fold, stuff, and pack the things. We didn't bring a lot, but it's getting a bit rumpled as we move through this damn place. I wasn't lying when I said I can't wait to get home. I'd like to have more comfortable clothes than dress up ones available and I miss my damn bed. It's a really fucking good bed and my back is feeling the lack of support.

What? I'm over thirty—even if I have superpowers, my damn back hurts like everyone else's.

"It feels like we're fugitives, doesn't it?" Benjy's voice pulls me back to the present..

"Doing the time without the fun of the crime sucks," I reply as my hands work methodically to stash our belongings. Escape is a strange bedfellow when you haven't actually done anything wrong; he's right about that. However, I also agree with Alistair that we're convenient scapegoats and anyone looking to avoid attention on themselves would sell us out for a fucking Snickers.

Or whatever the Fae equivalent is.

My eyes flick over to my ex-bully. Teddy's brow is creased deeply with worry as he continues brooding. He's determined to be our rock, but even boulders feel the weight of the world. I watch him for a moment longer, the tension in his shoulders speaking volumes about what's going on in his head.

"Teddy?" My voice is soft as I wrap my arms around his waist from behind. His body stiffens for a second, then melts against mine. "You're wound tighter than a spring. What's wrong?"

He exhales slowly before he responds. "It's nothing."

"Nothing doesn't look good on you," I counter gently, feeling the thrum of his heartbeat against my cheek. I grin a little, pinching his butt. "And not much looks bad on this ass."

His chuckle is a low rumble, but he doesn't elaborate. I splay my hands on his abs, humming a little as he leans into me. After a few moments, the others join us, forming a fortifying wall around my grumpy alpha. Wolfie steps in front, a protective barrier, while Benjy and Doyle flank us.

Their silent solidarity is a pact without words.

"Hey," I say, squeezing Teddy tighter, "whatever it is, you know we've got your back, right?"

There's a pause—an uncommon moment where Teddy's vulnerability shows—and then he nods, his hand finding mine. "Always," he says, and though the word is simple, it carries the weight of our shared history.

We stand there quietly for a few minutes until the urgency of our departure presses upon us once again. Finishing up the last bits of packing, we wait for Prez to return with the furry and feathered contingent. When he does, I wait for Teddy to grab his things and join us. With our gear slung over our shoulders, we step out into the inky embrace of the night, ready to face whatever lies beyond the threshold of the Court of Reaping.

Whatever the hell that might be.

THE WEIGHT OF OUR PACKED BELONGINGS PULLS AT OUR SHOULDERS as we stride out a back entrance to the castle. I can't help but break the silence, my voice barely above a whisper, "Are you guys that worried about this next stop?"

Wolfie's eyes are distant, reflecting a storm that's yet to break. "Alistair's info about my dad has me on edge," he admits, running a hand through his hair. "We don't even know what side he's on."

Doyle rolls his shoulders back, a defiant tilt to his chin. "I stopped caring who my father is a long time ago," he declares. There's a hardness in his eyes that tells me he's protecting himself. "Anyone who'd get involved with my mom is trouble. He'll be better at hiding than Wolfie's old man and ten times as dangerous. So no, I'm not worried about locating the git."

My eyes move to Benjy, who shifts from foot to foot with a rare unease. "I'm not scared, but I am worried," he says, his voice steady despite the confession. "It's more the people we care about... There's so much that could happen outside our control—things we might not be able to fix."

That's legitimate and pretty logical—which is why Benjy seems to be the eye of the storm lately.

Teddy just grunts, shaking his head—like a boulder refusing to roll downhill. His silence pricks at me until I can't stand it anymore.

Poking him in the side, I prod, "Come on, Teddy. We're family. You need to share, too."

He looks down at me, his blue eyes a turbulent sea. "I'm worried I won't be able to protect everyone," he finally says. There's a crack in his voice that mirrors the fault lines in our situation. "Not from our parents, the wacky shadowy villains, or the chaos snapping at our heels. I can't fail you again, Tilly, especially when there's even more at stake."

Silence blankets us, heavy as the darkness that shrouds the house we're about to leave behind.

Prez snorts, a smirk playing on his lips as he looks at our leader. "You can't control everything, Teddy. But that's okay. We look out for each other—that's how family works."

I think Teddy's going to slap the smug look right off Doctor McNuggie's face for a second, but he finally gives him a rueful grin. "Doesn't mean I don't *want* to control everything, you jackass. But I know you're right."

A line of cars greets us ahead, their engines purring softly as they wait. This is Alistair's people, ready to spirit us away. The ghostly gray vehicles seem almost spectral in the moonlight, the shine in their silhouettes promising both sanctuary and peril.

We have got to get out of this weirdly Gothic nightmare before I turn into Poe—what is with me?

Climbing into the car, I nestle against Teddy's side, his arm a comforting weight around my shoulders. I want to help him come to terms with the unpredictability we face as we head towards the last destination in our journey. Unfortunately, the steady rhythm of the road and the stress from whatever the hell happened last night hit me all at once. I know I'm getting sleepy and I can't help it.

As the miles unfurl like ribbons behind us, I'm passed from embrace to embrace—each one keeping me until I'm almost out. Eventually, exhaustion claims me, and I drift into sleep cradled between Benjy and Doyle, their steady breaths lulling me deeper into dreams.

Preparation for the final family can wait—we have time, even if people keep saying we don't.

Unsteady

Wolfgang

We've been on the road for hours, the hum of the engine a constant companion as landscapes merge and shift outside the window. Now, as we approach the border between the Midnight Court and the Court of Reaping, the world takes on an otherworldly glow. The sun cresting the hills is devoid of its usual fiery palette; instead, it's a glowing white orb hanging in a sky painted with grays and slates. Frost clings to every surface, icicles dangle like daggers from branches, and the ground is carpeted with snow that sparkles with crystalline accents.

Yeah, this feels like a place my twisted bio mother would be fond of.

"Looks like something out of a twisted fairytale," I murmur as my breath fogs up the glass.

Prez, ever the steady presence, nudges my side to get my attention. I lean into his warmth, feeling the coiled tension in my muscles ease just a fraction. He's doing his best, but there's no real comfort, not when I think about what—and who—lies ahead.

"Callie's always had a taste for the dramatic," I muse aloud. My mother is the infamous Cailleach and she could care less that she broke sacred laws when she and my bio dad conceived me. Hell, I wouldn't even put it past her to have done so on purpose to corner a powerful being. That would explain why they had to dump me in an enclave once I was born. Regardless of their arrangement, I'm here now, chasing down the specter of a man who could be steeped in rebellion and treachery.

My genetics aren't looking very promising at this point.

"Maybe he's just a hermit," Doyle offers out of nowhere, his tone laced with a wryness that doesn't quite mask his concern. "Sometimes rich, powerful people like to disappear into the ether to keep all the sycophants and sponges away."

"Or maybe he's playing a long game," I counter, pressing my palm against the cold window as the landscape rolls by. This journey isn't only about unearthing family secrets—it's about untangling a web that could ensnare us all.

Unfortunately, I've pulled Sugarplum right into the heart of all this drama.

"Sleeping dogs, Wolfie," Doyle says, glancing at me in commiseration. "Sometimes they're better left undisturbed."

"Right, because avoiding fleas is so important when you're dealing with a potential coup," I scoff. I know there's a kernel of truth in his words—some stones are best left unturned. But I've never been one to walk away from a challenge, especially not with stakes this high. Being the youngest person in high school, then veterinary school, and then in the Hollow's induction pool taught me that you can't simply let some things go.

I'm not a fan of conflict, but I know when it's necessary.

"Whatever's waiting for us," I say, pushing off Prez to sit up straighter, "we'll face it together. No one's going into this blind."

"Damn straight," Doyle replies, and I can hear the unspoken pledge in his voice.

The car begins its ascent up the final hill and the view expands before us. My heart beats a staccato rhythm against my ribs as we get closer. This is a precipice, and I'm poised on the edge. Jolene's strength,

Doyle's loyalty, Benjy's calm, Prez's quiet care, even Teddy's brash courage—they're the anchors in this sea of uncertainty. With them along, I know I can face whatever the hell it is I'm going to find when we locate my dad.

"Here goes nothing," I whisper, more to myself than to anyone else, as the Court of Reaping comes into full view.

As the first light of their false dawn spills over the edge of the world, it paints everything before us in a ghostly luminescence. It's like we've stepped into a fairy tale penned by a madman—beautiful and eerie all at once. I press my forehead against the cold window, watching the frozen landscape unfurl before us.

"Tilly," Teddy's voice cuts through the silence as he nudges Jolene awake. She blinks slowly, dragging her slender fingers through her tousled hair, pushing up her glasses with a practiced motion.

"Wha—?" Her voice is groggy, but she's alert in seconds, attuned to the tension that coils around us like a serpent. Her attention shifts toward me, and I can't help but lean into her warmth when she wraps an arm around my shoulders, her chin resting atop my head— a silent anchor in a sea of disquiet. "It's okay, little Wolfie. We've all got you."

I nod, smiling against her warmth. She didn't have to think of me before she even had time to fully awaken, but that's the kind of woman our girl is. "I know, Sugarplum."

"Worried about your dad?" she murmurs, reading me like one of the smutty books she and Teddy like to share.

"Something like that," I admit, my voice muffled against her jacket. "Thoughts of a father I never knew, hidden agendas... It's a lot."

"Join the club," Doyle chimes in, his eyes meeting mine as he stretches his legs out. "My dad's probably a grade-A asshole, and my mom isn't winning any Mother of the Year awards."

"Family's complicated," Teddy adds with a half-smirk, though his gaze stays fixed on the castle coming into view. "I'm an asshole with or without parental guidance. But change? That's the real bitch."

"Guys, really, you don't have to—" I start, but Jolene cuts me off with a soft chuckle.

"Let them bleed out some of that testosterone, Wolfie. Sometimes showing a bit of vulnerability stops them from being complete alpha holes. Helps make them more useful with our hosts, especially when they're being dicks to us."

"Point taken," I concede, a reluctant smile tugging at my lips as I sit up straighter.

The car slows, and we're suddenly face-to-face with the full spectacle of the Court of Reaping—an immense, glistening castle of obsidian and ice, carved into the very heart of the craggy cliff. The structure shimmers under the unearthly light, the trees surrounding it adorned with ice crystals that gleam like jewels.

Holy fuck, it's like Frozen and Nightmare Before Christmas had a baby.

"Damn," Jolene breathes out, echoing my thoughts. "These guys are *not* screwing around."

At the foot of the castle, a giant man waits for us, his sapphire attire offset by a raven beard laced with frost. His crown, a twisted amalgamation of dark stone and ice, sits heavily upon his brow. Beside him, the woman who must be his spouse radiates warmth despite the chill —a stark contrast with her fiery hair and crown bedecked with vines and gemstones. They are definitely the royals of this court, their lineage unmistakable in the faces of the four princesses and two princes beside them, gazing at us as we arrive with their partners a step behind them.

"Looks like they rolled out the red carpet for us," Doyle comments dryly, earning a grimace from Teddy.

"Should've known Alistair would send us into a den of wolves without so much as a how-do-you-do," he mutters as he pinches the bridge of his nose. "You all need to be on guard. Do you have your blade, Tilly?"

"Relax, guys," I say softly. I can't shake the feeling that every glittering eye on us is out to do us harm. "We don't know that Alistair told them. In fact, I'd bet he didn't; I think it's the work of the mole in Midnight. Regardless, they're just people standing there waiting right now."

"Huge people with unknown… influence," Doyle retorts with a sharp look at me. " who also come with a pet polar bear."

I blink, then I see the enormous white bear lumbering out of the snow to sit by the King's side with a suspicious look at the cars. "Could be worse," I offer weakly.

"Could be better, though," Prez says ruefully. "That's more threatening than I'd like."

"It could be exciting, though," Sugarplum says, her eyes alight with a spark of mischief that belies the gravity of our situation. "I've always wanted to pet a polar bear. Think they'll let me?"

Everyone groans and I smile a bit. 'Exciting' isn't the word I'd use— not when each step toward this castle feels like a descent into the unknown. But we've come too far to retreat, so we steel ourselves as Teddy shakes his head.

"Tilly, I am fully convinced you'll die trying to pet something you shouldn't. And since I don't want that to be anytime soon, she stays behind us until the animals are unloaded from the other car." He winks at her and she gives him a dirty look as we untangle our limbs. "Pup, I expect you to keep her from doing anything stupid while we deal with this formal nonsense, okay?"

I doubt anyone could stop Jolene Whitley when she has her mind set to do something, but I'll give it a whirl.

THE AIR FILLS WITH AN ICY TENSION THAT SEEMS TO CRYSTALIZE between us and the awaiting assembly. As we exit the car, I watch Jolene's shoulders tighten. Her breath mists in the cold as she peers out at the gathered crowd. "Someone definitely sang like a canary," she whispers.

"Or maybe a stool pigeon," I add, my eyes tracing the stoic faces of the younger royals. Their fear is a tangible shiver in the air—one they poorly mask with brittle smiles. Benjy catches it too, his head canted as he observes them from the corner of his eye.

"Scared heirs and their dates are becoming a familiar sight," he murmurs under his breath.

Teddy's gaze follows mine, landing on King Darragh and Queen Eabha, their expressions oddly mismatched to the gravity of the situation. "It feels like all the elder generations are puppets on strings. They haven't had a clue things are amiss—not in any of the courts so far. Some sort of… drug," he says as he looks at Prez and I. His tone suggests he's pondering that magic might be at play, but he can't say it in front of Jolene.

It's certainly possible, but that means this conspiracy goes much deeper than a few snitches in the courts.

"Let's not jump to conclusions," I caution, even though I'm already considering potential spells in my head. I'm not a caster —more of a 'natural magic' user. We'll need to talk to a more proficient spell user to get a better idea. Maybe we can text Alistair and Allora to look into it.

The frigid air bites at my skin as we wait for the animals to join us. What sends a chill down my spine isn't the temperature—it's the implicit understanding that every eye upon us has been watching since before we crested that final hill. Alistair's people unlatch the other car and release our animals, drawing the attention of everyone as they alight.

Jekyll, Hyde, Kali, and Hecate saunter out with a regal nonchalance, only to be met by the intense scrutiny of a massive polar bear. The stand-off is brief—Euryale swoops down from above to land beside Prez. Her screech echoes off the ice, commanding respect from the bear, which begrudgingly backs away.

I'll be damned.

Our girl chuckles at the exchange, a sound that softens the severity of the scene. King Darragh grins at her, a spark of mirth dancing in his eyes. "If you're as brave as your companions, the hunt will be quite the spectacle," he booms, his voice carrying across the frost-laden grounds.

"Nothing says 'welcome to our home' like chasing after wild beasts. Fucking Fae," Doyle mutters, the sarcasm dripping thicker than the icicles from the trees.

"Careful," I hiss at him. I don't want him offending the royals or breaking our damn oath just to get in a one-liner.

The King's laughter rumbles through the air, rich and deep, a counterpoint to the chilling silence that had preceded it. *He definitely heard and we're fucked.*

Queen Eabha steps forward while he chortles, her demeanor the blend of light and dark that seems to permeate this court. "No balls and gowns in the Reaping," she explains, her smile warm despite the cold. "We favor the thrill of the chase and the skill of the hunt."

"Thrilling," Teddy deadpans, exchanging worried glances with the rest of us.

It should concern me. A hunt here presents so many issues: what beasts they'll chase, what we'll have to ride, what weapons we'd use, and a multitude of things Jolene can't know about. I know all of it, but I can't help the grin that tugs at the corners of my mouth.

This is their game, but Sugarplum? She's made for this.

I know how she handles a horse, her ease with weaponry, and the way she moved with predatory grace in the battle at Midnight. She could outshine them all if given the chance—even without her supe sides fully emerged.

"Consider it a challenge," I say, feeling the adrenaline stir within me. It's a test, perhaps, but one we might turn to our advantage.

Jolene, undeterred by the audacity of asking your guests to compete, strides up to Darragh. She extends her hand in a gesture of good will rather than curtseying. His lips curve up at that, delight written all over his icy features.

"I look forward to meeting your hunt master once we're settled," she says, her confidence unshaken. "I hope your quarry is ready for me. I won several fox hunts during a stay in England."

That declaration makes me tilt my head—I'm fairly certain Sugarplum wouldn't kill an animal unless she had no option. *What's she playing at?*

As her fingers wrap around the King's, I feel something shift—a strong sense of readiness. This hunt may be unexpected, but so are we. And if they think we're the prey in this twisted game, they've got another thing coming.

The crowd all watch as the staff takes our bags and leads us toward the entrance to the castle. I look at Jolene, checking to make sure no one else is near us and whisper, "How did you win fox hunts without killing anything, Sugarplum?"

She gives me a wicked grin. "It's hard for anyone else to beat you if you gather up all the prey and take it back to the finish line with you. Sometimes, the best solution is around, not through."

Damn, she's clever.

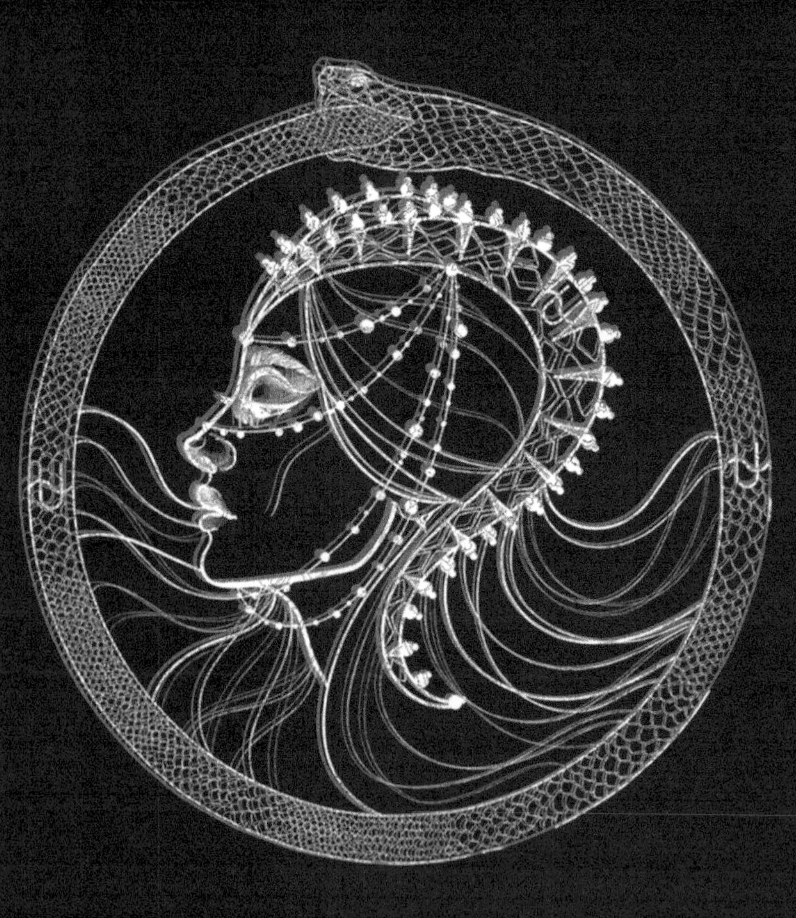

Landslide

Jolene

I KNEW this place was swanky when we walked inside and it had a double staircase with an immense, intricately carved chandelier in the foyer. The place looked like it was designed for a fairy tale LARP by an egregiously wealthy yet eccentric billionaire. I've been in three castles here and many at home and nothing I've ever seen prepared me for the Court of Reaping.

No wonder they let people call them ruthless killers—they want thieves to think twice before setting foot anywhere near this monument to opulence.

The door to our suite swings open, and I'm blasted with a gust of cold air that's somehow warmer than the icy chill in the hallway. My breath catches—not from the temperature shift, but from the sheer spectacle of our new quarters. Comfortable yet stunningly beautiful décor sprawls before us like a frozen kingdom, each corner meticulously carved from ice, yet emanating warmth. A monstrous four-poster bed commands attention, its icy pillars jutting up to support a canopy that glitters with encrusted jewels. Onyx, aquamarine, and diamonds wink at me as if they're in on my secret.

"Damn," Teddy murmurs beside me, his eyes wide as he scans the room. "I've heard of ridiculously wealthy homes built by movie stars and sultans, but this is…something else entirely."

"It's well past a bit much and on its way to offensive," I mumble, forcing myself to blink away the magical allure. My tame reaction is part of the act I still have to go through—despite the fact that pretending not to see the enchantments is getting old. Having to play blind when every detail screams to be acknowledged is harder than it sounds, especially with a group of men so attuned to my emotions.

For fuck's sake, there's a hot spring simmering inside of an icy whirlpool in the floor!

"The setup looks comfy, though," Wolfie chimes in, his attempt at casual undercut by the furrow of his brows as he strides toward the closet.

The sitting area boasts snowy white, fur-covered furniture so large and plush you could get lost within its depths. I take a whiff, my nose twitching until relief floods me when the synthetic scent confirms no animals were harmed for our comfort. It's a strange comfort, knowing we're lounging on faux luxury curated by someone who seems to know us intimately.

"Check this out." Wolfie emerges from the closet, his frown deepening into a scowl. "Clothes for all of us. Perfect sizes. Everything from casual to formal to night time included."

"Oh, wonderful," I say dryly, watching as the others poke through the selection. "Heaven forbid we look anything less than royal when we're sleeping."

Teddy is prowling now, his irritation tangible. "They've been tracking us closely—too closely for my comfort."

"Maybe asking ahead was someone's idea of hospitality?" I counter, hoping to calm him despite my gut twisting with intuition. This isn't just someone being thorough and I know it. Detail this intimate is invasive—a silent declaration that our supposed secrecy was nothing but a pipe dream.

"Look at this," Wolfie continues, gesturing to the sideboard adorned with a feast worthy of kings. Meats, cheeses, fruits—an entire perishable spread that would make Bacchus envious. Next to the Fae-style charcuterie display, there's crystal glassware and various types of drinks and on the floor, beds for our animal companions, complete with trays of food and water.

Okay, now I can't pretend it's someone being a good concierge.

"This is beyond stalking," I breathe, the words slipping out before I can stop them. "It's the work of the mole, for sure."

"Yep," Teddy agrees, his jaw clenched. "Time to check in with Alistair. Maybe we'll find out the douche bag gave this info to one of his 'spies' here and everything will be a little less creepy."

"If so, he's definitely as clueless as he claims. Anyone who gives up that much info to possible double agents is lucky they haven't been shanked yet. That's still better than being a traitor himself, though," I add as I frown.

The seed of doubt takes root as we continue looking at the items in this room specific to our family. I don't *think* he was lying; his worry for Allora was real. It's hard to trust anyone in this damn world, though, because they simply don't play by the same rules as the rich people in ours.

Big fucking surprise—supernatural elites are even more annoying than human ones.

As Teddy pulls me over to the comfy couches, I watch the shadows dance over the icy crystals. This place is so beautiful, but lots of pretty things are deadly once you scratch the surface. At least the ugly threats are honest. I turn to look at my grumpy ex-bully, tilting my head at him. "Are you just going to ask him point blank?"

Teddy's fingers fly over his phone, the screen a rectangle of blue light in the cavernous room. "Of course not, but Alistair better have some answers," he growls low, as much to himself as to me.

"Or you're going to kick his ass, I presume?" I lean in, trying to peek at the conversation unfolding on-screen. "That will be a feat all the way from here, Teddy Bear."

Prez laughs as he finishes stowing the rest of our things with Wolfie. The two of them join us on the big couch, dropping down on my other side. The doc's strong hands run over my shoulder and I groan low.

"Keep it PG, Tíogair, or we're going to make a mess before we get the answers we need," Doyle snarks as he flops on the big ottoman in front of us.

"Leprechaun's right, Tilly. Oh, and the prince claims he's clueless," Teddy snorts after a moment. There's an uneasy line between his brows as he responds to the next text. He's not letting this go at a simple 'wasn't me.'

"What else is he saying?" I ask as I peek over his arm. His damn privacy screen is blocking me and I punch his arm in annoyance.

"He's promised to check with his sisters to make sure they didn't contact anyone trying to be nice," Teddy continues, reading aloud the prince's response that flickers across the chat. "If they're not behind this, he'll send his own people to sniff out the traitor."

"As if that's any consolation," I grumble. "We're walking around blindfolded here."

Guilt gnaws at me—I'm withholding truths as heavy as the stones encrusting our ridiculous bed. So far, trusting the dream woman's advice about keeping them in the dark for their own good has worked out. Despite being attacked, the guys haven't let me out of their sight for a minute, and I think it's keeping us *all* safe.

At least, I hope so. I've never had dream woman hand down edicts before, so fuck if I know.

Before we can dissect Alistair's potential innocence further, a knock on our door shatters the stillness. The guys all jump to their feet as the animals bound towards the door. Growls fill the room and I rub my hand over my face, rising from the couch to greet whatever fresh hell is coming.

The door swings open to reveal a motley crew straight out of frost-bitten myth. A giant man looms, tusks protruding from beneath his bottom lip and eyes glinting with a chill that rivals the décor. Beside him, a fairy no larger than a child sparkles darkly, her wings a blur of shadow and shimmer. An earthy woman with a scent that speaks of wild forests and moonlit transformations nods curtly, while a stout Elven man, thickly dressed, clutches a ledger like a shield.

Dude, these people aren't even trying *in the Court of Reaping. What the hell would I be seeing if the Daybreak woman hadn't messed with my specs?*

"Evening," the giant rumbles, his voice like gravel tumbling down a mountain. "My name is Njord and we're here to prepare you for the hunt."

Teddy walks over, his scowl deepening as he looks at them. "We were told we'd have time to settle before you were sent."

"Preparation starts now, whether ye be ready or not," the elf says, his tone apologetic but firm. "Our skill is great, but not so much that we can sit around fiddling the day away."

"Alf is correct; our time to get you ready grows short," the shifter woman says, "and we aim to outfit you properly."

"Royal guests deserve nothing less. But do not fret! Both Bodil and I are as skilled as our fierce counterparts. You can ask anyone," the fairy chimes in, a twinkle of mischief in her eye.

"Revna speaks true, but we must take you in groups of two. We can focus more efficiently that way. Choose those who will follow us now, for we must make haste in order to finish for the late night hunt this evening." Bodil's eyes light on me and I try not to sniff the air to see if I can figure out what she is.

Doyle steps forward first, but Prez right beside him. They share that look—the one that means they're taking point to assess risks before they allow anyone near me. "We'll go ahead. We can speak with them about our specific...needs."

That translates to make sure they know our girl is currently under an information ban that's tying our hands behind our backs.

"I am not—" I protest, but Benjy's hand lands gently on my shoulder.

"Haggerty only means we should accompany you and the pup," he says, silencing me with a reassuring smile, "And not because you need protecting. Unfamiliar animals don't react well to me and Big Daddy over there."

Okay, that actually makes sense given what I shouldn't know about them.

"Same for Doyle," Prez interjects with a snort, folding his arms. "He can charm the pants off an old dowager, but animals look at him askance until they know him. It's probably his chaotic vibes."

"Please," Doyle huffs, a smirk lighting his features. "I've tamed more beasts than you in my lifetime, Hamilton." The doc rolls his eyes and they turn to follow the hunt team. His voice drops into a mutter, and I swear I catch the words 'Poseidon' and 'bastard horses' before the door closes behind them, leaving the rest of us to stew in a mix of concern and curiosity.

ONCE THE GUYS HEAD OUT, WE'RE LEFT TO LINGER IN THE OPULENT sitting room. Unease fills the air and I wrinkle my nose at the oppressive atmosphere. We can't sit around and worry, so I plop down on the couch again, gesturing for the others to do the same.

"Okay," I start, shifting the focus away from the gnawing concern for the others. "We've got one shot at getting the lowdown on Wolfie's dad during the hunt. Who has the best idea on how to approach these fuckers?"

Teddy rubs his chin thoughtfully, stepping into his element. "Diplomacy first. We keep it casual—feel them out during the ride. People love to talk about themselves, especially nobles. Maybe one of them will let something slip about the powerful people they know."

"True. You'd be amazed at the shit people say when they're drinking at the Speakeasy. The need to look important outweighs common sense all the time," says Benjy, nodding. "That's why I think we'll have more chances at dinner. Between toasts, small talk, and mingling—they're all opportunities to pick up clues."

"Exactly." Teddy paces, hands clasped behind his back. "We can't afford to spook anyone, so subtlety is key. I know most of us can do this, but someone will have to keep tabs on Haggerty. His natural inclination will be to cause trouble and that might seal lips."

"He's about as subtle as a flaming unicorn," I murmur under my breath, eyeing the abundant sideboard in distrust. "But he does have his strengths. He's excellent at loosening tongues when he's in his element."

"What an odd choice of words," Teddy murmurs, reaching for a piece of cheese and popping it into his mouth. His eyes widen, and he pauses mid-chew, turning to look at me.

Shit. Bad move, Whitley. Back it up before he figures it out.

"Is something wrong?" I ask, trying to sound nonchalant as I drift closer.

"Uh, cheese shouldn't taste this...rich." He watches me as I grab another piece and pop it in my mouth before he sighs in relief. "But it seems as though you like it. Should we venture out to that market we heard about so we can take some home, Tilly?"

I squash the impulse to blurt out why I have no desire to do that by biting my tongue. Crafty asshole thinks he'll trick me, but he's dead wrong. I pluck another piece off the tray and chew it enthusiastically. "Mmm. It's tasty as hell, so maybe we should. I'd like to see that place from the show."

Turning my back to the guys, I realize my face must betray my true feelings. Jekyll and Hyde perk up from their corner, tails twitching as they look at me. Their duet of delighted noises fills the space and I have to stifle a chuckle.

Obviously, they get my conundrum and sympathize—as much as cats can.

"Rich people are so fucking weird," I grumble as I contemplate whether to share this ludicrous luxury with my feline friends. The guys are still talking, but I'm stuck on this damn cheese like a skipping CD. My mind churns with the practicalities—or rather, the impracticalities—as I shake my head.

How rare are unicorns? How do you milk one? And how much does this shit even cost?

"Should I ask about the market tonight, then?" Teddy asks, oblivious to my inner turmoil over mythical lactation. "I think it would be a good place to look for clues, too."

"Maybe," I deflect, hoping I didn't miss too much when my brain took a curdled vacation. "We need to focus on finding out what we can about Wolfie's dad and anything we can about the people trying to kill the younger family members."

"Agreed," Benjy says, plucking his own piece of cheese but hesitating before biting into it. Teddy chuckles at him and the big guy frowns as he catches the words on the card. "We have to focus on our primary mission."

"Right," Teddy nods, his procedural mindset snapping back into place. "No distractions tonight. All our efforts have to be on getting what we need before we leave this place so we don't have to come back for a *long* time."

As if our collective will can conjure answers from this icy castle, we huddle together again—strategists plotting in the shadow of unicorn dairy treats and shadowy secrets.

If this damn cheese is the weirdest thing that happens today, I'll be a happy woman.

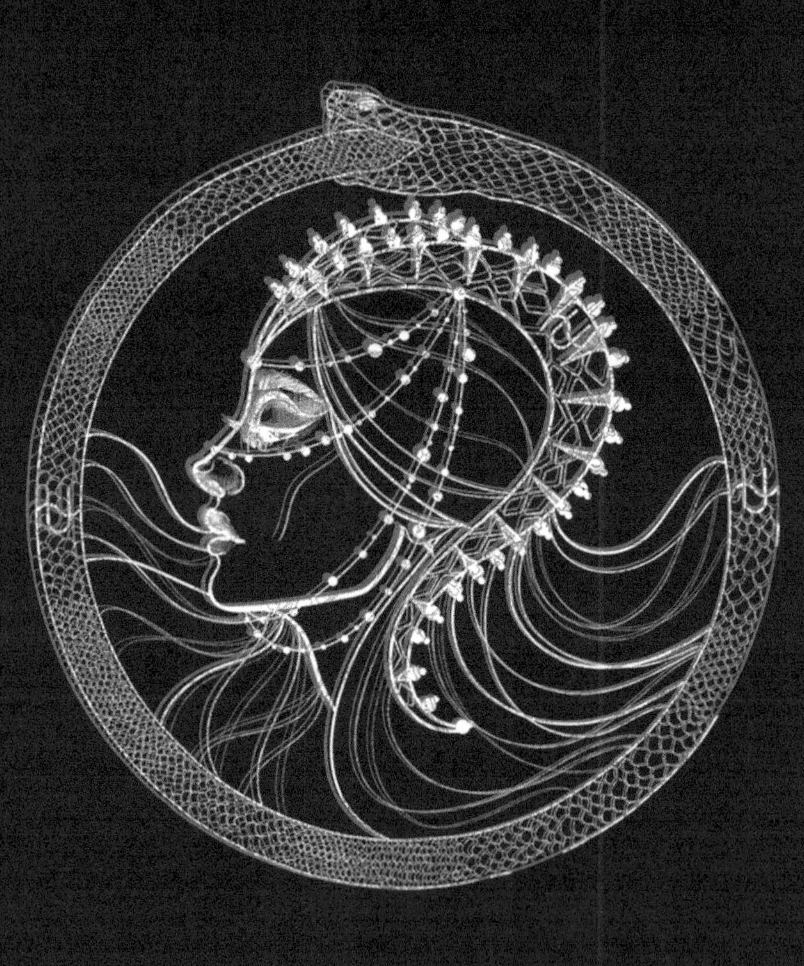

Protectors

Benjy

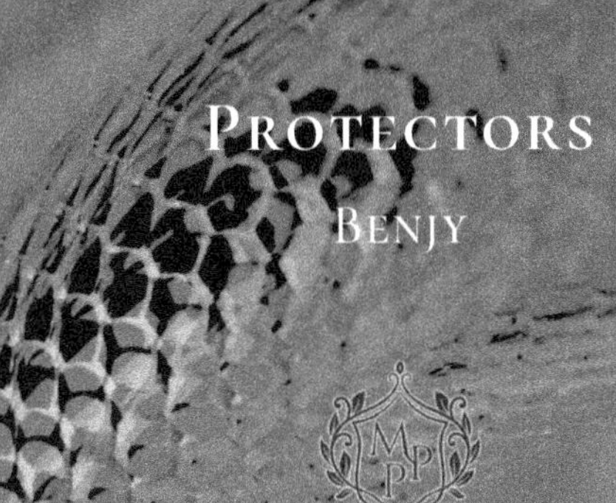

Tension prickles my skin as we walk back to the prep area with Bodil and Revna. Prez and Doyle are leaving their fittings, their expressions grim like bad omens. Their eyes lock on us—no, not us, Princess—and what I see isn't their usual bravado or laid-back ease, but a flicker of something darker.

It's a warning for me about what's to come and I need to take it seriously.

"Something's got them spooked, " I mutter to myself. "This isn't good."

Jolene is looking around the hallway curiously, watching as they approach her. She must have heard me because she scoffs as we get closer to them. "Spooked? Those two? Never. They look determined, sure, but we have to be, right?"

"I don't think it's that simple." I rub at the nape of my neck, feeling the prickly heat of unease. Doyle has seen a lot in the insane amount of time he's been on this planet; making him grimace like that isn't easy. The fact that neither stopped to fill us in means they couldn't figure out a good way to communicate without breaking the rules.

That's all bad fucking juju, as my mom would say.

Doyle throws me a glance over his shoulder, his brow furrowed in a way that would have sent lesser creatures scurrying. I catch it, but luckily Princess is oblivious. She's back to chatting away with Bodil and Revna about the Huntmasters' need to separate us into small groups. They're struggling to follow the rules—I can tell— so I distract our girl with a question.

"Are you looking forward to showing off, Princess?"

"Of course I am. But did you see their faces when I mentioned mounts?" she asks, amusement lacing her tone. "They acted as if they're asking us to ride unicorns or something."

"Unicorns might be less of a worry," I mutter to myself again.

My mind races with potential scenarios, each more unsettling than the last. These Fae could have any number of terrestrial or airborne mounts to hunt with—the myths and legends of what Fae do are so damn broad. Not one of us saw anything about this fucking hunt shit in the research we did at Harvest, so it must be a *very* well-kept secret. We couldn't prepare ourselves; hell, obviously even Alistair didn't know. Teddy would wring his neck for not warning us and he knows it.

Doyle probably wouldn't leave anything for my friend to strangle, but his temper is straight from a power that none of us really understand.

"Benjy, you're frowning like you're trying to solve a riddle," Princess teases, bumping her shoulder against mine. "What's got you brooding like Big Daddy Asshole?"

"Nothing," I reply as I force a smile. "I'm obsessing about the hunt and what it will require of us more than anything."

"Don't think too hard, big guy. We've got skilled riders and people trained in weapons since they could walk. Bless their hearts, we're from the South; they won't know what hit them." Her words are confident, but the sentiment doesn't quite reach her eyes—she knows something's up.

I may have overestimated my ability to wrangle our girl as well as Big Daddy can.

The image of Prez's worried gaze makes me feel like something big is coming, that involves the beasts we'll be riding. Teddy's words echo in my head—Jolene's skill set is as lethal as any weapon she wields. But how do you prepare someone for a monster when they're expecting a horse?

"Princess, you know whatever happens in this stupid game, you should stick close to one of us, right?" The plea slips out, wrapped in a half-joking tone, but it's real. I just found her and I can't bear to think about her getting hurt or worse. It's eating my gut like a damn virus as we take our final steps to the prep room.

"I will because I trust you guys to help, *not* because I need anyone protecting me," she replies in a strident tone. "We're a team, Benjy, and I'm doing my best to remember that after a long time where I took care of myself because I didn't have anyone else. It's not easy to unlearn that kind of hyperindepedence."

Just like that, her words lift my spirits and place the weight of responsibility on my shoulders at the same time. I have to keep her safe, even from things she can't see.

Hell, especially from the shit she doesn't know about yet.

"Benjy?" Her hand finds mine, her grip warm and reassuring as we approach the door. "We'll handle it together—whatever 'it' is."

"Of course, we will," I say, though the drumbeat of my heart tells a different story. We step inside, and it's all I can do not to let the fear show on my face.

Whatever 'it' is, I get the feeling it's going to be one hell of a ride.

THE SCENT OF LEATHER AND OILED STEEL MINGLES WITH THE TANG OF magic as Revna, the fairy seamstress, circles us with her measuring tape. She's a whirlwind of efficiency, her fingers dancing along the fabric like nimble spiders spinning silk.

"Deep purple for you, my dear," she declares, draping material over Jolene's shoulders to inspect it. "It'll complement your complexion splendidly."

Princess's face lights up, a stark contrast to her usual disdain for finery. We should have known she'd react this way to being given pants rather than a ballgown.

"Finally something practical," she mumbles as she admires the rich hue. "I was born to wear shit like this, not those ridiculous poofy things."

"I don't know, Princess. I think you look sexy as fuck in both." I wink at her and she wrinkles her nose. Guaranteed she would have flipped Teddy off, but somehow, she's okay with my statement.

Revna smiles, her eyes twinkling with mischief. "And for Benjy, black. He'll be a striking shadow to Jolene's vibrant flame."

If only she knew…

"Sounds perfect," I reply distractedly. We're being dressed for a hunt, but there's an edge to this prep that feels more warlike than sporty. That makes my animal twitch and I feel like I need to pace to work out the excess adrenaline.

Njord stomps in as I consider moving, his imposing half-orc frame casting shadows across the stone floor. His grunt is noncommittal as he sizes me up with expert eyes.

"Stand still," he rumbles, jotting down notes with a hand that looks capable of crushing stone.

"You don't seem like the kind of dude I want to irritate," I say, trying to lighten the mood. "Just tell me what you need and it's done."

"I'm not," he scoffs without looking up. It's hard to read him, but I sense tension in his posture. There's an unspoken warning in every mark he makes on his parchment and I have no idea what it's about.

Did Doyle piss this enormous motherfucker off?

"Alf will take care of your armaments," Njord grunts, finally stepping back with a satisfied look.

I didn't realize he was assessing both of us at the same time, but I nod. "Sounds good."

"This is my kind of fitting, big guy. I can't wait to see what they've got for us to choose from." Her excitement spikes again as we enter the armory. The walls are lined with an arsenal fit for gods, and she's like a kid in a candy store. Her gaze lands on a compound bow, sleek and deadly, its limbs whispering promises of power and precision.

"That's the one. I can *feel* it on my bones," she breathes out, her eyes never leaving the weapon.

"Are you sure? You have to use it while you're riding Princess, and—" My voice barely hides my concern. "That's a lot of weapon to use while you're moving unless you're from the Rohan."

"I've got this. Trust me." She throws me a look that's all fire and defiance and I crumble like a cookie.

Boone's going to fucking murder me when he finds out.

"If you're sure, then I won't try to talk you out of it," I relent. Holding my hands up in surrender, I smile before I head to the wall to look for myself. I select an ornate spear, noting that something makes it feel *right* to me as well, just like she said. Its heft is good in my hands—a balance of reach and lethality that suits my style.

"Now you come with me to the stables," Bodil urges, her voice a lilting song that can't quite mask the undercurrent of anxiety. I figured out she's a wolf shifter the second her earthy scent mixed with canine and pine hit my nostrils and I wonder how she's able to manage their animals with a predator inside of her.

Jolene catches up to her, chatting animatedly about the stables back home and what she does for Percy. It doesn't help my anxiety about this situation a bit, despite hearing how good she is with the Prince's horses. This isn't going to be high-strung thoroughbreds or show horses; that's obvious by the distance between the prep room and the damn building the animals are housed in.

I squint at the dark, brooding building Bodil identifies as the stables. It's a stark contrast to the polished grandeur of the prep area, both outside and in. As we enter, I see rows of stalls housing creatures that seem conjured from nightmares. Their fiery breaths puff out in angry clouds, and their red eyes gleam like coals.

"Jesus Christ on a boogie board," I mutter under my breath, hoping the Princess sees nothing more than impressively large horses.

"Look at them, Benjy. Aren't they *magnificent?*" Her squeal of delight cuts through the tension as she claps her hands. Our girl is enchanted by the entire group, but she's moving toward the most formidable of the lot—a jet-black steed with piercing blue eyes.

"Careful, Jolene," Bodil warns. "Antiope is not a normal beast; she's wilder than the wind."

"Wild suits me just fine," Jolene retorts with a grin. She's fearless as she steps into the stall without an ounce of protection. To my horror, she reaches out a hand, stroking Antiope's mane as if the beast is a gentle mare.

They're all going to kill me when this thing kicks her ass across the barn; I can see it now.

"Give her this," Bodil says, passing a carrot to our girl with a hesitant hand. "None of us have been able to get her to take anything from us, so that would be an accomplishment."

"See? She's a sweetheart," Jolene coos, feeding Antiope with a confidence that borders on insanity.

'Sweetheart' isn't the word I'd use for a creature bristling with power and malice that's huffing sulfur at us. But somehow, Jolene's touch calms the steed from Hades enough for her to swing up onto it's bare back.

"Looks like I've found my mount," she grins triumphantly. The horse glares at Bodil and I, her piercing blue eyes and snowy white mane eerie in the low light of the barn.

"Great," I say as I imagine the look on Big Daddy's face when he sees this damn thing.. "Just fucking great."

What the hell have we gotten ourselves into?

I GRAB TEDDY'S ARM AS SOON AS WE GET BACK TO OUR ROOM AND steer him away from the chattering trio. Jolene's animated voice fills the space, recounting her conquest of Antiope with a gleam in her eye that only adventure can ignite. She doesn't notice us peeling off; her focus is all on the hunt.

"Bro," I whisper urgently, "we need to talk."

His eyes lock onto mine, dark pits of concern that tell me he's already halfway to guessing what I'm about to spill. "What's up, B?"

"Princess chose the one damn horse in the entire stable no one has been able to hand feed, much less ride." I shake my head, still reeling from the audacity of it. "She's riding the beast no one in this court dares to approach, much less hop on. I couldn't stop her, man."

He grimaces, pinching the bridge of his nose as he lets out a long breath. "Prez suspected she'd do something like this. As soon as Wolfie told us he believed this 'wild hunt' isn't just a game or tradition, I knew the mounts had to be fearsome. This is the real thing—the hunt of legend—which makes it a survival test."

"Survival?" My voice pitches higher than intended, and I glance at Jolene, who's now wielding an imaginary bow, her movements fluid and deadly as she shows them what she plans to do. The hits just keep coming and this fucking oath is keeping us from warning her.

My gorilla wants to kill someone and he's usually not very 'King Kong.'

"All of this is what Wolfie feared," he continues. "And there's more."

"More?" I echo hollowly.

"Devil dogs." His voice is barely audible. "If the legends hold true, I'll have no choice but to shift and lead them. It's part of the hunt—a part I hoped was myth—but it means I won't be able to resist."

"Jesus, Teddy..." A cold shiver races down my spine. "Princess can't be part of this. Not when..."

He cuts me off, raking a hand through his hair. "We need to speak with the Huntmasters. We've got to find out what we're hunting and try to control the narrative. If it's humans, this could go sideways fast."

"Control the narrative? Have you lost your mind?" I scoff. "With hellhounds and whatever else they throw into the mix running around?"

"If I can keep the devil dogs in check, maybe it won't spiral out of control." Determination hardens his features. "I've sure as hell never met any of my kind before, but I've always been an alpha. Maybe I can wrangle them."

Dude's ego is writing a check his ass can't cash, no matter how rich he is.

And what, exactly, are you going to do to get them to follow you? Do you plan to gnaw through the prey in front of the Princess? Have you ever even *done* that Edgar Olivier Boone"

"I'll do whatever it takes to protect her," he says, the steel in his tone leaving no room for argument. "Doesn't matter if I'm fond of the idea or not."

"Mr. Boone," Revna's sharp cough slices through our hushed exchange. "We must leave. It's time for your fitting with Mr. Fletcher."

"Go," I urge, swallowing the knot in my throat. "We'll figure this out."

"Benjy..." He hesitates, his gaze flickering toward Jolene. "Keep her safe."

As Teddy strides away with Revna's fluttering presence guiding him, Wolfie follows. They both look like men marching toward their doom. I turn back to Jolene, whose laughter dances around the room as she continues to talk with Prez and Doyle.

"Benjy saw the way Antiope looked at me. It was like she knew I was the one to tame her. It's my specialty, you know," she boasts, oblivious to the darkness creeping at the edges of our reality.

"I saw you step into that stall without a lick of fear and the devil horse responded to you," I manage, my voice strained as I plaster on a smile that doesn't reach my eyes. "Together, you and that eerie looking mare are going to rock this hunt."

"Damn right," she replies, her confidence unshakable.

I watch her, the sinking feeling in my gut growing heavier.

Doyle's eyes meet mine from across the room, a silent understanding passing between us. The twinkle in his gaze tells me he's ready to revel in the chase. If anyone will be able to help us corral our enthusiastic mate, I think it's him. He's been alive far longer than us and he loves to pretend he's from this region.

Maybe he knows more than he's letting on; hell, I hope so.

Because Teddy and I?

We're bracing for a battle of a different kind—one that could very well change our entire lives in one fell swoop.

Yellow Flicker Beat

Jolene

Our room now smells of leather and steel—a sharp tang that nips at the inside of my nose. I'm hunched over our latest delivery, a collection of kits and gear laid out before us like a merchant's treasure. The armor from Njord gleams with an anticipatory luster, and Alf's weapons whisper promises of battles to come.

I feel like I'm gearing up for some real Games of Thrones shit and boy, did I never anticipate saying that sentence unironically.

"It's hard to believe this doesn't even phase us now," I murmur, my voice barely above the rustle of fabric as I run my hand over the sleek surface of my purple kit. The shining armor that will go over it is lightweight but promises durability, and I'm certain it will fit like a second skin for the hunt ahead.

"Best get used to it, Sugarplum." Wolfie chuckles from the other side of the room, his eyes scanning his own pile of equipment. "Every time I think I've seen it all, the world throws another curveball."

Benjy and Prez are just waking up, rubbing sleep from their eyes as they shuffle over to join us for dinner. We're nibbling on dried meats and hard bread—nothing too heavy; we can't afford to be sluggish tonight. After we all finished our time with the hunt masters we took naps in shifts to make up for the sleep lost last night. No one wanted to get tired by the time this thing started.

"I still can't get over their amazing horses," I say to Wolfie, and Teddy's eye twitches. Across from me, Doyle grunts, his attention fixated on sharpening a large sword. Its blade curves menacingly into a sickle-like protrusion. My frown deepens; it's foreign, not like anything I saw in Alf's armory.

Where the fiddling fuck did he get that *from?*

"How come he gets some weird mega sword?" I nod towards Doyle's weapon, my voice a conspiratorial whisper intended for Wolfie's ears alone.

He shakes his head in warning. "Don't ask him," he replies quietly. "Doyle and his mysteries are not safe topics on the best days, but he's been almost as grumpy as Big Daddy since he got back from the fitting."

"Revna and Njord took some liberties with his kit," I observe, watching as Doyle sets aside the sword and reaches for the ancient-looking helmet beside him. Its design speaks of old wars and older gods, which matches the weapon he's sharpening methodically.

"Everyone has secrets," Wolfie responds before he shifts the subject. "What do you think of your compound bow? Are you sure it won't be a hassle on the move? Benjy was really fussed about that."

I chuckle softly. "Darling boy, I've had my share of wild rides and most weren't on cowboys. Seer and I spent a couple months with travelers running a carnival in Eastern Europe. I picked up stunt riding while Seer dabbled in acrobatics."

"Is there anything you haven't done?" He blinks in surprise, and I shrug nonchalantly.

"Running around the world tends to fill your pockets with stories," I confess. "Especially when you're running from something and hoping it never catches up to you. One gets a bit… cavalier with mortality when they haven't worked through their shit yet."

As we talk, my gaze lands on Teddy. Unlike the rest of us armored to the teeth, he's traveling light, carrying only a curious bag clinking with metal. Its purpose is a mystery and I want to solve it. I open my mouth to question him when Bodil strides into the room, authority etched into every line of her face.

"Time to gear up," she announces. "The hunt begins within the hour."

We spring into action, each movement a testament to our strategy for surviving the night. I slip into my armor, feeling its familiar embrace, and grab my trusty bow. Tonight will be a test of skill—a dance of death and honor under the moon's watchful eye.

As much as the others may worry or keep their silence, I know one thing—we're a family.

And family looks out for each other, secrets and all.

THE STABLE IS A SHADOWED HIVE OF ACTIVITY AS RIDERS GET THEIR mounts ready. Anticipation and the musky scent of the creatures within fills my nose as we enter. I don't know if I'll ever get used to how much sharper my sense of smell and hearing are getting. I can't ask if it's a side effect of whatever the hell is going on with me, but I assume it is.

I glide among my companions as we find our horses. Each of us is clad in our colors and my armor hugs me like a second skin. The armor's design allows me freedom of movement, and the hue... well, it's always been a favorite. So I feel just as good in this battle gear with my hair tied back in a fat braid as I did in the glittering ball gown at Midnight.

Plus I get rocking fucking boots instead of stupid heels.

"Where's Teddy?" I ask Doyle as I squint at the empty space beside him. His emerald gear makes him look like a warrior from ancient myths, especially with that helmet casting his eyes into pools of mystery and the blade that pulses as if its alive.

"He'll be around soon enough," he says, his voice rough. "Just remember, Tíogair… stick close to us, but don't meddle in our fights. This hunt—you've got to prove your own worth."

I snort, pushing back a stray lock of hair. "I didn't come here to audition for these twats, but I guess we don't have a choice."

He grins, the metal of his gear catching the dim light. "You make it sound like a talent show."

"Isn't it though?" I shoot back, the corner of my mouth twitching upward despite the tension coiling inside me. "Just—" I hesitate, lowering my voice, "make sure we all get through this, okay?"

"Trust me. I've got your back." His words are more than a promise; they're an oath spoken by someone who understands what's at stake.

Internally, I catalog the silhouettes of shapeshifters as we line up at the edge of the forest. Their forms ripple between man and beast—a reminder of the hidden layers of this world and its inhabitants. Doyle shines like a beacon amongst them, Wolfie's aura flickers with enchantment, and the rest—the warriors—are an eclectic mosaic of danger and grace. The royals have provided us mounts that defy normalcy and their sides heave like bellows as their eyes glow with fire.

Keeping the fact that I can see all this damn nonsense silent feels like hoarding a cache of weapons so I can wield them when the time is right.

Then, the horn's call slices through the night, deep and resonant as it echoes off the hills.

An inferno leaps forth—an enormous armored hellhound, followed by a legion of smaller devil dogs. It takes me a minute to register that it's Teddy and that's why he didn't have the supplies the rest of us did. He's unmistakable even in this form as he leads the cacophony with howls that pierce the soul.

"Dammit, Teddy," I mutter, annoyance flaring hot in my veins. He should be here, where we can guard him as one of our own. "That jackass always has to be a show off."

Antiope snorts beneath me, her coat ablaze with ethereal flames. With a terse nod, I drive my heels into her sides, urging her forward. She responds with exhilarating speed, racing after the royal vanguard in a spectacle of fire and power.

Okay, I could totally get used to this shit. I feel like a goddamn Valkyrie.

Wolfie appears beside me, riding with the ease of a man born in the saddle. We're at the front of the pack with the elites simply because we ride better than most of the horde of hunters. But it's Doyle who surprises me most, charging ahead as if the very act of riding these hellish steeds was his birthright.

In the moonlight, his figure is outlined with an otherworldly glow. Helmeted and brandishing that bizarre sword, he's transformed. An epiphany crashes over me as I see the golden glow emanating from him: Doyle is not a mere mortal. No, he's touched by divinity itself— a god or demigod hidden in plain sight.

I'm going to flay him alive with a paring knife when I get a hold of him.

"Focus, Jolene," I chide myself silently, shaking off the shock as the hunters flow forward en masse, reaching a vast clearing.

Again, the horn sounds, a clarion call to the wildness within us and it's echoed by the chorus of Teddy and his devil dogs.

The hunt has truly begun, and with it, the unspoken challenges we each must face.

THE GROUND HEAVES BENEATH ANTIOPE, CRACKING WITH OMINOUS finality. Our large party has finally made its way through the forest to the Field of the Wild Hunt, but as soon as we cross the border, the earth began to shake.

I pull my horse up short as the soil beneath us ruptures, and from those jagged fissures, the lichs emerge. I don't know how I know what they are, except that they're a grotesque parade of decay. Their hollow eye sockets burn with malignant hunger as they seek anchorage in this world. My heart jolts against my ribs; these are not mere ghosts to be banished with a chant or a charm.

Even if I knew one—which I don't.

"Gods above," I mutter, a prayer or a curse—I'm not sure which.

The sky darkens above as if it heard me, and fae beasts come cascading from tears in the stratosphere like dark ink dropped into water. Their shrieks tear through the calm, and for a moment, it's all I can do to keep Antiope from bolting.

"Shhh, girl." I stroke her neck, and she steadies, fire in her eyes reflecting my own resolve.

My gaze swings across the clearing where a swarm of black clad riders approach like an omen of doom. It's a sight that chills me to the bone and for a second, I wonder what in the fuck we're going to do this time. I sure can't predict another burst of stuff like at Midnight. I look around at the hunters desperately, and amidst the fray is Doyle looking both radiant and terrible, his sword a beacon in the tumult.

"Dammit, Doyle." I spur Antiope toward him, the ground churning beneath us. When I reach him, I hiss. "Do something or we're all dead."

He whips around, his helmeted visage unreadable but for the flash of his eyes. He sees me—really sees me—and in that instant, recognition dawns. I know his secret, the divine blood coursing through him —not fae forged, but something far older. And that means I know my secret, too.

Come on, Lucky. Figure it out before they attack.

"Tíogair," he growls, the timbre of his voice resonating with an ancient power I've only read about in the dusty corners of libraries. "Take Antiope. Help Wolfie and Benjy with the royals."

"Like hell! You're—"

"Go!" His head jerks toward the others, his command leaving no room for argument.

I grind my teeth, fury roiling within me like a storm, but this isn't the time for our clash of wills. With a resentful nod, I wheel Antiope around, her flames blazing a trail through darkness and doubt.

"Stay alive, you stubborn asshat," I whisper to the wind, hoping it carries my words to him.

Antiope moves with otherworldly grace, parting the sea of combatants as we reach Wolfie and Benjy. The former is stringing arrows with lethal precision while the latter twirls his spear, a dancer among the dead. I wouldn't have believed it a few weeks ago, but I'll be damned if this isn't our goddamn life now.

"Need a hand?" I call out over the din, loosing an arrow from my compound bow with one fluid motion.

"Always," Wolfie replies, a wry smile on his lips despite the encroaching peril.

"Focus!" Benjy shouts, parrying a strike from a skeletal adversary. "We have to protect the king and queen and their children. That's what this shit is about."

"On it, big guy." I let another arrow fly then look over my shoulder for a moment.

Behind me, Doyle engages his foes with a ferocity that belies his usual calm. He moves like myth made flesh, every swing of his sword cleaving the shadows. That son of bitch is acting like a fucking hero and he's spent all his time convincing me he's a freaking bad boy.

He'll never live this down if I have anything to say about it.

"Alright, Antiope. Let's show these motherfuckers who they're dealing with," I say, drawing back my bowstring as I spur her on.

Together, we rocket across the field in a streak of black and purple. Once I get the feel of her gait, I push to my feet, standing in the saddle as I fire at one beast after another. The old fortune teller at the carnival we traveled with used to say I was born to do this kind of stuff and I always said my bruises told a different story.

But right here, right now? I kind of wonder if she wasn't crazy after all.

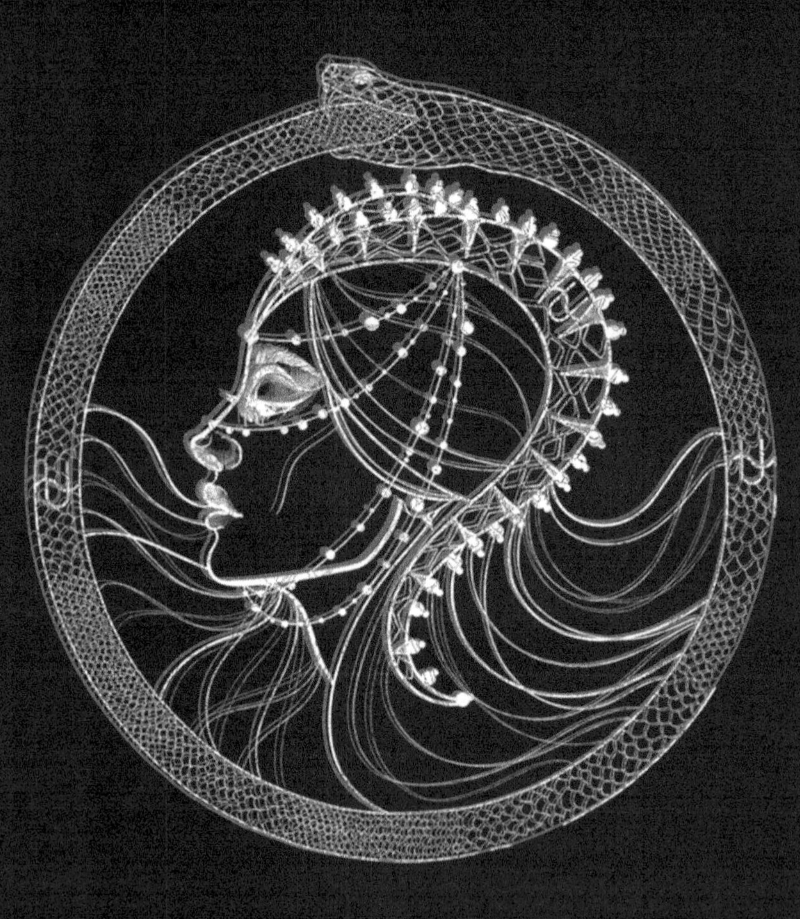

The Greatest Show

Doyle

I can't help but pause, the chaos around me fading into a blur as I watch Jolene. She's a comet of fury and focus, her form outlined against the darkening sky. Standing tall in her stirrups, she becomes part of the steed beneath her—her movements fluid and precise. Arrows fly from her bowstring, singing their deadly tune as they arc toward the fae beasts that swoop down maliciously. Without missing a beat, her aim shifts to the lichs scuttling around her horse, cursing at them as she takes them out.

It's not in the stars to hold our destiny, but in ourselves.[1]

"Damn that bard got it right every time," I mutter under my breath as an incredulous chuckle escapes me. How did the Fates stitch all these different souls together into this unconventional family? We're a smorgasbord of supes, each more different than the last, and all broken in various ways. It *should* be an absolute disaster.

My gaze is drawn westward when a howl echoes off the hills and I see Teddy has erupted into a monstrosity of wrath. He tears through flesh and bone as if possessed by a hunger for destruction. "I wouldn't have pegged you for a beast of Armageddon, Boone," I whisper to myself, admiration lacing my words.

A flurry of movement to the east catches my eye. Wolfie gallops over the field with his wings unfurled, trailing fae dust like cosmic breadcrumbs. His arrows cleave the air with deadly precision, finding their marks in the horde of advancing enemies.

"Nice shot, pup!" I shout, but my voice is drowned out by the cacophony of battle.

That's another one I didn't think had it in him, but look at him go.

My gaze moves to Prez as he wields his crossbow like an artist with a brush, painting death upon the undead skeleton men who dare advance. Next to him is Benjy, his gorilla roaring into the night and his spear a blur as he impales anything within reach. Those two don't shock me—I think they've had it in them all along, much like Edgar. They may be the calm in our family's storm, but their fierce love for our girl is fueling their rage.

"That's it, mates. Keep pushing them back," I mutter as I take in the rest of the field carefully.

Together, we're a symphony of mayhem. Yet, my Tíogair hasn't even tapped into her true potential. Her powers are lying dormant as she relies on her fighting prowess alone. She's beauty and grace… right up until she punches you in the face.

I think that's from some movie they made me watch…shit.

Focus, Haggerty.

"Time to even the odds." That decision sparks my inner desire to bend the world around me to its knees and I shudder in pleasure. Energy coasts over me as I tilt my head back in preparation.

I close my eyes, drawing deep from the wellspring of power handed down from the ancestors I know. The glow envelops me then spreads across the battlefield slowly. My horse, sensing the surge, grows restless beneath me. With a firm pat to its flank, I dismount, landing squarely in the midst of the fray.

"Now we'll show them why prayers are said on their knees," I chuckle darkly.

The air hums with energy as Harpe vibrates in my grasp. The famous sword of my relatives is hungry for release. I let the power swell within me, thrusting the sword's tip into the earth. A shock-wave erupts sending vibrations through the ground. Lichs stumble and fall like puppets with their strings cut, while my comrades ride through the tumult unscathed, their mounts surefooted amidst the upheaval.

"Yesss," I hiss as the field is cleared in one fell swoop. "Score one for cheating like the bastard you are, old boy."

Lifting Harpe, I press the blade to the golden helmet I borrowed. "Thank you, Auntie," I whisper, knowing she can hear me wherever she is. The gratitude is a fleeting touch, a moment of softness in the heart of battle.

Unlike my mother, she mostly gives a shit about me.

Once I pay my respects, I let out a cry that splits the heavens, then unleash all my pent-up fury. Golden magic arcs from the blade, striking out at the fae beasts like divine retribution. They plummet, one after another, in flaming spirals to their doom.

"Fuck yeah, you scraggly sons of bitches. Take that," I roar, my voice ragged with triumph.

Their bodies crash to the ground, and I can't suppress a savage grin. This is what I was born for—the clash of steel, the rush of power, the dance of death. The battle is far from over, and now that I've let loose the parts I keep shadowed, I'm thirsty for vengeance.

When I finally burn through the fury built up inside of me, sweat clings to me like a shroud. The rush of power that surged through me ebbs away, leaving an all-consuming fatigue in its wake. I tug the helmet off; it's suddenly suffocating. Tucking it under one arm, I lift my weary gaze.

"Damn," I mutter under my breath as I inspect the grim aftermath.

Supes and Fae are busy around me, their weapons rising and falling in deadly arcs, finishing off the remaining lichs and beasts in a cacophony of final screams and guttural cries. The air is thick with the coppery tang of blood and the sharp scent of burned magic.

We won, but at what cost?

Teddy's not far off, looking like hell in his canine form but moving with purpose. He corrals the devil dogs, his own wounds forgotten in the face of duty. Beyond him, the King props up the Queen, both battered but unbowed. My lips press into a thin line as I take them in; it's their fault we were all out here in the open. Despite their vicious reputation, the Court of Reaping was infiltrated as easily as all the others.

"Prez!" I shout, my voice cracking with strain. He's over with the royals' kin, playing medic and assessing injuries with a keen eye. The people in the Hollow trust him implicitly and the injured here seem to do the same. It's the gift of his kind and he wields that power with amazing efficiency.

A sob splits the night, pulling my attention to a wretched sight. One of the princes is kneeling, his form shaking with grief as he clutches a fallen figure. I swallow hard. The sight of his loss is too raw. I knew eventually these attacks would lead to something like this, but now it's real.

It's not even the first time I've seen someone die this year, but somehow, it hits differently now.

"Benjy? Are you okay?" I ask when I spot my comrade. He's pale as death, clutching his side, but nodding affirmatively. I know he'll live, but my relief is short-lived.

"Shit. Where are...?" My heart hammers, a sudden panic slicing through the numbness in my limbs. "Pup! Tíogair!"

"Find her," Teddy barks, his eyes wide with the same realization. We all fan out, urgency propelling our exhausted limbs. Prez and Benjy are kicking their way through the piles of bodies, checking to see if there are people underneath who might be breathing.

"Jolene!" I call again, my voice hoarse as we navigate the littered field.

Teddy's beside me, his nostrils flaring, sniffing for a trail or sign of them. He stops, then darts forward, leaving me to sprint after him. "Over here," he growls, his voice tight with dread.

We reach the forest's edge, where two hell horses, one of them Antiope,stand sentinel. Their riders are conspicuously absent.

My words catch in my throat. "Fuck, no..."

On the ground, Wolfie's and Jolene's weapons lie discarded. A nearby patch of earth tells a tale of struggle, the soil torn and trampled, and blood staining the grass.

This cannot be happening.

"They're gone. Jolene, Wolfie—taken, hurt." I can barely breathe the words without wanting to scream.

"Who would dare?" Teddy's voice is a low snarl of disbelief and rage.

Whoever did this has no idea of the storm they've just invoked.

"Someone's going to pay." My promise is ironclad, forged in the heat of my fury.

Teddy's immediate transformation is explosive,—a violent eruption of feathers and scales. His body elongates, snaking up into the sky, wings unfurling with a snap that echoes like a thunderclap. The giant Quetzalcoatl, soars above us, trailing flames and fury in its wake. My heart clenches watching him—this is his rawest form, the embodiment of his wrath.

"Find them," I growl, my voice barely audible over the beat of his massive wings. The bird glares at me as if it would like to peck my eyes out, but his head bobs before he streaks into the air.

Prez sprints over, his eyes wide as he takes in the form our leader never takes soaring through the air. "I'll go with him." His shape morphs into the white brilliance of his caladrius. Its healing light is stark against the darkened battlefield as it follows Teddy into the night.

A surge of helplessness swells within me. *I'm earthbound, so I can't join them.*

Benjy hobbles to my side, grimacing with each step. He's a mess of blood and determination, but his eyes stay locked on mine, searching for a plan in my gaze. "Dammit, Doyle, what do we—"

Before he can finish, the air sizzles, charged by an unseen force. Lightning cleaves the sky, striking the helmet under my arm. In a blink, it's not the same helm I'd tucked away. This one gleams sinisterly, its presence alone menacing. My skin prickles at its touch and I caress the curves and points with a wicked grin.

"Holy shit." Benjy's face blanches, his voice hushed as he stares at me. "Now we know who your fucking father is, bro."

Emerald and gold swirl in my vision, the colors of my heritage igniting within me. A smirk tugs at my lips; it feels foreign yet fitting. "Yes, we do," I muse, relishing the dread that ripples through the air.

Whoever has dared to take mine has unleashed the tempest.

"Did you have any clue? Do you think the people who took them know it's…"

"Someone they'll regret crossing?" I reply to the simian. The helmet in my grasp pulsates with a power that feels ancestral, divine, and diabolical all at once. "Likely not."

My mother's lineage may give me the divine power of persuasion, but my father's blood is a different beast altogether. It yearns for destruction—no, it revels in it. And right now, it's calling me to scorch the earth, to make ashes of whoever dares harm those under my protection.

"We hunt," I command, my voice echoing with newfound authority. "Now."

Benjy nods, swallowing hard.

Together, beneath the vanishing trails of Teddy and Prez, I smile as Odie and Eurayle herald the arrival of the animals.

The croaking raven doth bellow for revenge[2] *... and so do I.*

Read just a little bit more in the Revealed in the Hollow Bonus Scene!

Preorder Revenge in the Hollow now!

----

1. Julius Caesar, William Shakespeare
2. Hamlet, William Shakespeare

Reviews, Print, and Merchandise

If you have enjoyed this book, please leave reviews! It helps other readers find my work,
which helps me as an indie author.

Thank you!

Reviews for Revealed in the Hollow are appreciated on the following platforms:

Amazon
Goodreads
Bookbub
StoryGraph
TikTok
Instagram
Facebook

To purchase print copies or merchandise, go to The Worlds of Cassandra Featherstone

GET A SECRET BONUS SCENE!

For another secret bonus scene that follows *Revealed in the Hollow, click the link below, sign up for my newsletter, and get your freebie.*

Get your bonus scene here!

WORLD GUIDE & PRONUNCIATION

CHARACTERS

Jolene Athena Whitley 'Tilly', 'JoJo' , 'Sugarplum', 'Magpie', 'Tíogair' 'Peanut' (Joh LEEN Ah-THEE-nuh Wit-lee) we don't know her supe sides yet, only that she's unemerged, was bullied in HS in a big incident that got her named 'The Cotillion Catastrophe'. Calls Edgar Teddy, Wolfie is little Wolfie and McDreamy, Prez is Doctor McNuggies and McSteamy, Doyle is Lucky.

Jekyll and Hyde- serval cats who adopted Jolene when she arrived in town

Isis- rainbow reticulated python who appeared when Jolene was threatened in the *Hollar* office

Kali and Hecate- Edgar's King Dane dogs

Eurayle- A Harpy eagle that also appeared and adopted Jolene

Edgar Olivier Boone III 'Teddy' 'Daddy' 'Teddy Bear' 'Hound' 'Doggy' (ed-gar OH-live-ee-ay bOOn) triple hybrid—hellhound, incubi, and quetzacoatl shifts; calls Jolene Tilly and Wolfie Pup

Presley Hemingway Hamilton 'Prez' 'Doctor McNuggies' 'McSteamy' 'Birdman' (press-lee Hem-ing-way HAM-ul-ton)- town doctor, involved with Wolfie, caladrius. Calls Wolfie Lucy, Jolene Magpie.

Wolfgang Lucien Fletcher 'Lucy' 'Pup' 'Wolfie' 'McDreamy'(wulf-GahnG too-See-n Fleht-CHUR)- town vet, involved with Prez and Teddy, subbie, dark Fae and Calleich mother, adoptive mother in asylum. Calls Jolene Sugarplum, Teddy Daddy.

Doyle Aloysius Haggerty 'Lucky' (doy-UHL Al-oh-wishus Hag-ert-ee)- ancient but doesn't look it, works PR at Mayor's office, demigod hybrid, sent to Hollow to monitor, chaotic. Calls Jolene Tíogair, Edgar Doggy, Presley Birdman.

Odie- Doyle's secret raven companion

Hugo Atlas Macauley (hue-go AT-lass MACK-all-ee) only male o his species, acolyte of a goddess, related to other acolytes, teaches history at HS

Benjamin Louis Foster 'Benjy' (behn-JAH-min loo-ee Foss-tur) Old HS best friend of Teddy, owns Bottle 'N Cans, married to Sherilynn Foster Grant, divorced her when he realized Jolene was his, gorilla shifter; adopted children Scarlett, Simon, and Simone

Prince Dhameer Mirza Al Sharqi 'Amiri' (Dah-MEER MearZAH AL Shahrkey) djinn; owner of Mehdi; new contender in Jolene's life

Percival Whitman Atwater 'Percy' (purr-sive-uhl wit-man at-wahtur) owns Atwater's Store

Virginia Dolly Atwater (ver-GIN-n-yuh dahl-ee at-wahtur) Percy's sister, teaches English at HS, wants to date Teddy

Andromeda Bane (ann-dram-eh duh bay-n) guidance counselor at HS, was also counselor when Teddy and Jolene in school, clearly more than that

Isra (iz-RAH) the eternal guard of the Prince

Fazal (Fie-zahl) the butler of the Prince, his family worked for theirs for hundreds of years

Mehidi (MEH-ee-DEE) gorgeous thoroughbred horse belonging to the Prince that Jolene trains

Malik (Mah-leek) The Prince's favorite Arabian mount

Randall Keynes Barrington (ran-DULL KEE-nz BEAR-ing-tuhn) human; Chief of Police in the Hollow; father to Reese Barrington; married to Elyse Lance

Reese Emily Barrington (REE-ss ehM-ih-lee BEAR-ing-tuhn) member of Nip/Tucks; one of Jolene's bullies; hybrid of a TikTok and witch; manages Star Spangled Bank; married to Joseph Stephenson; adoptive mother to Carlotta and Cordelia Barrington

Amy Matilda Behle (AY-mee Muh-Till-duh BEEL) member of Nip/Tucks; one of Jolene's bullies; human, runs Hollow Hollar; daughter of Victoria & Reginald Behle; married to Lysander Behle; adoptive mother to Ariel, Dante, & Edward Behle

Lysander Marx Behle (LIE-san-dur MARR-x BEEL) unicorn shifter; interior designer; married to Amy Behle; children Ariel, Dante, and Edward

Edgar Osiris Boone II (ed-GAR OH-sigh-ris BOON) Teddy's adoptive father; Senator; Ouroboros agent; married to Margaret Emily Roth; human

Margaret Emily Roth (marr-GUH-ret EM-IL-ee Rah-th) harpy; Teddy's adoptive mother; married to the Senator

Eliot James Cantwell 'Jamie' (Eh-lee-ut Jaymz CANT-wel) Proprietor of Cantwell Farms, older than Jolene but a friend

Fidelia Violet Cantwell (fihd-AY-lee-uh VY-o-let CANT-wel) Percy's sister, owner of Dress Me Up Buttercup

Mina Cantwell (meenuh CANT-wel) Fidelia and Jamie's mother, retired horse farm owner

Aurelia Darcy Fletcher (AR-ale-ee-uh DAR-see Fleh-T-chur) Wolfie's mother, has been in an asylum since he was sixteen

Aoife (ee-FUH) pixie Fae; member of the *Laochra Na Peitil* in the Daybreak Court

Sítheach (Shea-u-ch) Fairy; member of the *Laochra Na Peitil* in the Daybreak Court

Ciarán (kee-RUN) fairy/angel hybrid; member of the *Laochra Na Peitil* in the Daybreak Court

Daire (Dah-RUH) Fae; member of the *Laochra Na Peitil* in the Daybreak Court

Taranis (tear-AN-us) Fae/goblin hybrid; member of the *Laochra Na Peitil* in the Daybreak Court

Dylan Marlowe Grant (dill-N MARR-low GRANT) pixie; runs Bound Together; Ouroboros inductee; companion Nostradamus a great horned owl; dating Detective Santos; parents Oscar and Zelda

Sherilynn Grant Foster (Share-UH-lin GRANT foss-tur) pixie/selkie; hybrid; runs Derby Pies; divorced from Benjy; companions Italian greyhounds Cleo and Marcus; adopted children Scarlett, Simon, and Simone; parents Oscar and Zelda

Zelda Louise Grant (ZELL-duh LOO-eez GRANT) pixie; owns Grant Home Furnishings; children Dylan and Sherilynn; husband Oscar

Aldous Basil Longworth (ALL-duss BAZ-UHL LAHNG-wurth) human, exec asst to Mayor; companions Sphynx cats Poe and Parker; married to Antigone Keene Longworth (deceased); children Ophelia Longworth

Ophelia Jane Longworth (oh-FEE-li-uh JAY-n LAHNG-wurth) siren/mage hybrid; father Aldous and mother Antigone; married to Beauregard Longworth; adopted children Brittania, Charlotte, Claude, and Vincent; runs Tame Your Mane; one of the Nip/Tucks

Saoirse Viola O' Flanagan (SEER-shuh VY-o-luh OH FLAN-uh-GAN) Guardian of Jolene; veela/valkyrie hybrid; cover job Fashion designer; adoptive parents Annabelle and Seamus; dating Julia, Tharin, and Zasha

Dorothy Elizabeth Hale (Door-O-thee ee-LIZ-uh-beth HAY-L) married to Jason Simmon (deceased); mother to Jillian Remington; Arachne shifter; runs WAP Florist;

Jillian Marie Remington (Jihl-ee-n Mah-ree Rehm-ing-ton) one of the Nip/Tucks from high school; Aranche shifter; owner Close Encounters of the Baked Kind; married to William Christopher Remington; Children are Brutus, Ernest, Blake, Octavian, and George

Julia Isabelle Ricci (Jooleeuh Iz-uh-bell Ree-Chee) Guardian; dating Saoirse, Tharin, and Zasha; Gorgon

Tharin Leonidas Drakos (TH-air-in Le-OH-nye-dis Dray-Kohs) dating Zasha, Julia, and Seer; Guardian; wyvern

Zasha Fyodor Petrov (Zah-shuh Fee-yo-door Pet-trawv) Guardian; dating Tharin, Julia, and Seer; Merman

Jackson Ellison Thorn (Jahk-son Eh-liss-on Thorn) Lawyer; ex-RA of Jolene at State University; retired agent; runs Thorn and Associates; has a Grey wolf companion named Fenrir

Andrew Justin Whitley (an-Drew Justin Wit-lee) Jolene's dad; human; professor at State University; deceased

Eloise Clara Whitley (Eh-low-ez Claire-uh Wit-lee) Jolene's mom; agent; professor at State University; witch

Bobbi Jo Ratliff (Bah-bee Jo Raht-liff) principal at WHFS; human

Cornelia Sykes (Core-neel-ee-uh sigh-ks) Mayor of Whistler's Hollow; chimera; pet lion Zareb; has harem of her own

Hazel Charlotte Thermapoulos- owner of Hazel's Diner; peacemaker; neutral zone; Laertes

Fiannula and Lorcan- guards at the doors of the Faerie

Deirbhile (DJIR vil a) part of royal design team Daybreak Court; brownie

Aimhirghin (AV er yin) part of royal design team Daybreak Court; goblin

Ríordán (REE ur dawn) part of royal design team Daybreak Court; Fairy

Ealadha (Elatha) part of royal design team Daybreak Court; druid/brownie

Draighean (DRAY un) part of royal design team Daybreak Court; witch/Fae

Áinfean (AWN f'yun) part of royal design team Daybreak Court; Fae

Prince Eógan (OH-uhn) Daybreak Court

Mick & Mack Stuart (MIK and MAK Stew-art) regents of the Harvest Court; leprechauns

Alistair Silkshine (al IS TAIR SILk SHYn) Unseelie Fae; royal interrogator; engaged to Princess Allora of Harvest Court

Princess Allora (UH for UH) Princess of Harvest Court, daughter of Hieronymous and former Queen; engaged to Alistair

King Hieronymous (HIGH Ron IM us) King of Harvest Court; scholar; father of Allora; married second time to Queen Rinah; first wife Magdalena died

Queen Rinah (ree NAH) second wife of Harvest Court King

Lukas (Loo KAS) husband to Elara, princess of Midnight Court; healer; from family of healers in Daybreak Court; Fae/hedge witch hybrid

Elara (eh-LAIR-uh) eldest Princess of the Midnight Court, married to Lukas

Julien (Joo-lee-N) fiance to Princess Celstine of the Midnight Court; former leader of Harvest Court's elite security service for royals; half orc/half Fae

Celestina (Ceh-les-TEE-nuh) Second oldest Princess of the Midnight Court, betrothed to Julien

Finntan 'Finn' (fihn-Tahn) fiance to the third oldest Princess Aubrette of Midnight Court; nephew to the King of Court of Reaping; hybrid Yeti/Fairy

Aubrette (ah-BRETT) third oldest Princess of Midnight Court; engaged to Finn

Declan- (deck-LAN) husband of Nissa, fourth oldest Princess of Midnight Court; full Fae; youngest son of magic trader from Midnight Court

Nissa- (NISS-uh) fourth oldest Princess of Midnight Court; married to Declan

Riordan (rear-Dan) fiance of Marin, fifth oldest Princess of Midnight Court; wizard/pixie and son of powerful Daybreak magical advisor witch

Marin (MARE-in) fifth oldest Princess of Midnight Court; engaged to Riordan

Keegan (Key-GAN) fiance of Siofra second youngest Princess of Midnight Court; Elf; son of the Duke of Elvin affairs in Midnight Court

Siofra (Seef-FRA) second youngest Princess of Midnight Court; engaged to Keegan

Angus (ANG-us) fiance of youngest Princess of Midnight Court; merman/Fae; heir to largest shipping conglomerate in Harvest Court

Flora (flor-uh) youngest Princess of Midnight Court

Darragh (Dare-AH) King of Court of Reaping

Eabha (Av-AH) Queen of Court of Reaping, originally from Daybreak Court

Njord (NY-ord) orc/Fae armorer from Court of Reaping

Alf (Ahlfuh) Elven weapons master for Court of Reaping

Bodil (beau-Deal) wolf shifter and beastmaster for Court of Reaping

Revna (Rev-Nuh) Fairy designer of vestments for the Court of Reaping

Whistler's Hollow- town where it all comes together

The City- nearby bigger city

State U- nearby college where supes go in the city

Atwater's General Store- town grocery store

Cantwell Farms- racehorse and breeding farm at the end of town owned by Percy's family. Jolene and Wolfie work there, Dhameer boards his racehorse there

Whitley Gallery- Jolene's studio and teaching spot

Whistler's Hollow Formative School- elementary school

Whistler's Hollow Finishing School- middle and high school (Jolene, Teddy, and Hugh work there)

Town Hall- home of the Mayor, her assistant Aldous, and Doyle's jobs

Wild Astor Plants- florist owned by Dorothy Hale

Star Spangled Bank- owned by the Barrington family

Hollow Hollar- town paper owned by Behles

Dress Me Up Buttercup- clothing store owned by Fidelia Cantwell

Bottles 'N Cans- liquor store and speakeasy owned by Benjy

Bound Together- bookstore owned by Dylan Marlowe Grant

Grant Home Furnishings- furniture store owned by Zelda Foster Grant

Derby Pies- pizza joint owned by Fosters

Longworth Family Mortuary- owned by Longworth

Tame Your Mane- salon owned by Ophelia Longworth

Close Encounters of the Baked Kind- bakery owned by Jillian Remington

Better Booties- gym franchise owned by Remington family

Thorn and Associates- mega global law firm now run by Jackson Thorn

Thermopoulos Diner- owned by Hazel, neutral zone

Howl- supe club in the city where Jolene and Seer got dosed, also where they first met Dhameer

Faerie- land of the four courts of the Fae, accessible only by gateway mounds across the world

Midnight Court- aka Summer

Court of Reaping- aka Winter

Harvest Court- aka Autumn

Daybreak Court- aka Spring

Laochra Na Peitil- The Warrior Petal; a welcoming committee in the Daybreak Court made of soldiers who handle high level visitors to the Court (Aoife, Cíaran, Taranis, Sítheach, and Daire)

Daybreak Court Royal Guest House #1- where the gang stays in the first week of their Faerie trip

Daybreak Castle- where the reel and the royals come together

Harvest Castle- where they are invited to meet the royals

Autumn Hotel- finest hotel in the Harvest capital where the gang stays

Court of Midnight Royal Castle- where the gang stays in Midnight Court with the royals

Winter Wonderland Marketplace- huge wintery market in Court of Reaping

Court of Reaping Castle- where the gang stays and the hunt is held in the Court of Reaping

The Fields of the Hunt- where the Court of Reaping holds the start of the Wild Hunt

Sneak Peek: Veiled Flame

Loser

Kat

The little blue icon on my app has been glaring at me all day, but I'm too damn nervous to open it. Everyone at Woodlawn High has been buzzing all day with their notifications and the squeals of joy and moans of despair were too much for me to take. My anxiety is through the roof—this is the moment I've been waiting for since middle school, but I can't seem to force myself to bite the billet and check.

Maybe it's because I don't have the support system most of my classmates have?

That's probably true, given I've always been a loner and I don't fit into any specific 'caste' here. It's hard to make friends when you get shuffled from foster home to foster home over the years. I've rarely stayed anywhere long enough to make a friend, much less a group of them.

I'm not delinquent or anything—the families I've been placed with just return me like a pair of pants that doesn't fit after a year or so. The caseworkers click their tongues sympathetically and hunt down a new placement, but I've never been given a reason *why* people don't want me around. One lady said I must be born under a bad sign and hell if I knew what that meant other than I'm not good enough to keep around.

It would be different, almost understandable, if I misbehaved or got bad grades. But I don't—I'm always in the top five percent of my class and I do everything I'm asked. I don't even lord my smarts over the other kids or adults. Being presentable and unassuming was something I adapted long ago to improve my probability of staying in a home long term.

Unfortunately, it never worked and though I should be a shoo-in for scholarships and acceptances galore, I can't bring myself to be rejected yet again.

So I wait for the last bell of the day, slinging my bag over my shoulder and trudging home to the latest in my temporary housing. I can't even contemplate looking at the possible heartache waiting for me in the college application system WHS insisted we use. The fear is too great and despite knowing I'll be on my own for good at the end of this year, I'm unable to risk the pain.

I hate being this way.

My court mandated therapist says it's some sort of attachment disorder that's common in foster kids, but I think that's bullshit. The problem isn't *me* not forming attachments; it's asshole adults not forming one to me. Being left at a safe haven in a fucking basket as a baby wasn't because *I* did anything wrong—again, fucking adults couldn't handle their commitments.

As usual, I arrive home to an empty house. There are two other kids who live here—Bryce and Blake—but they're at football practice. Of course, the Jamesons *love* them; they get to strut around at games because their strays are the stars of the team. I'm not mistreated, but I'm definitely an afterthought. Both of my 'parents' are still at work, so I drop my bag on the couch and head for the kitchen to get a snack:

Don't get me wrong. I *could* have been placed in far worse homes than any of the seven I've been in since elementary school. None of the ex-fosters starved, beat, molested, or abused me. They were all decent folks with jobs and houses that weren't hellholes, but they never liked me.

I have no idea why. I tried to be everything they wanted.

But when the end of each school year came, I was handed in like a textbook and off I went to some group home until the next contestant stepped up. It baffled everyone, not just me, but that's what happened every single time.

Sighing, I pull some fruit out of the fridge and grab a soda. I have homework to do and if I want to have time to work on my stories, I'll need to get it done before the house is full of people at dinner time. Bryce and Blake will have gotten messages about their applications, too, and I'd bet my pinkie toe those idiots got into some big sports school. Brett and Allison will be oozing happiness for them and I don't know if I'll be able to keep food down if I have to admit my failure when they ask.

Being eighteen sucks ass.

After I grab my books and tablet, I head down to the den. I have to give my current parents credit; they set up a very nice workspace for us to study in the converted basement. By the time they took me in, the Jamesons created a cozy room down here where the three of us could relax and do our work for school without being interrupted. It might have been more for the boys than me, but I appreciated it all the same. Desks, a couch, big chairs, and bookshelves fill the space, making it almost seem like our mini-library. They even put a small fridge for drinks and snacks in case we had to be up late to cram.

It's my favorite place in the entire house and I spend most of my time here.

I sink into the huge armchair, putting my drink and snack on the side table. It only takes a few minutes to arrange myself in the soft cushions and I pause to tug my headphones out of my pocket. Music always soothes my jagged edges and I need it to stay focused on the bullshit AP Calculus I need to keep my average up in. My course load is heavy, but I applied to tough colleges. I wouldn't have a chance to get in, especially on a scholarship, if I wasn't taking equally challenging classes in comparison to all the prep school kids.

As always, the sounds of Vivaldi carry me away as I scrawl equations on my screen and before long, thoughts of the blue notification completely fade away.

"Kat!"

The shouts barely register as I continue working on the problem set, gnawing on my lower lip in concentration.

"Jesus fuck, where is she? I could eat a hippo!"

"Kat!"

Thumping followed by what could pass for a stampede of elephants jerks me out of my math filled trance when Bryce and Blake come down the stairs. They smell as bad as the aforementioned pachyderm's cage, so they must have rushed home right after practice. The blond twins glare at me as if I'm the offending element despite being sweaty and covered in dirt and grass stains.

This doesn't bode well.

Usually, they're tired and hungry after practices so I'm used to cranky ass boys, but tonight, there's a light to their faces. That had to mean they've gotten their letters and dinner will be a gush fest in honor of their perfection. I'm going to need all of my strength to fake smile and nod as Brett and Allison fawn over them.

I don't begrudge them their success—not really. They work hard and play even harder on the field. It's not their fault they're the American dream teens and I'm the nerdy basement troll no one wants. But it's awfully hard living in the shadow of their bright light, especially when I'm no less intelligent or talented.

"I'm finishing the AP Calc, guys. What do you want?"

They roll their eyes at me before Blake scoffs. "It's not due until Monday. You're so hyper."

Duh. I take anxiety meds, douchebag; of course I'm 'hyper.'

"I can only be who I am, Blake." That earns me a snort from Bryce and I know it's because he thinks that's the problem. "Is dinner ready?"

"Almost. Get upstairs and set the table so we can shower—Brett's orders." Blake grins smugly.

The two of them seem to always arrange it so chores get passed to me for some half-assed reason and this is no exception. Sighing, I put my stuff aside, fully intending to hide down here after the dinner mess is cleaned up. Likely by me, but like I said, I could definitely live in worse foster homes so I let it go. Doing some chores isn't worth risking the group home for the last few months of my high school career.

They take off running up the stairs and I wait for them to disappear before I follow suit. My phone is tucked in my pocket and I feel like it's a stone of shame I have to bear. I know once the adults make over the twins' success, they will remember me, and I'll be forced to find out what disappointment lies in wait for me. The dread weighs on me, but I head into the sunny kitchen and pick up the pre-prepared pile of plates, silverware, and napkins on the counter.

Allison looks up from the stove and gives me a half-smile, nodding as I take the dishes into the dining room. Like I said, no one is mean or horrid, they just seem…obligated. After a while, it makes it hard to waste time trying to be bright and sunny. Being reserved makes it a hell of a lot easier not to feel rebuffed when they don't pay attention to you regardless.

"Make sure you include champagne glasses for your dad and I!" she calls from the other room.

The twins definitely got acceptance somewhere big. Brett must have gotten the bubbly on the way home.

Once I set the table, I return to help Allison bring out the roast and sides. I'm a little amazed at her efficiency when it comes to getting the housework done while working full time, but I suppose it's something people with real parents get taught as they grow up. My home life has been so fractured that I haven't learned how to cook more than very basic shit from YouTube videos. That may be a problem after graduation, but I've never felt comfortable enough to ask Allison if she'd teach me. I'm sure she would try, but it doesn't feel right.

"How was school, Kat?"

I look over my shoulder, seeing Brett in the entry to the dining room. He's already changed from work and smiling, but I see the distraction in his eyes. He's waiting for the boys to come down. "It was fine. I've got a Calc test at the end of the week. I'll be studying a lot to get ready."

"Good, good. No matter what happens with applications, keeping your grades up will ensure no one pulls any offers," he says.

Those words aren't for me. They are for the two wet haired boys who just appeared behind him.

"Kat's too much of a geek to ever let her grades slip, Dad," Blake says as he pushes past his brother and drops into his usual chair at the table. "Grab me a Powerade since you're in the kitchen, mouse!"

Both Brett and Bryce stare at me and I turn around, heading to the fridge despite the fact that I was *not* closer than the other twin. Out of habit, I take two of the drinks and a soda for myself. I've been here long enough to know Bryce will send me back to get him one as well. It would feel like typical sibling stuff, but for some reason, I just *know* they do it to fuck with me. I have no idea why I feel that way, but trusting my gut has been the one thing that helped me get through all the upheaval in my life over the years. It's a good gauge for knowing when I'll get booted or if people are being earnest in their reactions.

The therapist says that's some sort of trauma induced early trigger warning shit, by the way.

After I hand out the drinks, I sit down on my side of the table and we wait for Allison to come out. Brett is at his seat at the far end of the table and the twins are punching each other as they look at something on their phones. I know where this is all going but I drop my gaze to the table, swallowing the coppery taste of fear as it courses through my body.

I'm going to be exposed and there's nothing I can do to stop it.

Read the first three episodes free on Kindle Vella: https://www.amazon.com/kindle-vella/story/B0BSTMB1X3

Sneak Peek: Come Out & Prey

Just A Girl

Delores

Sighing, I look around my bedroom at the posters and decorations covering my walls. My obsession with pop music, musical theater, and high school rom-coms sickens my parents. They would prefer me to be into heavy metal and horror movies like the other kids my age.

Being the only child in a family as prominent as mine is difficult when you don't fit the mold. My parents—like their parents and all my friends' parents—are apex predators. Preds rule our world, and the division between us and prey is so severe that we regulate them to a completely different echelon of society. Prey shifters are weak and beneath our lofty abilities. The ruling class of elite predator families stretches back generations, and they've evolved into a bunch of assholes who only care about succession and greed.

My animal has not manifested yet, but it will soon enough. Luckily for me, none of my friends have manifested their inner animals, either. I'm part of the in-crowd at school, and my boyfriend, Todd, is the most popular guy in my class. While he and I aren't officially engaged yet, we've talked about it enough that I know it's only a matter of time before he puts a ring on my finger. I should be on top of the world, but I can't help but feel like my life just doesn't fit me the way it's supposed to.

Every teenager wishes their life was different, but I dream of becoming an entirely different person. Not inside, mind, because I'm pretty comfortable with who I am. I don't want to be part of this legacy, this society, or even this family. They are all focused on competing to be the richest, the deadliest, or the most powerful, and I want no part of it.

I walked over to my closet and pulled out the outfit that I had chosen for my tour of Apex Academy. My mother hired her personal designers to create a custom school uniform for today and expects me to present the 'appropriate' image of the sole heir to a Council seat.

I hate having to pretend to be like them because I'm nothing like them.

Regardless, I pull on the short, pink pleated skirt, three quarter length sleeve blouse, knee socks, and Mary Janes that comprise the uniform for my exclusive private high school. Since I'm using a 'college visit' day to tour the Academy, I'm expected to represent Shifter Secondary as well.

Shifter Secondary is the most exclusive high school for unmanifested shifter teens on the East Coast. Unfortunately for me, it was not my parents' first choice for my education. They hoped I'd follow in their footsteps by choosing to force my animal to emerge early. If I had done that, I could have attended *Apex Academy Lower School*.

I didn't have the stomach to use my body in that manner at fourteen.

Their heirs followed my lead, which made my mother and father furious and their hoity-toity council colleagues angry. My closest friends, the Heathers, also refused to force their animals to emerge, as did Todd and his friends. That was the first time the adults in our circle decided I was a bad influence. After that, I had to toe the line at every turn, ensuring that I followed all the strict rules and regulations that govern the heirs to council seats.

Everywhere I went, I had to dress in a manner befitting the next Drew to sit at the table. They forced me to take dance lessons, piano lessons, diction lessons, and other more humiliating tutorials to prepare for the day that I became a true predator. In our society, teenagers have no say in how we prepare for our animals to emerge.

Your parents make all the decisions, choose your friends, choose your mates, and decide every detail of your life down to what you eat every single day. At least, that's how it is in my family, because my mother is from the old world.

She came over from Slovenia when she was incredibly young and met my father on the society fundraiser circuit. Her idea of preparing her daughter for the future involves lessons in makeup, clothing, jewelry, and on how to keep your mate satisfied. Lucille is completely unconcerned about whether I end up happy, only that I attend to my council seat and my husband's *needs*.

Once I get dressed, I grab my vintage Vuitton bag and peek at the mirror for a last check before I head downstairs. I tuck my perfectly highlighted blonde tresses behind my ears, and the smokey eye and winged liner are on point with this year's fashion trends. I apply a quick swipe of cherry red lip gloss and open my mouth, inspecting my teeth to make sure they are pearly white. Even though once I develop threatening incisors or sharp fangs, something will inevitably cover them in blood, my parents want my smile to look like a tooth-paste commercial.

It's all such utter bullshit.

I take a deep breath and turn on my heel, heading for the door. I can already hear my parents yelling in a Scotch and vodka induced rage in the drawing room. It's only eleven thirty in the morning, for Hera's sake.

Lucille and Bruno don't fuck around with cocktail hour. They are nicely sauced by ten a.m. every day, without exception. I can't remember a time when my parents didn't get drunk off their asses at an event or party, much less in our 'home'. They liquor up and fight until they part for the day, and then start again once they arrive home from their daily commitments.

I brace for the barrage of criticism my mother will subject me to when I cross the threshold. Closing my eyes, I whisper words of encouragement to myself via lyrics to some of my favorite songs, desperately trying to hype myself up before she can tear me down.

"Delores! I hear you breathing at the top of the stairs, darling. Come down this instant and let your father and I inspect your presentation."

My mother's purr *sounds* friendly, but believe me, it's not. I roll my eyes as I make my way down the stairs, knowing my mother won't hesitate to send one of the staff if I don't acquiesce to her command. Most of their staff would gleefully jizz themselves with being chosen to drag me downstairs for inspection.

At this time of day, the only servant in the drawing room will be Matilda—my ex-nanny turned personal assistant—and that request would test her loyalties. As the only person in my household who has my back, I don't want to put her in that position, so I answer. "Yes, Lucille. I'm on my way."

I'm not allowed to refer to her as 'mother' because it makes her feel old. 'Lucille' is always what I've called the woman who supposedly gave birth to me. I'd be tempted to disbelieve we shared any DNA at all if it weren't for our similar bone structure. She's about as nurturing as a rattlesnake, and if it weren't for Matilda, I might have died as a child. If the kitchen staff whispers are accurate, I have to accept that my mother neglected to feed me much of the time.

"You coddle her far too much, Lucille," my father growls. "As the heir to our family seat, Delores will come without being instructed to do so. We will not tolerate her insolence after her animal emerges. She will behave as I command or suffer the consequences."

The last of Bruno's rant echoes off the marble walls of the foyer as I step onto the hideously expensive, endangered teak floor. Schooling my features into the mask of indifference I wear whenever I have to deal with them, I enter their den of drunken fights with my spine steeled for an emotional assault.

"I apologize for my tardiness, Father. I only wished to perfect the image I will present during my tour of Apex Academy. I realize it is imperative I impress the Headmistress and her staff."

The humanoid features of his face shift seamlessly, and the hungry crocodile inside of him gives me a toothy smirk. "You will impress them, daughter, or so help me… I'll send you to Bloodstone Isle."

My stomach drops like a stone as I barely suppress a shiver.

Bloodstone Isle is a reformatory school. It's surrounded by spells and enchantments to prevent students from escaping—a feat that has only happened once in its one thousand years of existence. The most feared cat group in the shifter world—the Khan ambush—runs the school, and they're rumored to consume errant students when the Council allows it.

It's the threat both rich and poor shifter parents used to keep their children in line. Wealthy parents like mine use it as a method of controlling any heirs that refuse to conform to the rigid structure of our society. Predators don't value the lives of those who are weak, and they label heirs who refuse to take their rightful place at the top of the food chain weak. Everyone knows Bloodstone is full of criminals, miscreants, and psychos, and even they don't seem to survive.

Bloodstone is a death sentence—pure and simple.

"Y-yes, Father. I understand," I croak out. As if the pressure of touring my new school isn't enough, now I worry the Dean will relay something to my parents that gets me shipped off to Death Island.

"Bruno, darling, if you scare her, she'll frown. That causes wrinkles. Delores, chin up and smile for us."

Swallowing the lump in my throat, I flash my mother my brightest smile. Her blood-red lips curve, and her leopard fangs burst free as she all but purrs. "I will not have you sullying the family name, Delores. It's bad enough that your education gave you ideas about your value beyond breeding stock. You will take the seat on the Council when it is time, but the husband we select will control the business—as nature intended. Do you hear me?"

My eyes narrow briefly, and for what is possibly the millionth time this week alone, I nod at my mother to appease her temper. "Yes, Lucille."

"Excellent!" The leopard fades as she claps her hands. "Matilda!"

The tiny woman steps up, her eyes wide behind her glasses. She's a pred, but the smaller size of hawk shifters puts her in the servant class. I believe she genuinely lives in fear of one or both of my parents deciding to eat her. "Yes, madam?"

"Fetch Bruiser. He will accompany Delores to the academy for her tour. Tell him to take the Escalade—it won't do for her to arrive in a tiny car—it will draw attention to her extra weight. We must make an impression."

Matilda nods, and I feel the fear radiating from her, and I don't blame her. Bruiser is one of my parents' bodyguards and our frequent chauffeur. He's a Komodo dragon shifter and the house staff are terrified of him. It's hard not to be, given that he prefers to play with his food, then eat it after it's dead. The kitchen crew believes he 'handled' the gardener that looked too long at my mother when I was ten. He disappeared without a trace.

Once Matilda scurries away, I watch my parents drink and bicker about their plans for the day. Bruno is going golfing with a congressman, and Lucille is going to the spa. We all know that both outings will include stops at the homes of their current pieces of ass for a quickie, but no one talks about it. The appearance of the loving couple has to be maintained, although neither of them has slept in the same room since I was a baby.

They don't give a damn about fidelity; I learned that at an early age. Children often discover things they shouldn't because of adults discount their ability to understand the conversations happening around them.

I stopped keeping track of who they're boning long ago, because I'd need an assistant to keep the affairs straight.

While my parents' marriage is a sham, I remind myself that my boyfriend, Todd, isn't like them. Yes, his parents only own half the live entertainment industry, but my father allows me to see Todd. The other parents will force the Heathers to accept an arranged betrothal, and I'm grateful I'm lucky enough to have found the perfect match on my own as my high school sweetheart.

"Delores, Bruiser is ready to escort you to Apex. He's pulling the car around now," the hawk shifter says softly.

Snapping out of my reverie, I smile at the trembling woman. Bruiser must have scared the living hell out of her. For no other reason than it amused him, I'm sure. He's as much a brute as his name implies, and I don't look forward to riding alone to the academy with him.

Something about that shifter gives me the creeps...

SNEAK PEEK: BLOODTHIRSTY

QUEEN BEE

They dim the lights in the club, and the spots click on as the curtain slides open.

It's a full house tonight in the little burlesque club off the Rue Pierre Montaine.

Chez Arc En Ciel is not well known compared to the *Moulin Rouge* or *Le Lido*, but the wealthy from both sides of the Seine gather here for shows four nights a week. If you pass the various layers of security checks to even be permitted to book a reservation, you also have to be able to afford the two thousand Euro per guest cover charge. If you don't eat or drink anything, that's all it will cost; however, that would get you blacklisted.

Intro music pumps through the speakers and I stand on my mark in the opening position. My cane is resting on the wooden boards of the stage by my front foot as I pretend to lean on it. Roars of applause echo through the room as our troupe of dancers catch the lights, sequins sparkling like diamonds when the stage lights rise. We're dressed in pinstriped black pant suits and fedoras to match the big band style opening to the song. As soon as the horn-filled intro finishes, the dance begins.

I follow the routine with precision, snapping and popping my hips to the beat as we spread out across the stage. You wouldn't know by the fake smile on my face that I'm scanning the crowd. Two fan kicks later, I've rotated past the proscenium, and I think I've found my mark. Twirling, I stop in the place I need to be for the bridge, singing along as if my life depends on it. It might, to be honest, because I need to sell my cover tonight, so no one notices me.

The Guillotine moves in the shadows, but tonight, she's in the spotlight.

My ass shakes as I dance my way through the song, swinging the prop cane I'd replaced with one of my design. You wouldn't know by looking at it, but it's not the painted balsa the other dancers have for a very specific reason. I need it to complete the mission that forced me to spend two months in Paris working my way into this job at *Chez Arc En Ciel*. If I can't strike tonight, the surveillance, counterintelligence, and time spent building this cover are wasted because my mark is leaving for Asia tomorrow.

Tonight, the Cobra dies for his sins.

The break of the song slows the music and the dancers pour into the crowd to wiggle around the rich assholes. It's choreographed, but it's also to advertise each girl for private dances in the lounges upstairs. We're not strippers—not that there's a damned thing wrong with a woman using her body to support herself—but we do bare more skin in the closed rooms. The *laissez-faire* attitude of the owners means as long as we kick them thirty percent of the fees for those dances, they don't care what any of the girls do in the rooms. I'd find it sleazy, but the girls who work here are highly skilled performers who choose to make thousands of dollars a night rather than peanuts in some ballet troupe or chorus line.

By the time I've flirted my way to the VIP tables, the Cobra is staring intently at all of us. Spotlights pin each one of us on the floor at the bass hits, and I swivel my hips as my free hand slides down to the secret spot on my jacket. In unison, we tear the jackets off to reveal rhinestone studded bras with straps crisscrossing our waists like shibari ropes. A lift of the fedora and pop of my hip, along with the beat, draws the fierce-looking brawler's eyes directly to me. I pout prettily and stalk towards his table with the swagger of a tiny dicked asshole that owns a monster truck.

His thin lips pull back over the famed curving fangs he had implanted. Dark, glittering eyes follow every move I make as I approach, and I pretend to whip my hair from side to side as I check for his guards. They're here somewhere, but I need them to be far away so I can beat my escape before they notice. When I get within inches, I tap his leg with my cane and spin around to shake my ass in his face. The grunt of approval makes me want to heave, but I turn, holding onto the prop with both hands. My feet click on the floor in a soft shoe step as I make 'fuck me' eyes at the dirty bastard. He leans back, his pants tented as he gestures towards his lap.

Fucking gross.

I don't care about his weapons trade or what happens when people get the shit he moves. I have no clue why I have to take him out. The reason they have sentenced him to death isn't part of my contract, and I'm nothing if not a dispassionate observer of the darkest parts of human desires. Twelve years at *l'Academie* ensured I care very little about anything that isn't directly related to my ability to complete my jobs.

Sighing, I dance closer and drop onto his rather unimpressive erection and wiggle. There's plenty of cloth between us to prevent him from doing anything I'd make a scene over, so I focus on the task at hand. I slip the cane behind his head, resting the wood against his neck as I tug him forward. The move reads as playfully bringing his face to my breasts, but at the last second, I click the release built into the custom weapon. One end slides open to reveal the razor sharp garotte and before he can say a word, I yank it through.

Faint gurgling is the only noise besides the end of the song, and I carefully slide the sides of the cane together. Climbing off the nasty fucker, I put my hands on his cheeks so I can pretend to flirt with him while I arrange the head so it looks as if he's leaning back in the booth. It needs to look realistic to allow me to return to the stage with the others. When I have it settled, I back away from the booth, blowing fake kisses as I walk backwards through the crowd. I almost collide with a dark-haired guy with his collar pulled high as I head for the stage, and I roll my eyes. Whatever celeb that is trying to keep their face away from the paps is doing a shitty job of it.

The entire troupe takes a few bows and shuffles off of stage left to the wings. I exhale a sigh of relief when the next group enters on the opposite side. I haven't heard shouting yet, so I don't think the Cobra's men realize he's down. Now I take this emetic pill, have a vomiting episode, and I'll get sent home.

That's when Arabella Montaigne, the burlesque dancer, will cease to exist, and Remy Arsine Benoit will re-emerge.

I smile to myself as I chew on the tablet that will have me retching my guts out in a few moments. This is a more complex extermination than I usually prefer, and I can't leave my normal calling card behind. The Cobra's head had to remain in the booth rather than get delivered to his home in a basket.

Such a shame, that. I quite enjoy the reactions my little gifts engender when they're discovered.

Walking into the dressing room, I carefully strip my costume off, putting all the pieces in my bag. Every item in the locker room that belongs to gets placed in the duffel carefully as I wait for the effects to hit me. It won't do to leave loose ends, even if my prints have never touched a single surface in this place. My gut roils and I turn, facing one of the other dancers as the vomit finally comes. Gracelia screams like she's being skinned when I hurl on her and it's everything I can do *not* to smirk through the chunks.

"C'est la merde!" she shouts, running for the showers as if she's on fire.

It takes less than a minute for the owner to send me home for the night. I walk out the back door of the building with everything just as the sirens scream.

Perfect timing, as always.

I jump into the first cab I can hail, directing him to the *Hôtel de Crillon*. Their suites are the ritziest in Paris, and it's my go-to hideout when I'm here. I used to only stay in the Bernstein Suite, but some rich fuckwad purchased it six months ago. If I could track them down and beat the hell out of them, I would, but I booked my schedule until late 2025. Assassins with my skill set and accuracy are getting harder to find. They forced the old guard into retirement because they refuse to adapt to the digital age. Too many cameras, crime labs, and hackers running about to do everything Cold War style.

The future of murder for hire is millennial, people. We're old enough to be stable, but young enough to be agile with new technology. Plus, most of them are broke AF from crooked ass student loans.

It's not an issue I have, but I've been in the business since I hit double digits. You don't survive *l'Academie des Invisibles* if you haven't killed someone before the end of primary school. It's unheard of.

I was eight the first time I used the weapon that would become my signature.

Shivering, I tap on the window of the cab and bitch the driver out. He's taking a longer route than necessary to raise my fare, and I'll have his guts for garters if he doesn't knock it the fuck off. A string of curses in French erupt from him when I voice the accusation, and I slam my palm on the window with enough force to crack the plexiglass barrier. He almost drives into another car, but when he regains control, he makes the requested adjustments to our route.

We arrived at the front entrance after a few more arguments and a traffic jam around the *Champs*. I throw the euros at him in disgust, memorizing the medallion number for later. He's not worth my time, but I have quite a few contacts who might be interested in blackmailing a cabbie in town. Getaway cars are cliche in the crime world now. Most ne'er-do-wells like myself find greater comfort in anonymous taxis or ride-share accounts hacked through the deep web accessed on burner phones. If your ride doesn't know you're a villain, there's no one to flip if law enforcement comes looking.

I never look the same for any job—ever.

I will not use Arabella Montaigne as a cover in the future, and once I move to the location of my next job, I'll ensure that she meets with a terrible fate. It's a lot more work to slowly kill off my alters once I've used them, but it's also why I've never even come close to being caught. The dancer with long wavy red hair, freckles, and big green eyes will never grace the streets of Paris again after I hop a plane. She will, however, get a minor story in the paper and an obituary when I decide how she tragically dies.

The Guillotine will rise from her ashes and be reborn.

Sneak Peek: Children of the Moon

PROLOGUE

Twenty-one years ago…

A powerful wave of apprehension hits me as we approach Claridon's house. Pausing at the edge of the forest, I wait until we can see what awaits us. The silence is deafening as we take in the wreckage of what was once the home of our dear friends.

They splintered the heavy cabin door in pieces littered around their yard like an explosion sent the shards flying. When the wind shifts, the foul stench of death and rot slams into us, making my wife gag. Lights are flickering ominously in the shattered windows and another scent—burnt food—catches the breeze as we approach.

"Cast protection before we reach the porch," I murmur.

"*Ego invoco deus ab mihi. Protego mihi ab hostili et malum.*[1]"

I nod solemnly, repeating her words to invoke our Goddess' watchful eyes on me as well. The scene in front of the house does not inspire confidence about what we will find inside.

The air is thick as we step onto the porch and another smell wafts towards us—blood. Its metallic tang invades our senses almost to the point of tasting copper on my tongue. Climbing over the debris, I look at the once cozy living area. Shredded cushions, torn drapes, stuffing, and other destroyed furnishings lie scattered around the room. When I bend to examine the destruction, I find coarse animal hairs embedded in the remnants. I pick some up to sense the aura of the creature it came from, but all I feel is death.

The bloody hoof prints puzzle me—I do not recognize them as belonging to any creature I'm familiar with. Whatever came to this house was not a normal shifter, nor was it a common magic user. The level of malice and lack of emotion concerns me. Its aura is like that of a necromancer or one of their creations.

I follow a set of heavy prints to the hallway leading to the dining area and kitchen. Swallowing hard, I prepare myself for the carnage I know will appear. The rotten food and decomposition scents are so bad I have to raise my shirt to cover my nose before I vomit.

It is certain our friends are dead; no one can lose the amount of blood that coats the surfaces and walls while staying alive.

"What made those claw marks? I've never seen such deep furrows," my wife whispers.

I shake my head, holding a finger to my lips to keep her quiet. I've never seen that type of mark, either, but we don't know if there's anyone still here. We must stay silent while we explore. The food on the stovetop is burned and has flies on it—that's the rotting smell. Wood is barely burning in the oven, just a few embers remaining, but it tells me our friends were caught unaware.

It means the malevolent being that attacked the wolves did it within the past few hours.

My heart stops when I remember their baby girl. Feray had to be here when it happened; it's the New Moon and both of her parents stay home during the start of the new lunar cycle.

"Freya, forgive me. I almost forgot the baby," I hiss at my wife.

Her eyes widen and her hand flies to her mouth. I see the tears forming as she thinks about what the condition of this place means for a defenseless infant. Together, we leave the kitchen, intent on heading back through the outer room to the stairs.

Just beyond the landing, we stumble over the body of Claridon. His corpse is mutilated, but I recognize those battered hands anywhere. He clearly put up a hell of a fight to keep the intruder from making it past him. Despite that, it ripped his chest open and his intestines are hanging out. Blood spatter decorates the once lovingly decorated walls, painting them vermillion and signaling his desperation to protect his family.

Swallowing again as I look at Imogen, I tilt my head at the trail of bloody hoof prints that lead to the nursery. We were here when they found out they were expecting, when they assembled the room, and even after Feray was born. Now the beauty of that memory has been sullied by the scene before us.

We have to be strong…

Once we're both ready, we follow the prints to the door of the baby wolf's room. The sight that greets us is horrific: it splayed Lyra out as if nailed to a cross and impaled her head on a post of the baby's crib. Blood is dripping down the whitewashed wood, making its way to the pink carpet. Dead eyes stare sightlessly at us as we hold our breath and enter. The injuries to our friend are a testament to how hard she fought to protect her child, though in the end, she also failed.

I don't want to see what this monster did to the baby we considered a sister to our child. Forcing myself to approach, I stare at the empty crib in astonishment. There's no sign of Feray, nor that it harmed her in this room. I whip my head around to look at my wife in shock.

Was this a kidnapping? Why would they kill everyone so brutally instead of simply sneaking in to snatch the baby?

My eyes dart around the room until I reach the closet. I stalk over, throwing the door wide. There's a pile of dirty linens and blankets in the bottom, which is unlike Lyra. She always kept everything tidy, so much so that we all teased her about it. Tossing the clothes over my shoulder, I dig down until I reach the floor. I call for light and my magic brightens the dark space enough for me to see a tiny seam at the baseboard.

Claridon was always paranoid, and I never understood why. We both lived simple lives in a small town of magic users and shifters, well outside the dangers of the big city. He was a master craftsman and Lyra ran a bakery; there was nothing to worry about. Humans were far away from our little town and the stench of corruption from the gangs and Councils doesn't exist in Silver Falls.

But I recognize a bolt hole when I see one, so I search frantically until I find the lever that will spring the door open. It takes several tries to successfully open the door—Claridon was top-notch at his trade—but when it swings out, I gasp.

There, wrapped in her father's shirt and Lyra's clothing, is Feray. She has the warding amulet Imogen made for her on her chest, and I realize that even while scared for their lives, Lyra and Claridon ensured the beast wouldn't find their child. Between the magic of our amulet and their scent swaddling her, the baby is hungry and tired, but safe.

I lift the tiny infant out of the hole gently, my eyes filling with tears. Her baby scent makes my heart hurt for my fallen friends and I clutch her to me tightly. It's our responsibility to take care of her now; I know that. Imogen nods when I look at her with a sad expression, then walks over to the dresser, opening a drawer. When she hands me the baby sling, I know she feels the same.

Once I secure Feray to my body, we make our way back to the stairs and head out of the house. It will need to be burned to keep that creature or anyone else from following the scent trail to our home. We don't want anyone to know Feray is alive; she will be safe with us as long as we continue to have her wear the amulet that suppresses her wolf.

Raising her with our daughter, in a new town, is the only way to keep her alive.

I didn't wake up this morning knowing I'd have to abandon my entire life and our home, but I know as surely as the sun will rise tomorrow what we must do to protect this baby. Looking down at her curiously, I ponder the situation again. A magical beast used as an assassin seems like overkill if their target was the infant. Slaughtering her family was also unnecessary—that thing could have slipped into her room and killed her before anyone knew it was there.

Lifting the magic on her amulet for a moment, I wait until Feray opens her eyes. That's when I realize why my friends put it on her. My wife walks up beside me and runs a finger over her cheek. Her red hair looks very much like mine and as long as we keep the magic refreshed for the spell, she will look as though she is our natural daughter.

"We must pack up and move immediately," Imogen says as we walk out. "The capital city is vast, and no one knows us there. That will allow us to raise her as our own—a sister to Fiadh."

"Yes," I murmur. "I will send a message to the local council to inform them we are moving. The death of our friends and their daughter are too much for us to bear here. You simply need to keep her secret in our home until we leave."

She nods. "What about the monster who did this? Who would send it to kill a baby, and why?"

"Someone who scared Claridon enough to make a secret bolt hole in the nursery and forced Lyra to ask us for that amulet. I don't know what they were up to, but obviously, it was much bigger than our tiny town."

Imogen frowns. "We made three amulets, love. Why weren't Lyra and Claridon wearing theirs?"

"I don't know, Gen. Whatever the reason was, they took theirs off and someone powerful hunted down their daughter. Nothing is what it seems here, but we must protect Feray. We will keep her wolf suppressed for as long as possible—up to her Ascension if we can. She'll grow up and if she's destined for something bigger, she'll be able to assume that mantle when she's ready."

Taking this baby on and keeping her secret violates our coven laws; we both know it. Hiding her means we will always be on the run—we need completely new identities when we flee to the capital. It's a lifetime commitment, but the look on my wife's face tells me she's certain this is the right thing to do.

I know without a doubt that being was pure evil, and it came with one purpose: *assassination.*

Tomorrow, we begin our lives on the lam with two babies—there is no other option .

Get it now: **https://books2read.com/newmoonrisingCOM1**

1. I call on the gods. I protect myself from enemies and evil

About Cassandra Featherstone

Cassandra Featherstone has channeled her lifelong passion for writing into a flourishing career, a journey that started when she first grasped a pencil as a gifted child with ADHD.

Her debut novel, born during the solitude of COVID lockdown in March 2020, draws on a tapestry of personal encounters and insights that resonate deeply with her readers.

An international bestseller, Cassandra has topped Amazon charts in categories such as LGBT Anthologies, LGBTQ+ Mystery, and Bisexual Romance, among others. Her works navigate the complexities of bullying, PTSD, body dysmorphia, mental health struggles, personal reinvention, and the empowerment of claiming one's own space. Importantly, Cassandra offers a thoughtful and respectful portrayal of LGBTQIA+ relationships, subtly reflecting her own connection with the community through her narratives.

Her literary repertoire spans sci-fi fantasy, urban fantasy, paranormal, and comedic genres in academy whychoose settings, with a strong commitment to portraying consensual, safe, and accurately depicted BDSM and kink lifestyles. Her books are an invitation to explore transformative stories that are both inclusive and engaging.

Often affectionately called 'The Muppet' for her wacky theater kid personality, she resides in the Midwest with her tech-savvy husband, their creatively inclined college student, a literary-minded dog, and four scheming cats.

READ MORE AT CASSANDRA'S WEBSITE OR HER FACEBOOK PAGE. SIGN UP FOR EXCLUSIVE CONTENT AND UPDATES HERE.

FIND HER ON ANY OF THE SOCIAL MEDIA BELOW AS SHE **LOVES** TO CHAT AND **NEVER** SLEEPS!

Yo-Ho Holes (Book One)

CHILDREN OF THE MOON-
WITH SERENITY RAYNE

New Moon Rising (Book One)

Waxing Crescent (Book Two)

Waxing Gibbous (Book Three)

Full Moon (Book Four)

Waning Gibbous (Book Five)

APEX ACADEMY CAPERS

Come Out and Prey

Let Us Prey

In Prey We Trust

Oh Holy Spite (3.5 novella)

Eat. Prey. Love.

FAETAL ATTRACTION

Hell on Wheels (Book One)

RISE OF THE RESISTANCE

Ream Exclusive Prequels

Hooked on a Feline (Book One)

Book Two (TBA Title)

KINDLE VELLAS

Blood on the Ice (Secrets of State U S1)

Veiled Flame (Discordia University S1)

Blood From A Stone (Denizens of the Dark S1)

Hell on Wheels (Faetal Attraction S1)

Forbidden Fates (Agents of the Ouroboros S1)

ANTHOLOGIES

Unwritten

Shifters Unleashed

Jingle My Balls

Love is in the Air

Silent Night

Snowed In

All Hallows Eve